SEVEN

ECHOES IN TIME - BOOK THREE

By M MacKinnon

Printed in the United States of America
Paperback ISBN: 978-1-965253-16-8
Ebook ISBN: 978-1-965253-17-5
Library of Congress Control Number:

DartFrog Plus is the hybrid publishing
imprint of DartFrog Books, LLC.
301 S. McDowell St.
Suite 125-1625
Charlotte, NC 28204

www.DartFrogBooks.com

CONTENTS

GLOSSARY

blootered–very drunk.
bonnet–a traditional woolen cap worn by Scottish men, also called a tam-o'-shanter.
bonny–pretty, good-looking.
claymore–a large, two-handed sword.
dinnae; didnae–don't; didn't.
dinnae fash–don't worry.
dreich; oorlich; plowetery; smirr; stoating–words to describe miserable Scottish weather.
eejit–idiot.
gie–get.
greetin'–crying.
gybe (ho)–accompanies the start of the boom swing across the centerline of a sailboat.
ken; kent–know; knew.
leanan (Gaelic)–sweetheart.
mo ghràdh (Gaelic) my love.
noo; th' noo–now.
numpty–a fool, idiot.
rig–the furrow characteristic of Scottish farming.
sgian achlais (Gaelic)–an armpit dagger, concealed under a man's arm.
skelp–to beat or slap.

snood-a narrow circlet or ribbon fastened around the head and worn by unmarried women.
trews-trousers.
uisge beatha (Gaelic)-water of life, whisky.

PROLOGUE
JULY, 1651

eat crept beneath the young clansman's collar. It snaked under a shirt sodden with sweat and dampened a face already reddened by the frenzied flight from the battlefield. Midges swarmed and were blinked away unnoticed.

This running was futile, a retreat from sure defeat at the hands of a venomous enemy intent on claiming its last victims. It was a complete rout, the future of his clan—nay, of Scotland itself—almost certainly lost. Still, they must press on. Surrender was not a word heard in the auld tongue; certainly it had never touched the lips of his clan.

They could not last much longer in this heat, but stopping was not a choice. Close behind, they could hear the pandemonium of men crashing through the brush, fed by the anticipation of victory. A ravenous army intent on delivering the final blow to its enemy.

Damn the English! Damn this endless war that had raged through the three kingdoms for over ten years. Damn the kings who used their subjects as pieces in a chess game with no beginning and no end. They could all go to hell. Let them argue with Satan over who was right and who should die.

The clansman suspected he might be in hell already; perhaps he and the men who fought beside him had slipped into death without knowing. Hell could very well be an eternity of marching, running, and killing.

Sweat dripped from his brow into his eyes, imbuing the path ahead with a misty glaze.

Path? He wiped the sweat from his eyes and tried to focus on the way ahead. The sounds of pursuit had diminished as the men of his clan ran without the constraint of gorse and bramble thickets that had impeded their escape until now.

There was something odd about the wilderness here. It was . . .groomed, as if God had finally taken notice and was offering solace in their last moments. Ash, birch, and elm stood alongside a pathway that meandered through a carefully tended forest. Ahead, an opening in the trees beckoned.

The exhausted men burst from the trees and stood, panting. Across a manicured lawn stood a castle. Symmetrical, with gabled roof and dormer windows on the upper floors, its two wings reached out to the sides as if to enfold them into its embrace.

Their chief signaled and the clan moved forward, a new sense of hope buoying their spirits. Surely here they would find sanctuary, among fellow Scots. The small windows on the ground floor and lack of an obvious entrance suggested that this place had been built as a fortress and would provide safety from the pursuing English.

The chief strode to the base of the castle and called

for help in the name of their king, his voice ringing with the strength borne of his heritage and responsibility. They waited in a silence heavy with anticipation.

A face appeared in a window and stared at them, taking in their Highland clothing and bedraggled appearance. In the next second, a stone was launched from the parapet above, striking one of their number on the shoulder and taking him to the ground. The face disappeared and a shutter closed over the window.

The man scrambled to his feet, clutching his shoulder, and stared at the others in shock. From the forest behind them came the clamour of mad voices, as the enemy drew closer to where they stood in the open, exposed and vulnerable.

Men emerged from the trees and paused, shock written across their faces. Here stood their enemy right out in the open, waiting like lambs in the slaughter pen—with no hope of retreat. The soldiers moved forward almost leisurely, weapons held loose in their hands. There was no rush now.

With a muffled curse, the chief drew his sword and held it high. "Bàs no Beatha!!" he roared. "Death or victory!" As his men echoed the war cry of their clan, all knew which it would be. As one, they moved toward their destiny.

More men poured from the woods and the lawn became a frenzied mass of screaming, cursing bodies as the two sides engaged. In moments, the grass became slick with Highlander blood.

The clansman dodged one soldier and parried a thrust from another. He winced as a sword nicked his left arm, then shook off the pain and turned to face the threat.

"The chief!" came a cry, and the clansman turned to see his chieftain go down, clutching at his belly. As if galvanized by the wounding of their enemy's leader, soldiers converged on the fallen man.

A Highlander stepped forward to stand in front of his chief. "Airson ar ceannard!" he screamed. The words in the auld tongue rang into the air. "For our chief!" The man stood, legs braced apart, and stared fearlessly into the face of his enemy.

There was a pause, and then three swords met the challenge. The Highlander sank to the ground beside his chief and was still.

Another stepped forward, sword drawn. "Fear eile airson ar ceannard!" he shouted, "Another for our chief!" He stood his ground in defiance, and in the next moment, he too was cut down by the swords of the enemy.

"Fear eile airson ar ceannard!" Four times more the cry was heard, as one by one the chief's men stepped forward to stand guard over their wounded leader. The clansmen fought with skill and fury, though outnumbered ten to one. The outcome was inevitable. The men were dispatched in turn by the power of the opposing force, and fell to lie next to their chief in a tangle of limbs.

"I am all that remains," the clansman murmured. "I am the last." For the briefest of moments, he wavered. A voice murmured in his mind, "I want to live." Then he pushed the thought away and stepped forward to take his place, sword held before him.

"Fear eile airson ar ceannard!" he called, and waited. For a moment the enemy stood immobile, humbled by the courage of these men who had stood bravely before them, willing to sacrifice their lives for their chief.

But it was war, and the moment passed unmolested. Men surged forward; blades glinted and clanged in the sunlight. The clansman whirled and parried, and for a few moments was able to withstand an attack by more than six soldiers determined to put a finish to this conflict.

The odds proved too much. Overwhelmed by the sheer numbers against him, the clansman sank to his knees, falling at last to lie on his back next to his brothers on the killing ground. He stared at the summer sky as his vision dimmed and the sounds of battle faded.

"Airson ar ceannard," he whispered.

CHAPTER 1

ISLE OF MULL, SCOTLAND, 1628

CRÌSDEAN

"Tell us anither 'un, Ma!"

Anna Maclean narrowed her eyes and looked at her young audience. Ranging in age from three to eleven years, the six little boys sat on the floor before her, hands clasped in their laps and innocence radiating from wide eyes.

She wasn't fooled for a single minute. This was a nightly ritual. They'd demand a story, and when that was finished, another, and another. It would have been lovely if their enthusiasm was the result of her talent as a storyteller, but she knew better. After the story came bedtime, and none of her children ever seemed to embrace that idea.

Her children. All hers, and all boys. She loved every one of them to distraction. She adored her husband as well, but the result of that love always culminated in another pregnancy—another boy.

Anna gave an inward sigh. She was going to tell Arthur tonight that it had to stop; she simply could not bear him another child. She was thirty-one, a once-young woman with the body of an old crone. She sometimes wondered why he still found her attractive, still wanted—never mind, it didn't matter that she liked it too. It had to stop.

It wasn't so much the bearing; it was the raising. Six lads, all so different one from the other. Bearnard, at eleven years already sure of his role in the family and his place in the clan. A big, sturdy lad who spent much of his time trailing after his cousin Hector, the chief's young brother, like a devoted hound.

Giles, her scholar. Dark and handsome already at ten, he was reading as usual. Giles preferred books to people and had to be pried from the library for meals. He would have the lassies chasing him in a few years, hoping for a glance from those long-lashed blue eyes. *Good luck to them,* thought Anna—unless a lass existed as words on a page, she likely would have no chance with Giles Maclean.

Dànaidh was watching his mother, hazel eyes hooded and unreadable. Always watching, was her Dànaidh, with eyes far older than his seven years. He was the one she worried about most. He seemed always on edge, restless, his rare smile saved for his brother Ealar.

Her eyes moved to the five-year-old next to him, and she smiled. Ealar sat scrunched up so close to Dànaidh that he was nearly in his brother's lap. She was waiting for the day Dànaidh lost patience with this hero-worship, but he seemed to have an honest affection for his younger brother and seldom pushed him away. Maybe Ealar was what Dànaidh needed—his little guardian angel, proof of his worth.

She pulled herself back to the moment and eyed the empty space next to Ealar with irritation. When had the twins sneaked away?

"Where are Fergus an' Pàdraig?" she demanded. The lads, except for Giles, looked around in surprise and then shrugged.

"Prob'ly in th' larder," Bearnard said. "Th' cook'll shoo 'em out 'n a minute."

Sure enough, the door flew open and Duart's cook stood in the doorway, a squirming three-year-old under each arm. "Th' little heathens was at me pies again!" she announced, but there was no heat in her voice.

The twins were the pets of the keep, coddled and tolerated like kittens, adorable and wild. *An' growin' wilder by th' minute*, Anna thought. *I'm too auld fer this. I'm tellin' Arthur . . .*

She nodded wearily to the cook, who set the lads down and pushed them forward. Freed from restraint, they raced across the floor and skidded to a stop in front of their mother, red-faced and panting, before clambering into Anna's lap.

"Fergus, get th' thumb outta yer mouth. Ye'll ruin yer teeth!"

The child pulled the offending digit out of his mouth and studied it. His brother poked him in the stomach and he erupted into giggles.

"'At's it! Doon ye go!" Anna dumped them off her lap and pointed at the space on the floor. "Thanks t' ye weans, there's only time fer one story t'night. Ye'd best hope yer brothers dinnae take a strap t' ye." The twins grinned at their older siblings, unfazed by a threat they'd heard many times before.

"Tell us th' one abit th' Lady on th' Rock!" Ealar said.

"Agin?" Anna said. "Ye heard that 'un jist yesterday."

"Agin!" they chorused, and the little lads chimed in, "G-in!"

Anna smiled and began. "More than a hunnerd years ago, th' Macleans were havin' trooble wi' th' Campbells. The chief o' th' Macleans was called Lachlan, jist like our chief now. He was verra clever."

Bearnard broke in. "All Maclean chiefs 'r clever."

"Aye," said Anna. "An' if ye interrupt, I'll let ye tell th' story!"

Bearnard subsided with a sheepish smile. "Aye, Ma."

"As I was sayin', Lachlan had 'n idea. Instead o' goin' t' battle wi' the Campbells, he decided t' marry one. He thought th' children wouldnae want t' fight if their parents were from both clans."

"Bit it didnae work," muttered Dànaidh, "cause th' Campbells are rotters."

"Dànaidh !" his mother said, her voice stern. "It wasnae only the Campbells' fault that it didnae work. D' ye wannae hear th' story, 'r no?"

Dànaidh sat back and scrunched up his face. "Sorry, Ma."

"Aye, ye should be. Anyway, it didnae work, b'cause

Lachlan an' his wife nivver had children. An' they did-nae get along—in fact, they grew t' hate each other. An' th' next part," she paused and fixed Dànaidh with a long look, "wasnae th' fault o' the Campbell lass, it was all doon t' Lachlan Maclean himself. He kent his idea had been a failure, an' decided t' rid himself o' his wife."

None of the children said a word—this was their favorite part of the story.

"So, one dark night at low tide, 'e sent 'is men t' carry his wife oot t' a rock in th' sound, an' they tied 'er down an' left her there t' drown when th' tide came in. Lachlan sent a messenger t' her kin t' tell 'em his wife had died in 'n accident, bit when 'e arrived at the Campbell keep later t' help wi' th' mournin', 'e saw 'is wife sittin' amidst her kin, safe 'an sound. She'd been rescued by a passin' fisherman an' returned t' her family.'

Anna lowered her voice. "Lachlan barely escapit wi' his life, an' after that, th' two clans went back t' battlin' each other."

Her audience sat in rapt silence except for Fergus and Pàdraig, who hadn't understood much of the story and were now rolling around on the floor, trying to stick their fingers in each other's ears and laughing like monkeys.

Anna rolled her eyes and sat back in her chair. "Sae let that be a lesson t' ye!" She pinned her sons with gimlet green eyes. "Ye have t' be verra careful when choosin' a wife. There are clans that cannae be messed aboot wi', if ye're t' have peace 'n yer home."

"Weel, I'm never gettin' marrit, so none o' that's fer me," said Dàinaidh. "Lassies 're wretchit." He crossed his arms over his skinny chest and stuck out his chin.

Ealar watched his brother with admiration before mirroring his actions. "Wretchit," he echoed.

"Careful wi' yer words, lad," his mother waggled a forefinger at Dànaidh. "Things'll look a wee bit diffrent when yer older, aye?"

"An' ye dinnae ken any lassies, so how are ye so sure whit they're like?" Bearnard ruffled his brother's hair. "Some lassies are nae so bad."

Dànaidh wrinkled his nose and pursed his lips. "Nivver gettin' marrit," he repeated. "Nivver."

"Me neither," said Ealar. "Nivver."

His mother pressed her lips together to keep a smile from breaking free. "Aye, lad. We'll see."

Suddenly she looked up, realizing the hall had gone quiet. The twins were nowhere in sight. Anna sighed.

"Giles, love, will ye fetch the wee ones fer me? They always listen t' ye."

Giles, who had returned to his book as soon as the story ended, looked up and blinked. "Wha-? Oh, aye." He scrambled to his feet and was out the door, calling the toddlers' names down the hallway.

Dànaidh looked after his brother and sniffed. "Dinnae ken why ye ask *him*. He uses sich big words they cannae even ken whit he's sayin'."

Bearnard cuffed the smaller lad across his head. "Dinnae be mean, Dàn."

Anna clapped her hands. "All right, lads, git. It's time fer bed an' ye're pure wearin' me out."

Giles returned with the recalcitrant Fergus and Pàdraig in tow. The boys lined up, and each kissed his mother's cheek before they all disappeared out the door.

Anna sat back in the chair and let the blessed silence seep into her soul. They really had worn her out tonight, more than usual. She couldn't remember the last time she'd been this tired so early in the evening.

A fist wrapped itself around her heart and she sat up straight. The last time she'd been so tired . . .

Anna Maclean stomped into the bedroom she shared with her beloved Arthur, murder in her eyes. Her husband backed up nervously.

What is 't, *mo ghràdh*?" he asked anxiously.

She plopped down on the bed.

"I'm wi' child!" she moaned. "I'm havin' anither bairn—anither lad!"

Arthur patted her arm. "Bit 'at's wonderful. Ye love bairns, an' maybe this un'll be a lass."

Anna glared at him. "It willnae be a lass!" she hissed through clenched teeth. "It'll be a lad. An' I'm namin' him Crìsdean, 'cause maybe the good Lord 'll sit up an' take pity if the wean's named after his own son."

"Crìsdean," Arthur said. "It's a guid name." He folded his wife into his arms. "An' he'll be th' seventh. Seven is a verra lucky number, aye?"

Anna pulled away and looked deep into her husband's eyes.

"Hear me noo, Arthur Maclean. I dinnae care if 'tis lucky or nae. Ye ken I love ye, but there'll be nae more bairns after this. Crìsdean is the last!"

CHAPTER 2

ISLE OF MULL, SCOTLAND, 1645

KENNA

The world had been at war for as long as Kenna could remember. She suspected it was much longer than the thirteen years she'd been in it, and nothing looked likely to change in the future.

It was the nature of men. Never satisfied with what they had, always eager to take away from others or bend them to their way of thinking. *Their* politics, *their* religion. Kings, clan chiefs, rectors—they were all men.

The world doesnae need more men t'fight. What th' world needs is women who can fight like men. Women hae more sense. They think afore they act. So why'd they let men make all th' rules?

Why her parents had thought things would be different here in Mull, Kenna could not begin to fathom.

"Ye'll be safe at Castle Duart, *leanan*. War willnae touch ye there," her mother had said. "Th' Macleans 're good people; ye'll thrive amongst 'em. Ye'll find a husband, raise a family in peace awa' from war an' bloodshed."

How wrong they were, she thought. And how little they knew their own daughter!

From her hiding place in a corner of Duart Castle's great hall, she watched the men readying themselves for another battle. It took all she had to stay still when every nerve in her body wanted to propel her into their midst. She flexed her hand and imagined it holding a sword.

Find a husband, indeed! The castle was overflowing with men, of every age and temperament. Some of them were even good-looking, and most were kind. None of them knew her heart.

She didn't want to marry one of them. She wanted to *be* one of them.

Kenna pulled up the woolen trews and tucked the homespun shirt in as well as she could, given the fact that everything was ridiculously overlarge. She gathered the top of the trews and pulled the makeshift rope belt twice around her waist before tying it in a lopsided bow.

The clothing was the best she could do under the circumstances. It had taken days to gather what she needed, and if she was stopped now, she might never have another chance.

Thank God the twins were slight of build. They were tall, but at least she wasn't lost in the shirt. Sleeves and cuffs could be rolled up.

She glanced down at her treasured black boots. Found in the bottom of Fergus's trunk, tucked under the rest of his mess, they'd obviously been outgrown long ago and forgotten. The heels were worn and the laces frayed, but if she wore her heaviest stockings, the boots would fit.

All she'd needed was a weapon, and that had been a challenge. Men might be slovenly with their garments, but they kept their swords and muskets as close as a lover.

Claymores hung in the great hall, but they were far too heavy even to lift, let alone wield in any useful fashion. She'd settled at last on a *sgian achlais*, the secret dagger meant to be concealed in a man's armpit.

Kenna lifted the cuff of her trews and studied the lethal-looking thing with some trepidation. The blade was too long, but at least her boot held it fast and the trews almost hid it from sight. If she needed the dagger, she would have to bend down and pull it free carefully; otherwise, she'd likely slice herself.

A cut was the least of her worries. If Pàdraig discovered it missing and figured out she was the culprit, he'd track her down and skin her alive. For that reason, she would have to return it to its place in his room each time after practice and hope he didn't change its location.

She'd been watching the younger men of Castle Duart for some time, ever since she determined to learn the skills of war. The older clansmen were too frightening. She shuddered to think what Dànaidh or Ealar would do if they caught her messing about in their room.

Bearnard and Hector were out of the question. Bearnard had a wife, and women knew when other women were up to something. Hector would be clan chief someday, and Kenna needed to stay in his good graces. What she was doing was already against all the rules; stealing clothing or weapons from Hector, even temporarily, would be a personal betrayal.

Giles probably wouldn't care—he never seemed to care deeply about anything outside of his books—but he wouldn't help, either. The only one of the lads she might have gone to was Crìsdean, and Kenna would rather run naked in the great hall than allow him to see her in men's attire.

She sighed, remembering. From the first moment she'd entered the keep a year ago and laid eyes on Crìsdean Maclean, her fickle female brain had turned on her. Sea-green eyes under a mop of wild russet hair that refused to be tamed. A mobile mouth that seemed always to be smiling. A dimple on one side that did something funny to her heart.

If I was t' marry, t'would be him.

Kenna pinched herself, and the traitorous thought fled. Marriage was not in her plans, no matter how comely the lad. She would not become a man's property, condemned to sit in the solar and ruin her eyes with needlework, forced to empty her mind of all but domestic concerns. She was born for greater things.

But he was so bonny . . .

It had not begun well. At his mother's call,

Crìsdean had left off sparring with an older lad and come to stand dutifully before them while Kenna was introduced.

"Crìsdean, this 's Kenna Macleod," Anna told him. "Her parents 're kin t' yer aunt Mary, an' she's t' be ward t' her an' yer uncle Lachlan. You're the closest in age; I expect you to see 'at she's made welcome."

Crìsdean's response had been immediate and harsh, like a bucket of cold water upended over her head. "I dinnae have time t' coddle a bairn."

"Did I say sommut ye didnae understand?" his mother asked in an even voice. Something about the tone must have been familiar, because her son took a deep breath and straightened to his full height.

"Nae, mam," he said. "I heard ye fine. Come on, then," he said to Kenna, "I'll show ye around."

As soon as they were around the corner and out of earshot, he'd rounded on her. "Dinnae think ye'll be followin' me around," he hissed. "I'm a man noo, I cannae have a lass gettin' unnerfoot. How old 're ye, enyway?"

"I'm twelve years," she had mumbled, fighting to keep the tears at bay. *How dare he?*

She stared him down. "How old are *ye*?"

Kenna watched as he straightened to his full height and gave her a lofty look. "I'm fifteen."

"At's nae so old," she said. "Bit 'tis old enough t' 'ave learnt some manners when talkin' t' a lady."

Now, a year older and wiser, Kenna huddled in the corner of the keep and watched as the men moved in the dance of combat. Forward, backward, thrust, parry, block. Her eyes went from man to man, assessing their skills.

Pàdraig and Fergus faced off against each other, as they always did. The twins did everything together, but Kenna thought that made little sense when training for battle. *Your enemy isnae goin' t' be a man ye ken better than yerself.*

As if he'd felt her watching, Pàdraig turned. His eyes widened as they caught her attire, and then he shook his head and turned back to block his brother's move.

Kenna shrank back into the shadows, heart racing. *Thank God 'twas him*, she thought. Paddy wouldn't give her away. If it had been that numpty Fergus, now . . .

A hand grasped her arm and she was swung around. A pair of furious green eyes pinned her in place and she felt her heart plummet. Crìsdean ran his hands through his hair and took a long, deep breath, as if fighting for patience.

"Jist wha' d' ye think ye're doin' here—an' wha's 'at ye're wearin'?" he hissed. "If Mam or Aunt Mary were t' see ye—"

"S' none o' yer business, Crìsdean Maclean!" Kenna felt the tears gather behind her eyes. "Gie on, go join th' men an' leave me be!"

His hand grabbed hers and he pulled her away from the hall and up the stone stairs to the living quarters. He was stronger by far than she; she had no choice but to follow. Outside her room, he stopped.

"Ye are no a man, Kenna Macleod! Wha' d' ye mean by dressin' in men's trews an' . . . an'. . ." he bent suddenly and yanked the sgian achlais out of her boot.

"Whit th' hell, Kenna!" He brandished the weapon

in front of her. "Whose is this?"

Kenna studied the floor. "Pàddy's."

"Weel, I'll take care o' returnin' it," he said, and tucked the dagger into his belt. "I dinnae want t' see ye near th' hall when th' men're trainin', ever agin. D' ye unnerstand?"

Crìsdean turned and strode off down the hall, throwing words back at her. "An' fer God's sake, pit on a dress!"

Kenna waited until she was sure he was out of earshot.

"I hate ye, Crìsdean Maclean!" she yelled, and listened as the words echoed off the stone walls and came back to mock her.

CHAPTER 3

CAPE BRETON ISLAND, CANADA, PRESENT DAY

*Unrequited love does not die; it's only
beaten down to a secret place where
it hides, curled and wounded.*
—Elle Newmark

"r. Maclean, can I talk to you after school? It's real important."

Brian clenched his fists. Meghan Reynolds, again. What was going on with her? She'd always been an attentive student—asked questions, participated readily, but in the last months she'd begun lingering behind when class was over, asking him for help with assignments or clarification on homework that she'd never had trouble with before. Seemed to be happening more often too. How many times had it been this week? Two, and it was only Thursday.

Besides, what could she need help with? Finals were over, and even though he still gave homework, the students knew as well as he did that it didn't mean anything with only a few days of school left.

He should talk to her guidance counselor. If there was trouble at home, she'd be the one to deal with it.

He took a deep breath.

"I don't think I have time today, Meghan," he began, and watched her face fall. "Have you talked to your counselor?"

"She doesn't get me." Meghan's voice was sulky. "Not like you do."

An alarm bell began to sound in Brian's mind, and he could feel a headache building at the back of his eyes. *Get me? What did she mean by that?* Didn't sound good.

Suddenly he was very much aware that they were the only two in the classroom. He focused on the eleventh grader in front of him. Her makeup was overdone, caked on in an effort to hide teenage acne. The brown eyes were made up like a doll's, mascara and eyeliner applied liberally and without regard to excess. Her lips were coated with a lipstick that should never have seen the light of day—bright red like an apple . . . or blood.

Her shirt was unbuttoned to show the lacy edge of a black bra, and he could guess without seeing it from his seat behind the desk that the skirt was probably too short. The part he *could* see was definitely too tight. Did her family not notice, or not care? He knew Meghan had several brothers and sisters; her brother Jimmy had graduated just last year. Nice kid, not terribly interested in algebra, definitely not interested in whether his teacher *got* him.

A shiver ran up Brian's spine. He should have noticed the changes in Meghan, paid attention to the signals she was sending. The child was trying to look older, more womanly, but the truth was she just looked sad. The headache intensified.

"Meghan, I'm flattered that you think I understand you, but I'm your math teacher. I'm not qualified to be a guidance counselor." He paused. "You know, I'm sure there are other students who need help with some of the assignments. You've given me a great idea—next term, I think I'll offer a group session once a week for those who are interested. What do you think?"

Meghan stared at him. She shook her head slowly, and then her glossy lips curved in a smile.

"I don't think you get it, Mr. Maclean. Or maybe you do, and you're just being shy."

Brian felt as if the air was being sucked out of the room. What was happening here? None of this was appropriate, in any world!

"Meghan," he fought for breath, "this isn't funny. I'm your teacher, and—"

"I like you."

The words dropped into the classroom like a lead ball. Silence filled the space between them, while Meghan continued to smile and Brian fought for breath.

He jumped to his feet and backed away from the desk.

"Meghan, stop it!" He heard the incipient panic in his own voice, but he was helpless to stop it. "I'm your teacher, and you're my student. I'm an adult and you're a child!"

It was the wrong thing to say. The girl's eyes filled, and the smile dissolved into a quivering pout.

The door opened and the tenth graders began to file in. Meghan stood and gave him a long look. Then she shrugged her shoulders.

"Okay." She lowered her head and shuffled to the door, looking like a prisoner who has been told she was about to be beheaded.

Brian realised he was sweating. He forced a smile and summoned his thoughts in preparation for his next class. Thank God he'd headed that off before it could escalate.

I'd better see the counselor about Meghan; she'll be in my class again next year and I don't want it to be awkward. She's just a kid; summer should take care of things.

School would be out in a week. Just five more days, and then he'd be on the lake, with nothing to worry about besides the usual issues that befall sailors. Hulls crack, sails turn to ribbons, ropes jam, goosenecks snap, and water finds its way into tanks. Right now that sounded like heaven.

When his last class was over and the closing bell had rung, he closed the classroom door and sat at his desk with his head in his hands, letting the tension drain out of his body.

Why didn't I see this coming? Am I that oblivious?

"*Of course you are.*" His sister's voice sounded tart in his head, as if she were right in front of him instead of across the pond in Scotland. "*You think you care about people, but you don't, not really. I told you this would happen.*"

When he'd come home with the news that he was going to be the math teacher at Central Cape Academy, Fiona had teased him that he was too good-looking to survive an onslaught of teenage girls.

"You're going to have to pay attention," she'd told him. "You'll be dealing with tenth through twelfth grade girls. They're not going to be able to concentrate on algebra or geometry once they see you, what with all those hormones jumping around."

"You only think I'm handsome because we look alike," he'd countered.

"Really?" his sister had laughed, "that's all you heard? My point is made."

It was true, though—about the looks. Fiona was the younger sibling by fifteen months, but the two had often been mistaken for twins. They had the same thick russet hair and green eyes, and both had inherited their father's wide, ready smile.

Brian's thoughts returned to the present. He wished he could talk to Fiona about this thing with Meghan. She'd deliver the obligatory "I told you so," but she would give him sound advice. After all, she was a woman; she could put it all in perspective.

His sister was about as far away as anyone could get, though—off in the land of their ancestors with her Scotsman. Even though they talked on the phone at least once a week, this wasn't the sort of thing that could be discussed long distance. It had been months since the wedding; he should make some time this summer to go over and visit her.

After the regatta, of course.

The Bras d'Or Regatta in August took precedence

over everything in Baddeck, and soon the lake would be filled with sailboats of every size and sailors of all experience levels. It would all be over by mid-August, so that gave him nearly three weeks before the start of school. Plenty of time for a trip to Scotland.

The oppressive silence of an empty school intruded on his meandering. Time to go; the lake was waiting. They'd have time for one practice run before dinner, and they needed all the practice they could get if they were to have a chance in August.

Brian and his friends, Liam and Sean, had been sailing on Bras d'Or since childhood and knew the lake's every whim. Sam was a newbie; he'd only started sailing two years ago when his parents had come up from the States and bought a second home—and a sailboat—in Baddeck.

Sam's father was a Star Wars fanatic, so the boat was named *Millenium Dolphin*. Nobody cared what the name was though, as long as they could be a part of the crew. And to be part of the crew, they had to teach Sam how to sail.

The kid had talent and good hands, but inexperience could make the difference between glory and disaster in a race, so they needed vigilance, perseverance, and luck in equal measure. And practice.

Brian's spirits lifted as he walked toward his car. The silver Audi was the only vehicle left in the parking lot. He stopped fifty feet away and grinned in anticipation. The convertible was the only one of its kind in Baddeck, a totally unsuitable choice for an island that saw warm temperatures for only a few days of the year, but today was one of those days.

He'd wanted a convertible for as long as he could remember. When he was a teenager like the kids he now taught, Brian had endured the raised eyebrows of family and friends and scanned the magazines strewn around the waiting room at MacInnes Motors until the perfect vehicle drove off the pages of *Car and Driver* and into his heart.

For months, his family was subjected to lists of descriptions and attributes of the banana-yellow MG he was sure would change his life.

"What do you want with a cloth-top in a town that gets snow from October to May?" his father asked, before disappearing behind his newspaper.

"Why do you need such a fast car, dear?" his mother put in, her eyes worried. "There aren't any high-speed roads on the Cape."

"Will you let me drive?" Kirsty, at fourteen, had a gleam in her eye that Brian chose to ignore.

"And how will you pay for this work of art?" his father's voice came from behind the paper. "Will a part-time job at the yacht club do the trick, on top of college expenses—hmm?" The question was followed by a snort.

In desperation, Brian appealed to Fiona. "You get it, don't you, Fee? Help me out here."

His hitherto silent sister gave him a look of apology and cleared her throat. "I don't know what you're all worried about. Look at him; he's already six-one. He won't fit."

Brian shook his head. Trust Fiona to have her finger on the pulse. Ten years later, when he finally had the chance to try out his dream car, he found that once again she'd been right. He felt like a sardine, squished into a cockpit that closed in around him, pinched his knees, and gave him instant claustrophobia. The dream died a quick and painful death.

Then one day Mr. MacInnes had pulled him aside after sailing practice. "You still want a sports car?" he asked. "Just got in a 2012 Audi TT. Owner's moved up from Virginia and wants to sell it."

"What's wrong with it?"

Mr. MacInnes shrugged. "Just needed the brakes aligned. It's in pristine condition, otherwise."

"So why is he selling it?" Years older and wiser than his teenage self, Brian was not taking the bait like he once had.

"Says it's impractical," Mr. MacInnes said. "Quote— only a crazy man would want a convertible in Nova Scotia." He winked. "So I thought of you."

And shortly thereafter, Brian found himself sitting in the surprisingly roomy cockpit of a classic car. A convertible. She was his first love, and he named her Juliet.

Brian smiled at the memory. He'd never regretted a single moment with his girl, and she looked as good today as she probably had when she rolled out of the factory in 2012.

Something intruded on his reverie. Something was off. It took a full minute for the truth of what he was seeing to sink in. From the front panel, all along Juliet's gleaming silver finish, a thin line of paint was missing. He stared in shock at the damage, ran his finger over the rough edges.

Somebody had keyed his car.

He looked around the lot, but there was no one there. A movement caught his attention and his eyes focused on a figure across the street from the school.

Someone was staring at him, standing perfectly still and just watching. Then the figure turned and ran into the trees that formed the boundary of the school property and was gone.

Brian stared from the ugly slash on the side of his car to the trees, unable to process what had just happened. A chill began at the base of his spine and worked its way up to lodge in his chest, and his stomach flipped over.

What the hell?

CHAPTER 4

INVERNESS, SCOTLAND, PRESENT DAY

*Telling an introvert to go to a party
is like telling a saint to go to hell.*
—Criss Jami

The dark figure crouched in the shadows, hand steady on the hilt of his sword. A gift from his father on his fifteenth birthday, the lethal blade glinted in the dim light cast by a waning moon, promising death to anyone unfortunate enough to test its resolve.

Soft footsteps sounded on the path. The swordsman tensed; this was the moment he had waited for—the culmination of ten years of bitter waiting. The next few seconds would make the difference between victory and failure for him and his master.

The footsteps moved slowly, drawing ever closer, and now he could hear the soft breathing of his prey. Another second . . . and another—

A knock on the door broke the silence, and Sophie's head jerked up from her book. *Damn it*, just when she'd gotten to the best part! She groped for her bookmark and placed it carefully in her copy of *The King Exemplar* before placing it on the side table. It looked as if the assassin would have to wait a few more minutes to complete his murderous task.

She dragged herself to the door, her mind still on the plight of the hapless Sir Anthony. *Will he sense the danger and avoid Morgan's lethal blade?*

Sophie looked through the peephole and sighed. She swung the door open and managed a wan smile for her best friend. Deirdre Clarke pushed past and ran into the sitting room, sprawled on the couch, and looked up at her friend with a gleam in her eye.

"What's up, Dee? Why are you here so late?" Sophie's eyes slid to the book on the side table. *But Sir Anthony's still injured . . .he can't fight . . .*

"I can't stay; I only have a minute. But Soph! I got them!"

"Got what?" *His best option is to escape . . . maybe Lady Anne will arrive in time and . . .*

"The tickets, numpty! For Saturday night! Are you paying attention?" Deirdre's red curls bounced and her brown eyes danced with excitement.

Sir Anthony and his potential assassin whooshed back into the pages of *The King Exemplar*, forgotten. Sophie sat down with a thump.

"Are you serious? Alasdair Fraser and Natalie Haas? How?"

"My dad's the solicitor for Eden Court now. I asked him to keep an eye out, and the old man came through! And the tickets include a question-answer session with the musicians afterward. Am I not the best friend in the world?"

"You are the best friend in the universe. Without a doubt." Sophie looked across the room at her violin and gave it a thumbs-up.

"I'm glad you realize it," Deirdre's amused voice purred. "There's one thing you have to know, though."

Sophie's heart dropped. "Is this where the other shoe drops? What's the catch?"

"Eden Court is a theatre. A public place. It'll be full of humans . . . you know—*people*." Deirdre lowered her voice to a dramatic whisper. "Can you cope with that?"

"Oh, shut up," Sophie laughed. "You're such an arse."

"I'm an arse?" her friend snorted. "You hide yourself in this huge place all by yourself." She looked around the dark sitting room and shivered. "You spend your time playing that damned violin or reading romantic drivel," she indicated the book on the side table and pursed her lips, "about people who never existed."

"And your point is?" Sophie's response sounded puzzled. "Reading increases your vocabulary. I'm not good enough at the violin, so I have to practice."

"When's the last time you went out?"

"Don't be an eejit. I went to Morrison's yesterday."

Deirdre blew air through her lips. "Not to the market—when's the last time you went somewhere you might have to actually interact with real people?"

At Sophie's blank stare, Deirdre sighed and stood up. "Honestly, I don't understand how you can be so oblivious to the fact that there are humans sharing the planet with you."

"I'm not oblivious. I know they're out there. So what?"

Deirdre gritted her teeth. "My point is, you never go anywhere. You're always huddled up in this big mausoleum, interacting with things. There's a world full of people out there, and half of them are men!"

"I don't really care for people," Sophie said. "And men are just larger versions of people."

Her friend threw her hands in the air and stood up. "I swear, I don't know why I deal with you. You're so beautiful; I'd kill for your looks. You could have any man in Inverness, but you freeze them all out and spend your time holed up in this gothic mansion talking to a stringed instrument."

"That's enough." Sophie laughed and pushed the other girl toward the door. "Go home; it's late and I want to discuss the news with Oliver."

Deirdre rolled her eyes and appealed to the ceiling for help. "And she's named her violin. That's not the least bit weird."

She sighed. "Okay, I'm done with you."

Sophie noticed her friend eyeing her tartan pajama pants and faded grey fleece. "What?" she said.

Deirdre rolled her eyes. "I'll pick you up on Saturday. Wear something sexy; you never know, maybe you'll meet a man who isn't made of wood and strings."

She gave Sophie a hug before turning to go.

"*Oliver*," she muttered under her breath. "Why do I bother?"

Sophie closed the door and leaned against it, wondering if she'd ever be totally comfortable with Deirdre's extroverted personality. She was a darling, but the truth was, she could be exhausting. Still, they'd managed to be friends since primary school, closer than sisters.

At least I suppose we're like sisters. I never had a sister my age, and the brothers are . . . well, brothers. The truth is, none of us are really close.

It wasn't anybody's fault. When Mom had died, Dad's spirit had died with her. He became distant, cold, and even contemptuous toward his children, as if they had no right to exist if his beloved wife didn't. Toward Ewan, whom he blamed for his wife's death, he was hateful and mean. It was no wonder Ewan had left home the minute he turned eighteen.

Izzy had tried to be both mother and father to her younger brothers and baby sister, but she'd been only fourteen, crushed by the weight of her own grief. The truth was they were more like a collection of orphans than a family. What had once been a warm and loving home was like a jungle choked with weeds of anger, despair, and regret.

The older MacArthurs had begun to leave home as soon as they came of age, until only the youngest two remained. Father had sent Daniel to his brother Ranald, leaving sixteen-year old Sophie alone in a house that no one else could bear to live in.

The joke was on them; she loved it. Being raised in an environment surrounded by people who tip-toed around each other for fear of attracting Father's attention, she had learned very early to be quiet and not draw the gaze of others. A natural introvert, she turned more and more in upon herself. After a while, the empty house became her solace. She knew its secrets, rejoiced in its strength and solidity.

And now it was hers. When Father had died, his will left the house to Izzy, as the oldest, and she in turn had signed it over to Sophie, free and clear. It was hers to decorate, to furnish—to hide in.

Sophie wandered back to her chair and picked up *The King Exemplar.* She opened it to the bookmarked page and searched for the last place she'd been. Morgan and Sir Anthony were right where she'd left them, waiting for her to read them through this latest quagmire.

With a sigh, she tossed the book aside again. Right now, she didn't really care about their problems; they could fend for themselves for a while. Her mind kept going back to Deirdre's comments.

You're always huddled up in this big mausoleum, interacting with things . . . You spend your free time playing that damned violin or reading romantic drivel about people who never existed.

Sophie looked across the room at the violin, leaning against the wall and minding its own business. "She didn't mean it, Oliver," she told the instrument. "She's not me. I mean, you and I know people are annoying. They're not predictable."

They're not safe.

A bitter smile crossed her lips. No one except Deirdre had noticed when she dropped out of The Royal Conservatoire after three years, and even her best friend didn't know why.

"It just wasn't right for me," she'd said. "I'm not good enough."

"But you were good enough to get in," Deirdre had protested in confusion. "You even got a merit scholarship! Did they say you weren't good enough, or was that your own decision?"

"Let it go, Dee. Please." Sophie had forced the words through lips numb from the effort to keep from crying. "I'll just study at home."

Thinking about those words now, Sophie's lips curled in self-derision. Not good enough. Deirdre thought she had meant the violin, but the truth was far worse than that. She'd been good at the violin—very good. Her professors had praised her for the magic she created with a bow and strings, told her that in time she might play in one of the best orchestras in the world.

What she hadn't been good at was people. Reading people, sensing when a kind facade hid something dark and evil. She hadn't known that such depravity even existed.

She didn't have a mother to teach her about that. No one to advise her about things women should be wary of, nobody to tell her what could skulk on the other side of a handsome face and laughing eyes.

There'd been no one to hug her and tell her it wasn't her fault. No parents to see that justice was done. She had four older brothers, and not one of them knew. Not one was close enough to his baby sister to sense her despair, or to fight her battles and tell her everything would be all right.

Sophie took a long drink from the water bottle on the side table and willed the nausea to go away. It had been three years, and she still woke screaming some nights, struggling to get free. She still found herself in the dorm room, a small voice whispering, *Don't go! Something's not right.* Why hadn't she listened?

She'd dropped out the next day. Left it all behind—the scholarship, the accolades . . . her future.

What had followed her home was shame, guilt, and the raw feeling of disgrace. It accompanied her if she dared to leave the house, lurked in dark corners of her mind, waiting for the chance to remind her that strangers couldn't be trusted. It filled everyday activities with tension and anxiety, whether she was pushing a cart at the market or walking down High Street. The only place she felt safe was in her home, surrounded by inanimate objects that didn't judge.

She told herself she wasn't the only one in her family to endure trauma. At least three of her siblings had faced issues from their family's dysfunction, just like she had. Ewan had struggled for years with feelings of guilt about their mother's death. Daniel had turned to alcohol to cope with hidden things he never shared. Izzy was now divorced from a husband who had turned out to be the worst kind of rotter. Every one of them had faced it alone. So who was she to think she was any different?

Maybe their family was cursed; it would explain a lot. Perhaps a MacArthur ancestor had offended God in such a way that doomed his descendants to suffer unspeakable personal loss, always alone.

At least she had Deirdre. One good friend was all an introvert needed, after all. Her friend sensed there was something wrong, but after that one time, she hadn't pushed. Sophie's idiosyncrasies became just another part of her natural tendency to avoid people, maybe a little more pronounced than before, but manageable. According to Deirdre, she was just Sophie.

"It'll be okay, Oliver," Sophie said. She picked up *The King Exemplar* again, and settled down to another night alone, surrounded by things and objects—and people who didn't exist.

CHAPTER 5

BADDECK, NOVA SCOTIA, PRESENT DAY

*For the first time in his existence,
he knew he was drowning and he
wasn't thinking about survival.*
—Christine Feehan

"Mr. Maclean, could you see me for a minute after school?"

Brian looked up from his lunch to see the school principal, Mr. Dunn, in the doorway.

"Sure, no problem."

The principal backed out of the lunchroom without another word. *Odd,* Brian thought. Ralph Dunn prided himself on being 'just one of the guys"—his own words. Most days he ate lunch with his staff, taking turns sitting with each group during their lunch period. But today, he'd seemed eager to leave.

Mr. Maclean? Why so formal?

Brian shrugged. End of the year tension, probably. He didn't know how they did it, the administrators.

All those reports—analyzing test scores, interacting with colleges, working head to head with the guidance counselor to juggle scholarships and summer work programs; he'd go mad if he had to give up the kids for paperwork.

He knew that a lot of the teachers at Central Cape were involved in the educational leadership process; it seemed all they wanted was to get out of the classroom and away from students. Some days he could understand, but those days were rare. Teaching wasn't a job; it was a calling.

The last eight years had been the best of his life, and he couldn't imagine doing anything else—except maybe sailing, but that didn't pay as well. On the contrary, it sucked money out of you. He grinned to himself; he didn't know a single Caper who regretted the loss of money because of sailing.

The smile faded as a thought returned to tickle the back of his brain. Something about the principal . . . no, the guidance counselor. He hadn't seen Lynn Buchanan about Meghan Renolds, and school was over in three days.

He admitted to himself that he didn't want to discuss what had happened three days ago with the girl; it was embarrassing. But after what happened to his car . . .

Did he really think Meghan could have done that? She'd been in class the next day, and nothing she'd said or done since alluded to anything resembling guilt.

Sure, she was avoiding eye contact, and she'd stopped participating in class, but he didn't really blame her for that. She'd embarrassed herself; it would be natural for her to avoid him.

His face heated at the memory of those words, uttered in a voice so low he could almost make himself think he hadn't heard them correctly.

I don't think you get it, Mr. Maclean.

I like you.

No, it had definitely happened, and he was going to see Lynn about it. Even if she didn't think she could act on it now, since school was almost over, she'd be prepared to help the girl and keep a gentle eye on her when the fall term began in September. After all, Meghan would be in his class again for her senior year.

He took a deep breath and let it out. He'd see Lynn today if Mr. Dunn's meeting didn't take too long, and if it did, he still had tomorrow. And then he could wash his hands of the whole situation and concentrate on the regatta.

Except that somebody had keyed his car. What were the odds that such a thing could happen the same day that a sixteen-year-old girl had bared her soul to her male teacher and been rejected?

There'd been someone watching him as he stood in shock and assessed the damage to his beloved Juliet. Someone small enough to be female. He hadn't reported the vandalism to the police; he wasn't sure why. He had made an appointment at Peter McInnes' shop for the first week school was out and tried to shrug it off. Some people just needed to ruin other people's things.

But the ugly gash mocked him every time he saw his car, and he couldn't get the thought out of his mind—*what if it was Meghan?* He didn't want to get the girl in trouble, although the primitive part of his brain envisioned dunking her in the lake until she confessed.

If it was her. The school parking lot was accessible to the street; there was no fence to keep random people out. Anyone could have damaged the Audi, and maybe he'd just missed seeing the gash. Maybe it had happened the day before.

He knew that wasn't possible, though. He parked his car in the same spot every day, and that horrible scar had been the first thing he'd seen when he crossed the lot. No, it had happened sometime that day, for sure.

Maybe he should tell Ralph Dunn about it this afternoon—get another opinion. Just the thought of sharing the incident took a huge load off his mind. Yes, the principal and the guidance counselor should both know, just in case. If she'd done this, she needed help. You just couldn't take things too lightly with teenagers.

As soon as the last bus pulled out, Brian headed down to the main office. Best to get this over with; ratting out a student without firm evidence had never been his style and it made him uncomfortable.

As he raised his hand to knock on Ralph's door, it occurred to him that this meeting hadn't been his idea in the first place. He'd been summoned. He shrugged and rapped twice on the door.

"Come in."

As soon as he crossed the threshold, Brian knew something was wrong. Dunn sat behind his desk, his posture stiff. The customary smile was missing, and there was an odd, unsettled look about his eyes.

Brian sat in the chair in front of the desk and smiled at his principal. The smile was not returned.

"Erm . . ." Dunn said. "I really hate having to have this conversation . . ."

A frisson of unease slid through Brian's stomach. He furrowed his brow and waited.

Dunn cleared his throat. "Brian, I've always thought highly of your teaching, you know that." He paused, and a thick silence settled on the room. Brian stared at his boss in confusion. Was he being praised? It didn't seem like it.

"I've received a letter from one of our student's parents," the principal continued, "and I wanted to address it with you first, before we go any further."

Go any further? Was somebody complaining? Ralph always backs his teachers when parents complain. He sat up straight, his heart beginning to hammer in his chest.

"Yes?" he managed. "What's the problem?"

"Meghan Reynolds' parents are accusing you of inappropriate behavior toward their daughter," Dunn said.

"What?" Brian wondered if he had heard it right over the pounding in his ears. "What are you talking about?"

"They said you sought her out after school, under the guise of giving her extra help, and . . ." Dunn's lips twisted. "You made advances to her."

Time stood still for an eternity before Brian found his voice. "Ralph, that's ridiculous! You know me! She's the one—" he stuttered to a stop.

"She's the one? You mean it's true?" Dunn's eyes

widened and his face radiated astonishment. "You kept her after school?"

"No!" Brian could hear his voice rising in panic. "I mean, yes, she stayed after school a few times for help, but she's the one who asked!"

"Was she doing poorly in your class? Why would she tell her parents something like this?"

"No! Meghan is one of my best students! I don't know why she'd say something like that—she—she's the one who came on to me!"

As soon as the words left his lips, Brian wanted to grab them back. He'd just made it sound as though something had really happened! What could he say now? The roaring in his ears reached crescendo pitch, and he was suddenly afraid he'd black out. Why hadn't he gone to the guidance counselor the next morning? Why hadn't he gone to Ralph immediately?

The principal was watching him, horror dawning on his face. Brian opened his mouth and closed it again, afraid to say another word. His thoughts were a churning mess, and he felt light-headed.

Fiona was right. He *was* oblivious. He'd never seen this coming. For God's sake, he'd cared more about his damn car than about the real danger, and now his world was falling apart in front of his eyes.

Brian found himself in the parking lot shared by the Bras d'Or Yacht Club, the Freight Shed restaurant, and several other businesses without knowing how he'd gotten there. He'd been in a trance since leaving the principal's office. He locked the car and walked across the lot, shuffling like an old man.

Suspended! With three days of school left, he'd been suspended "pending further investigation of his case."

His case? There was a *case*? How could Dunn even think for a moment that he would do such a thing? How could the man listen to the words of a teenage girl over his?

His own words filtered back into his brain. "Mr. Dunn . . . *sir*, you don't need to suspend me. If you believe this nonsense for even one minute, I don't belong here. Consider this my resignation."

He flinched at the memory. The words didn't sound so brave now. In fact, quitting his dream job just made him sound guilty. And it wouldn't stop an investigation—hell, he *wanted* an investigation! Surely the truth would bear him out. Surely—

"Brian! Where's your head?"

Brian looked up to see Liam Macleod leaning out of the window of his car.

"Huh?"

"I almost hit you! What the hell are you thinking about?"

Brian took a deep breath. "Nothing. Sorry."

Liam parked and the two walked into the club. His friend said nothing more, but Brian could feel concerned eyes boring into the side of his skull. He made an attempt to shake himself out of his fugue; there was no room for error on a racing sailboat, and one misstep could mean disaster for them all. It was hard enough with Sam on board; two sailors not at peak performance was an accident waiting to happen.

He pushed his problem ruthlessly to the back of his mind as the four pushed the *Millenium Dolphin* into Bras d'Or Lake. A seventeen-knot wind, gusting at times to twenty-five knots, churned the waves into whitecaps and pushed the J70 sailboat from side to side, as if the lake resented the intrusion of such a small creature and wanted to assert its dominance.

Despite the rough conditions, the lake was dotted with the usual plethora of jet skis. From his place at the tiller, Brian caught Sean's eye and grimaced. Jet skis were the bane of a sailor's existence, rented for the day by people who knew little or nothing about sailing. They were like noisy gnats, buzzing in and out of a sailboat's path with barely controlled speed, sure that the larger boats would maneuver around them.

Of course, there would be no such nuisance during the regatta, but practice runs were rife with near misses. Tangles with sailboats weren't the only hazard for unprepared jet skiers; Brian remembered an incident two years ago where a party of four college kids had ventured out in high winds on rented jet skis and only three had returned. They'd found the body of the fourth the next day, several miles away from the point of origin.

Sam was staring at the jet skis, his lips taut. His position in the bow guaranteed a good soaking, but his attention never wavered.

He's doing fine, Brian thought, and felt a surge of pride in the younger man. He looked at the other two, intent on their tasks.

"Gybe ho!" Liam called. They began a controlled gybe, maneuvering the stern of the *Dolphin* through the wind. This turning required concentration no matter how many times they did it, and especially in high winds.

"The fool!" Sean yelled. "He's trying to cut us off!"

Brian turned in his seat. A jet ski was about twenty yards off, running parallel as if the idiot thought he was racing them. Without warning, it sped up and angled toward the bow of the *Dolphin.*

Brian stood up to see, but from this angle he couldn't see the jet ski under the jib.

"Brian! Look out!"

He turned just as the boom whipped across at lightning speed, caught the side of his head and sent him flying—over the side and into the water of Bras d'Or Lake.

The lake folded him into its embrace, and he felt himself drifting in a world of color, helpless to move. Oranges and yellows and greens expanded and contracted like a kaleidoscope, ever changing. It was the most beautiful thing he'd ever seen, and suddenly he knew.

He was drowning. He waited for the water to fill his lungs, but nothing happened. Instead, there was sound—grunts and bellows, the clang of iron on iron.

That's weird. Brian gave himself up to the sounds and waited. He didn't want to miss the end.

Something clutched his hand, and he felt himself being pulled upward. The colors were gone, but the clamor intensified, and now he thought he could identify the sounds. Men fighting with swords, like in the movie *Braveheart.*

Someone was patting his cheek. It was annoying, so he lifted his hand to brush it away.

"Crìsdean!" A woman's voice, far away. *What was a woman doing on their sailboat?* Maybe he should open his eyes and find out.

He wasn't on the boat. He was lying on the ground, his head cradled in the arms of a young woman. The fear on her face gave way to relief and she clutched him close.

"I was so feart; dinnae ever do 'at t' me agin!" she scolded. "Are ye awright?"

Brian gawked up at the stranger who was holding him so tight he could barely breathe. A young girl. Long blonde hair, impossibly blue eyes. She stared back at him, confusion replacing the fear in their depths. He struggled to sit up, and looked around in shock.

The *Millenium Dolphin* was gone. Bras d'Or Lake was gone. Behind the girl, a group of men parried and feinted with swords, cursing and grunting with the effort. And behind the men rose the grey and brown stone walls of a castle.

CHAPTER 6

ISLE OF MULL, SCOTLAND, 1646

KENNA

Kenna smoothed her gown, grateful for the yards of material that encircled her waist. No one would suspect that underneath the gown's full skirt she wore men's trews, or that in one boot nestled the sharpest kitchen knife she could find.

Well, Crìsdean might, but there was no way he was going to find out. She grinned at the idea of Crìsdean Maclean lifting her skirts to check for a weapon. Nae, she was safe from that kind of attention at Duart Castle. A strange, mingled feeling of relief and regret fluttered through her like the wings of a newly hatched bird.

Her cheeks grew warm. What was happening to her these days? During the year since her first aborted attempt to join the men in their training, she had dutifully "pit on a dress" as Crìsdean demanded. But recently she'd discovered a look of approval from her erstwhile adversary that caused an odd upheaval in her stomach, as though a kaleidoscope of butterflies had taken up residence there.

She was almost fifteen now—a woman. It was becoming more difficult to disguise herself as a male when she sneaked out to train. Parts of her were emerging where no man should have such protuberances, while her height had remained frustratingly lacking. She looked like what she was—a young lass.

Until she took off the gown and stuffed her long blonde hair under a man's woolen bonnet. Odd how clothing defined a person. In the gown she was a lady, in trews, a long shirt, and a slouchy bonnet, a lad. If she didn't get too close to the men who knew her best, she could watch them and learn.

It wasn't an ideal way to train, but it was the best she could do. Kenna had convinced Albert, the head kitchen lad, to spar with her when no one was around so she could practice what she observed in the yard.

He was balking at being used as a target, though; she'd cut him once or twice by accident and he was being such a bairn about it. But he was all she had, so she'd given him her treasured boots as compensation.

It had taken her three months to pilfer another pair—this time from Pàdraig. He was as messy as his brother, which was a double boon when foraging for clothing. Neither twin threw anything away, and both usually wore whatever they found on the floor.

Kenna worked her way through the castle corridors, keeping to the shadows where possible, until she reached the door that led to the kitchen yard and the outbuilding where the castle's food was prepared. From there it was easy to see the yard where the men were training.

She retraced her steps to an alcove and stripped off the gown, rolling it into a ball and stuffing it behind the bench that was more ornament than furniture. She'd never seen a soul actually take time to sit there, which was why it was her favorite nook in the castle. Close to the outer door, too shadowed to allow reading or needlework, it was perfect for her purpose.

Behind the bench she had stored her "training weapons," a lofty term for the broomstick that became a sword when facing off against Albert, and the two round wooden trays he had stolen from the kitchen. The broomstick was wrapped in cloth at her adversary's insistence; *I dinnae need eny more bruises, ye ken?* he had told her. Kenna snorted at the memory. *Wee cowart.*

She pulled out her supplies, and a moment later a young lad sauntered out of the alcove and headed for the door to the yard. Kendrick Macpherson, if anyone asked, was a kitchen lad, just one of many. It was the only job Kenna could think of that would allow her the freedom to move unnoticed and give access to the yard where the men practiced at swords. Kitchen servants had the run of the castle, and they were invisible unless bearing food or drink.

She pulled the bonnet lower so that it drooped over her face. It wouldn't do to let her eyes show; too many had commented on their unusual shade.

"Ye're goin' t' be a beauty," Mary had told her when she arrived. "I've ne'er seen eyes th' like; so big an' blue with bits o' green mixed in. Like t' the sea on a summer day."

Being bonny had never been Kenna's goal—until recently. Things had taken a disturbing turn since Crìsdean Maclean grew to a lean six feet and sprouted muscles. Since he began looking at her in a new way.

She felt like two different people, depending on the clothing she wore, and it rankled. It shouldn't have to be that way. Of course she couldn't fight in a gown, but why the need to hide what she was? She ought to be allowed to train with the men, to carry a blade proudly and stand ready to defend Duart like the others.

Women 'ave been defendin' castles fer centuries. Kenna frowned and juggled the two trays and her broomstick while trying to push the door open with one foot. *Didnae Jeanne d'Arc pit on men's clothes and fight along with her men? Why cannae these stoobern Macleans see 'at?*

Albert was nowhere in sight. Kenna leaned one tray against the stone wall and hoisted the other in her left hand, hopeful that no one would notice the lack of anything on the tray.

She made her way toward a sound of clanging metal mixed with grunts and curses of men engaged in combat. Kenna found her spot, deep in the shadow of a tower wall, and let her eyes rove over the scene before her, searching for one particular figure.

Her heart gave an odd jump as she spied Crìsdean, partnered today with Ealar. The older brother was the better technician, but Crìsdean's energy made up for his lack of experience. Kenna watched as Ealar lunged, and she clenched her fists even though she knew he would never hurt his brother—at least not deliberately.

Crìsdean dodged to the side. Suddenly he stepped forward quickly so that his brother was thrown off balance and forced to back away. Ealar responded by planting his left foot and thrusting forward with his sword, stopping his blade an inch from Crìsdean's chest.

A swift parry wiped the smug look of triumph from Ealar's face as Crìsdean moved his sword into the path of his brother's blade. Before the older man could react, he twisted his forearm and struck Ealar's sword, deflecting it with a loud clang that rang out over the yard.

Ealar lowered his sword and regarded Crìsdean with grudging respect. "Ye've improved, lad. Keep at 't, 'an ye might jist no get kilt in a real battle." He clapped his brother on the shoulder and strode off to find his next opponent.

From her vantage point near the castle wall, Kenna watched the exchange with pride. Ealar was one of the best swordsmen in the clan; everybody knew it. A word of praise from him was worth two from most others.

'O course, he doesnae use his full strength on his brothers, but still . . . I wisht I could learn from him. Kenna caught hold of the errant thought and strangled it before it could take root. Ealar, or any of them to be honest, would rather die than admit a woman could practice swordcraft. For now, this was all she could do—watch from the shadows and swing a broomstick around.

She sighed. It was the way of things. She swept the threatening sense of depression away and squared her slim shoulders. No one was going to stop her from learning to fight. Who knew; someday she might save one of these arrogant Macleans. Then they'd sing a different tune!

She shrugged and ran over the moves she had just seen in her mind. *Lunge, dodge, thrust, parry, sweep.* She moved further into the shadow and practiced until she could execute the moves without reciting them in her head.

"I dinnae think ye need me eny more," a voice said at her ear. Kenna spun around to face Albert, standing with his arms akimbo.

"Do ye mean 't?" Kenna asked him. "Or are ye jist scared I'll whack ye wi' my wee sword?" She narrowed her eyes and brandished the broomstick. Albert snorted and turned to watch the action on the field.

"Wha's a matter wi' Crìsdean?" he asked. Kenna's eyes followed Albert's pointing finger.

There *was* something wrong with Crìsdean. He stood alone in the yard, both hands clutching his head. As they watched, he took two staggering steps to the side and swayed on his feet before his knees folded and he collapsed onto the packed dirt.

Kenna forgot she was hiding, forgot she was dressed as a lad. The sound of weapons diminished and she was in motion, racing across the yard to where Crìsdean lay, unmoving. She sank to her knees, put her arm around his shoulders, and pulled him toward her.

"Help!" she screamed, into a void of chaotic sound. Out of the corner of her eye, she saw the Maclean clansmen sparring, unaware of her distress. She gave up and focused on the still figure in her arms.

His eyes were closed, face pale. Sweat beaded on his brow and his breath came in gasps. What had happened? She'd been watching the whole time; no weapon had touched him.

"Crìsdean!" She heard the quaver in her voice and clutched him tighter. "Wha's wrong?"

He opened his eyes, and she allowed herself a deep breath of relief and gratitude. For two years those eyes had laughed at her, narrowed in frustration countless times, crinkled with mirth. They were a clear green that held all the colors of the forest. Kenna knew his eyes as well as her own.

A chill slithered through her as she gazed into them. There was just one problem. These weren't Crìsdean's eyes.

She was holding a stranger in her arms.

CHAPTER 7

ISLE OF MULL, SCOTLAND, 1646

CRÌSDEAN

The fog rolled in off the sea, grey and formless and silent. It reached into Crìsdean's mind with slender fingers, grasping at his senses with a cold rapacity that seemed almost sentient.

Nausea formed and coiled itself into a ball in his stomach, like a snake. Its tongue whipped back and forth, looking for the danger it knew must be present. Like a blind creature desperate to escape, but knowing it was no use.

Like a blind creature . . .

He wasn't blind, yet his brain refused to give up the pieces that formed the images wavering in front of him. He wasn't deaf either; harsh sounds were resonating from somewhere in the fog. He drifted toward the sounds, but each time he thought to catch them, they broke and were lost again in this formless, convoluted world.

He could feel. Soft bands circled his body and held him tight, but he was grateful, for he sensed those bands were all that kept him from floating away in the fog.

Light penetrated the shadows, and images coalesced and danced in front of him. A head floated in and out of the shadows, its face pale and weightless. Young and ethereally beautiful. A lass, perhaps, yet not dressed as a lass. Strangely familiar, too, but he could not find a name. Surely he should remember the owner of a face so lovely.

A lass not dressed as a lass? He found his senses returning with the challenge of this new mystery. Now he recognized the harsh clanging as swords meeting in combat. His vision cleared and he realized he was being squashed against a chest that, despite the rough homespun shirt, was definitely female.

A lass not dressed as a lass. *Kenna.* For a moment a sense of profound relief overwhelmed him, an understanding that if Kenna were here, everything was going to be all right.

Even so, there was something wrong. Crìsdean could smell something rank and metallic in the air, mixing with the fog that refused to lift. *Fear,* and it was coming from the lass who held him in her lap. Which was ridiculous—fear was not something he'd ever associate with Kenna. Foolhardiness, perhaps, pigheadedness, absolutely. But Kenna feared nothing. He opened his mouth . . .

"Wh-where am I?" his lips said.

Wha? Why would he ask such a thing? He knew exactly where he was; the walls of Duart Castle loomed behind him, rising out of the fog like a mountain, strong and impregnable.

"Who are you?" he asked, in a voice that shook.

The creeping sensation was back. None of those words were his.

"Crìsdean!" The girl was shaking him, and now he knew for certain it had to be Kenna. But his mouth wouldn't form the words he needed; it was as if he were a marionette and a stranger was pulling the strings, making him say things he didn't mean.

And suddenly the fog was gone. It didn't dissipate, as an ordinary fog would. It simply vanished. He was lying on the ground, Kenna Macleod's worried blue eyes searching his face. He struggled to sit up, and looked around.

"Are ye awright, noo?" she asked him. She pushed his hair off his face and felt around his head.

Crìsdean pushed her hand away and sat up fully. "I'm fine."

"Ye're no fine when ye jist faint away fer no reason," she countered. "Ye're no fine when ye dinnae ken where ye are or who ye be!" She sat back and crossed her arms over her chest. "An' quit lookin' at me like 'at!"

Crìsdean snorted and stood up, swaying on his feet. "Mebbe ye should find a glass an' take a look at yerself," he said, grateful that the words coming out now were what he meant them to be. "Seems like ye've lost yer gown some'ere. Or did ye forgit who ye are when ye got up this morn, by chance?"

Kenna glared at him, and he put his hands up in defense. "Awright, I give up. S'no like ye'll listen, enyway." He shuffled a foot in the dirt of the yard. "How long were ye oot here, afore—um—"

"Afore ye decided t' take a wee nap in the middle o' practisin'?"

Crìsdean opened his mouth to deliver a retort that would put the lass in her place, and then he took a second look and shut it again. Long hair straggled from under the over-large bonnet. The shirt had come out of the trews on one side and hung almost to her knees, which were filthy from kneeling in the yard. Her face was paler than usual and smudged with dirt, and her eyes dark and wild like the sea on a stormy day. She was so beautiful.

The realization brought back the memory of her arms around him, her panicked voice echoing in his ears. A voice not his own speaking through his lips. Crìsdean remembered the fog that had come and gone like no fog ever would, the feeling that he'd lost himself in his own body. He shivered, and Kenna's eyes narrowed.

"Somethin' happened t' ye, didnae 't?" she asked quietly, never taking her eyes from his.

He didn't want to talk about it, didn't want to remember that unnatural fog. He opened his mouth to tell her that, to insist it was nothing to worry about.

"I wasnae myself," his voice said. It wasn't what he wanted to say, but at least the thoughts were his own. That much was a relief. He took Kenna by the arm and led her away from the practice field and into the shadows cast by the castle.

"Ye were passed out proper," Kenna said, her head nodding in recollection. "Ye jist . . .fell." She studied the ground at their feet, and when she looked up her eyes were clouded with memory. "I was that worrit, Crìsdean. I thought ye were—" She shivered. "D' ye remember whit happened jist afore?"

He thought for a moment and then forced his eyes to meet hers. "I dinnae ken," he said, his voice low and serious. "I remember Ealar walkin' away from me, an' then th' fog came an' I couldnae see enythin'."

"Fog?" Kenna's brows were furrowed. "There isnae eny fog t'day. Look at th' sun." They both turned to look at the unusually blue, cloudless sky.

"There was fog," Crìsdean insisted. "'Twas . . .*inside* me. It filled me up an' I couldnae see. I tried t' talk, but it was like someb'dy else had my tongue, like it wasnae mine enymore. I heard him askin' daft questions, but I wasnae 'n control. I couldnae stop him. Do ye think I'm brain-cracked?"

Kenna grinned, and then the smile dropped away at the look in his green eyes. She patted his arm.

"Nae, I ken ye're no mad. I-I had a feelin' when I was holdin' ye, like ye didnae ken me. Like ye werenae there." She took a long breath. "Like someun else was."

She kens, Crìsdean thought, and a wave of relief washed over him like a tidal surge. He nodded and swiped a hand across his face.

"Aye," he said, his voice thick. "Like someun else was."

He could feel tears threatening and turned away quickly. Out in the yard, his clansmen continued their swordplay, heedless of the two figures in the shadows.

They didnae see it. None o' it, Crìsdean thought in disbelief. He turned back to Kenna and pointed his index finger at her.

"Dinnae tell enybody abit this, ye ken? If ye do, I'll gie ye a skelpin', be ye lassie or lad. I mean 't. An' fer God's sake, pit on a dress!"

Without waiting for a reaction he knew he wouldn't like, he strode across the yard and through the side door, unable to stifle a grin. He was halfway across the great hall when another voice hailed him.

"Seven!" He turned at hearing the pet name his mother had given him, and the smile died.

Frances.

His sister-in-law's lips curved up in a smirk that reminded him of a cat toying with its prey before consuming it. Frances knew how much it bothered him to hear that name from anyone other than his mother. It was why she did it.

It would be no exaggeration to say Dànaidh's wife wasn't his favorite person in the castle. She was beautiful, all long, black, glossy hair and wide black eyes, but did no one else see the look of a predator in them? She seemed to take pleasure in teasing him—not the way Kenna and his brothers did, an easy byplay under which a current of love ran free. Frances' wit came with barbs, sharp jabs that left scars. Knowing that he wasn't her only target helped little when it was his turn.

"Hullo, Frances," he said, careful to keep his voice light. He turned quickly and entered the castle, taking the spiral stairs two at a time. Risky, as the stone steps were so narrow, with worn spots from centuries of Maclean boots marching up and down. He made it to the great room, turned, and there she was, right behind him.

Frances grinned, a wide, knowing smile that boded ill. "Whit were ye up to, out there in th' yard jist noo?"

Wha d'ya mean?" His voice sounded dull and dimwitted to his own ears. How could she do this to him every time? Reduce him to a sodden lump of stupidity?

"I saw ye. Lyin' in another's arms, th' two o' ye all comftable as can be." Frances walked the length of the huge room, trailing her fingers along the massive table. Then she returned to stand before him, her eyes bright with malice.

"Ye an' a kitchen lad. Do th' others ken?"

"It wasnae—" he stopped short. If he saved his pride, he'd be outing Kenna. Damn it, why did the lass have to make a bollocks of everything? *I'm goin' t' strangle her when I see her next.*

"Hullo, cousin," said a voice behind Frances. Kenna stood there, smoothing the folds of her gown and looking impossibly young and innocent. The difference between the two women was not lost on Frances, who stiffened and narrowed her eyes.

"I couldnae help overhearin' whit ye were sayin' t' Crìsdean jist noo," Kenna said. "I ken ye saw what I saw, bit it wasnae how it looked."

"Aye?" Frances sniffed. "An' what was it, then?"

Kenna laughed, a low chuckle that rolled out like honey. "Weel, it was my fault, t' be true. I asked Albert, th' kitchen lad, t' sneak up on Crìsdean an' gie him a wallop on his backside when he wasnae lookin'."

She avoided Crìsdean's appalled glare and went on. "I didnae think he'd take me fer real, ye ken, but th' next thing I knew, the wee numpty up an' smacked 'im, awright—but in th' heid!"

She paused and clutched her bosom. "I was that afeared, when I saw our Crìsdean lyin' there, an' I chased Albert all th' way back t' th' kitchens wie a broomstick." Her head bobbed earnestly. "Reckon ye missed 'at part, eh? I promised not t' tell on him, bit I dinnae want enybody t' git th' wrong idea, ye ken?"

Frances's face wrinkled as if she'd swallowed something sour. "Weel. If ye say so. Better get yer heid checked then, lad." She turned her glare on Kenna. "Dinnae ye think it be time fer ye t' act yer age an' quit playin' childish pranks?" Without another word, she hefted her skirts and sailed off toward the staircase to the upper floors.

Kenna stared after her. "I dinnae like her much," she said.

Crìsdean's heart grew lighter, and he grinned. "I ken one thing. I'm beginnin' t' feel sorry fer Dànaidh."

CHAPTER 8

CAPE BRETON ISLAND, NOVA SCOTIA, PRESENT DAY

*You can't stop the future . You can't
rewind the past. The only way to learn
the secret . . . is to press play.*
—Jay Asher

The world was rocking. Brian felt nausea working its way into his throat and lay still, trying to fight it down. After a while, he decided he *might* not be sick if he dared to open his eyes.

Faces loomed over him, and for a moment he wondered who they were. His mind cleared and he realized he was lying on the hard, wet floor of the *Millenium Dolphin*. His head pounded a fierce rhythm, each beat sending a wave of pain to his brain. *What the hell?*

"He's awake! Hey Brian, can you hear me?" Liam's voice, sounding scared and relieved at the same time.

Brian coughed up salty water and struggled to sit. An arm came around his shoulders and helped him into a half-sitting, half-lying position in the cockpit. The nausea returned and then receded, and he looked at the surrounding faces in confusion.

"What happened?" he asked.

"That damn jet ski turned into our path, and you got hit by the boom and sent overboard," Sean told him. His face was pasty. "We thought we'd lost you for a minute; you should have seen how fast Sam here jumped in to grab you! Who knew he was a champion swimmer back in the States?"

Sam blushed and shrugged his shoulders. "Shut up; you can all swim as well as me. I was just the closest."

"Well, anyway, thanks," Brian said, and managed a smile at the pleased look on Sam's face. "You're my hero." He closed his eyes again as a new wave of pain ratcheted through his skull.

"Just lie still and rest." Liam patted his shoulder. "When we get back to the dock, you need to get your head looked at; you were knocked out and swallowed a lot of water."

Brian lay back and kept his eyes closed. Images swam through the pain; water filling his nose and mouth, darkness giving way to light. Clanging. *Why had he heard clanging underwater?* Someone holding him—that must have been Sam.

No . . . not Sam. There had been a woman cradling him. A girl, really. A beautiful girl who called him by someone else's name. Chris? John? The names skittered away like frightened rabbits.

More memories found their way to the surface. The clanging had come from swords, like in those movies about the Middle Ages; men hacking away at each other like old-time warriors.

A castle. There'd been a castle—*underwater?* No, there was no water in this memory. He was lying in the dirt, and the castle loomed behind the girl and those fighting men, dark and menacing.

I've seen that castle somewhere before. Brian tried to remember, but thinking just made his head hurt more, so he gave it up. He opened his eyes. The others were manning the sails, heading for the dock, but Sam still sat next to him, as if he'd made Brian's well-being his personal project.

"Sam," Brian said, his voice raspy and thick, "do you know anything about what happens when you drown?"

The younger man blinked. "Well, I took a course in college. Um . . .if you're conscious you struggle, then try to hold your breath, and then feel light-headed before water enters your lungs."

"Does a drowning person . . . hallucinate?" Brian asked. "Like, see things that aren't possible?"

"I don't know. I guess once you can't get oxygen, you might," Sam said. He paused. "But you were knocked out, so you wouldn't have been able to hold your breath. You would've started to breathe in water right away; hey, let's not talk about it, okay?" Sam's face had gone pale. "We got you in time—that's all that matters, right?"

The boat bumped the dock and was tied off. Liam and Sean got an arm under Brian's and helped him out of the *Dolphin.* He didn't think he'd ever felt anything as good as ground that didn't move under his feet.

His friends got him into Sean's car and drove him to the emergency room of Victoria County Memorial Hospital. After a CT scan, it was determined that Brian's head injury was a concussion. The near-drowning was of more concern, requiring myriad tests including a chest X-ray and a complete blood count. Both conditions meant a hospital stay overnight.

By the time his family arrived, Brian was in full grump mode, and these people, those who loved him best, were the ones he could take it out on. He frowned at his mother, waiting.

"How are you feeling, sweetheart?" she asked.

"My head hurts, my throat hurts, and they've been using me as a test subject since I got here," he began. He listened to the whine in his voice with a perverse enjoyment. "They stuck me with needles, took blood I'm sure I need, won't let me sleep, put things down my throat, sent me through weird machines, hammered on my back." Brian took a breath and glared at his audience. "Oh, and they asked me if I'd been drinking, and told me I should take a boating safety course! Seriously?"

"It's their job, Brian," his sister Kirsty said, exasperation colouring her tone. "They're trying to make sure you're okay, so why don't you put your big boy pants on and suck it up?"

Brian intensified his glare. "Why don't you try it, then? Oh, wait—I forgot. It'll never happen to you because you won't sail. It might mess up your hair, right?"

"I won't sail because it's dangerous!" she huffed. "And maybe your throat would stop hurting if you didn't talk so much."

"All right, you two, knock it off," his father said, in the weary voice of someone who had been through this too many times to count. "Kirsty, can you spare a bit of kindness for your brother this time? He's been through quite an ordeal."

Kirsty hmphed and subsided, but Brian caught the glint of tears in her eyes and felt his own grow damp. She cared about him; they all did. If you were going to vent on your family, you had to take the consequences. His mother's face was pale and she looked as if she'd aged years since the morning, and his father's brows were drawn together in an unaccustomed frown.

"Brian," a voice intruded on his thoughts. A hand found his and held tight. "Are you sure you're going to be okay?"

Worry etched Niall's normally open face, and his voice wavered. Brian reached over and tousled his fourteen-year-old brother's brown curls.

"I'll be fine, really. I just don't like hospitals, and I'm taking it out on you guys. I'm sorry."

Niall grinned. "Good. How 'bout I find your doctor and tell him you don't need a boating safety course?" he asked earnestly. "You know everything about boats!"

Brian laughed and tried to ignore the pain in his throat. "That's okay, Squirt. Kirsty's right; they're just doing their job."

Over Niall's head, he caught his father's eye. William Maclean blinked at him, and then said to the others, "All right. Let Brian get some rest. He'll be home tomorrow, and you can pick on him then." He ushered them to the door. "I just want to give him some information about the check-out process. Meet you at the car."

William closed the door and returned to his place at his son's bedside. He sat for a minute, saying nothing, and Brian felt an ominous sensation spread through him. This wasn't about check-out instructions.

He glanced at the window of his room. Darkness had settled outside, mirroring the gloom on his father's face. He held his breath and waited.

"I called your principal to let him know about your accident," he said after a moment. "He told me you've been suspended—and that you quit."

Damn! He'd forgotten all about the thing with Meghan Reynolds! His stomach flipped and he thought he'd be sick all over again.

He took a deep breath. "Did he-did he tell you why?"

"No," his father said. "He said that information was yours to tell, and he said he hoped you were okay. That's all."

Brian nodded. He stared at the blanket and cleared his sore throat. "Someone—a parent—called and told him his daughter said . . . she said I, I came on to her." Shame coursed through him and his throat closed. "Sexually." He looked up at his father and forced words through the mass that was choking him. "I didn't, Dad! I would never!"

William Maclean grabbed him by the forearm. "I *know* that, son. Don't ever think you need to say such a thing. Not to me." He nodded twice, and kept eye contact until Brian let his breath out and returned the nod.

"I'll contact our lawyer tonight," his father said. "We'll talk about it when you're home, all right? It's all going to come out; the truth always does. We'll be fine." He patted his son's shoulder and stood up. "I have to get back to the others. Keep this to yourself for now, okay?"

Like I want to tell anybody else, ever. Brian thought. *Except Fiona—I have to tell her.* He could feel the bitter tears swimming behind his lids, and forced them to stay where they were. Crying wouldn't help. Kirsty was right; time to pull up his big boy pants and face this.

The rest of his family would believe him, just as his father had. Immediately and with no need for proof. His friends would believe him. Surely his reputation as a teacher and staff member would prove how ridiculous such a charge was.

By the time he was discharged the next morning, Brian's mind was a morass of competing images. Waves crested as high as houses, tipping a small sailboat and rolling it relentlessly back and forth. A dark castle loomed over a muddy field where men dressed in strange costumes brandished swords and glared at him with accusatory eyes. "Suspended!" they called, in voices with strange, guttural accents. A girl with impossibly blue eyes held him tight and called him by another man's name. Nausea reared its ugly head every time he moved.

He clutched his head with both hands.

"Are you all right, son?" His father glanced over from the driver's seat with anxious eyes. "Did they give you something for the pain?"

Brian sighed. "Yes, but I don't want to take it unless I have to. They said the headaches could pass in a day or two, or last for a week. I might get dizzy off and on for weeks." He turned bleak eyes toward his father. "No more sailing this year."

"I would think you'll want some time away from boats and water, so that's not such a bad idea," his father said.

They drove in silence for a few minutes.

"Did you call your sister?" his father asked. Both knew which sister he meant.

"Not yet," Brian said. "Thought I'd wait until I get home and can be alone."

"Well, good luck with that." William grimaced. "Between your mother and Niall, you'll be lucky to get a moment of peace." He glanced over and then returned his attention to the road.

"The attorney returned my call this morning," he said after a moment. "I'll fill you in on what he said later, after you've settled in. He was optimistic, so don't spend too much time thinking. Okay?"

Brian nodded but said nothing. There was nothing he could do to stop thinking; the fractured thoughts ran around like cats chasing their tails, till he thought his brain might be turning into a poisonous vegetable soup.

His mother had gone to even greater lengths than usual with breakfast, but for the first time in family history, Brian couldn't eat. He pushed the pancakes around on the plate and rolled the sausages with his fork, before giving it up and taking himself off to his bedroom on the second floor of the farmhouse.

He woke in the afternoon, feeling better than he'd expected. The throbbing in his head had subsided, and the nausea was gone. More important, he was hungry. His father and the lawyer's report were waiting downstairs, but first he had to call Fiona.

"They did *what?*" His sister's voice rang out over the distance as if she sat right next to him. This was what he'd needed; no amount of *I told you so*'s could ruin the warm feeling that spread through him at the sound of her voice.

"What the hell, Brian! You've worked for that ass for eight years! And he has the unmitigated gall to listen to a love-struck teenager's words?"

"He has the school's reputation to uphold, Fee," Brian said. "He can't be seen to be taking sides until the evidence is in."

"It'll never be the same, Bri." Fiona's voice was low, as if she were holding back. "Will it?"

"No." The words were out. No matter how this turned out, the damage was done. Even if they apologized; hell, even if they welcomed him back with a brass band marching down Chebucto Street, he was finished as a teacher here.

It felt like a death in the family.

"Fee?" he said, voice thick with the realization. "How would you like a visitor?"

"Waiting for you to ask. And you know the answer. How long are we talking?"

The warmth spread further, cleansing the corners of his mind that had been steeped in gloom and shadow for the past two days.

"I don't know. A week? A month? Maybe forever?"

"Gotcha. You clean things up there, and Ewan and I will be ready"

"Fee?" Brian's whisper swirled through the phone and across the Atlantic. "Thank you," he forced the words through a suddenly thick throat, "for being you."

CHAPTER 9
INVERNESS, SCOTLAND, PRESENT DAY

People come into your life for a reason. They might not know it themselves. You might not know it. But there's a reason. There has to be.
—Joyce Carol Oates

Sophie pushed the basket around Morrison's listlessly, wondering why she needed so much food when there was only one of her in the house. Cooking was one of many things she didn't care about; cooking was for eating, and she didn't do much of that either.

The purpose of eating was to stay alive. It was a necessary part of her routine, like bathing and sleeping, but Sophie found little else to recommend it. The only time she enjoyed food was if Deirdre came over, bringing weird ingredients that mingled into something that smelled and tasted delicious.

A small boy careened around the corner, bounced off the edge of her basket, and bounded away, mumbling "Sorry" under his breath.

"Jemmy!" A woman appeared and narrowly avoided the same fate as the boy. "Excuse me," she said, "have you seen a wee lad? Looks like an angel, but believe me, he's not."

Sophie pointed down the aisle in the direction the angel had gone, and the woman blew the hair out of her eyes and followed in his wake.

There are worse things than being alone, and they all involve people. Sophie checked both directions and headed for the cereal aisle. She needed more porridge.

"Was she worth it?" came a male voice from the next aisle. Sophie froze, one hand on the basket. Her heart thudded in her chest and a creeping anxiety took hold of her heart. That low, sibilant voice. *Could it be? No, impossible.*

He wasn't from Inverness—not even from the Highlands; there was no way he would be here. She was becoming paranoid, letting a voice from her nightmares intrude on her daily life. This had to stop. It had been three years; he couldn't possibly know where she lived and had no reason to seek her out. She needed to get a grip and move on.

Don't think you can get away from me; I'll find you. The furious voice, sounding above her pounding heart as she ran. *I'll find you.*

She peered down the aisle at the front windows of the supermarket and shivered. Full dark, and for the first time she questioned the wisdom of her shopping preferences. Morrison's closed at ten, so she'd made it a habit to arrive an hour before closing time, when there were fewer people.

"Jemmy!" The harried voice of the angel's mother drifted from several aisles over. What was that woman thinking, allowing a child out so late? He should be in bed; tomorrow was a school day. But strangely, knowing he was there settled her. He was normal; innocent as only a child can be. She took a deep breath and pushed her cart toward the registers.

As she loaded her few purchases into her bag, Sophie glanced back toward the supermarket aisles. There was no one in sight. She hefted the handles of the shopping bag over her shoulder and left, perhaps a little more quickly than usual. Something had creeped her out tonight; she'd probably be having the nightmare again.

She added her basket to the queue outside and retrieved her coin. Should she get a taxi? Home was a quick walk over the hill past the High Street; such a short distance. She could do this. It had been her choice to shop at night; if the consequences of such a decision were an enhanced sense of weirdness, so be it. But one thing was for certain—she was shopping in daylight from now on. It didn't matter how many wee hooligans caromed into her path; more people meant safety.

Does that mean I'm improving, or going backwards? Sophie shrugged and picked up her pace. *Does it even matter?*

She crossed the High Street and took the Market Brae steps, listening to her footsteps tap on each stone. At the top, she paused to catch her breath.

Darkness eased around her like a soft blanket, and Sophie raised her head to take in the sounds that made up her city at night. A door opening and closing in one of the huge guesthouses that lined both sides of the street. A dog barking away to the west, near the river. Closer by, the flutter of wings, possibly a bat?

Familiar sounds, comforting sounds. Sophie took a deep, cleansing breath, switched her shopping bag to the other shoulder, and moved on. Home was near; Oliver was waiting.

Here on top of the hill, Ardconnel Street stretched before her in all its glory. Huge stone homes loomed like stately dowagers from the turn of the century, refusing to admit that fashions had changed. The wealthy families who owned them had bowed under the weight of taxes and expenses necessary to keep them running, and now most had evolved into inns, restaurants, and B&Bs.

Her own place was one of the few on this street that had not followed the trend. Izzy had given her the house and enough money to keep it going for the foreseeable future. It was her home and sanctuary.

She knew none of her neighbors because they were always changing. Accents and languages from all over the world came and went week by week, mingling with the familiar Scottish cadences of those who used Ardconnel as their shortcut from the High Street to other roads, other neighborhoods.

Sophie shook herself out of her daze. The breeze was picking up; it swirled last autumn's leaves that, even now in early summer, seemed intent on sticking around. She smiled at their desperate tenacity and wished them luck with that plan. Her mind strayed to the new book that was waiting on her side table, and she hurried her steps.

Other steps sounded behind her, and she turned her head. No one was there, and the footsteps were silent. Only her imagination, then, brought on by the darkness and her own meandering thoughts. She turned back, and there they were again. Definitely footsteps—as if someone was playing a game, trying to match his footsteps to hers.

A chill crept up her spine, one that had nothing to do with the wind. It was not her imagination; someone was following her. She stopped again and peered into the darkness at the top of Market Brae. Nothing.

She remembered the male voice she had heard at Morrison's. "*Was she worth it?*" uttered in a sneering tone that had seemed familiar.

Suddenly an unreasoning panic took hold, and she was running down Ardconnel as if pursued by the hounds of hell. She could taste the fear; it was sour and bitter in her mouth. Her home was just at the end of the street—so close. She dared not spare the time to turn around again, but she didn't need to. She could hear the footsteps running lightly, getting closer.

There was a vacant lot just ahead, a singular piece of real estate in this area. The lot was all that was left of a home that had burned down years ago, still empty due to issues with the owner's estate. Now it was choked with weeds and the odd bit of charred wood. She'd explored it once; there were stone steps at the back that led down to Castle Street, busy even at this hour. There was a fence, but perhaps she could get over it—lose her stalker in the darkness, get down those steps, and—

Sophie came to an abrupt stop and stared, confusion overcoming the fear that had sent her running.

What the hell?

The vacant lot between Numbers 24 and 28 Ardconnel Street was gone. Where it should have been was a tavern; slate-roofed and built of sandstone, like every other building on the street. An engraved plaque proclaimed it Number 26. The red wooden door stood open below a weathered sign that read *The Dancing Unicorn* in Celtic script, and below the name, the mythical beast cavorted on its hind legs.

Laughter and shouting vied with the sound of drums and bagpipes that poured out into the night, and Sophie could smell smoke that reminded her of the peat used in her family's distillery.

A noise from the darkness behind jolted her back to the present, and panic returned to drive her up the three steps into the pub. She crossed the taproom and raced behind the bar to stand wild-eyed and panting, eyes fixed on the doorway and the darkness outside.

"Er, ahem." A voice found its way from her ears to her brain, and Sophie dragged her eyes away from the door to find a man staring at her with surprise and some concern, a cloth in one hand and a dripping beer mug in the other.

He was the tallest man she'd ever seen—several inches over six feet, with broad shoulders straining against a homespun shirt. He wore a kilt and leather boots, and wiry red curls sprouted from a grey bonnet that had seen better days. He looked like a clansman from another century, which Sophie supposed was the idea. Whatever the intent, it worked.

"Did they hire a new barmaid and forgit t' tell me?" he asked. His brogue matched his look; rough and musical at the same time. Then his words sank in, and she blushed.

"Oh! I'm s-so sorry!" She stayed put, though, eyes riveted on the bartender. Whoever he was, he looked more than a match for anyone who might be out there in the dark. He looked . . .safe.

The man stuck out a hand like a paw, and she watched her own disappear inside its grip.

"Name's Caomhainn," he said. "Folks call me Wee Caomhainn, fer obvious reasons." He winked at her. "An' this is Biscuit." He waved his free hand and Sophie spied a black cat sitting at the end of the bar. Its yellow eyes stared at her, and for a second Sophie could have sworn the creature nodded. She shook her head in confusion and returned her attention to the barman, who was still shaking her hand up and down as if he'd forgotten about it.

"Uh—I'm Sophie," she said.

"An' whit's brought ye t' the Unicorn, an' most important, t' me bar?" He dropped her hand and grinned, enjoying her discomfiture. "Are ye lookin' fer a job, then?"

"N-no," she said. What could she tell him? *Someone was walking behind me. Did he attack you? No. Threaten you? No. What did he do? Nothing.*

Now that her breathing had slowed to something approximating normal, her panic seemed unrealistic, silly even, borne out of an overactive imagination and a fear spawned by old demons. An unreasoning fear that she would never share, especially not with a stranger.

"I live just down the street . . . I've wondered about this place, thought I'd stop in and have a wee dram." She squared her shoulders and faced the man called Wee Caomhainn. It was true—she *had* wondered about this place, for the five seconds she'd known it existed. She had no earthly idea why she'd mentioned a dram; wasn't it what you ordered in a pub?

Sophie hated whisky. Despite coming from a family that had made its money distilling the stuff, she loathed the smell of barley and hops and had thought she might vomit the only time she'd ever tasted it.

The man's lips quivered. "Ahh," he said. "Weel then, let's git ye proper settled. I'll bring ye a sample o' our best." He took her elbow and shepherded her around the corner of the bar. Almost as if he'd conjured it, an empty table appeared in the corner, and Caomhainn seated her as if she were a duchess and he her doting valet. "I'll be right back with yer drink, aye?" He winked at her and, rather than returning to the bar, disappeared through another doorway.

Sophie sighed. Too bad she was such a twit; she was going to waste perfectly good whisky because she had the courage of a housefly and the instincts of a born liar. She put her shopping bag and her purse on the chair next to her and looked about the room.

This place was a tourist's dream—thick, smoke-blackened beams, rough wooden trestle tables. A stone fireplace dominated the long wall opposite the doorway, and even on this summer night a peat fire was blazing. People raised mugs and glasses in toasts shouted over one another, and ignored the band on a small stage in another corner that was trying its best to be heard over the din.

She studied the performers with a musician's eye. An odd collection of instruments; there was a very enthusiastic drummer, a piper, a guitarist, an accompanist manning a spider-legged digital keyboard, and a young lad doing something to a violin that could only be described as torture.

Other than the child, the musicians were quite good. Sophie's eyes went to the bass drum, which was labeled with two large letters: HP. *Odd name for a band—the leader's initials, perhaps?*

The bass guitarist leaned over and spoke to the lad with the violin. The boy looked abashed and lowered his bow. The guitarist smiled and patted him on the shoulder before returning to his instrument, and the lad raised his bow again. This time he pretended to play, but the bow never touched the strings.

Sophie's heart went out to him. She remembered when she was just beginning to learn; there was nothing worse than violin played badly, and sometimes a student who wasn't quite ready was encouraged to mimic playing during a concert, out of consideration for the audience's ears.

"Welcome t' th' Unicorn, lass," said a soft voice, and Sophie turned to see a tiny woman dressed in a seventeenth-century gown and bearing a tray. The woman resembled a small brown bird, with bright black eyes that crinkled when she smiled. She set the tray down and Sophie noted with surprise that it held a cup of tea.

"Thank you," she breathed, and the woman smiled again. "But how did you know?

"At th' Unicorn, we give ye whit ye need," was the cryptic answer. "D' ye fancy th' music, then? 'At's our house band, the *Highland Players*."

"Well," Sophie began, and stopped. Something told her that lying would never work with this woman. "They're very good, but the poor lad on the violin—"

The woman burst out in a musical laugh. "Aye, 'at's wee Tommy. Our fiddler moved away, an' Tommy's jist fillin' in till we find some 'un t' replace him. Do ye perhaps—" she eyed Sophie with unblinking little bird eyes— "know eny body 'at might play th' fiddle?"

CHAPTER 10

INVERNESS, SCOTLAND, PRESENT DAY

From one moment to another memory
steps back to rediscover the past.
—Munia Khan

Fiona MacArthur studied her brother through narrowed eyes. His were red-rimmed and heavy-lidded from lack of sleep, which could be put down to the overnight flight from Halifax and the three-hour train ride from Edinburgh to Inverness. Could be, but . . .

"Are you all right, Brian? Really?"

He blinked and focused on her. His shoulders sagged. "No. Not really."

Fiona glanced at her husband. Ewan gave her a helpless look that plainly said, *This one's on you.* She sighed and returned her attention to her brother. "Well, you still have your teaching certificate. That's good."

Brian's tone was bleak. "Oh, yeah. I can still teach. But do I want to? I mean, you were right, Fee, as usual. I am totally oblivious. I never saw that coming. Never."

Fiona got up and crossed to sit beside him on the couch. "Are you waiting for the 'I told you so'? Sorry, I'm not that cruel." She patted his hand. "At least the little bitch confessed in the end. That's something."

Brian's head jerked up. "Don't call her that! She's a troubled teen—one of many, unfortunately. They don't think of the consequences. And it had to have taken courage for her to come clean to her father like that."

Fiona grinned. "See? You're not that oblivious after all. You do have empathy when you choose to use it."

Brian gritted his teeth. "Sure. Whatever. She also ruined my career."

Fiona hesitated. "So, it may or may not be the right time to ask, but is this going to just be a visit, or—?"

Brian's voice came out low and ragged. "I'm not going back, Fee. At least, not to the school. And what other job could I get in Baddeck? I don't know what to do." He looked up at his sister, and tears shone in his eyes. "I'm a teacher. It's all I ever wanted to be, and now I've lost that."

"Didn't they give you your job back, though?"

"Oh, sure. They removed the suspension, even apologized." Brian looked up and now his green eyes glinted with unaccustomed anger. "But they shouldn't have had to. They *knew* me. They should have believed me in the first place. I could barely look at Dunn; I just wanted to punch him in the face. So instead, I resigned."

Brian's fists clenched and unclenched, and the next words came out on a choked sob. "I don't think I can ever set foot in that place again. The worst part is, I'm not sure about teaching in *any* school. I don't know if I could walk into a classroom of teenagers and act as if I don't know what's hiding under the surface. I'm scared, Fee—scared of kids!"

Ewan spoke. "Brian, you don't have to decide anything yet. Stay with us as long as you like."

Brian gave him a grateful glance. "Thanks, Ewan. But I don't want to hang around like a stray dog you've brought in out of the rain. I'll have a visit, be a proper tourist, and then I'll go back. To what, I don't know."

His brother-in-law gave a soft laugh. "Oh, don't think you'll get off that easy. I'll give you some time to look around, learn about the Highlands a wee bit, and then ye'll be put to work." He thickened his brogue. "Ye're a Scot, after all, even if ye got lost and wandered across th' pond, and Scots hae t' work fer a livin'. Ye'll be helpin' me wi' th' tours," his eyes glinted, "an' ye'll be learnin' a wee bit o' scramblin'."

A snort came from Fiona. "Oh God, Brian. You're going to need more than a nap."

He was drowning. The water filled his nose and ears and he could see only shadows, cold fingers reaching for him in the murky darkness. With a sense of profound despair, Brian let his lips part and waited for the water to rush into his lungs. It was over. He lay back and gave himself up to the finality of it.

Nothing happened. He forced one eye open, and was stabbed by a shaft of light almost painful in its intensity. *What the hell?* He opened the other eye and gazed around an unfamiliar room. *Where am I?* Receiving no helpful answers, he lay still, and slowly the images took shape and became thoughts.

Ewan's house in Inverness. He was in Scotland. His heart rate slowed, returned to a regular rhythm, and after a minute, he managed to sit up. Fog still clung to the inside of his head and he felt as if his brain was soaking in molasses.

He looked at his watch, surprised to find that it read 9:00 p.m.—then he remembered that his body thought it was only 4:00 p.m. More surprising was the fact that he'd slept at all. Maybe the insomnia that had dogged his nights since the end of June was finally easing its grip.

About time. Brian Maclean had never had a problem sleeping before; maybe a little jet lag was just what he needed. He shook his head to clear it, stood up slowly, and worked his way down the stairs and into the small sitting room, feeling disoriented and muzzy.

The windows were open and a soft breeze lifted the curtains so that it seemed they were dancing. Ewan and Fiona sat in tartan armchairs on either side of the stone fireplace, pamphlets strewn over the side tables and in their laps.

"Ah, you're up." Fiona beamed at her brother. "We've been going over some of the touristy things, but don't worry; we won't make you do anything until you're ready. It's a tough trip, and no easy way to get here." Her eyes met Ewan's and both of them grinned at a private joke. "But believe me, it's worth it."

Brian looked away, embarrassed by the emotion that lingered in the air between his sister and her husband. "Get a room," he muttered under his breath. *I'm not here to find love and romance. God forbid.*

His inner voice sounded sour, even to himself, and he gave himself a mental slap. *You're just tired—and jealous. Your favorite sibling has found her happy ending, and here you are wallowing in envy.* He pasted a smile on his face and looked around. "Why is it so bright out?"

"Summer in the Highlands," Fiona said. "The sun doesn't set until 10:00 p.m., and you'll probably wake up around 4:30 a.m. to daylight. Takes some getting used to."

"I never realized how far north Scotland is," Brian said. "I always felt as if Nova Scotia was the Great North."

"Are you hungry?"

He shook his head and yawned. "Nope. Whatever the sun wants to do, I'm going back to bed. I just got up and I feel as if I haven't slept for a week."

Ewan nodded in sympathy. "I get you. I've never been able to sleep much in those flying tins, myself. Why they have to make planes so uncomfortable, I'll never understand." He rose to his feet and started for the door. "Get ye t' bed, laddie. The scrambling can wait."

Brian gazed after his brother-in-law. "What *is* scrambling, anyway?"

Fiona grinned at him. "I think I'll leave it up to Ewan to explain." She patted his shoulder and looked him over. "You're an athlete; it won't kill you. At least I hope not." She laughed at his expression and pushed him toward the stairs. "Good night."

The next morning Fiona found her brother in the sitting room, poring over the pamphlets on the tea table. "How long have you been up?" she asked him.

"Since four," he told her. "I didn't sleep much anyway, so I checked out the tours." He held up two of the brochures. "What torture do you have planned for today?"

"Well, Ewan thought you might want to start with a walking tour of Inverness, take it easy on the first day. Or we could do bikes."

"Whatever you want," he said. "You know your town best. And isn't your husband a tour guide?"

"Ahh," said Ewan as he entered the room. "You're not ready for my kind of tours yet; we'll start with the simple stuff. But for the first order of business, let's introduce you to a full Scottish breakfast, aye? Sit tight, I'll serve it in here."

A few minutes later, Brian held a fork over his plate, unsure of what to do with all the odd things on it.

Ewan laughed. "Don't be afraid to ask."

"Okay." Brian pointed with the fork. "The bacon and egg I get, and the toast. I assume that's sausage, right? Mushrooms, and baked beans." He looked up at his sister. "Baked beans for breakfast?"

She gave him an encouraging nod.

"But what're these round things, and this flat triangle?"

Ewan laughed. "The flat triangle is a tattie scone." At his brother-in-law's frown of confusion, he elaborated. "Potato. That's haggis there, and that one's black pudding."

"Black pudding? What's in it?"

"Now *that* you probably shouldn't ask, at least until you try it."

Brian shrugged and took a miniscule bite. His eyes widened, and he took another bite, bigger this time.

"It's good!"

Fiona patted his hand and grinned. "That was your first trial. Your blood is Scottish; I knew you'd be okay."

By the time he'd been dragged through the streets of Inverness and along the river into the deep greenery of the Ness Islands, Brian had forgotten his fatigue and was beginning to congratulate himself on his decision to come here. There was something magical about this city—similar and yet so different from his own tiny island back home. It felt less like flight and more like returning.

Maybe it was the sheer age of the place, or maybe it was the castle perched on the hill overlooking the river. Whatever, his head wasn't aching for the first time in weeks. An ocean away from Central Cape Academy and the creeping feeling of failure and shame that had dogged him since his summons to Dunn's office that day in June, it was easy to believe none of it had ever happened.

The feeling of euphoria lasted until they got home, when he sat down—just for a second—and fell asleep.

In his dream, a castle stood on the hill near the city centre. Not Inverness Castle—this one was much older, and it stood against the grey clouds like a sentinel. Instead of warm brown sandstone, this fortress seemed to have been constructed with whatever was at hand, making it seem as if it had sprung out of the very land itself. The waters it guarded were vast and turbulent, lashing the rocks and sending spray far into the sky. In the distance, he could hear the clang of metal mingled with grunts and curses and the occasional cry of pain.

The picture changed; the castle wavered and resolved into the face of a girl. Very young, blonde, with a careless beauty borne of nature rather than artifice. Her sea blue eyes stood out against the harsh landscape like a beacon and did something to his heart that he couldn't understand. It was ridiculous, so he woke up.

He lay still for a minute, listening to the comforting sounds of conversation mixed with the clatter of dishes. Ewan's rich Scottish brogue blended with Fiona's familiar Canadian accent, and suddenly Brian didn't want to be alone. He needed people.

He stumped down the carpeted stairs and followed the noise into the kitchen.

"Sit." Fiona pointed to the table.

Obediently he sat, and looked around the kitchen for the first time. The countertops were a deep marbled granite, the double sink sparkled in its stainless steel glory. The cupboards were a soft white that blended perfectly with the satin finish of the refrigerator.

Dominating the far wall was a monstrosity. A stove of some kind, incongruous in its bright red ceramic enormity, it seemed to say, "Yes, it is I who rule this kitchen." It had two strangely capped circles on its cooktop, and four oven doors in front. He'd never seen anything like it.

Fiona grinned at her brother. "The iconic British appliance, our AGA. Isn't it wonderful?"

Brian nodded, not sure there was a proper answer. In his experience, stoves and ovens existed so that his mother could churn out copious amounts of food, which he was happy to consume. He'd never really paid attention to what the object looked like, as long as it did its job. He had to admit, however, that this one was rather impressive. It was so red.

"Stays on all day, even in summer," his sister said. "Heats the house, dries the towels." She pointed to a line above the cooker, over which two hand towels had been draped. "Don't you think Mom would love it?"

But Brian had stopped listening. He'd noticed something else about the thing; there were no smells of cooking food coming from it. Fiona wasn't the world's best cook, but at least there should be an odour of slightly charred dinner, shouldn't there?

"We're going out," she told him, having read his mind again. "There's a new pub right up Ardconnel, and we haven't tried it yet. Grab your coat."

They walked down Culdathel and turned onto Ardconnel Street. Brian's eyes widened as they passed the huge stone houses lining both sides of the street.

"Must cost an arm and a leg to live in one of these," he said.

Ewan winced, and Brian gave him a questioning look.

"Ewan grew up in that one," Fiona whispered, and pointed to a large house on their left. Brian stared at the palatial sandstone building in awe.

"We own a distillery." Ewan shrugged. "To be truthful, *I* own a distillery. Unfortunately."

Unfortunately? Brian glanced at his sister, and she gave him a tiny shake of the head. "That's a story best left for another time," she said. "For tonight, we're off to find my starving brother some of Scotland's finest cuisine—pub food."

The music reached them first. The fiddler—a good one, if Brian was any judge—was playing a tune he recognized as strathspey, the dotted rhythm punctuated by short notes followed by longer ones reminiscent of bagpipes.

The last remnants of insomnia drained out of him, and he felt totally alive for the first time in a month. This was the music of Cape Breton, of home. His step quickened toward a sign featuring a whimsical creature in a kilt under the words, *The Dancing Unicorn.*

"Seems to have gone up almost overnight, but it looks as old as all the other buildings on the street," Ewan was saying. "Amazing what these modern builders can do."

Brian barely registered the words. He was already through the door, drawn by the music. The taproom reeked of age, down to the uneven wooden floor and smoke-blackened beams.

Across the room next to a huge stone fireplace, a young woman stood on a small stage. She was dressed in a white blouse and long tartan skirt, and her shoulder-length blonde hair swung in time to the music. She cradled a fiddle as if it were a part of her being, and the bow danced across the strings like a living thing.

Her eyes were closed as she swayed to the music, but somehow Brian knew they were blue. He remained frozen as the last notes of the tune trailed from the instrument and the girl opened her eyes and smiled at her audience.

Yes, *blue*. Brian felt his breath stop. The last time he'd seen those eyes, they had been filled with fear . . . for him.

It wasn't possible, but he *knew* this girl.

CHAPTER 11

ISLE OF MULL, SCOTLAND, 1646

KENNA

There *was* something wrong with Crìsdean. Kenna watched him under hooded lids, as she had every day following that strange collapse on the training grounds. On the surface he seemed fine; the old, obnoxious lad was back in force.

She furrowed her brow and kicked at the carpet. *If enythin', he's worse. I cannae go enywhere bit he's there, lurkin'. Starin' at me as if he kens whit's in my heid.* She caught at that thought and flushed. *Mebbe it's no Crìsdean 'at has somethin' wrong wi 'im,* she thought.

She shook herself out of her worries and continued to the library to fetch the book Mary had requested. Running errands for the chief's wife accomplished two things; it endeared Kenna to the mother of the future chief, Hector, and it gave Kenna freedom to wander at will. As long as she returned in an appropriate space of time, no one needed to know where she went.

"'Tis th' new book o' poemes by Alexander Montgomerie," Mary had announced, clasping Kenna's hands and nearly dancing with excitement. Kenna smiled and flashed a brilliant smile in return, hoping the dear woman would never know that she hadn't the sliver of an idea who Alexander Montgomerie was, and that reading poetry was the last thing she would ever do willingly.

Th' Cherrie an' th' Slae, Th' Cherrie an' th' Slae, Kenna muttered to herself as she searched the shelves. *What sort o' name is 'at, enyway?*

But there it was, a thin volume sandwiched between other books in a corner of the library—right where Mary had said it would be. Kenna grabbed it and started for the door, eager to get out of this musty place, when a voice stopped her.

"What're ye doin' so long in th' librarie?" A woman's voice came from the alcove where Giles spent most of his free time. Kenna shrank back against the shelves and listened. Who was this person? Giles hated to be bothered when he was reading.

Crisdean's older brother could usually be found hidden away in the alcove if anyone was looking for him; the man seemed to have few interests beyond reading. But who was he talking to? Kenna had been up here many times on errands for Mary, and she'd seldom seen anyone else in the library but Giles.

It was a shame he was such a recluse; he was undoubtedly the handsomest of the Maclean brothers—after Crìsdean, of course, even if he was an old man of twenty-seven. His black wavy hair, full lips, and bright blue eyes drew every woman's eye and elicited many longing sighs from female visitors. Kenna had trailed around after him for weeks like a lovesick puppy when she'd first arrived at Duart, but that was before she grew up—and before Crìsdean.

To his credit, Giles had been kind about her hero worship. He was always kind; he just didn't spare much time for anything or anyone who didn't reside between the pages of one of his books. He'd probably die without a wife, but he'd surely have a book in his hand.

Still, she felt protective, in the way a little sister watches over an adored older brother. He needed protecting; always on some other plane of existence or with his head in the clouds . . .unless he was at practice.

With a sword in his hand, Giles was another person, a magnificent warrior, like someone from the ancient stories. He had studied every aspect of warcraft and put it to use on the training field, and the brothers all had bruises to prove it.

"Ye prob'ly missed yer lunch, ye silly goose," came the voice again. Simpering, fatuous, pitched to sound coquettish. "So I brought ye some cakes from th' kitchen."

Frances.

This is interesting, Kenna thought. *What is Dànaidh's wife doing hanging about up here? Surely it isn't to further her knowledge of domestic duties.*

"Thank ye, bit I'm no hungry," Giles' answer was short, with a ring of finality.

"I'd be glad t' fetch ye yer books, so ye dinnae have t' stop yer readin'," Frances said, and now the voice held a pout.

Kenna covered her mouth and nose to stifle a snort. Did the woman not understand rejection?

"No, thank ye." Giles voice was low and clipped; how could Frances miss the annoyance in those few words?

"Bit ye're always up here wi' yer nose 'n yer books. We miss ye doonstairs."

"I'm fine. Thank ye."

"Awright, I'll leave ye t' yer readin'. I was jist tryin' t' help."

Kenna stayed still in her shadowed corner and tried to blend into the shelf behind her, but she needn't have worried. Frances seemed oblivious to anything but her quarry, whose head was back in his book. After a moment she shrugged, turned, and sashayed out of the library, nose held high.

There was an audible sigh from the alcove. Kenna waited another minute and stepped out into the center of the room. Giles was staring at the door with an odd look on his face.

"Hullo," Kenna said. "Mary sent me fer a book o' poetry." She brandished the volume to prove her reason for being there.

"Aye," Giles said. He shook his head and looked down at his book.

Sensing dismissal, Kenna headed for the door.

"Kennie."

She turned to find Giles staring at her, a spot of color high in his cheeks. His brows were furrowed and his blue eyes narrowed.

"Did ye hear 'at?"

"Aye," she said. "Hard not t'."

He said nothing for a moment. Then he looked up and fixed worried eyes on her. "Ye're a woman."

Kenna flushed. She'd once caught him eyeing the toes of her boots where they peeked from under her gown, but unlike that lump Crìsdean, he had not judged her or lectured on propriety. So his opinion mattered the most.

A warm feeling spread up from her stomach and ended as a flush on her cheeks. If Giles thought she was growing up, did others? *Did Crìsdean?* He might not approve of her activities, but he had kept her secret, and lately it seemed he might be wavering just a bit.

"I mean, you ken whit women 're thinkin'." Giles' voice intruded on her thoughts.

Kenna didn't stifle the snort this time. "If ye're talkin' abit our Frances, I dinnae thynk I kin help." She saw the look of confusion deepen on Giles' face, and took a deep breath. It was very apparent that despite his advanced age, he was a lamb and Frances held the knife.

"Frances doesnae *thynk*, she plots," she said carefully. "Ye need t' take care, Giles. From whit I heard jist noo, she fancies ye."

He looked up, confusion mixed with horror now. "Bit she's marrit!"

Kenna shook her head. "Aye, she is. An' Dànaidh has a temper. So ye need t' be mindful, ye ken?"

"I nivver gave her eny reason—I nivver said—I dinnae—" Giles was nearly incoherent from shock and vexation.

"I ken 'at; everbody does. Naebody would put you as the villain, Giles. Weel, most naebody. I dinnae ken abit Dànaidh."

Giles shook his head. "How does a wee thing like ye unnerstand so much?"

Kenna cocked her head. "Ye said it first. I'm a woman. An' ye cannae find everthin' in a book, Giles. Not about wimmen, enyway."

With that, she turned and made her way down the stone staircase to the rooms occupied by the chief's family, feeling as if she'd crossed some sort of boundary. *I'm a woman,* she said to herself, and looked down at the gown that proclaimed her status. Never mind that there were trews under the gown— *I'm a woman.*

Mary met her at the door, eyes aglow at sight of the volume she held. "Ah, Kenna! Ye're a darlin'!" She grabbed the book and retreated into the solar, eyes already fixed on the words in front of her. Kenna turned away, wondering. How could people spend so much of their time with their eyes fastened to a printed page? Didn't they know there was a world out there?

Mary was such a dear, and so often alone. Maybe for her, books filled the gap left by the absence of her husband. The existence of a clan chief's wife wasn't as glorious as Kenna had first thought when she arrived at Duart. Even for her—a lass who straddled the gap between the world of men and the duties of women more often than not—life in these days was ofttimes boring and lonely. Aye, there were men—plenty of them—but their minds were on war, and they waited for their chief as ardently as did Mary Maclean, albeit for different reasons.

When *was* the last time Lachlan Maclean had been home? It couldn't be easy for him, either. During the war that ravaged the three kingdoms of Scotland, England, and Ireland, Lachlan had taken up his duties as chief and gone off to join the Cavaliers in their continuing battle against a Parliament rife with discontent and strife. As Royalists, the Macleans of Duart stood ready to protect their king at the call of their chief.

Or so Giles had told her, much of it going over her head. What war meant to the women of Duart could be seen in the lines on Mary's face.

Lachlan had been gone since February of last year, never home for more than a fortnight. In his absence, men trained . . .and women waited.

CHAPTER 12

ISLE OF MULL, SCOTLAND, 1646

CRÌSDEAN

Crìsdean sat alone on his favorite boulder, a nice flat one above the spray of the crashing waves, and stared out at the sound. He held his head between his hands gently, as if afraid it might fall off if he left it alone.

His dreams were getting worse. Filled with impossible things, things his imagination should never have been able to dredge up. Every time he closed his eyes, there they were.

An odd building stood on the horizon. A lighthouse, but this one had red and white stripes, like the pennants in a village festival. There were men dressed in what looked like undergarments, short trews and odd shirts without buttons or ties but with portraits on them. Shoes with strange symbols and no stockings.

More shocking was the fact that the men seemed to be outdoors, where anyone could see!

The men in his dream numbered three. They seemed unaware of the impropriety of their attire as they grappled with the sails of a small ketch, the like of which he'd heard about but never seen. He knew that there were small sailboats like this in these modern times. It was said that nobles in England used such vessels, sailing down the Thames while they drank and caroused, but there was no use for them here. The waters of the Sound of Mull were far too rough and men had no time for mindless pleasures like that.

He grasped his head tighter, as if squashing his brain would rid it of these images. Something had happened to him on that day in the yard. He had lost consciousness and then all control of himself; only for a few minutes, but it had been enough to strike terror into his soul.

Crìsdean climbed down off the boulder and searched until he found a sharp-pointed rock about the size of his fist. He stood at the base of the rock and began to carve the images he had seen into the soft sandstone, not understanding why but convinced that his sanity depended on his remembering them. Then he threw his rock into the sound and made his way back to the empty training yard. He sat with his back against the castle wall and let his thoughts roam, glad that for the moment at least, they were his own.

Was he possessed by some evil demon? He didn't remember hearing of any demons who entered a human's dreams and took over his body, but who knew what the vile creatures that roamed the hills and lochs of the Highlands could do? Maybe his dreams were brought by a *caoineag*; it was just the sort of thing a banshee like that would do.

A chill spread through his body. A *caoineag* was known to foretell the death of a clan member by crying during the night, and it loved lochs and firths. Was that why he was dreaming of ketches and water? Was something going to happen to one of his clansmen? But there had been no crying in his dreams, and why would the caoineag choose him as its messenger? His shivering intensified as a thought occurred to him. *Because I'm the seventh son?*

He thought back over the stories his mother had told as he was growing up. Anna Maclean held no superstitions about the ghosts and goblins that lurked in the wilder places of this land, but she was not above using them to punish her sons when they pulled at her last bit of patience. And she'd always told him he was special because he was the seventh . . . the last.

Could he share his fears with Kenna? She'd been there; it was she whose eyes shone with worry when he awoke in her arms, right here where he was sitting now. That look made it all real; he wasn't the only one who knew something weird had happened. Somehow, he knew Kenna would understand; she'd said as much.

I had a feelin' when I was holdin' ye, like ye werenae there. Like someun else was. Yes, Kenna would understand.

No. He stiffened his spine and sat up straighter against the wall. *She'll think me weak.* Why that mattered so much, he didn't want to contemplate, but the thought of Kenna MacLeod finding him wanting was something too daunting to bear. No woman was going to have that kind of power over him.

And she *was* a woman. Kenna had turned fifteen last week, and he was all too aware that she was different now. Crìsdean forgot about the caoineag and the demons who haunted men's dreams as his childhood nemesis floated into his mind. His face reddened. Still a wee little midgie, but other things were changing about her—things that made his pulse race when he saw her in a gown.

He knew there were men's trews under those skirts, but he'd stopped bothering her about it, turning a blind eye when she sneaked into the alcove by the side door and came out dressed as a lad. Her skills with a broom handle were improving too. The kitchen lad sported more bruises after one of her visits, and Crìsdean had spied him running to hide in the woodpile more than once when the castle door opened.

The wee pudding thought her sneakery was unobserved. A smile crawled across Crìsdean's face. Then it turned to a frown and his brows furrowed. He wished he hadn't been so mean when he'd discovered the knife that first time; maybe she would have confided in him and he could have helped her. If she was going to persist in training to go to battle, what was wrong with it? She'd never be allowed to go, at any rate. Maybe he should take a chance and help her. The smile returned.

"Whit're ye grinnin' aboot, like a mad fool?" A rough voice intruded on his thoughts. He jerked as his brother Dànaidh plunked himself down and leaned against the wall next to him. The older man stared into the yard, his brow creased, and his hazel eyes hooded.

There was something dark about Dànaidh these days. His temper seemed to waver between anger and melancholy much of the time, and his patience was on a short tether, even for him. He'd always been testy; the brother who was first to find fault with everyone around him, except maybe Ealar.

When he'd gone off with Ealar to Lochaber last year and come home with a bride, the family had eagerly embraced the newcomer. It didn't matter that Frances was a Cameron, a clan with whom the Macleans had an uneasy relationship. She was cheerful and outgoing, and she made Dànaidh happy—for a while.

"Whit's amiss wi' ye?" Crìsdean ventured.

"Nuthin'. Mind yer ain." Dànaidh ran both hands through his light brown hair and stared out at the empty yard.

The silence deepened and became uncomfortable and Crìsdean was relieved when the others filtered into the yard and he could spring to his feet and join them. They moved onto the field for practice.

When Giles emerged onto the field, Dàinaidh pushed himself off the wall and ambled over.

"I'll take Giles," he announced. Crìsdean thought he saw a wary look cross Giles' face, but he nodded and moved to join Dànaidh on the field. The others paired up, Crìsdean drawing Pàdraig as his sparring partner.

Out of the corner of his eye, he watched a small kitchen lad slip through the door and lean against the wall, watching with narrowed eyes. He grinned and resumed practice with new energy.

For a while, nothing could be heard but the grunts of men and the clanging of swords. Then a cry of pain and an oath had heads turning to find Giles, lying on the ground with the point of Dànaidh's sword at his throat. His brother stood over him, red-faced and panting.

"Whit're ye doin'?" Giles gasped. "That was a foul move!"

"All's fair 'n battle, brother," Dàinaidh snarled. He didn't remove the sword.

"Dàinaidh!" Bearnard stalked over from the other side of the training ground. "This isnae battle! Ye ken 'at. Whit're ye thinkin'?"

"Giles kens whit I'm thynkin'," Dàinaidh hissed, never taking his eyes off the man on the ground, who had gone very still. "Take 't as a warnin' . . . brother." He moved his sword away from Giles' neck, stuffed it into its scabbard, and stalked off the field without a backward look.

Giles got slowly to his feet and turned to face the others. He shrugged, but the look in his eyes was wary, as if the unwarranted attack hadn't altogether surprised him.

Crìsdean felt eyes on his back and turned to find Kenna staring at him. She blinked and looked away, but the message was clear. She knew something about this.

Bearnard studied Giles. "Are ye awright?" he asked, his voice low.

"Fine," Giles said. "He didnae hurt me." He mustered a smile that didn't reach his eyes. "Like 'e could. If 'e's goin' t' use trickery like 'at, I'll be ready next time."

Bearnard nodded and clapped him on the shoulder before crossing the field again, while the others resumed their stances.

"Whit was 'at all aboot?" Pàdraig whispered.

Crìsdean raised his eyebrows. "I dinnae ken," he said, "bit 'tis sure Dànaidh has sumpthin' up 'is arse." He glanced over at Giles, who was now sparring with Fergus. "Seems he's in a worse temper 'n usual, though . . . an' it looked personal."

The usually sunny Pàdraig nodded solemnly. "Aye. Giles better watch 'is back fer a wee while, I'm thinkin.'"

CHAPTER 13

INVERNESS, SCOTLAND, PRESENT DAY

Hell hath no fury like a man
embarrassed by a woman.
—J. R. Rain

Brian stood immobile in the doorway. The laughter of patrons, the crackle of the fire, the smell of old wood and whisky—his senses shut it all out, and he was alone with the music and the fiddler.

The moment was too beautiful to last, though. The song ended to loud cheers and clapping, and a voice at his side broke the magic it had conjured.

"Sophie!" Ewan called out. The girl looked up, surprise and delight breaking over her features. She said something to her bandmates and they nodded, set their instruments down, and stepped off the small stage. Brian barely noticed; his attention was on the girl heading in their direction.

"Surprised?" she asked.

Fiona hugged her. "How long have you been here—doing this, I mean?"

The girl grinned and grabbed Fiona's hand. "Come sit, and I'll give you the story." Brian trailed after as she led them to a table near the bar, behind which the largest man he had ever seen was washing glasses. The giant glanced at Ewan and then winked at the girl.

"Family?" he asked.

"How do you *do* that, Caomhainn?" she demanded. "Sometimes you're positively spooky!"

The big man grinned and reached for another glass. "If I told ye, t'wouldn't be fun, aye?" He let the silence lengthen for a minute, then gestured between Ewan and Sophie with the glass. "It's not magic, ye wee numpty. Everybody in your family looks alike, ye ken?"

Sophie looked confused. "We do not! We all look totally different. And what do you mean, 'everybody'? You know other MacArthurs besides me?"

The man she'd called Caomhainn shrugged and gave his attention to the whisky glass, which was already sparkling. "Cannae say. Mebbe."

Sophie gave up. "All right, you win. Keep your secrets, then. You're right; this is my brother Ewan, and his wife, Fiona." She turned to them. "The mysterious fellow here is Wee Caomhainn."

Caomhainn nodded. "Nice t' meet ye. An' I'm thinkin' our other guest is Fiona's brother?"

Sophie looked startled. She turned and focused on Brian as if noticing him for the first time, and color suffused her face. "Oh."

Brian flushed. *Oh? What a rude little—I'm sitting right here!*

Fiona gave him a covert glance and then flashed the gentle smile that had deescalated arguments and pacified Maclean siblings for as long as he could remember. "You're right, Mr. er . . . Wee Caomhainn—" she eyed the giant bartender—"Brian's my brother." She pulled Brian forward. "Brian, this is Ewan's sister, Sophie."

Brian pasted a curt smile on his face and prepared to give the girl a noncommittal nod, but his attention was arrested by movement behind her on the bar. An object moved, stretched, and resolved itself into a small black cat. The animal's luminous yellow eyes fixed themselves on Brian as if challenging him to a staring contest. Then the cat jumped gracefully off the bar and wandered over to sit next to his chair, eyes still locked on his.

For some reason he felt better. *At least somebody cares.* "Hello, there," he said, and bent to pet the animal.

"Dinnae!"

He jerked his hand back. A tiny woman appeared at his side and scooped the cat up in her arms. "Not unless ye fancy losin' a hand." She smiled at Brian to soften her words. "To be fair, it's no yer fault. I'm surprised she came t' ye like that, Biscuit doesnae usually give strangers the time o' day."

The woman released the cat and it stalked back to its spot on the bar, tail held high. The tiny woman held out her hand. "I'm Mary Duncan. My husband Henry an' I manage this pub. And did I hear ye're all related t' our Sophie, here?

"Just Ewan," Sophie told her. "Fiona is my sister-in-law, and Brian is her brother."

"Well, make yerselves t' home at th' Unicorn," Mary said, in a musical voice that reminded Brian of a songbird. In fact, he thought, everything about the woman resembled a small brown wren, from the mouse-colored hair to the bright black eyes. Even her attire, a muted brown and green tartan skirt and homespun cream-coloured blouse, gave her an other-worldly look, as if she'd just emerged from a forest hut.

Like a tiny benevolent witch, Brian thought, and wondered where that thought had come from. This country was doing things to him. Somehow though, he felt that, witch or no, Mary Duncan was someone to be trusted.

A plump, middle-aged waitress came over and handed them menus. "Hullo, I'm yer server, Betty," she told them. "D' ye know our Sophie, then?"

Introductions were made for the third time, and then Brian gave his attention to the menu, printed on paper made to look like old-fashioned parchment. The usual Scottish bar fare was headlined by odd-sounding names like Cullen Skink, Haggis, Neeps and Tatties, and something called Cock-a-Leekie. *Sounds like something a man should go to the doctor for*, Brian thought. *There. Fish n' Chips. That's probably safe.*

Decision made, he let his eyes wander around the room. He took in the sandstone fireplace, the white stucco walls, and the tartan throw rugs scattered everywhere, but no matter how hard he tried, he couldn't keep his eyes from wandering to Ewan's blonde sister, across the table.

That feeling he'd had, that he'd seen her before, lingered just outside his memory like a wispy shadow. It couldn't be; there was no way he'd forget a face like hers. Brilliant blue eyes, a solemn, unsmiling mouth—he bet she would have dimples if she smiled. Naturally blonde hair cut in a sleek modern style—a bob, the high-schoolers called it.

The blue eyes caught his and he flushed a deep red. *Caught staring, damn it.* The next second she looked away, and he felt as if a cloud had covered the sun.

Ewan was talking, and Brian forced his attention back to the conversation.

"So, Soph, do you play here often? I haven't seen you in ages, and here you are—in a pub, of all places." Her brother looked around the tavern. "I only live a few blocks away, and I never knew this place existed!"

"Neither did I, and I live right down the street." Sophie followed his gaze. "Looks old, doesn't it? But I walk down this street all the time from the city center, and I swear I never saw it before a week ago. So weird."

She paused. "To answer your other question, I—um—stopped in on my way home from Morrison's."

Brian saw a shadow cross her face, and then it was gone.

"There was this lad trying to play the violin. Lord, he was awful, poor thing. Mary asked if I knew anybody who could play, and the next thing I knew, I was the fiddler at *The Dancing Unicorn!*"

Ewan gave his sister a puzzled look. "But you hate places like this."

Sophie raised both hands, palms up. "Mary can be very persuasive."

Brian said, carefully, "You play beautifully. That was a strathspey, wasn't it?"

Sophie looked at him with surprise. "Yes. Do they play them in Canada?"

"In our part of Canada, yes. Fee and I are from Nova Scotia. Cape Breton Island."

"Are you a musician?"

"No. A teacher."

"What do you teach?" Sophie asked politely.

"Um, I, well . . ."

Fiona spoke up. "He's a high school math teacher, the best they have. His kids love him—oh—" she broke off and sent her brother a stricken look. Brian's face coloured, and he looked down at the table. Was he doomed to spend the rest of the evening red-faced?

Like a chubby savior, Betty chose that moment to return. "Ready?" she asked.

Brian mumbled his order and spent the next minutes with his head down, studying the whorls on the wooden tabletop and wishing he could disappear.

It's not Fee's fault; you'll have to come to grips with this sooner or later, so get on with it! But why did he have to be such a bumbling idiot? And why did that matter so much right now?

The orders came and everyone else dug into their food as if they hadn't noticed anything wrong with Fiona's brother. *Right.* Brian was sure his fish would taste like cardboard, get stuck in his throat, he'd puke all over everyone at the table, and the evening would slide into a puddle of misery, just to make it all perfect.

But the food was good. Better than good. And whatever else might be going wrong in his life, Brian Maclean could eat. He'd seldom missed a meal that he could recall, and he wasn't going to start now. As he bit into the soft haddock, his mind settled and his heart slowed its racing beat to something resembling normal. He even let the conversation around him filter into his consciousness.

"I'm really happy you're doing this, Soph," Ewan was saying. "You needed to get out of the house more."

"I know. I just—well, never mind. I'm here, and I love it."

"Really lucky that a job came up just as you walked into the place."

"Aye. It's weird. I've been here for a week, but I feel as if I've known these people all my life. They make me feel safe."

Brian forgot his own embarrassment and tuned in. *Odd thing to say; they make her feel safe. Didn't she feel safe normally? Strange girl.*

Maybe it was better not to get too close to Sophie MacArthur. She could be a certified weirdo for all he knew. Fiona had told him a little about the MacArthurs, and now he tried to dredge up what she'd said.

They owned a distillery, a successful one. Apparently it had gone to Ewan when their father died. No, not just died; murdered by a close family friend. That would be enough to screw anybody up.

Ewan seemed to have come through it pretty well. His sister would never let herself fall for a guy who was a nutcase. But he was the oldest son, probably a year or two older than Brian's own twenty-nine. So maybe he'd had the maturity to cope.

Brian looked at the blonde girl across the table from him. How old had she been when that happened? It was a year ago, and she looked to be no more than twenty-two or three. Was she there when it happened? Was that why she didn't feel safe? He wished he'd paid more attention to Fiona's limited information, but in his defense, he hadn't known any of these people and never expected to be here.

And you're oblivious. He could hear his sister's voice as if she was saying it out loud. He glanced over at Fiona, but she was listening raptly to whatever Sophie was saying.

Wee Caomhainn appeared at the table with four small glasses and a bottle of amber liquid. The bottle bore the image of a sprig of green leaves with purple flute-shaped flowers and the name *Wild Thyme* 25 in Celtic script.

"Thought ye should taste some o' the finest whisky in Scotland," he announced, before pouring a small amount of the stuff into each of the four glasses. "Wild Thyme, in honour of our Sophie."

"Stop it, Caomhainn," Sophie said. "It's not for me. I don't drink whisky and you know it. You're just showing off for Ewan."

"Is that your distillery?" Brian asked.

"Aye," Ewan said. "Much as I complain about having to deal with it, I'm pretty proud of the stuff we turn out. Do you drink whisky?"

Brian huffed. "Just because I'm from across the pond doesn't mean I've forgotten my roots. We Capers are Scots through and through. I'll let you know if it's any good." Even to his own ears, the words sounded defensive and obnoxious. What was wrong with him tonight?

Ewan just laughed. "Aye, lad, you do that."

The first dram was lovely, the second necessary, and the third stole away all his tension and inhibitions. At some point, Brian held his empty glass aloft and proclaimed, "'Tis fine stuff." He felt lighter than air and happier than he had in weeks. "I b'lieve I'll have one more."

Fiona eyed her brother with concern and opened her mouth. But it was another voice that penetrated the pleasant haze and splashed cold water on his euphoria.

"Does he drink like this all the time?" Sophie asked. "He's fair-on blootered, isn't he?" Brian sat up straight, made a great effort to focus, and fixed both of her with a righteous glare.

"I'll ha-v y' know, I can hold my liqu'r 's well as th' next man."

He knew he should have stopped at the second dram; he could hear himself slurring. He was exhausted and not really much of a drinker, despite what he'd said. But that voice pulled something out of him that needed to escape, and released a frustration that had been building for weeks. He couldn't let that snooty little girl put him down.

He reached across the table for his glass and the world slipped sideways as he slid out of his chair. His head cracked against the edge of the wooden table on his way down, and the last thing he remembered was the appalled look on Sophie MacArthur's face.

INVERNESS, SCOTLAND, PRESENT DAY

Death never comes at the right time,
despite what mortals believe. Death
always comes like a thief.
—Christopher Pike

Rachel loved the walk home from MacKay's, almost as much as she hated the bar itself. Well, not so much the bar; it wasn't the pub's fault. MacKay's was one of the oldest pubs in Inverness and oozing with old-word charm, which made its location on Union Street perfect for the tourist trade. The bar was fine. It was one of the people in the bar. Specifically, her boss. *Fat, randy git.*

Some days this walk home in the wee hours of the morning was the only thing that kept her from screaming. It gave her solace, a welcome respite from the noise of the pub during tourist season.

She put her earbuds in and turned on her music app, matching her pace to the lively sounds that only she could hear and hoping to dispel the image of Archie MacLeish and his leering, sweaty face. The street was empty, tourists all gathered at Hootanany or Gellions, or tucked into bed after a long day on buses or trains.

She didn't want to quit her job. Rachel loved waitressing at the pub, meeting people from all over Europe and across the ocean. Especially the Americans; they usually tipped even when they knew it wasn't expected.

She liked the kitchen staff too. Franklin and Harry and Ian had all been there since before she started, and they'd taken her in as if she were family. The other girls on the waitstaff were friendly and didn't seem so jealous of the attention Rachel got from the male tourists, like the girls at her last place. Still, she knew they talked about her behind her back.

Could she help it if she had great genes? She hadn't asked to be graced with good bone structure, naturally blonde hair, and long-lashed blue eyes, and she had a good figure because she worked at it. It took effort to look good, and there was no shame in it.

But there were consequences. Once in a while, a visitor who had one too many drams thought that she came with the whisky, and went a bit beyond flirting. She could handle them, knew how to let the air out of their balloons without losing the review on social media.

And it was those times when her hero stepped in. The latest addition to the staff was young, handsome, and seemed to know just how to defuse a situation that looked to be getting out of control. If a patron put his hand on her wrist, he was there instantly to cajole the drunk and make him think he was better off without touching the waitresses at MacKays. She couldn't have asked for a better ally.

But the problem wasn't the tourists. No one else knew about the hot breath and loose hands of Archie MacLeish because she didn't want them to know. The men would blow it all out of proportion and she'd end up without a job, and the other girls would judge her. Women always did.

She could handle him herself. The bastard couldn't take the chance that someone would see what he was up to and slip a note to his wife. He was a coward, and thank God for that.

If her mum knew the things he whispered though, the way he let his beefy paw run across her arm in the narrow hallway between kitchen and toilets, she'd come down to MacKay's and give him a skelping he'd never forget. And then she'd skelp her daughter too. And for what? Rachel would be fired anyway.

She needed this job. Mum didn't know it, but most of her daughter's savings were going into an account at the Bank of Scotland on High Street. As soon as she had enough, she'd move into an apartment of her own. She was nineteen years old; it was time she left the nest her parents had built and feathered her own.

She turned left onto Church Street and walked the short distance to turn right onto the lane that led to Castle Road and the River Ness. In all the time she'd worked at MacKay's, not once had she seen another human being on this street. It was narrow and dark, hemmed in by the windowless sides of buildings that loomed over the land.

It might have been frightening to some, but there was something about Inverness in the wee hours of the morning that called to her. It whispered in her ear and assured her that everything was fine because she owned the city, it was hers, and she was the only one in it.

Or was she? Was that a footstep somewhere behind, back on Church Street? Rachel stopped and took out one earbud, but all she heard was the wind whistling up the narrow street from the river. Still, she turned off her music and pocketed the earpieces.

The night wind was picking up; more rain was on the way. Rachel turned back toward the river and picked up her pace. Suddenly, the city seemed colder, less friendly. Maybe she should have taken her friend up on his many offers to walk her home.

There. It *was* a footstep, followed by another, and they were coming up behind her. A primitive instinct of fear took hold and she began to run. If she could just get to Castle Road, surely she could flag down a taxi. There were always tourists at the end of the High Street where it met the bridge, even at this hour.

"Rach! Rachel!" A voice brought her to a standstill, and relief flooded through her. She turned to welcome the familiar figure.

"What the hell! You scared the shite out o' me!"

He came up close and smiled; she could see his perfect teeth in the dim light of the streetlamp up ahead by the river.

"I knew you needed me," he said.

She punched him lightly in the arm. "I don't need you, but I'm glad you're here."

"Of course you need me. I don't know why you have t' be so independent."

His voice had dropped to a low murmur. He leaned down and brushed the hair back from her face. "Stop fooling around. I know you like me too."

"What?"

He reached for her hand and held it, perhaps more tightly than he needed to. He bent his head until she could feel his breath on her cheek. "You've been teasing me, haven't you, lass? Trying to make me jealous, flirting with that bawbag MacLeish?"

"What are you *talking* about?"

"I'm disappointed in you, Rachel. You're just like all the rest, I guess. Lead a man on, and then act as if he's just a friend because you think there's a richer catch out there. MacLeish is married, didn't you know that?"

Rachel could feel the blood pounding in her ears. She tried to pull her hand free, but he had anticipated that and held it in a grip that hurt.

"Please, stop it! This isn't funny!"

The slap came out of nowhere. The shock was instant and enervating, and the strength drained from her body. Her knees wobbled; she sagged against him and would have fallen had he not wrapped his arms around her to hold her up.

"There." The words were a whisper in her ear. "That's more like it. I knew you wanted me. You were just playing hard to get, weren't you, sweetheart?" His hands moved up and cupped her head so that she couldn't move if she'd had the strength to do so. Escape was impossible.

She could barely hear him for the roaring in her ears. She leaned back and tried to see his face in the darkness, but what she found there made her wish she hadn't. This wasn't the friend who had her back when things got rough at MacKay's, the sweet, handsome lad who flirted harmlessly with all the female tourists.

This was someone new. There was something different and raw and vile about this man who held her in a grip so strong she could feel his fingers digging into her scalp. The eyes that bore into hers weren't the warm dark brown she remembered, eyes that crinkled when he laughed. There was no laughter in them now; they glinted black with anger and seared her vision.

How had she never seen what he really was? This was a monster, strong and implacable and merciless. She kept silent, sensing that anything she might say would only make things worse.

Holding her tightly, he moved sideways toward the building at the near side of the lane where two rubbish bins stood, darker shadows against brick walls. A large cardboard box had been flattened and placed between them, and it was there he was dragging her, into the deepest shadows cast by the bins and the overhanging rooftop.

If she didn't loosen his grip somehow, she was lost. She brought the heel of her trainer down onto his foot with all the remaining force she could muster and wrenched at the wrists grasping her head.

He laughed. The beast laughed at her while he tightened his grip.

"Did you think a wee trainer would hurt, love?" His voice hardened. "It was a good try, but all you've done is prove that you really are a hooer, after all. Nasty wee lass."

The last words came out on a sibilant hiss.

He shook his head. "Tsk, tsk. You need to be punished."

Panic ripped through Rachel's chest and lodged in her throat, choking the scream before it was born. She fought to stay erect, understanding that if he brought her to the ground it was all over. She no longer wondered what he had in mind.

It didn't matter what she thought. Larger, stronger, fueled by a self-righteous rage at her refusal to give in, he forced her to the ground on top of the flattened cardboard and knelt over her, one hand over her mouth and his knees on either side of her heaving body.

"Be still!" The words were a whip crack. "Don't make this more difficult than it needs to be."

Rachel kept squirming until he hit her again. Her head exploded in pain and her hands fell loose at her sides. Tears streamed down her face and she looked up into the black eyes, searching for any sign of pity.

The demon stroked her hair away from her face and smiled. "That's my lass. Just lie still now, and take your punishment like a good girl."

His hands moved down her body slowly until they reached the skirt of her uniform. The cool night air brushed her thighs, and then she felt a searing pain that seemed to go on and on, amidst grunts of pure animal pleasure.

At some point, she must have passed out. When she opened her eyes, he was lying on top of her; she could hear his frenzied heartbeat thumping against her chest, feel his hot breath on her neck. When he saw she was awake, he sat up, zipped and fastened his jeans, and pulled her skirt back down, taking all the care in the world. Then he knelt over her again.

Rachel looked up at the face of the monster she had called friend.

"P-please . . ." The word was an incoherent whimper. A strange lethargy spread through her, and she found herself unable to look away from the black eyes that pinned her in place.

He smiled. "Now, wasn't that better than you expected?" The voice was soft. His hands came up to caress her face, and he tucked a strand of hair gently behind her ear. His fingers wiped the tears from her cheeks, trailed across her lips, and then moved down her neck.

He grinned again, placed his thumbs in the hollows of her throat, and squeezed. Rachel's hands came up and scrabbled at his wrists. She thrashed and gasped and choked, but the relentless band only tightened around her throat. A red mist rose and obscured her senses, and all that was left was the pain.

Rachel stared into the black eyes as her vision dimmed. Her hands slid away from the iron wrists, and she floated away from herself, over the building and into the clouds far away from the dark lane. Like a wisp of smoke, formless and empty, she drifted with the night wind until it carried her down again to hover above the scene.

A girl lay on the ground between two rubbish bins, a man's hands around her throat. Her wide blue eyes were fixed and empty, and her mouth open in a silent scream. On a whisper, Rachel drifted away again and was gone, into the early Inverness morning.

The man stood and looked down at the still form. A small smile played about his lips, and he sighed. He leaned down, grasped the girl under her arms, and dragged her further into the gap between the bins. He placed her tight against the wall and crossed her hands over her stomach. Finally, he pulled the sheet of cardboard over her body so that the top edge leaned against the wall, and stepped back to inspect his work.

He dusted his hands off on his jeans and walked away toward the Ness River, humming a tune he remembered from another time and place. A classical violin piece, played by another girl with blonde hair and blue eyes.

CHAPTER 15

INVERNESS, SCOTLAND, PRESENT DAY

*Only fear can defeat life. It has no
decency, respects no law, shows no
mercy. It goes for your weakest spot,
which it finds with unnerving ease.*
—Yann Martel

Sophie MacArthur sat in a straight-back wooden chair at the edge of the stage in the silent pub and plucked aimlessly at the strings of her violin, listening to the rain out on Ardconnel Street. Her muscle memory guided the bow; people hearing the sound might think they were hearing a beautiful Highland melody, played well.

The reality was, she had no idea what she was playing. Her mind's eye was fastened on a scene in this very room, almost five hours ago. Fiona's brother lying unconscious on the floor, blood from a gash in his head seeping into the cracks between the ancient boards while everyone looked on in shock.

It had all happened so fast. How had no one realized he was getting so drunk? She suspected he hadn't realized it himself. Tourists came over and thought they could hit the first bar they saw, even though often they were jetlagged after an overnight flight and exhausted from a long train ride. They were seduced by good single malt and acted as if they needed to drink it all in one go, in case the low prices were an illusion.

He didn't seem like an eejit, though. A teacher, he'd said, but didn't sound very proud of the fact. There had been that odd exchange with Fiona, and that's when he hunched into himself and begun mumbling nonsense—as if there was shame in teaching math. Weird guy.

Good looking, though. Russet-colored hair that fell over his forehead, bright green eyes like his sister's, a tall athletic frame, and muscles in all the right places . . . She put Oliver down and pulled out her mobile.

This is Fiona MacArthur. I can't come to the phone right now; please leave a message and I'll call you right back.

So they were probably still at the hospital. A worm of worry slithered through Sophie and curled up in her heart. He must really be hurt; he'd still been unconscious when the ambulance arrived. Paramedics had brought in a stretcher and made quick work of taking his vitals and administering initial care before loading him into the emergency vehicle and carting him off to Raighmore, while everyone in the pub looked on, confused and frightened.

"I'll take you," Caomhainn had announced and trundled Fiona and Ewan off in the ambulance's wake.

Mary had come up to Sophie and whispered, "We need someone to get up there. Can you do it?"

Now the band was finished and gone. When Caomhainn returned, he and Henry put up the 'Closed' sign and Mary had shepherded patrons out as soon as they finished their meals and drinks. They all left smiling and clutching their tiny bottles of Wild Thyme whisky, having forgotten the drama they'd been witness to. And now, at barely half-nine, Sophie sat alone and played reels and strathspeys to an empty pub without paying attention to what was coming out of her instrument.

For the first time she could remember, she didn't want to go home to her empty house. She wanted to be around people. She wanted to know how Brian Maclean was doing.

Caomhainn came out to clean up the bar, and Sophie made a decision.

"Caomhainn, will you take me to the hospital?"

"Aye, lass," was all he said, and she loved him for it. There was something about Wee Caomhainn, actually about all the people who ran *The Dancing Unicorn*, that was . . . otherworldly. They knew things. Even Biscuit the bar cat had a look that said, *I know what you're thinking and I'll keep your secret if you stay away from me.* It was a continuous source of amazement to Sophie, but somehow comforting. She grinned at the big man and followed as he turned off the lights and closed the wooden door behind them.

Together they sloshed through the rain to his Land Rover. On the way to the hospital, Caomhainn said nothing, which suited Sophie fine. She didn't know what she was doing or why she was doing it, but she decided she'd face that when the time came.

It's because he's Ewan's brother-in-law, she told herself, and heard a mocking echo in her head. *No, really. I just want to be there for Ewan and Fiona.* And until she knew what she really did want, her head would just have to deal with the confusion.

At Raighmore, she pulled herself together enough to ask for a visitor's pass at the front desk. The young woman consulted her computer.

"It's after visiting hours. Are you family?"

"Yes," Sophie heard herself saying. The girl gave her a disinterested look and reached into a basket.

"Mr. Maclean has been moved to the general wards. Sign here, take the lift to the third floor, and turn left. They'll guide you." She gave Sophie a wrinkled paper pass. "Turn this in when you leave."

Sophie left Caomhainn in the lobby and followed the directions to the third floor, where she found Ewan and Fiona sitting in the hallway. They looked up in surprise to see her.

No more surprised than I am. Is it too late to just turn around and leave?

"How is he?"

Fiona looked up. "The doctor's in with him now. He's been for a CT scan, and we're just . . .waiting." She looked up and down the corridor and shivered. "I was hoping I'd never have to see the inside of this place again. Once was enough."

Ewan nodded and clasped her hand. "Aye." His blue eyes were bloodshot and shadowed. "That was not fun. But it all turned out fine, and so will this. Raighmore is a good hospital."

The doctor came out and closed the door behind him.

"The CT scan is negative for any trauma," he said, "but--"

"But what?" Fiona demanded. "Is he awake?"

The doctor shook his head. "That's the curious thing. All the tests are negative. I would have expected him to have regained consciousness by now."

He surveyed the three people who stood anxiously before him. "Has he had any previous head injuries?"

Fiona turned pale. "Yes. He was in a boating accident a month ago. He had a concussion. Why?"

"Ahh," said the doctor. "That may account for it." He hesitated. "You need to understand, head injuries are always serious. People watch TV and the hero gets knocked out every episode, but he jumps right up and gets his man. The truth is, the brain doesn't find that amusing." He paused. "I don't want to scare you, but even a concussion is serious, and every time someone loses consciousness from a blow to the head, it's because there has been some damage to the brain."

Fiona gasped, and he put up his hand. "However, the human body is resilient, and the brain is no exception to that. As long as there is no pressure or internal hemorrhaging, there is every expectation that he should recover with no residual effects. He needs to be watched, though, and the staff can't be there every minute."

"I'll stay," Fiona said. She turned to the MacArthurs. "Ewan, will you take Sophie home?"

"I'll stay with you," Sophie said. "We can take turns."

Her sister-in-law looked surprised. "Sophie, that's very nice of you, but it isn't necessary."

"I'll stay." Sophie's voice was firm. "You can't sit up all night. He'll need you when he wakes up."

Ewan gave his sister a grateful look. "Thanks, Soph. Really."

"Oh!" Sophie said. "Caomhainn is waiting downstairs. Can you tell him to go on back?"

Ewan nodded. He hugged his wife and prepared to go. "I'll be back tomorrow. Let me know when he wakes up," he said, and moved quickly down the hallway toward the lifts.

Fiona watched him disappear around the corner. "Ewan hates hospitals," she said. "Particularly this one."

Sophie nodded. "This is where Mum died. He was only eleven. "She was rushing him here because his appendix burst, and they got into an accident. Dad blamed him for years."

"I know," Fiona said. "He's told me. And then I ended up here, which nearly sent him round the bend. I'm so proud of the man he became, despite all that."

She turned and looked at her sister-in-law. "He wasn't the only one in your family to experience trauma, though."

Sophie turned pale, and then let out a breath and gave Fiona a weak smile. "Oh, you mean Daniel . . . aye, sometimes I think we're cursed." She eyed her sister-in-law. "But you Macleans are doing pretty well in that department yourselves. "First you, and now your brother." She smiled and patted Fiona's hand. "No need to keep up with the MacArthurs, ye ken."

Fiona took a deep breath and smiled. "I'll try to remember that," she said. "Let's go see Brian."

They stood by the hospital bed and studied the patient. Brian had a bandage on the side of his head and an IV was hooked to his hand, but other than that and the beeping machine beside him, he just looked as if he was taking a nap.

He really is handsome, Sophie thought, and gave herself a mental slap. *Not in the market,* she reminded herself. *That's not for you.*

"Look," she nudged Fiona. "His eyelids are moving. Is he dreaming?"

"Maybe." Fiona made a fist and brandished it in the air. "Would be just like him, the lazy thing. I'd like to give him a punch. Jerk."

Her voice had a quaver in it. Sophie looked sideways and saw tears running down her sister-in-law's face. She grabbed the fisted hand and held it tightly.

"He'll be fine," she said, her voice soft. "You can punch him after he wakes up, eh?"

They took turns in the cot provided by the hospital, but sleep was elusive for both. The wan morning light filtered through the curtains at the window at three-thirty to find both women standing by the bedside, staring at Brian as if they could will him awake.

Sophie wandered down to the lobby at six, looking for coffee. As she stood in line at the cafe, her phone buzzed.

"Aye, Mary?"

"How's our patient?"

"Doctor says he'll be fine, but he's not awake yet."

"When were ye thinking t' come back?"

"Just getting Fiona a coffee, then I'll take the bus back. Ewan'll be by later."

"Listen, lass. Caomhainn is on his way." There was an edge to Mary's normally calm voice that Sophie hadn't heard before. "Dinnae get the bus."

"Oh, that's so sweet of him, but he doesn't have to come; the bus is fine."

"Dinnae take the bus." It was an order. Sophie felt the hairs on the nape of her neck sit up and take notice.

"What's the matter, Mary?"

"There's been a murder."

Sophie's heart clutched. *What the hell? A murder? Someone she knew?* Her heart ran any number of names through her brain in a second, starting with Deirdre's, but her tongue was locked. She waited.

"No, lass, no one ye ken. Sorry to scare ye. But . . ."

"What? Mary, what's the problem?"

"D' ye remember last year, there were three young women raped in Glasgow?"

"Y-yes."

Glasgow was where the Royal Conservatoire was.

Three young women . . . raped . . .

She swallowed the sick feeling. "Mary, Glasgow's a rough city. Lots of drunk hooligans, especially after football games. Wait—are you worried about me?" A wave of affection washed through Sophie, followed by a new burst of anxiety. Mary never worried. She took care of things so she didn't have to. If Mary was worried . . .

"There was another woman attacked a few months ago in Stirling, and then one in Fort William," she was saying.

"I read about it."

"And two nights ago a young woman was found strangled, right here in Inverness. The police are saying she was raped."

"B-but—"

"Lass, all these woman were young, and all of them had blonde hair and blue eyes. The police are saying they think it's the same man, that he has a type."

Time stopped. Sophie's mind brought up a map of Scotland. *Glasgow, Stirling, Fort William. Towns on the way to Inverness. Blonde hair, blue eyes.*

The Royal Conservatoire, three years ago. The night her life changed forever.

A night last week, footsteps following her home from Morrison's.

Mary's voice came to her out of the murk. "Lass. Are ye listenin'?"

"I'm l-listening."

"Caomhainn will be there. He'll be drivin' ye home today, and walkin' ye home after work from now on. Ye'll not be going anywhere alone until they catch this cursed animal."

The words she'd said just last night to Fiona echoed in Sophie's memory. *Sometimes I think we're cursed.*

CHAPTER 16

ISLE OF MULL, SCOTLAND, JUNE 1647

BRIAN

There were voices all around him, but he didn't recognize any of them. His head ached like hell, and the raucous call of seabirds above the crashing waves didn't help. Nausea swelled and receded with each breath he took. He'd read somewhere that you should close your eyes and face forward if you were suffering from motion sickness, so he kept his eyes screwed shut and resisted the temptation to look.

Odd—he never suffered from motion sickness, but the rolling was definitely coming from inside his stomach. His memory flashed and flickered, and a picture formed against his eyelids.

The pub. Fiona and Ewan. A fiddler playing a reel that reminded him of home. That bratty girl—Sophie?

Yeah, that was it. Ewan's baby sister. A giant pouring whisky. Fish and chips.

Ugh. His stomach heaved again. He shouldn't have had that third drink, damn it. What had he been thinking? Sure it was good, but that was no excuse to drown himself in the stuff. He didn't normally drink much, and when he did, he preferred craft beer. So what had brought on that bout of idiocy?

Maybe he'd been more tired than he thought. Certainly his decision-making had been impaired, and when that girl implied he was a lightweight, his pride had jumped in and sacrificed him to the gods of drink.

No, it had started before that. He'd already been playing the fool, acting as if his country's honour was at stake, and he had to drink Scotland dry to save it.

The girl had asked if he was a teacher. That's all she did—she didn't mean anything by it; she couldn't have known, but it had released all the anger and grief he'd been holding in since his career imploded.

Does he drink like that all the time? He's fair-on blootered. The memory of her voice, dripping with condescension, triggered another wave of nausea. He turned to the side just in time and threw up.

"Seven!" A woman's voice reached him. Not one he knew, so he opened his eyes to see. The face of an older woman hovered over him. Pretty, even with the circles under her eyes and the tiny lines around her mouth that suggested she smiled frequently.

She wasn't smiling now. Her brow was furrowed and her face pale and she was gripping his hand so tightly it hurt. Was she worried about him? He struggled to a sitting position and tried to smile.

Immediately she pulled him in and enveloped him in a hug that threatened to suffocate him in the folds of her gown.

Wait. Her gown? Brian leaned his head back as far as he could while being squashed. The woman was wearing a gown of heavy muslin, with a silver brooch centered by a crystal of some sort holding her shawl in place. It was the kind of dress the actors wore every year at the Tempest Grove Renaissance Faire, across Bras d'Or Lake from his hometown.

He'd been there once or twice with a date and thought the posturing and the games rather silly, but the ladies seemed to like it. Had Ewan and Fiona somehow dragged him to one of those events while he was drunk?

That would explain a lot. The clothing, the medieval look of the room, the name they were calling him. So, was his name to be Cris-something here? And where were those two perpetrators—his sister and her husband?

I'm going to get them back for this.

For now, best to play along. He ran his eyes around the room, taking in the stone walls, arched windows, and heavy draperies. The room was huge, anchored by a stone fireplace that took up most of one wall. In the center of the mantel was a carved shield.

Brian focused on the woman who was still holding him, a little too tightly.

"Does an actor's fee include mauling the guests?"

She stared at him, the picture of confusion.

Jeez, she's good!

"Where's my lovely sister?"

A look of pain crossed the woman's features, and morphed into anger. "That's purely ruide, Crìsdean!" she said. "Ye dinnae have call t' mock me fer givin' birth only t' sons. D' ye think I wanted it this way, ye oaf?" She punched him hard enough in the arm that he winced. "Ye were s'posed t' be a lass!"

Snickers sounded somewhere behind her. "Mebbe he is a lass, Mam," said one of several young men standing by the fireplace. Brian looked over the woman's shoulder and studied the speaker. He was dressed in woolen trews and a white shirt with wide cuffs at the wrists. Around his shoulders he wore a tartan sash, held in place by a large pin that Brian knew well because he had one at home. It was the same as the shield above the fireplace.

The Maclean clan badge. A tower embattled argent, with the motto, "Virtue Mine Honour," emblazoned around the top edge. He looked around at the other men in the room, and a shiver worked its way up his spine. Several of them wore similar badges. That clinched it. What were the chances that these actors had just coincidentally been cast as members of Clan Maclean? He was going to skin his sister alive.

He looked down and realized that he was wearing the same period clothing as the others—clothing he'd never seen before. His sash was fastened with the Maclean clan badge. How had they done that?

"I mean," continued the young man who had found him amusing, "he sure faints like a lass."

The woman who had been embracing Brian whipped her head around. "Haud yer tongue,

Fergus!" she hissed. The man grinned and held his hands up as if to fend off her anger. "Sorry, Mam, I was jist playin'."

Brian decided that half-lying on a cold stone floor was not helping anything, so he struggled to his feet. His head still felt muzzy, as if he had a head cold, and he swayed a little before gaining his balance.

Why am I the only one being pranked here? When does the joke end? Where's my damn sister?

"Crìsdean!"

A young girl flew into the room and caromed off the jerk who had been laughing at him. She came to a halt and grabbed both of his arms in surprisingly strong little hands.

"I heered ye fainted agin. Are ye awright?" The girl peered into his eyes and stiffened, the color draining from her already pale face.

"I-I-y-you," Brian stuttered. "Who—?"

The girl clapped her hand over his mouth and grabbed his hand. "Aunt Anna, he's awright. He jist needs somethin' t' eat—I'll take 'im."

She dragged him out of the room and down the spiral stone staircase to the next floor, away from the crowd of strangers. Once in the lower hallway, she shoved him up against the wall and glared at him.

Brian stood speechless, staring at the girl he'd last seen playing the violin at The Dancing Unicorn. The beautiful blue-eyed sister of Ewan MacArthur.

"S-Sophie?"

"Who?" the girl demanded. "Who's Sophie?" She searched his face for a long moment, and then dropped her voice to a whisper. "An' who are ye?"

But Brian wasn't listening. This wasn't Sophie Maclean. This girl was younger, barely in her teens. And her hair wasn't cut in a bob; it fell to her waist in thick blonde curls. It could have been a wig, he supposed. Like the others in this reenactment, she was dressed in period clothing—a long tartan skirt and wheat-colored blouse with a shawl like that of the older woman back in the huge room.

"I said, who are ye?" the girl demanded again. Her voice held anger with an edge of panic. It wasn't Sophie's voice.

"This isn't funny!" Brian said, desperation edging his words. "Where is Fiona? I don't want to play this stupid game anymore! I hate this stuff!"

The girl's eyes widened and she stepped back from him. "I kent it," she muttered to herself. "When it happened afore, I kent ye were someun' else. Bit how—?" She pinned him with those blue eyes again.

"Who are ye?" she said, her voice low and soft, as if she were speaking to a patient in a psychiatric institution. Those words, and that stare, were the most frightening things Brian had experienced so far in this upside down world.

This wasn't a Renaissance Faire. Not a reenactment. Fiona wouldn't do this to him; she would never take it this far.

Suddenly he remembered where he'd seen this face before. This was the girl who had held him in her arms after the sailing accident, when he was drowning in Bras d'Or Lake. She had called him Christian then too. Or something like that. She had saved him; he was sure of it—but he didn't know how.

A chill gripped him, and he looked around the hallway in sudden terror. The same grey rough-hewn blocks, the same arched stone windows. Outside the nearest window he glimpsed waves, rolling toward the land and breaking against more stone.

Something bit into his arm, and he looked down to see the girl's fingers latched on like talons. "Tell me yer name," she said, more quietly.

"Tell me yours first," he said, desperate to regain some control over this impossible situation.

"I'm Kenna."

He nodded, as if it all made sense. "I'm Brian."

She blinked, then shook her head. "No, ye're nae Brian. Yer Crìsdean Maclean. "At least, 'at's who ye're s'posed t' be."

CHAPTER 17

ISLE OF MULL, SCOTLAND, 1647

KENNA

Crìsdean's eyes were vacant and he looked as if he might cry. Kenna understood; she felt close to tears herself. Her best friend, the one person in the castle who knew and kept her secrets, was losing his mind, and he was as terrified as she.

Who are you? he had asked.

She believed he thought he was someone else, and she would support him to the end, but such a thing was impossible. And yet . . .

This man's hands were Crìsdean's hands, calloused from practice with a sword. Like all the Maclean clansmen, he stood with his legs slightly apart, balanced on the balls of his feet, and braced for combat.

His hair was Crìsdean's hair, thick auburn curls that refused to stay in a queue and kept falling into his eyes.

His voice. His voice was wrong, the accent flat and harsh. He was using words she'd never heard before, not from Crìsdean, not from anybody. But that wasn't all.

Her heart skipped a beat. *It was the eyes.* Eyes didn't lie. They were windows into the very soul of a man, the source of his being. Though they were the same clear green, these were the eyes of someone she didn't know, a man much older than Crìsdean's eighteen years. A stranger.

But if she believed that, she had to believe there was someone out there named Brian who had found himself in Crìsdean's body, twice now. And she couldn't. To do that was to risk her own sanity when she needed it most to help her friend.

Still, this man before her, looking so like Crìsdean Maclean and begging with those eyes, needed her. Her heart went out to him, and without thinking, she reached out and pulled him close.

He didn't resist. He put his cheek down on the top of her head and let his breath out in a long, ragged sigh. Her small hands patted him on his broad back until his breathing slowed and settled into a normal rhythm.

When he lifted his head, she looked into his face again and let out a sigh of her own. "Come. I'll show ye th' castle. Ye'll need t' ken yer way, and fer as long as yer here, I'll help ye, aye?" She patted his hand as if he were a small child.

He nodded, his eyes clearing for a moment, and the tiniest of smiles lifted the corners of his mouth.

Wha' a wonderful thing it must be t' be believ'd, she thought. She didn't, of course. She didn't believe any of this, not for a minute, but absent any reason that made sense, she would give it all she had. She took his hand and led him down the staircase to the ground floor of the castle and out into the yard where the men practiced. Today it was empty; everyone was indoors waiting for dinner, so Kenna knew it would be safe.

"This is where we train," she said.

"We?" he said. Kenna shot him a sharp look, but his expression was one of simple curiosity. "You train with the men?"

She puffed up and put her hands on her hips. "O' course," she said. She waited for him to call her out, but he gave her a weak smile and made a fist with his thumb pointing up.

"Good for you," he said. He wandered around the yard, gazing up at the stone walls with an odd expression on his face. Then he turned to face her.

"I know this place," he said, his voice low. "I was here before. You were here too. You were—mm—holding me."

It had been a year ago, but Kenna hadn't forgotten those few moments in the yard, and she doubted she ever would. Watching Crìsdean's legs fold and his sturdy body collapse into the dirt of the yard had been one of the most frightening things in all her fourteen years on this earth. Heedless of the men's clothing she had been at such pains to conceal from other's eyes, she'd raced across the training ground and gathered him into her arms.

When he'd opened his eyes, she'd been grateful beyond measure—until she saw the impossible in them. They weren't *his* eyes. And now she understood.

"'Twas *ye*." She glared at him. "Most a year gone. Only fer a minute, bit ye took my heart oot an' squeezed it so's t' make me think I was dyin'."

The man laughed. The green eyes that belonged to Crìsdean Maclean crinkled at the edges, his lips tipped upwards at the corners just like Crìsdean's when he was teasing her. And just for a second, everything was all right.

Just for a second. The smile fled, and lines appeared again on the forehead of the man who called himself Brian. Kenna's shoulders slumped.

"Brian who?" she asked suddenly.

"What?"

"Do ye have a surname?" Kenna planted her hands on her hips. *Now we'll see. If he's havin' me on, he will- nae have an answer fer that 'un.*

"Oh. Right. It's Maclean. Brian Maclean."

"Weel, o' course it is." Kenna nodded. Crìsdean Maclean was a fast thinker, she'd give him that much. She sighed. "Let's gie on."

Together they explored the castle, careful to avoid other people when they could. It was fortunate that most everyone was at supper; the halls were nearly empty. The family were used to seeing Crìsdean and Kenna together, and no one paid them attention.

For the first time Kenna was grateful for her small stature and her age. No one was terribly interested in the exploits of the youngest members of the family when food was on the table. If they missed supper, there was more for everyone else.

It occurred to Kenna that if someone did come, Crìsdean would have to stop the pretense of being someone else. His brothers wouldn't stand for that nonsense, and she'd get to watch them teach him a lesson.

But if he *wasn't* pretending? She couldn't explain why, but she didn't want to find out that way. She was the only one who'd seen those eyes change. It was her secret, hers to protect.

Over the next few hours, Kenna tried various times to catch Crìsdean out, but the light in his green eyes was amazement, as if he was seeing his birthplace for the first time.

Finally they stood together in the great hall, everyone having eaten and moved on to other pursuits.

"Thank you," he said. "It's amazing, really." A shadow crossed his face and he looked around as if unsure what to do next. "Er," he said, stopped, and started again. "What year is this?"

A surge of fear swept through her, followed by a red wave of anger. No.

"Why?" she demanded. "Why are ye doin' this? 'Tis b'yond a jest, Crìsdean."

A thought occurred to her. "D' ye have a wager on wi' Pàdraig? Are ye gettin' yer own back fer me dressin' as a lad an' foolin' ye? If ye are, I'll kill ye!"

She stared at his face, waiting for a smirk, a wink, *anything*. But all she saw there was confusion. Losing patience, she reared back to give him a sharp kick in the shin and stopped, one small foot in the air.

Someone was coming carefully down the spiral staircase from the upper floors. A moment later Frances rounded the corner, her brows drawn downward in a frown and her lips taut. She stopped in front of Kenna and Crìsdean and glared at them.

"Ye . . . ye . . ." she spat. "Dinnae ye say *anythin'*!" She gathered her skirts and stomped off down the hall, leaving the two with gaping mouths.

"But we didnae," Kenna said. She shot a glance toward the steps. "I'll wager she's jist come from th' library." A slow grin spread over her face. "Guid fer ye, Giles," she said under her breath.

Brian was still gazing after the departing figure.

"Who's she?" he asked.

"Stop 't!" Kenna barked. "Ye ken weel enough it's Frances."

"I don't like her," he said, in a low voice. "There's something about her eyes."

Kenna gazed at him for a long moment.

"'Tis 1647," she mumbled, under her breath, and looked away from him.

A man rounded the last step from the floor below. His expression mirrored the one they'd just seen on Frances, but he'd been coming *up* the staircase, not down. He too stopped in front of them.

"Hae ye seen Frances?" he snapped. His brows were furrowed and his face red.

"She came down—ouch!" Brian yelped and grabbed his foot.

Kenna assumed what she hoped was an innocent smile. "We didnae see 'er, Dànaidh. Mebbe she's wi' th' aunts."

Dànaidh glared at them, then shot a glare at the steps leading upward. "Fffft," he spit out, and stomped off in the direction his wife had taken. In his wake, silence filled the hallway again.

Brian was staring after Dànaidh.

Kenna let out a breath. "I dinnae like it," she mumbled. "She's jist askin' fer trooble. She needs t' stop an' remember 'at she's a woman marrit."

"I ken it. Dànaidh doesnae deserve 'at. He loves 'er so much."

Kenna gasped. She clasped a fistful of his shirt and dragged him back around to face her. His eyes were clouded, and his brows narrowed in frustration.

"Wha'?" he said. "Am I nae right t' be worrit? An' whit are ye grinnin' aboot, like a wee fool?"

Crìsdean—*her* Crìsdean—was back.

CHAPTER 18

INVERNESS, SCOTLAND, PRESENT DAY

*People from the past have a tendency to walk
back into the present, and run over the future.*
—Anthony Liccione

The shadows receded. Or rather, *he* was receding, flying backwards as if propelled by an unseen force—a strong wind or waves. He couldn't see the castle anymore, couldn't see the oddly dressed girl, or the stone walls, or . . .

"He's waking up!" A feminine voice with a Scottish burr to it. Soft, earthy, vaguely familiar. Brian struggled to open his eyes and immediately closed them again as light stabbed his retinas like hot needles. He took a deep breath and tried again, more carefully this time, and found himself staring into a pair of sky-blue eyes. Kenna's eyes, no, these were different somehow.

"Thank God!" He recognized Fiona's voice this time. The relief that coursed through him brought tears to his eyes and blurred the image of the two women. Embarrassed, he turned his head away and concentrated on the throbbing pain in his head.

He reached up and felt for the source of the pain. There was some sort of bandage covering the side of his forehead.

A hand grabbed his. "Don't touch!" his sister ordered. So he lay still and focused on the room he was in. The walls were a stark institutional white. There was a TV on a wall mount across from him, and a tray table beside his bed. The bed was too short; his feet pressed against the footboard.

Bed? Why was he in bed? He turned to look for his sister, and squinted against the light coming from a picture window across the room.

The images solidified and forced away the memory of rough-hewn stone walls, the sound of waves crashing somewhere in the distance. The castle was gone. The smell of the sea was gone, replaced by an antiseptic odor that was oddly familiar.

He was in another damn hospital.

His eyes sought and found those of the other girl. Not Kenna; it was that girl from the pub—the fiddler. Ewan's sister. What the hell was she doing here?

"Ladies, I'm going to need you to leave for a few minutes while I check on my patient," a brusque Scottish voice broke into his thoughts. The two women retreated and a door closed.

"I'm Dr. Buchanan." A man in a white coat pulled a rolling stool to the side of the bed and leaned over Brian. He peeled the bandage back from the side of his forehead and clucked his tongue. "You've gotten yourself a nasty gash there, lad," he said. "You need to be careful when sampling our fine whisky, aye?"

Brian could feel the heat rising in his face. Uninvited, his memory conjured up the pub with its roaring fire, the music so reminiscent of home, his own hand pouring dram after dram into a tiny glass. He closed his eyes and willed the world to go away.

The doctor lifted his lids and shined a penlight into his eyes, took his blood pressure, and tested his reflexes. Then he sat back on the stool and crossed one knee over the other.

"It's odd, though," he said. "That cut is on a part of your head where the skull is pretty thick. It should hurt, aye, but you've been unconscious for the better part of a day." He peered at his patient and drew in his brows. "Your ladies told me you had a head injury not long ago?"

"Y-yes, sir," Brian's voice sounded rusty to his own ears, as if he hadn't talked in weeks. "I was in a sailing accident a month ago. Got a concussion."

"Ahh," Dr. Buchanan nodded. He turned Brian's head to the side and felt through the hair on the back. "Ach, aye, you've got a nice scar back there," he said with some satisfaction. "You know, any head injury that causes you to lose consciousness is considered brain damage."

Brian sighed. "Yes, they told me that." *At this rate, I'll be a drooling fool pretty soon.* Didn't much matter; these people probably thought he was a drunk at the least. *Note to self—no more whisky!*

The doctor's eyes narrowed. "You have to take better care, lad," he said. "I'm going to keep you here another night, run some more tests, and if everything looks good, you can go home tomorrow. Aye?"

He stood to go, and then turned back. "Have you ever suffered from insomnia?"

Brian's eyes widened. "Yes. Since the accident. How did you know?"

The doctor shrugged. "I didn't, not for sure. But insomnia can be triggered by trauma or stress, so I'm not surprised."

Trauma or stress. *Well, doc, if you only knew. Thanks again, Meghan.* He felt the bitter bile rise up in his throat.

"The point of my question," Dr. Buchanan continued, "is that alcohol can be a factor in insomnia, and too much drinking can aggravate the fugue state caused by chronic lack of sleep."

"No problem there. I'm really not much of a drinker," Brian said without thinking. The silence following that remark resounded in the antiseptic environment, and he cringed inwardly as he watched the doctor's eyebrows rise. "This insomnia," he said quickly. "Can it be cured?"

"Well, it's not a disease, lad. It's a sleep disorder. But certainly it can be treated. I'll have a nurse come in and give you some suggestions. And don't worry too much; since it was likely triggered by your previous accident, it may not be chronic."

He patted Brian's hand. "I'll send your lassies in, then. They'll be wanting to make sure you're back in the land o' the living."

After the doctor left, Brian lay back and let the words circle around in his head. *Brain damage, insomnia, fugue, alcohol, trauma . . .*

Trauma. He hadn't told the doctor everything. Did trauma cause you to dream about places you'd never seen? *Times* you knew nothing about? Did trauma have names like Christian, or Kenna, or—what was it—Danny? He knew no one with those names.

The door opened quietly, and his sister tiptoed into the room as if the floor was made of eggshells.

"Brian?" she whispered.

"Fee."

"Oh, Brian!" Fiona rushed across the room to his bedside and enveloped him in a hug. "I was so worried! They wouldn't tell us anything, and you wouldn't wake up—you scared me so much—" she broke off to stare into his eyes. "Are you really all right?"

"I'm really all right," he said. "I'm just an ass. Why'd you let me drink so much?"

"I'm sorry, I'm the worst sister ever. I wasn't paying attention, and all of a sudden, you were rambling on about keeping the honour of Canada alive or some nonsense, and then your eyes rolled up in your head and you went down like a ton of bricks." She punched him in the arm. "You're not an ass, just . . . well, yeah, I guess you are an ass, but I love you. Don't ever do that to me again, you hear?"

Brian managed a laugh. "Just tell it like it is; don't spare my feelings or anything." He straightened suddenly and looked past her. "Where's—um—where's the girl who was with you? Ewan's sister."

"Sophie? Oh, she went home with Caomhainn. We took turns waiting for you to wake up, and she has a gig tonight at the pub."

"Why?"

Fiona looked concerned. "Because she works there. Are you sure you're all right?"

Her brother glared at her. "I know she works

there! Does everyone think my brain was removed in surgery?" He took a deep breath. "I mean," he said carefully, "why did she take turns with you? She doesn't even know me."

Fiona shrugged. "Well, she is Ewan's sister, so she's family."

Brian lay back and let that filter into his scrambled thoughts. Right. She was family. She probably thought of him as an annoying brother, that was all. He shook off the odd feeling of disappointment and focused on his sister.

"What did the doctor say?" Fiona asked.

"He said I probably shouldn't hit my head anymore."

"Well, duh."

"And I should be careful about drinking." He narrowed his eyes and waited.

"You're not really much of a drinker, though," she said.

"And that's why you're my favorite sister."

"Eh?"

"Never mind. Fee . . ." *How to put this?* "Um, do we know anyone named Kenna?"

She considered. "Don't think so. Why?"

"How about Christian?"

"Not offhand. I think one of Kirsty's boyfriends was called Chris, but I think it was Christopher. What's this about, Brian?"

"Nothing." He paused. "Have you ever been to a castle near water? I'm pretty sure it's in Scotland."

Now she was openly staring. "Brian, do you have any idea how many castles there are in Scotland? And a great many of them are near water. It was a strategic location." She put a hand to his forehead. "Are you *sure* you're okay?"

He brushed the hand away. "I'm fine. Forget it—guess it was a dream. It's just that it's happened a few times now. The same dream."

Fiona's eyes went wide. She left the bedside and went to stand by the window, looking out over the hospital parking lot and the distant hills. When she spoke, her voice seemed to come from far away. "Brian, do you remember the weird dream I kept having back home—before I came to Scotland?"

"Yeah. You looked like death warmed over when you had one."

She turned back to face him, hands twisted together in front of her. "Well, it was always the same dream, and it followed me here."

"Well, wouldn't it? I mean, it was your dream."

Fiona crossed from the window and pulled up the stool. She leaned her elbows on the bedcovers and covered her eyes with her hands. "I never told you how I met Ewan." She pulled her hands down, but she kept her eyes closed. "He was in the dream. Not him exactly, but someone who looked just like him. He was on a battlefield, and he was trying to protect me—"

"So, what's weird about it?" Brian interrupted. "Dreams are like that."

Fiona opened her eyes and stabbed him with a glare. "What's weird about meeting your future husband in a dream *before* you actually meet him? Gee, I wonder."

It was Brian's turn to widen his eyes. "Sorry. Okay, that is weird. Go on."

His sister shook her head. "The point was, I did meet the man of my dreams. Literally. He—Brian, what's the matter?"

Her brother had gone still, his hands fisted in the covers. As she watched, his breathing returned to normal, and he worked up a smile.

"Sorry, I'm fine. It's just that—" he cleared his throat. "In my dream, there was this girl named Kenna."

"And you think you'll meet her in real life?" Fiona's voice was low, almost a whisper. She didn't sound as surprised as he thought she would be.

"I already have." His eyes were wide with something between wonder and disbelief. "Kenna is the spitting image of Sophie."

Fiona stared at him.

"Sophie? Ewan's Sophie?"

"Yep. I'd already had one of those dreams when I met her at the pub. It was when I was in the hospital after the sailing accident." He winced in memory. "When I met Sophie, I had no idea who she was, only that I knew her from somewhere."

"What?"

"She wasn't quite the same. The girl in my dream was much younger. A kid, really. And she was dressed in old-fashioned clothes. Her hair was longer too."

Fiona let out a breath. "Then maybe it's just a coincidence," she said. "Did you say anything about it to Sophie?"

Brian snorted. "That one? I only saw her that one time. She was quite busy putting me in my place, if you remember, and I was quite busy deserving it.

When would we have had the time to talk about our dreams? And I have no intention of ever getting close enough to her to do that. She may be your sister-in-law, but she's a judgmental little twit."

Fiona looked at him, and a tiny smile creased her lips. "Whatever." She thought for a minute. "You said there was a castle in your dream?"

"Yeah, but it might have been just my imagination because I was thinking about Scotland."

"Brian," his sister said slowly, "you weren't thinking of Scotland when you had that first dream. You said it was after your accident. You hadn't called me yet. You didn't know you were coming here."

"Oh. Right. Let me think." He lay back and closed his eyes, letting the images float to the surface. Sandstone. Spiral stone stairs. The sound of water crashing. People dressed in old-fashioned clothing, swords, clan badges . . .

"Fiona." He sat straight up. "Do we have a castle?"

"What?" She blinked at him. "I think I'd remember moving into one if we did."

"Shut up and think—you worked at Gaelic College. I don't mean us, specifically; I mean the Macleans. Don't most of the Highland clans have a castle or two in their history?"

"Oh." She considered. "Sure. Several, actually. One of ours is still owned by the family. The chief lives there." She pulled out her cell phone and googled Clan Maclean. "Here it is," she said. "Duart Castle. It's over on Mull." She handed him the phone.

Brian took it from her and squinted at the small image of Duart Castle. Even in the small thumbnail it was a magnificent fairytale structure, a brown sandstone structure that sat alone on a promontory in the middle of the sea, like a sentinel. He tapped 'images.'

Shock swept through him, and he forgot to breathe. There were the spiral stairs down which that angry woman had swept. There was the courtyard where the girl named Kenna said the men practiced swordcraft. The great hall with the Maclean crest carved into the fireplace. The furnishings were different, but it was the same place.

The details were perfect; things he couldn't possibly have known. Unless he'd *been* there.

CHAPTER 19
INVERNESS, SCOTLAND, PRESENT DAY

Truth is not something outside to be discovered,
it is something inside to be realized.
—Osho

The sound of a violin string breaking is a tiny pop of air audible to only the closest listeners, but to the fiddler it is as momentous as the cry of an injured child. You want to stop everything and tend to the hurt, but the show must go on.

Sophie continued for a few bars on the other strings, adjusting the tune to compensate for the lost one. Then she brought the instrument down and stepped back. The others nodded and moved into another tune; one that didn't call for strings of any kind.

Anything can cause a string to break. The weather, a fault in the instrument, a sharp edge on the tuner. Or a lapse on the part of the musician.

"I'm sorry, Oliver," Sophie murmured to her violin. "I let you down." She felt over the remaining strings and cursed herself. Strung too tight; a beginner's mistake. She restrung and adjusted the fiddle and set Oliver carefully in his case, wondering at such an unusual oversight. Where had her mind been these last two days?

In the hospital, her inner voice told her, a note of snark in its tone. *With that Canadian lad you claim not to care about.*

"Well, I don't," she said.

"What was that then?" Sophie looked up to find that the band had taken a break, and all four of her mates were staring at her.

"Ye don't what?" the drummer said.

"Oh, nothing, Jack. Was just talking to myself."

"Is wee Oliver all right?" Concern wrinkled the piano player's weathered features.

"Oh. Aye." Sophie looked at her bandmates with affection. They all called the fiddle Oliver now, and every member cared about his welfare as much as that of their own instruments. They had to be. Jack's drums, Steve's keyboard, Hugh's pipes, and Roger's guitar—they were all a part of the family their little band had become in just a few weeks.

She thought back to the first time she'd seen them. They'd all been here that first night, along with Steve's nephew Davy, the poor lad who'd been gallantly trying to man the fiddle. Davy was the one most excited by her entrance into the band because it meant he could retire at the ripe old age of fourteen. He'd since relegated himself to the position of equipment manager, and gratefully accepted pay in the form of fiddle lessons from Sophie.

"Ye've been woolgathering these days, lass," Jack observed. "It's not like ye."

Sophie sighed. "I know, and I'm sorry. It's nothing; haven't had enough sleep, that's all. I've been helping my sister-in-law watch over her brother in hospital."

"The tourist lad who took a header into his whisky and met the table on his way down?" Hugh said. "Is he all right?"

"I think so. Fiona told me he woke up yesterday and he's fine. It was scary, though." She shivered at the memory of that handsome face, pale as chalk and bleeding from a cut on his head. "I doubt he'll be back anytime soon."

A pang washed through her at the thought, unwelcome and raw. He was just visiting; she might never see him again. She nodded to herself. Aye, that was for the best. But maybe she should stop by Ewan's in a day or so, bring some biscuits or something.

The door banged open, and there he was. Still pale, but walking on his own two feet. The corner of a bandage poked out from under his russet hair, and his eyes darted around the pub as if checking for people who might have been there to witness his humiliating performance in the pub. *As well he should, the numpty.*

Then the incredible green eyes turned on her like a beacon, and her knees threatened to give out. Before they could, Sophie gave a curt nod and turned away. She picked up a music stand and moved it two inches to the left, then three inches back to the right. When she felt the strange connection ease, she risked looking up and saw that he had moved over to the bar and stood talking to Caomhainn.

She felt a mingled feeling of relief and loss. He was a stranger to her—an invasive, annoying one at that—and it was obvious he felt the same way about her. Maybe he didn't even remember her.

He turned suddenly and caught her eyes again, and just like that she froze, as if trapped in a beam of alien light. What was happening to her these days? There was no room for this nonsense in her life. *He's a man*, she reminded herself. *Not to be trusted.*

To assert her emotional sovereignty, Sophie squared her shoulders and stepped down from the small stage. She sauntered over to the bar and pulled herself up on the only available stool and then turned to the man standing beside it.

"Oh! Hullo." *There. Did that sound suitably nonchalant?* "How are you feeling?"

Brian gave her a weak smile. "Hi. I feel much better, thank you. Um . . ." The nonconversation dribbled itself into silence.

"I'll have a tap water, Caomhainn," Sophie said.

"Ginger ale for me," Brian said. The barman nodded and fetched the glasses, and both watched as if the procedure was the most interesting activity in the world.

Sophie squirmed. She was usually so comfortable with silence; what was going on with her? Her eyes settled on the cat, sitting in her usual spot on the end of the bar and licking her paw.

"Uh, be careful not to pet the cat," she said. "Biscuit's very suspicious of strangers, and you have enough injuries already."

Brian flushed, and Sophie gave herself a mental slap. *Way to go, eejit.*

The cat had looked up at the sound of her name, and now she stood up, stretched, and ambled over to sit in front of Brian. She yawned, showing a pink tongue and several sharp teeth, and then extended one paw and patted his nose gently. Brian lifted her carefully and settled her into his arms, scratched her under her chin, and gave Sophie an angelic smile.

"I like cats," he said. "We've always had one or two around the house."

Sophie glared at the animal. *Wee betraying dobber.* Biscuit cocked her head and stared back with unblinking yellow eyes.

A cough from behind the bar had Sophie switching her glare to the big man, who cleared his throat and grinned at her. "I heard our Sophie here watched over you in hospital," he said to Brian. "Ye should feel privileged; *she's* the suspicious one if ye ask me." He gave his full attention to an invisible spot on the bar, rubbing vigorously at it with a towel.

Brian looked up and his face flushed again. "Oh, yeah. I heard you were there with Fiona. Wh—th-thank you," he said to Sophie. He paused. "You didn't have to do that."

Sophie opened her mouth to say something clever and innocuous, but nothing came out. Fortunately, she was saved from further stress when the pub door opened and a voice carried over the noise in the room. "Soph!"

Sophie and Brian turned at the shout. Beyond grateful, Sophie waved Deirdre over.

"What are *you* hanging out at the bar for?" her

friend asked. "Make way for the drinkers. Hullo, Caomhainn, I'll have a gin and tonic, please. Hi, cat."

Biscuit yawned and closed her eyes.

"What's up?" Sophie asked, but her friend wasn't listening. Deirdre assessed Brian from head to foot as though he wore a *For Sale* sign on his forehead, and then turned back to her best friend.

"Who—?"

"Oh. This is Brian. He's Fiona's brother. From Canada. Brian, this is Deirdre."

Brian extended a hand and smiled. Deirdre took the hand and held on, a little longer than necessary in Sophie's opinion.

"*Very* nice to meet you," she purred. "So you're a Maclean, then? My mother's cousin is a Maclean. From Coll, I think. His name is Hector. But then again, most of the Macleans, at least the important ones, are named Hector. I'm a Clarke, which is a sept of Clan MacPherson, but you probably wouldn't know about that, being from Canada. Anyway, a lot of Highland clans are septs of other clans. A sept is a clan that has a different name from the main clan but is really the same family. Like Sophie. MacArthur is a sept of Clan Campbell, but you might know that, since her brother is married to Fiona. Oh, wait— that's your sister, aye? What an eejit I am! So I guess you two are related, in a way."

"We're not—" Brian and Sophie spoke at the same time, but Deirdre had swept on, heedless of the interruption.

"I don't usually talk this much, but I'm curious because I never see Sophie with a lad, let alone a hot one, and since she's my best friend I guess we're connected too, in a way."

Caomhainn thrust a glass at Deirdre. "Yer G 'n T, lass. Drink up, ye're probably thirsty. 'At was a long speech, even for you."

Deirdre grinned at him and took the glass. "Sorry, I get carried away by a pretty face." She turned to Brian and fluttered her lashes, before giving her attention to her drink. "Mmm. You're the best, Caomhainn. Now, where was I?"

Brian glanced at Sophie over Deirdre's head and rolled his eyes. She grinned back, suddenly happier, and he gave her a conspiratorial smile that had her toes curling.

"Wait," Deirdre said. She put her drink down and pointed at Brian's head. "Sophie told me someone got hurt here the other night. Was that you? Are you all right?"

Brian flushed. "I'm fine. I just slipped and hit my head. It was embarrassing enough. Let's not talk about it." His eyes flicked back and forth as if he were waiting for rescue, and Sophie decided to answer the call.

"He's really fine, Deirdre. Fiona and I took turns watching him, and—"

"You watched over him? You're that close? How long have you two known each other?" Deirdre's hazel eyes had narrowed. "Why didn't you tell me about him?"

"Excuse me." Sophie hoped her voice didn't sound as desperate as she felt. "It's time for another set." She hopped down off her stool and turned to face the empty stage. "I'd better round up the guys." She caught a look of betrayal on Brian's face and allowed herself a tight smile. "Caomhainn, can you find these two a table in the front?"

"Aye, lass, looks like one's just opening up now. Deirdre, over there. Sit doon and give yer tongue a rest, aye?"

Sophie reached the stage and turned around in time to see Deirdre grab Brian's sleeve and pull him over to the table. A new feeling slithered through her stomach and climbed up to her chest to reside there. It stayed as the band reassembled and took their places and began tuning their instruments, persisted through the tuning and warming up, and settled into a dull throbbing as Sophie watched Deirdre lean across the table to give Brian her best smile.

He didn't seem to mind; he was smiling right back, the wee pudding. Acting as if every word that flowed out of her friend's mouth was a pearl of wisdom and charm. And why should that bother her?

"Sophie!" Hugh hissed. "What the hell? You're on the wrong bar! Are you all right, lass?"

Shite! She sent a look of contrition to her bandmates. "Sorry, I'm fine."

She grasped her bow and returned herself to the music, quickly finding her place in the tune. A look around the pub confirmed that most of the Unicorn's patrons were conversing with each other, raising drinks and forks, unaware that anything had gone amiss with the band. Some probably hadn't noticed there *was* a band.

The life of a musician in a pub. Sophie sighed and concentrated on her playing, being careful to keep her eyes focused somewhere away from the table where Brian and Deirdre sat. She didn't know if those two were listening or not.

And I don't care. The words sang out of her fiddle to the beat of the music she was playing. *I can't care. I don't know how to care, and I don't want to.*

Another word sang off Oliver's strings, sly and knowing.

Liar.

CHAPTER 20

INVERNESS, SCOTLAND, PRESENT DAY

We are all humiliated by the sudden
discovery of a fact which has existed very
comfortably and perhaps been staring at
us in private while we have been making
up our world entirely without it.
—George Eliot

His cell phone buzzed, and Brian flinched at the number he now recognized. How could anyone with a modicum of intelligence not remember a number he'd seen at least six times over the last week? He grimaced and let the call go to voice mail.

Deirdre. She couldn't seem to understand that he had no desire to hang out with her, and Brian had never been very good at letting women down. He didn't want to hurt their feelings, and he didn't want them mad at him, so he hemmed and hawed and ended up making things worse by getting their hopes up.

He also had to admit he wasn't very good at picking up clues. If a woman was nice to him, he was nice back. It was that simple. He couldn't seem to get the hint that she liked him until it was too late and she wanted to take it to the next level.

"You're the stereotypical Canadian," Fiona had told him more than once. "Too nice. I'm glad I don't have that problem."

"Ha!" he'd retorted. "Really? Is running away your solution then? I seem to remember that a certain someone flew to Scotland to get rid of an old boyfriend, hmm?"

"That's not what happened!" His sister had rounded on him, righteous indignation written on her face. "Dad sent me to Scotland, and Greg didn't want to wait for me. Turned out for the best, though, didn't it? He wasn't the right one, anyway."

A sharp gust of wind jolted Brian out of his thoughts. He shoved his hands deeper into his jacket pockets and walked along the pathway on the east side of the river toward Ness Islands, his favorite place for thinking these days. There were always people in the park, walking their dogs or herding their children, all of them minding their own business and enjoying the beauty of the little islands nestled in the middle of the river.

The huge trees gave him a sense of serenity and seemed to whisper to him, *Go ahead. Think all you want, we won't judge.*

He sat down on a wooden bench, one of many carved from tree trunks into whimsical shapes by local artists, and stared out at the waters of the Ness river. In some places, the water had to make its way around an impediment of some kind—a large rock or a sandbar, and the river rippled and gurgled at the barrier before making its way out into the center and flowing north to the Beuly Firth.

He'd read about it. Only six miles long, one of the shortest rivers in Europe, the Ness made the most of its length. Several walking bridges crossed it at strategic spots in the city, providing pedestrians with a stomach-tickling bounce that children often intensified by jumping up and down.

Now he stared out at the swirling eddies near the bank and thought about Deirdre Clarke. She'd monopolized him last week at the Unicorn, sending him admiring looks while she sipped her drink, brushing her hand against his when she passed the vinegar for his chips, and *talking*.

Lord, that girl could talk. She seemed to take silence between two people as an evil void that must be filled, and fill it she did—with a remarkable litany of history, local news, and who knew what else—he'd zoned out numerous times and missed a lot.

She was rather sweet, though. Much of what she said was actually interesting. She had a great sense of humour, and she didn't seem to mind that he wasn't listening half the time. She was perfectly fine carrying the burden of conversation, and nothing she said required an answer from him. Attractive in a girl-next-door kind of way, with those red curls and wide brown eyes in a smiling, freckled face. Cute.

He just wasn't interested. He hadn't come to Scotland to throw himself into a peat bog. He was too raw these days, too cautious. He should have left, instead of sitting at the table, letting her go on for an hour. *Oblivious*, his sister's voice sang in his head.

After the experience with Meghan Reynolds, Brian had told himself to wake up and tune in more. He had to stop being so unaware, quit letting himself be carried along like flotsam in a stream. He was trying, but he knew that most of his effort involved avoiding any real connection with a woman. Any woman. It wasn't an ideal solution, but it was safer that way.

He had no desire to go back to Baddeck, at least not right now. There was nothing to go back to, and the thought of being in his home town in September, watching the school buses carrying students to Cape Central High School, filled him with shame, embarrassment, and anger.

If he stayed here, in Scotland . . .

An image formed at the back of his mind, unbidden. Blonde hair, brilliant blue eyes, a generous mouth that should smile more because that smile, when it came, was breathtaking. Sophie MacArthur was probably the most beautiful woman he'd ever seen. And that was the problem, the reason he was sitting here in the Ness Islands talking to himself.

His phone rang again. He glanced at it and let it go to voicemail. He was going to have to do something about Deirdre Clarke and soon. She was Sophie's best friend, and in Brian's forced state of awareness, it was apparent that she liked him. If he told Deirdre how he felt, she would be unhappy. She would probably tell Sophie, and Sophie would dislike him even more. If he let the girl continue to pursue him, Sophie might very well approve, but *he* would be the unhappy one. Shite, as the Scots would say.

He pushed himself up off the log bench and made his way over the bouncy bridge to the west side of the river. Dusk was settling, and he was feeling the first pangs of hunger. Maybe if he took the long way round, he'd arrive at The Dancing Unicorn just before the band started to play.

As he walked north along the Ness Walk, making his way through the hordes of tourists, his spirits rose. History was his dad's thing, and his sister's, but it was in his blood nonetheless, and Fiona's new home had plenty of it. By global standards, Inverness wasn't even old, having only been granted city status in 2000, but it had been a settlement since the sixth century, and to someone from the New World, it was ancient.

He passed a sandstone building and paused to read the sign that proclaimed it as the "University of the Highlands and Islands." A *rather grandiose name for a university*, Brian thought. The building wasn't much larger than Cape Central High School. He shrugged off the pang that memory brought and moved on.

Inverness Castle rose on his right across the river. He wondered what the original structure had looked like back in the days when Mary Queen of Scots visited, long before Jacobites fleeing the Battle of Culloden had burned it to the ground. It was closed now, and a ridiculously incongruous fence—wooden planks painted a garish shade of orange—wrapped around the castle. Ewan had told him that a major renovation was underway.

Maybe he'd be here when it reopened. He shook his head. That thought seemed to emerge more and more these days; he'd have to deal with it at some point.

On his left loomed the huge hotels that catered to tourists from all over the world, grey behemoths standing side by side like giant warriors from a time long past. The Palace, opened in 1890 and now owned by Best Western, and the Columba Hotel, named for the saint who had visited Scotland sometime in the mid-sixth century with the hope of converting the Pictish Brude to Christianity.

He suddenly had a vision of Saint Columba and King Brude sitting together at the outdoor cafe in front of the great inn, discussing religion over a latte, and grinned to himself. Time had a way of blending and overlapping in this place.

"Mom," a shrill voice piped up and he stepped sideways and avoided a young boy wearing a New York Yankees cap. "Does the Loch Ness monster swim this far down the river?"

Brian smiled at the child. Nessie would have a hard time with that one, since the river beside them was no more than a foot or so deep, and the rock-strewn bottom could easily be seen under the flowing water. He marveled at the ability of a child to ignore the obvious in favor of the possibility that a huge monster might rear its head out of the water right next to him.

He gave the kid a mental thumbs-up and turned right to cross over the Young Street Bridge toward the city centre. People thronged the intersection on their way to one of the many music venues or pubs that catered to the tourist trade. Everyone seemed happy to be in the city called the Capital of the Highlands.

He glanced to his left, where the encroaching darkness of evening met the opening to an even darker alley behind the shops and restaurants of Bridge Street. *No place is perfect.* Somewhere in the soup of information Deirdre had ladled out last week, she'd told him she was carrying pepper spray now because a girl had been murdered just off this street.

"Strangled, can you believe it?" Deirdre's face had flushed with excitement. "Just thrown out near the bins like rubbish."

Her enthusiasm was both startling and a little off-putting, as though the possibility of meeting a murderer was somehow thrilling, but he'd given her a wan smile and murmured something about being careful.

Later he'd asked Fiona about it, and wormed out of her in what he thought was a cleverly devious way that Sophie was being escorted back and forth by Caomhainn these days.

Sophie. She'd be playing soon. He picked up his pace and hurried up the High Street past stores that were closing now, the tourists having left the shops for the pubs and restaurants a few streets over. By the time he gained the top of the Market Brae steps, it was full dark and he was breathing hard from the climb, but further down Ardconnel Street light spilled out of The Dancing Unicorn and he could hear instruments being tuned.

The light was magical, pulling him in. He quit wondering why a man who wasn't supposed to drink kept visiting a bar and just went. It made him happy, and that was enough. It had nothing to do with the alcohol, the decor, or the food. Maybe it was the music. *Yeah, that was it.*

The pub was full, as always, and Brian found his eyes going to the stage as if caught in a tractor beam. She wasn't there. A shaft of disappointment surprised him in its intensity, but he fought it back, made his way to the small bar in the back, and pulled himself up on the only available stool.

Caomhainn looked up and nodded, reaching automatically for a glass and pouring a ginger ale without being asked. Biscuit left the corner and minced her way along the bar to give Brian a pat on the nose before returning to her position of vigilance.

Mary was circulating around the room, laughing and joking with the patrons as if every one of them were a member of her immediate family. *She would have made a great teacher,* Brian thought. He was pretty sure she knew more about Scottish history than most, and she would deliver it with wit and humor—and a little vinegar. He'd like to see the teenager who would cop an attitude with Mary Duncan. The kid wouldn't last long.

As if she could sense his thoughts, Mary appeared at his side.

"We're seeing ye here often, lad," she said. "Ye like the chips 'at much, do ye?"

Brian narrowed his eyes, pretty sure she was messing with him, but those little black bird eyes gave nothing away. He shrugged.

"Well, it's no th' whisky, ye ken," he said in his best

brogue, and surprised a laugh out of her—whether at his words or the lame attempt at a Scottish accent, he couldn't be sure.

"No, I s'pose not," was all she said. She gave him an appraising look. "She's here, lad. She'll be out soon."

Brian widened his eyes and stared at her. "Who?"

Mary rolled her own eyes and gave him a disgusted look before rounding the bar to whisper something in Caomhainn's ear. The big man had to bend nearly double to reach her.

Then the two of them turned to look at Brian. Mary studied him as if she were a hungry bird and he a tasty worm. "Aye," she said to Caomhainn. She patted the barman on his massive forearm and disappeared through a door at the back of the bar.

Caomhainn turned to replace a bottle on the shelf. "Boss says ye should walk our Sophie home t'night. I cannae do it the noo," he said over his shoulder.

A new feeling swept through Brian and settled in his chest, making it difficult to breathe. *Our Sophie.* They trusted him to keep her safe, as if he were a part of that *our*, and they acted as if they knew he would. He couldn't put words to the feeling, but it was lodged somewhere between pride and wonder. He felt . . .*chosen.* He hadn't had that feeling since he'd received the news that he was to be a teacher at Cape Central High School.

The band started their first number, and he turned again to the stage. She was there, fiddle in hand, foot tapping to the reel and fingers dancing over the strings. Her eyes were closed, but as he watched, they opened slowly and came to rest on him. Those eyes were the skies over Cape Breton, the waters of Bras d'Or Lake on regatta day. The colour of home.

She smiled at him and he melted, all his organs oozing into a puddle in his gut. He didn't like her. She didn't like him. She was too young for him. She was bad for his self-esteem.

But right now, in this moment, none of that mattered. He was going to protect this woman with his life. The feeling was threatening, exhilarating, humbling. It rocked his world and scared the shite out of him.

CHAPTER 21

DUART CASTLE, 1647

KENNA

The clanging of arms seemed incessant now. The men trained for much of the day, and their weapons were never far from their hands, even at dinner. They were always ready, resigned to the inevitability of impending battle.

Women have their own war, thought Kenna, as she put on her battle dress. Not the floppy trews and leather boots she wore to practice; this was her most becoming gown, accompanied by a blue snood to hold back the heavy bulk of her blonde hair. At the last minute, she added the silver bracelet Mary had given her two months ago on her fifteenth birthday. There was no need to dress so finely for just another day of household chores, but this was a different sort of battle.

She stared into the small glass and studied her reflection. Not too bad; her skin was clear and her lips needed no tint. Face painting was for the older women like Frances, who slathered on ceruse with abandon even though everyone knew the stuff was poison. There was no way Kenna was going to paint herself into an early grave, not even for Crìsdean.

She admitted she was a wee bit ashamed of herself for dressing to please a man, especially one so annoying as Crìsdean Maclean. He probably wouldn't notice, anyway; as long as it was a gown, he was satisfied, the wee fool. For him, nothing had changed.

Or, maybe it had. For the past few months he'd stopped baiting her, quit scolding when he caught her in her training clothes. He still grumbled she should put on a dress and act like a woman, but the words were half-hearted and carried no heat. And last week he'd come upon her sparring with Albert and had sent the kitchen lad off, to that one's gratified relief.

"I'll take over th' noo," Crìsdean told him, earning the lad's eternal loyalty. "Ye needn't take eny more bruises from this madwoman, eh?"

Kenna had glared at him until he circled behind her and reached around to change the position of her broomstick.

"Ye're holdin' it wrong," he said, the words a whisper in her ear. "Ye'll git yerself kilt in two minutes flat."

Kenna shivered at the memory. That hoarse whisper had done something to her insides, melted them into a broth of confusion seasoned with a strange excitement. Afraid to move, she stood as wooden as her makeshift weapon and allowed him to adjust the broomstick in her hand.

Her eyes widened when he stepped around and took a stance five paces in front of her, his own sword held ready.

"Show me whit ye can do," he ordered.

For the next few glorious minutes they had sparred, until a sudden parry from Crìsdean's sword sliced her broomstick in half.

"Ye did 'at a' purpose!" Kenna sputtered, as he stepped back and executed a courtly bow.

His face radiated innocence. "S' mebbe ye should go pit on a dress noo, aye?"

Hands fisted at her sides, she watched him stride off toward the castle entrance. "There be many brooms at Duart!" she called after him.

"I ken 'at," he threw over his shoulder. "Find one, an' meet me here t'morrow. Ye need a lot o' work."

True to his word, he had met her in the empty yard before training the next morning, and much to her surprise, he was a good teacher. Patient, understanding, even kind. He adjusted the lesson to her diminutive frame and gave her advice on grip, stance, and movement, without sarcasm or mockery.

Kenna floated through the week, running Crìsdean's instructions through her head while she went about her chores, executing his footwork in the hallways when no one was around, hearing his voice in her ears. And somewhere in the swamp her mind had become, something filtered up and hung in the air before her eyes.

I like him. Nae like a brother . . . like a man. I like Crìsdean Maclean.

It was glorious, exhilarating, and frightening at the same time. Without giving it much thought, she found herself wanting to dress like a woman—for him. And was she imagining the glint she saw in his green eyes? Was it just chance that had him seeking her out at odd times, asking her questions that any of his brothers could have answered? Probably.

Kenna shook herself out of her latest foray into a world she knew next to nothing about and made her way upstairs, her arms full of washing. She paused outside the room occupied by Crìsdean's eldest brother Bearnard and his wife Dorcas, shifting the garments in preparation to knocking.

Voices—two of them—were muffled by the heavy wooden door, but the words carried a tone that had Kenna freezing in place with her hand upraised.

Dorcas was crying.

"It willnae happen, Bearnard, I ken it. I was so sure this time, bit my courses came agin. I'm so aggrieved fer ye."

Bearnard's voice was low and soothing, the words indistinct. Kenna's heart dropped. The whole castle knew they had been trying to have a child; Kenna had heard the other women discussing it in low voices, faces sad. Dorcas was twenty-nine. If she hadn't become pregnant by now, it was likely she could not.

It isnae fair. Dorcas is th' kindest person 'n the cas-tle; she watches o'er everbody else's bairns, naebody deserves a child more. Kenna had added Dorcas to her prayer list long ago, but apparently she was in no better standing with the Lord than anyone else at Duart.

She shifted her pile of wash again, turned to go—and bumped into Frances, her head cocked in an effort to listen.

"Oh," Kenna said, "pardon me. D' ye need somethin'?"

A small smile twisted itself onto Frances' face. "Oh, nae, I was jist comin' t' see Dorcas abit my needlework, bit it seems she's busy."

Kenna snorted. "I didnae ken ye were interested in stitchery, cousin Frances. I've ne'er seen ye wi' a needle, or enythin' sharp. In yer hand, 'at is."

"Weel," Frances sniffed, "'at shows how much ye ken, lass. If ye spent as much time wi' the ladies as ye do wi' th' men, mebbe ye'd nae have t' be sae curyus." She raised her nose in the air and glared at Kenna. "I'm thinkin' mebbe this isnae th' best time t' talk t' our dear Dorcas, so I'll be off." She spun on her heel and flounced down the hallway toward the great hall, but not before Kenna caught a calculating look that distorted the pretty features.

Kenna watched her go, swallowing the sour taste she always had after a few moments in the presence of Dànaidh's wife. She made her way to the next room, delivered her load of wash to Mary, and indicated the remaining items.

"I wonder if ye could gie this t' Dorcas later?"

Mary raised her eyebrows, and Kenna lowered her voice. "She seems upset."

A look of pain crossed Mary's kind features. "Ahh, anither disappointment, I think." She shook her head. "Thank ye, lass, I'll see she gets her wash later, aye?"

With a heavy heart, Kenna returned to the hall and made her way up the spiral staircase and out onto the castle's parapet. She leaned her elbows on the rough stone wall and gazed out into the Sound of Mull. This was her place, close to the heavens and open to the world. It was high tide, and the salt spray rose from the rocks below and sparkled in the afternoon air like jewels.

Beyond the castle walls, men battled each other for power and pride, for the right to impose their politics, their religion, their king. It never stopped. But here, at the confluence of two great waters, it seemed as if Duart floated in the clouds, above and beyond it all. As if the sound and the loch held the small peninsula upon which the castle perched in a fierce embrace, safe from the bedlam that reigned on the mainland.

"I kent I'd find ye here," came a triumphant voice from behind her, and Kenna felt her heart flip as she turned to face Crìsdean. He looked like a god, outlined against the sky with his feet braced and his hands on his waist. His hair blew in the wind, flicking across his face and into green eyes that danced with humor. "Hurry; we'll be late t' supper, an' ye ken whit happens if Fergus an' Padraig git a start—"

"Awright," she said, laughing. "I dinnae ken there's ivver been a time when we went wi' out food, though."

"Allus a first time," Crìsdean said. He held out a hand and then seemed to think better of it, tucking his fist into his trews before he started toward the castle door. Kenna stared after him.

Was he thinkin' o' holdin' my hand? The thought was like honey.

There was plenty of food left, of course. The

room was a riot of talk and laughter, as always with so many people gathered around the great tables. Wine flowed and meat was passed. A few punches—and sometimes a meat bone—were thrown as the clansmen traded insults. The mayhem was accompanied by the scolding of mothers and wives, usually to no avail.

Kenna glanced around the table and felt gratitude well up inside her. She wasn't a Maclean, yet they had taken her in without question and accepted her as one of their own. They teased her relentlessly and bullied her when it suited them, but no more so than they did to their own family. She was one of them. She belonged.

Her eyes stopped at one figure who stood out amidst the activity around the table. Dorcas sat still, her eyes fixed on the table, and pushed a piece of potato around her plate with a wooden spoon. Next to her Bearnard was uncharacteristically quiet. His brows furrowed and he watched his wife with concern, but said nothing.

It was Dorcas' nature to be cheerful. She would move on, surround herself with the castle's children, make herself useful. Until the next time. Kenna wondered how long she would be able to keep hope alive, and worried that someday her regret might break her. Dorcas was made to be a mother.

Suddenly Frances stood up and cleared her throat loudly. When that produced no result, she grabbed a serving spoon and banged it against the pewter mug in front of her. She waited for the din to subside, eyes hooded.

"I want t' tell ye all o' my news," she said, and looked around to be sure that all eyes were on her. Her lips curved up in a wide smile that rang false to Kenna, and her black eyes were wide with innocence. "I wisht it t' be a surprise." Another dramatic pause—*had her eyes shifted to Dorcas?*

"I am . . . with child! Isnae 't wonderful?"

In the ensuing clamor of well-wishes, Kenna stole another glance at Dorcas. Bearnard's wife sat immobile, eyes fixed on Frances. Her hands were clutched so tightly that the knuckles were white. As Kenna watched, Dorcas took a deep breath, stood up, and made her way to where Frances stood. Without hesitation, she wrapped her arms around Dànaidh's wife and hugged her.

"I'm that happy fer ye, sister. Truly."

From across the room Kenna watched the triumphant smile fade from Frances' face. Maybe her distaste for the woman had something to do with it, but the new look seemed to be one of . . . what? Disappointment? Had she expected the other woman to fall apart?

Good fer ye, Dorcas. Ye spoilt 'er game.

The door banged open, sounding like a musket shot in the silence engendered by Frances' announcement. Fergus, whose turn it was on watch, stood in the doorway. His usual smile was gone, and tension radiated from his body.

Another bang followed the first, and then another. Not the door, then.

"'Tis th' Campbells," Fergus announced. "They're here."

CHAPTER 22

DUART CASTLE, 1647

CRÌSDEAN

"Dinnae ye e'en think aboot it."

Crìsdean turned in the doorway to face Kenna. She looked impossibly innocent, in a gown of brown and black checks topped by a black woolen waistcoat. About her shoulders a white shawl was fastened with a pewter brooch,

The gown was very like those that every other woman in the castle wore to go about her daily tasks. Very nice. Very appropriate. Very *not* Kenna.

Lately she'd been making more of an effort with her appearance—at least she was no longer looking as if she'd thrown on the gown as an afterthought when she got up in the morning. But there was something about this apparel.

His eyes narrowed. Instead of the expected laced ghillie shoes, the toes of brown leather boots peeked from beneath the gown. If someone were to force him to a wager, he'd say with confidence that underneath those feminine skirts was a pair of men's trews.

"I dinnae ken whit ye mean," Kenna said, blue eyes as wide and clear as the North Sea on a spring day.

He held her gaze until she looked down at her feet. When she looked up, her face was pink.

"They're most comf'table."

"I didnae ask."

"Weel, then."

Crìsdean restrained the urge to throttle the lass and let out a breath slowly. This was going nowhere. The siege was into its third week, with no signs the Campbells were planning to leave anytime soon. There was no worry about water, thanks to the well inside the castle walls. For now, the food they'd stored was enough to last weeks, more if they were careful, but they were prisoners in their own home and it was taking its toll. Tempers were fraying about the edges. He had no time for this; his brothers were waiting.

Attempts by the Maclean clansmen to harry the invaders had so far done little more than annoy the enemy, like midges dancing about in front of their eyes. The white tents remained in place just outside the range of Duart's cannons, and several times a day the attackers made a dash toward the castle walls, carrying ladders and firing muskets at the defenders arrayed on the parapet above. It was a war of nerves.

The ladders were easily dislodged. Only one man at a time could climb the three storeys to the top, and boiling water or an arrow in the eye discouraged all but the most intrepid of the government soldiers.

Govermint? Crìsdean's mind wandered from the problem in front of him and considered that. *Who was the govermint these days?* This was a civil war—Englishman against Scot, Scot against Scot. Even the Irish and the Welsh were involved in this never-ending parade of armies.

The government was supposed to be the king, was it not? Granted, Charles was a large part of the problem; he seemed to be fighting with everyone. His own parliament was locked in a power struggle between the Cavaliers, who agreed that the king had ultimate authority, and the Roundheads, who wanted to make the rules themselves.

Then there were the religious zealots, the Covenanters, who hated Catholics and wanted Charles to drop his ideas of High Anglican power over religion. And to make the mess complete, the Catholics in Ireland kept pushing for their own agenda.

Giles had tried to explain the politics to him, but most of it had gone over his head. He only needed to know one thing—the Macleans had always sided with the king, as it should be. The idea of limiting the monarchy was nothing short of treason. There would always be a king; anything else was unthinkable.

Crìsdean's attention was caught by a furtive movement, and his eyes snapped back to the young woman in front of him. No longer in front. Kenna had slid to the side and was attempting to slink out of the room. He grabbed her by the wrist and swung her back to face him.

"This is war, Kenna! Th' Campbells mean t' take Duart, an' they dinnae care if they have t' do it o'er our dead bodies." He raked his hands through his hair, making it stand on end. "Th' war has come t' us. It's a siege, an' th' men must go out t' rid us o' th' enemy else we'll all starve here, ye ken? The *men!*"

His emphasis on the last word was not lost on Kenna; her face stiffened and sparks flew from the blue eyes, dark now like the sea on a stormy day.

"Aye, th' *men!*" She planted her feet and glared at him. "Nivver mind that wimmen 're th' ones left behind t' protect th' castle whilst th' *men* 're out peckin' at each other like roosters. So gie on wi' ye. Go fight. I'm no stoppin' ye, so leave me be!"

She turned to leave, only to be pulled around again to face Crìsdean's furious green eyes. "Promise me ye'll no try t' sneak out this time, Kenna. I cannae pit my head into the fightin' unless I ken ye'll mind. Please!"

His eyes clouded at the thought of what he would do if something happened to her. She'd tried it before, and when he turned around and saw her following like a small shadow—where in the bloody *hell* had she gotten that damn sword?—his heart had flipped over and he thought he'd throw up. She'd seen him watching and turned back, but she'd been out there. Outside, dressed as a lad, ready to fight the Campbells.

His mind filled with a mixture of pride and frustration. She was so stupid—stupid and pig-headed and . . . brave. She didn't understand what she was doing to him. She didn't realize she could get him killed.

"Kenna. I ken ye want t' help, I ken ye thynk ye can hold yer own, and mebbe ye could, if th' Campbells brought their baby lads wi' 'em t' fight—" He saw the fury darken her eyes and rushed on. "Bit if somethin' happened t' ye out there, I couldnae live! Dinnae ye unnerstand?"

"Wh-wha'?" She had gone still and was staring at him.

"I love ye, ye stoobern, woolly-heided lass!" He heard the words as if someone else was saying these foolish things, but the tension, the fear, and the anxiety of the long siege surged through him and there was no stopping. "Aye," he hurled the words at her, "I love ye, an' I'll no see ye kilt afore my verra eyes."

He reached out and gathered her into his arms, heedless of the choking, gasping sounds she was making, squashing her to him as if he could somehow transfer his fear to her and make her understand.

"Aw-awright." His woolen jacket muffled Kenna's voice. "I promise." She pulled back and stared into his face, as if searching for something. "Bit ye're no playin' fair." Her lips quivered. "I promise," she said again. "I dinnae want t' see ye hurt fer worryin' aboot me, so I'll bide." She turned again to go, and at the door turned back, a wide grin spread over her face. "'Cause I love ye too, ye big oaf!" And she was gone.

Crìsdean allowed himself to dwell on what had just happened until he slipped and nearly fell down the spiral stairs. He caught himself on the rope rail and stood for a second, panting, then pushed the scene ruthlessly to the back of his mind. If he didn't stop thinking on it, she was going to get him killed before he even saw battle.

Lachlan was waiting with the other clansmen gathered about him. "We'll use th' tunnel an' circle round th' keep," the chief told them. "I ken some o' ye havenae seen real battle afore, bit ye've been trainin' for this. Divide int' two parties; Hector, take yer men th' south way and Bearnard, ye take yers round th' other side. Use the brush an rocks fer cover, an' wait fer my signal."

Faces taut, the Macleans of Duart nodded, and one by one they disappeared into the tunnel at the rear of the empty dungeon and emerged on the seaward side of the castle. Crìsdean shivered in the raw night air and followed close on the heels of Giles and Ealar, careful to watch his footing amid the rocks and scrub surrounding the keep.

Though full night had fallen, there was a weak moon tonight. The men took care and held to the darker shadow cast by Duart's stone walls, waiting for the signal from their chief. A hundred yards ahead, they could just see the white tents of the invaders, with the Campbell standard flapping in the sea wind.

Silence reigned over the night for a long moment. It was broken by a shriek in the darkness, ripping through the air like a sword. "*Bàs no beatha!*" rang out the voice of their chief, Lachlan Maclean, and a second later every man took up the battle cry, screaming "Death or victory!" in the auld tongue.

The clansmen rounded the corners of the castle and rushed at the white tents. They fired their muskets once and dropped them to be picked up later, drawing their swords and continuing the charge into the enemy camp, where a sudden pandemonium had broken out. The watch was overwhelmed without a fight.

It was all over in minutes. The Campbell soldiers picked up what they could and ran, back over the road and away from the castle, leaving their tents and supplies behind. The Duart defenders chased them for a few minutes, and then returned to gather around their chief once more.

The rout was a complete victory. Not a single Maclean clansman had been injured during the mad dash through the enemy camp. Crìsdean followed the others back to the keep, entering this time through the main gate, and the great wooden door slammed shut behind them.

There would be no celebration this night. No one would relax until daylight broke, and it was sure the Campbells would not return. But it had been a good battle, one they could be proud of. They had broken the siege and returned unscathed.

Crìsdean sat with his brothers, listening to their laughter as they recounted tonight's adventure, but his thoughts were elsewhere and his lips curved upward.

"I love ye too, ye big oaf!"

The wee pudding. Tomorrow he'd have it out with her again because her promise to stay out of men's affairs could never be trusted. But for the first time, he felt as if he'd already won. There were different sorts of battle, after all.

CHAPTER 23

INVERNESS, SCOTLAND, PRESENT DAY

*Something unnamable fit between them and
for now it was too delicate to put words to.*
—Allie Ray

Sophie and Brian walked side by side through the lamplit darkness of early morning Inverness, the silence a suffocating blanket thrown over them.

Sophie shifted the violin case to her other hand. The only words Brian had uttered were an offer to carry her violin for her. She probably sounded rude when she said no, but nobody was allowed to carry Oliver but her. Ever.

Say something! Sophie told herself. The words of a popular song drifted through her head. *Say something, I'm giving up on you.*

On whom, though? She'd given up on herself long ago, as far as communication with the male species went, and she'd been fine with that. Anyway, she hated small talk, especially with a stranger. So why was the silence so oppressive now?

Was Brian Maclean really a stranger, though? He was her sister-in-law's brother. She'd sat through the night by his bed in hospital. She'd even exchanged a few words with him, albeit snarky ones. She was glad he couldn't see the flush on her face in the darkness. *Why was her house so far away?*

Say something.

"So . . ."

"So . . ."

The word, uttered in tandem, shattered the quiet night with its simplicity. Something bubbled up from deep in Sophie's stomach, and suddenly she was laughing. The laughter was brittle and fragile and totally unsuited to the situation, but it was noise. And it felt good.

She laughed until she hiccupped. Brian had stopped on the sidewalk and turned toward her, and at the look on his face, she was off again. He patted her tentatively on the back, but it didn't help. There was nothing at all funny about the word so, but she felt better than she had in a long time. She gave up and allowed the laughter to have its way.

"So," Brian was saying again when she finally caught her breath, as if there was nothing unusual about hysteria over the English language. The word threatened more strangled laughter, but she grasped her self-control and held on for dear life. "Your house is that one at the end of the street?"

"A-aye," she managed. "I-I'm s-sorry. I don't know what came over me. I'm not laughing at you. Really."

"That's good," he said. "It would be a nice change."

She rounded on him. "What?"

He put both hands up in a gesture of surrender. "I was kidding, sort of. Are Scots always this prickly?"

"I'm not prickly!" she announced. In the light of the streetlamp she could see the look of profound disbelief on his face, and it almost sent her off again.

She sniffed. "Well, when I met you, you were working your way through a bottle of single malt, and babbling about Capers and Scots or some such, and then . . ." Her words trickled to a stop. The *and then* hadn't been funny at all. She should just stop talking. That would be best.

"Never mind," he said. "I'd really like to forget that, if it's all right with you. It wasn't my finest hour. Or many hours, to be honest." He turned and started walking again, as if eager to get this unfortunate encounter over with.

She hurried to catch up. "I'm sorry," she said again. "That was really inconsiderate of me. I'm not usually this obnoxious."

He turned to face her, and his face, caught in the glow of the street light, broke into a beautiful smile that disappeared when he pursed his lips together in an effort to keep them still—and then it was his turn to laugh. A low chuckle began in his throat and spilled out into the night air, and Sophie watched as he laughed until he clutched his stomach and bent double in an effort to stem the flow.

Finally he straightened, stopped wheezing, and wiped the tears from his eyes.

He shook his head. "We're quite a pair."

"Aye, we are that," Sophie said seriously. "And I probably should mention that we passed my house a few minutes ago. That intersection up ahead is Castle Street."

Brian looked behind them, up the long length of Ardconnel Street, and Sophie followed his gaze. In the distance she could see the light spilling out of The Dancing Unicorn, like a beacon in the darkness. As they watched, the light blinked out.

In renewed silence, they turned and walked the hundred or so yards to her house. The silence was different this time, lighter. In it she could hear the echo of their shared laughter. She stopped at her gate and turned.

"Um, I know it's late, but would you like to come in for a cup of tea?"

He looked at her, his face expressionless. "Yes," he said after a long moment, "I would."

Inside, Sophie placed Oliver's case carefully on its cushion in the sitting room and led Brian to the couch.

"This is where I spend most of my time, when I'm not at the Unicorn."

"Oh," he said. "It's . . . huge. And nice. And, wow, you live here? Alone?"

"I do," she said, pride welling up at his reaction. She suddenly wanted him to like it, to understand just a little bit the love she felt for this place where she'd spent all her life. This *mausoleum*, Deirdre called it. She watched his face.

"Wow," he said again.

Sophie hid her grin until she reached the safety of the kitchen and plugged in the kettle. She arranged two cups on a tray, and when the whistle shrieked, she threw two tea bags into a pot and poured the hot water over them.

Then she went foraging for something to eat. Sophie didn't eat sweets, and the only person she entertained was Deirdre, but fortunately her best friend considered it her mission to bring a package of biscuits every time she came over. Usually the ones Dee didn't eat sat in the cupboard until they were stale and then went into the bin. But there was always hope.

Brian Maclean looked like someone who liked food. The way he'd tucked into the fish and chips at the Unicorn was a clue that he didn't turn down many offerings. But all she found was a package of spaghetti, a bag of rice, a jar of peanut butter, and a box of porridge. Maybe she could offer him the peanut butter and a spoon?

Sophie envisioned the look on his face and sighed. She placed a sugar bowl and pitcher of cream on the tray and took the meager offering into the sitting room. Brian was sitting on the couch where she'd left him, engrossed in a book. When he looked up, his eyes had that faraway glaze she recognized—Deirdre had pointed it out many times when Sophie was reading and trying to be polite at the same time.

He closed the book and smiled at her, and she felt her knees turn to water. She concentrated on placing the tray on the coffee table, then pointed to the book in his hand.

"*Where's Me Plaid?* Funny, isn't it?" she said. "I bought it for the title. It's by a guy from Ohio, but I really liked his take on Scotland. You might relate; it's about the Macleans. You can borrow it if you like."

"Thanks," Brian said. "I never thought I needed to search for my roots. I know a little about Clan Maclean; hard not to when your dad's the dean at the Gaelic College. It's entertaining and, as you say, funny. I'll take you up on that offer, thanks."

And you'll have to come back, if only to return it, the thought whispered across her mind. It circled and returned as she poured the tea and made excuses about the lack of anything edible. *You'll have to come back.*

He spent an hour, staying long after the tea was gone. They talked about politics and sports and music and by the time he left, she had made a mental note to go shopping the next day and stock the place with biscuits. And steak—or whatever it was men ate. She should probably call Deirdre.

He watched them disappear into the house. His pulse hammered, and a red wave almost obscured his vision. He forced it back and considered his options. He wanted their reunion to be perfect, but it was proving to be more difficult than he had imagined, and his patience was wearing thin.

The bitch never seemed to be alone these days. She rarely left the house, except to shop or walk the few paces to her job at that creepy pub, and when she did, someone always accompanied her.

First it had been that giant bartender who walked her to and from her house, but now it was this guy. Who the hell was he, anyway? His accent said he was American, or maybe Canadian—they all talked the same over there, and it didn't matter. Unlike the giant, this one would be no match for him, not with the advantage of surprise on his side. He'd prefer to avoid confrontation, but if push came to shove, he'd take him on. No contest.

He fondled the handle of the dagger he kept tucked into his belt and smiled. Were they an item? He hoped so; it would be fun to see the look on her face when she saw her boyfriend bleeding out in front of her. Anguish, fear, panic—those emotions kept him going, fed his desire.

That need, the surging, blinding fire that never left his gut, nearly rose to engulf him, and he fought it down with difficulty. Not yet; he couldn't afford to lose himself right now.

He knew everything about her daily life, what there was of it. She got up, puttered around all day alone in that huge mansion, waited for her escort, and walked with him to the pub. When it closed, she repeated the procedure in reverse.

He had enjoyed watching her from his seat in the pub's corner, listened to her playing that violin just like she had the first time he'd seen her three years ago. Did she even know how good she was? Why the hell was she wasting her time and talent here?

He'd made sure not to go too often, and he always wore a facemask. Many people still wore masks these days in public places. *Thank you, pandemic.* He couldn't risk being noticed by that weird little woman who ran the place; he'd caught her staring at him once or twice. There was something about her that had the hairs on his neck standing on end. Like she could see through the mask and knew what he was.

He hadn't dared go back in the last few days. He rubbed at the long scratch on his left hand, courtesy of that fucking cat. It was almost as if the thing knew something—cats were spooky bastards; he'd always hated them. The creature had come slinking up to his table in the corner, swishing its tail, and sat there staring at him until he reached out a hand to pet it. Almost as if it was challenging him.

Then it had swiped at him, claws on full display, and raked the length of his hand so fast he never saw it coming. He'd let out an oath and grabbed for a serviette to staunch the blood pooling along the cut, but not before people at the tables closest to him had turned to see what had caused the disturbance.

He hadn't been back since. He missed the place, though. Well, not the pub; he missed her. She was his by rights, and he wasn't about to let a demonic cat get in his way. He was a hunter too, just like the animal. If he ever saw that beast outside the bar, he'd strangle it in two seconds to show it who the alpha was.

He needed to retreat for a while, pull himself together, and think about how to do this. He knew the police had tracked him to Inverness; the thing last week with Rachel had put them on high alert. Maybe if he backtracked, went back to Glasgow for a while, it would throw them off. He'd leave a trail to confuse them, and then he could come back for her—the one who mattered. The one who thought she'd gotten away.

CHAPTER 24

INVERNESS, SCOTLAND, PRESENT DAY

*When we illuminate the road back
to our ancestors, they have a way
of reaching out, of manifesting
themselves . . .sometimes even physically.*
—Raquel Cepeda

Brian lay on his back in the dark and stared at the ceiling. His eyes had adjusted to the darkness, and he could make out shapes on the plaster caused by rainwater leaking through the old roof over the years. *A mountain, a dog, a castle.*

"It's on the list," Ewan had assured him. "The roof's fixed, so you don't have to worry about anything dripping on you. Old houses never stop giving you ideas for how to spend your money, eh?"

His brother-in-law's words swirled through his tired brain, bringing with them an image of the ceilings in the old farmhouse back home. His own room had similar darker areas, and when he was young, he'd made a game of identifying and naming the shapes.

A *rabbit, a crow*, and, if he stretched his imagination, *a sailboat*. They had accompanied him through his childhood, a comfortable part of his past.

An edge of homesickness sliced through him. The regatta was over now; school would start at Cape Central in another week. Someone else would greet the kids in his old classroom, directing their attention to the number chart and the graphs. The whispers would circle through the staff lounge. *Didn't you hear? He would never . . .Where there's smoke . . .*

Nausea coiled in his stomach. Why couldn't he stop thinking about it? Why couldn't he sleep, dammit? Could you die from insomnia? No, the doctor had told him—not directly. More likely you'd just wander out in front of a car while in that fugue state caused by sleeplessness. Sounded like fun right now.

Brian gave himself a mental shake. He wasn't a negative person, and he refused to allow himself to give rein to the depression that was always waiting in the background of his mind these days. *This too shall pass.* He returned his attention to the shapes on the ceiling.

Definitely a castle. A little lopsided, only one tower, and maybe a chimney. It didn't really look like his castle at all.

His castle. Duart. He cast his mind back over the vision of stone walls, the sound of men fighting, the young girl telling him that the men trained in the courtyard every day. It had all seemed so real. That's because Duart Castle *was* real. A real place that he'd never heard of before but had somehow seen in an illusion.

Things were becoming clearer now, his memory offering up clues to this strange hallucination. It had been twice now, the second time lasting much longer than the first. And there was something odd about the girl in the vision—the one who looked like Sophie MacArthur. He concentrated, comparing the two events, and it clicked.

She'd seemed older the second time. He was sure of it. Granted, the first hallucination had been much shorter; he'd barely had time to register the castle and the girl. She'd dressed as a boy that first time, so maybe that was the difference.

But no—what had she said? A *year gone*. In that weird accent, like the Scots language used in old movies about Highlands history. A colleague at Cape Central showed *Rob Roy* and *Braveheart* to his history classes every year. He'd told Brian how he used the movies to illustrate the historical inaccuracies and laughed with the kids at Mel Gibson's blue-painted face and out-of-time kilt.

Now that he thought about it, none of those men in the castle's great room had dressed like Mel Gibson. Not a kilt in sight—they'd all worn homespun shirts and woolen trews with sturdy boots. He had thought they were part of a reenactment troupe, like a Renaissance faire. But groups like that usually wore kilts to look more Scottish to tourists, didn't they?

A chill, out of place on this warm day, wormed through him. *'Tis the year 1647*, she'd said. *Kilts hadn't been around in the seventeenth century.*

It made sense, if it was Duart Castle. Why the men were all named Maclean—why the Maclean clan crest was carved into the fireplace. All the men in his illusion had been wearing the clan badge. Had he merely conjured the crest he knew best? He *must* have seen a picture of this castle before; he just couldn't remember.

Relief flooded through him. That's what it was. His mind had taken the easy route, using his own clan to fuel a dream more detailed than anything he'd had before. A dream; that was all it was. That was probably why the girl looked like Sophie too.

He stopped congratulating himself on his cleverness when another thought pinged. Why had he named his dream girl Kenna instead of Sophie? He'd never met anyone with that name, and weren't dreams supposed to come out of experience? Were there even rules about such things?

The details were amazing. The girl had seemed annoyed when he told her his own name. Her emotions—the fear, the anger, the sympathy—it all seemed so real. She was worried for him. No—for the man she called Christian. Of course he had known students named Christian over his years of teaching, but none that had made a special impression on him. And she'd given it an odd pronunciation—more like *Crees-jun*. Was it even a Scottish name?

Brian realized he was pacing the room. He forced himself back into bed and closed his eyes, but it didn't help. Images fused on the backs of his eyelids like a badly edited video, mixing in a wild maelstrom of sound and action.

Sailboats raced past an ancient castle, chased by jet skis driven by men dressed in medieval clothing and brandishing swords. They came closer and reached for him, trying to pull him into the roiling sea.

Sam called to him out of the wind, his words harsh and abrasive. "Whit are ye up to, lyin with a lad? D' th' others ken?"

Brian tried to explain, but Sam had morphed into a woman whose dark beauty was marred by a sulky expression.

"Dinnae ye say anythin'!" the woman snarled.

The scene shifted again and became the taproom of The Dancing Unicorn. The black-haired woman was there, but now she was pouring whisky into a tall drinking glass, laughing as she filled it to the brim. Sophie sat across the table and watched, shaking her head in disgust as Brian picked up the glass and chugged the entire thing down. Men with blue-painted faces cheered him on, clanking their own glasses and hooting drunkenly.

"Somebody ought to stop the eejit," Sophie said to a black cat who occupied the chair next to her at the table.

"Aye," said the cat. "He should probably wake up now, don't you think?"

"Wake up! Brian, wake up!"

Brian's eyes snapped open. Someone was shaking him. The grey light of dawn filtered into the room and he stared into his sister's worried eyes.

"You were having a nightmare," she told him. "Yelling things about too much whisky and it's not your fault and 'Stop it, Frances!' Who's Frances?"

Brian felt as if he were crawling through mud. He took a deep breath, pushed himself to a sitting position, and dangled his legs off the edge of the bed.

"Fee," he said, "Where can I find out more about Duart Castle?"

His sister was becoming used to his odd questions. She reflected for a minute. "Your best bet would be to go see Jeremy."

"Who's Jeremy?"

"A researcher at the university. He's the one who helped me find my ancestor when I first came to Scotland. I doubt there's much about Highlands history he doesn't know—or can't find out." Her green eyes lit. "Why don't I take you now? I don't have to start work till this afternoon, and Jeremy loves to talk about the clans, trust me."

Brian jumped up and pushed his sister toward the door, heedless of the fact that he was wearing nothing but a tee shirt and threadbare boxer shorts. Fiona shielded her eyes.

"Whoa!" she laughed. "Slow down; there's time. It's best if you change into clothes first. I'll be downstairs making porridge."

Brian wolfed down the porridge in record time and was waiting impatiently next to the car when Fiona emerged. She arched her brow but held her tongue.

They wound their way through the convoluted streets of old Inverness, crossed the A9, and finally turned onto a newer road that led to a complex of modern college buildings.

"It's so new!" Brian exclaimed. "I thought the university was in Inverness."

"This *is* Inverness," his sister laughed. "You're

thinking of the old building along the river, right?" At his nod, she explained, "That's just the headquarters. The University of the Highlands and Islands has campuses all over northern Scotland. Jeremy has an office at headquarters, but right now he's here on the main campus because he's teaching a course this term."

They left the car in the visitors' car park, waded through growing crowds of returning students trying to find their way to advisors' offices, and ended in front of an office on the quieter second floor. 'Dr. J. Brown' was rendered in Celtic script on a nameplate next to a door. Fiona knocked and waited.

"Come in," a voice called.

They entered a space that reminded Brian of a library, except he'd never seen a library this messy. Bookshelves lined three of the walls, tables cluttered with ominous looking tomes teetered on tables in the center of the large room, and along the fourth wall were desks holding an assortment of desktop computers and stacks of laptops. Wires snaked across the desks to disappear behind the computers, probably finding their home in a bank of power adaptors hidden somewhere out of sight.

A man in his late thirties looked up from a stack of papers. He grinned at Fiona and ran both hands through his thinning brown hair. "Thank God—I needed an interruption. How do you like my new pad?"

Fiona looked around the room and shook her head. "It's three times the size of your other office, yet there's not an inch of space left to put anything on. How do you do it?"

The man dipped his head and grimaced. "I don't know. If you figure it out, please tell me." He smiled. "And this must be your brother."

Brian blinked. "How did you know?"

The smile widened. "Is he serious?" he asked Fiona. "Lad, you two could be twins." He came out from behind the desk and extended a hand. "Nice to meet you; I'm Jeremy Brown."

Brian took the proffered hand. "Brian Maclean."

Jeremy eyed them. "So what brings you here to the madhouse?"

Fiona laughed. "I know you're getting ready for classes, but my brother has some questions. Is it a bad time?"

"Never a bad time when it's you," Brown told her. "I hope it's another mystery." Eagerness shone from the intelligent brown eyes.

Fiona wandered off toward the shelves, and Jeremy gave her brother his full attention.

"Well," Brian began. "I need to know about the people who lived in Duart Castle in the past."

Jeremy blinked. "Well," he said, "that's a tall order. Duart has had several owners over the centuries, but most of the time it's been the Macleans. Let's see." He ushered Brian over to the computers against the side wall and started tapping keys on one of them.

"The present castle was built in the thirteenth century," he said. "The Macleans held Duart until the mid-seventeenth century, then they lost it, and it became a ruin for a while."

Brian fixed on the date. "What happened in the mid-seventeenth century?"

Jeremy tapped some more keys. "A lot happened in the mid-seventeenth century. The Wars of the Three Kingdoms, the execution of Charles I, and Oliver Cromwell's conquest in 1649." He looked up from the computer. "The monarchy was abolished for eleven years."

"I've heard Dad talk about that," Brian said. "Didn't they throw the king out and then invite him back later?"

"Aye, that was Charles II," Jeremy told him. "But what in particular do you want to know? Can you be more specific?"

"What about 1647? Or 1646? Did someone named Christian live there then? Or Kenna?"

Jeremy stood and crossed to the bookshelves. "All the clan histories are here, but you have to understand that written history is mostly concerned with the chiefs and their families. Individual clansmen merited little recognition."

At Brian's crestfallen expression, he put up one hand. "I didn't say it was impossible." He pulled a book from the shelf. "This is the most comprehensive history of Clan Maclean, as far as I know."

He leafed through the huge volume until he reached a page about a third of the way through.

"Almost all the Maclean chiefs have been named either Lachlan or Hector. Their troubles started in 1631 with the sixteenth chief, Sir Lachlan, who insisted on maintaining an unswerving loyalty to the royal family. It eventually cost the clan the castle and all their lands." He scanned the pages, stopping now and then. Finally, he looked up.

"I'm afraid those names aren't here," he said. "I think your best bet is to visit the castle; maybe they have more on the individual Macleans who lived there. I've been there myself several times; the castle is open for tours daily. Oh! You said 1647? There was a siege by the Campbells in 1647; it's pretty well-known, so likely these people you're looking for would've taken part in that."

Brian felt his blood quicken. "Is the castle hard to get to?"

Jeremy shook his head. "Nowhere is hard to get to in Scotland, lad. It's about a three-hour bus ride to Oban, and then you catch the ferry to Mull."

He looked at his watch and stood up. "I'm sorry to cut this short, but I have to spend some time on the job they pay me for." He hurried them to the door, hugged Fiona, and shook Brian's hand again. "Good luck, I'll keep looking. If I find anything else, I'll let you know."

Brian was quiet on the way home, thinking. If the people he was searching for weren't in Jeremy Brown's books, they were either lost to history or had never existed in the first place. The castle was his last hope.

He didn't know when it had changed, but it wasn't just curiosity driving him anymore. The people in his dreams were real, and he was sure the castle and its long dead occupants held the answer. There was something he had to find out . . . or something he had to do. And nothing could shake his conviction that until he found the answer, he would keep having those visions or dreams or whatever the hell they were.

He realized with a shock that he was looking forward to his next trip to the past.

CHAPTER 25
INVERNESS, SCOTLAND, PRESENT TIME

*If you are ever going to have other people
trust you, you must feel that you can
trust them too—even when you're in
the dark. Even when you're falling.*
—Mitch Albom

"An AGA is more like a musical instrument *than an appliance. One needs to tune recipes to its frequency and patiently practice if one wishes to produce the harmony that will make one's cuisine sing."*

Sophie straightened from the manual, pushed an errant strand of hair out of her face, and glared at the ceramic monstrosity that dominated the kitchen. What a load of rubbish! It was a damn stove, for God's sake. She knew musical instruments, and this creature was not one. It didn't need to sing; it just needed to cook.

The AGA had been here since before she was born, but she had rarely seen anyone cook on it. Her mother probably had, but Mum had died when she was only three, and Sophie's memories of her were hazy.

Izzy had tried to master the thing, but she'd been only fourteen, a teenager who should have been hanging out with friends and talking about the lads instead of cooking for four younger brothers and a baby sister.

It was only when she became a teenager herself that Sophie appreciated her sister's sacrifice. The boys spent as much time away from the house as they could and moved out the minute they turned eighteen without a backward look. And now it was all hers, including this ceramic monster that apparently thought it should be in an orchestra.

Sophie put the manual aside and bent over the cookbook for the thousandth time. It was like being plunked down in a foreign country and realising you had no idea what language they were using and no way of asking where the toilets were. She was in trouble.

She'd always thought that cooking would be simple if she ever really wanted to get beyond the microwave; there was no mystery, it was just simple math, after all. Litres, grams, degrees Celsius. But there was so much more to the translation from recipe to table. And Brian was coming in less than an hour.

Why hadn't she begun with something simple? Like a complete meal out of the box, or takeaway from the Unicorn? She'd seen him devouring the food on that menu; he'd probably love it.

But here she was on her one day off, hair falling into her face and sticking to the damp sweat that was only partially due to the heat from the AGA, trying to make the thing sing to her. Bollocks!

The doorbell rang, and Sophie jumped. He couldn't be here already, could he? She still had to cook the potatoes, and the roast had an hour to go! At least, that was what the cookbook said—who knew what the AGA was thinking?

She ran to peer through the peephole, and then flung the door wide to admit Deirdre.

"Thank God you're here! I'm having company, and I lost my mind and thought I could cook. Help me!" She pulled her friend inside and raced back to the kitchen.

"You're cooking? You never cook! Who is this company, anyway?"

"Tell you later. If you help me figure this out, you can stay for dinner."

"Deal." Deirdre threw herself into action, and soon the smells of roasting beef were wafting through the kitchen.

"I love you," Sophie said.

"As you should. What sides are you having besides the potatoes?"

"Sides?"

Deirdre rolled her eyes. "Sides, numpty. Like vegetables, salad?"

"Oh. Carrots. Men like carrots, right?"

Deirdre stared at her in shock. "Men? Your company is a man? In this house?"

She put the back of her hand to Sophie's forehead,

and then to her own. "No fever. Have you hit your head?"

"Shut up. It's just Fiona's brother. Remember? You met him at the pub."

Deirdre froze, a wooden spoon clutched in her hand. "Brian?" she said, drawing out the word.

Sophie's forehead furrowed. "Yes. Are you okay?"

"You're having him to dinner? Alone?"

"Yes, he's been walking me home from the pub the last few weeks, and I thought it would be nice—" She broke off. "What's wrong?"

An odd look had come over Deirdre's face. "Oh, nothing. He's been walking you home? Every night? For weeks?"

"Yes. I thought I told you."

"You didn't." Deirdre put the spoon down with great care. "It's ready. You can put the carrots on yourself." She walked toward the door.

"Dee! What's the matter? Aren't you staying? Don't you like Brian?"

Deirdre's face twisted as if she'd eaten something sour. "Oh no, I like him fine." She paused, one hand on the door handle. "I wondered why . . . never mind. Nothing's wrong. I just remembered I have something to do, so I can't stay." She turned on the step and blew Sophie a kiss. "See you later. I love you, have fun." And she was gone.

It wasn't until a few minutes later, when the carrots were bubbling in their pot and the table was set, that a thought percolated through her head. *What did she come for, if she was too busy to stay?*

The doorbell rang again, chasing thoughts of her

friend's strange behavior out of her mind. Brian stood on the step, a bottle of wine in each hand.

"I didn't know what you were making, so I brought red and white," he announced. "See, Canadians have class." He grinned at her. "And that's pretty much where it ends. I'm no wine expert."

Sophie laughed. "I'll take your word for it. Come on in."

She preceded him to the kitchen. "We're having beef, so I guess that means red." She put the bottle of white wine in the refrigerator and turned to face him. "I know you're supposed to chill white wine, because we Highlanders have class, ye ken? And that's pretty much where it ends for me too. I have no idea how to open a bottle of wine, but there is a wine opener here somewhere."

"Ahh, allow me." Brian rummaged through drawers and eventually produced a corkscrew. "I can be useful sometimes." It only took two tries before the bottle yielded its cork with a satisfying pop, and Sophie handed him two wine glasses.

"I'm not supposed to drink much, after . . . you know," he said, "but one glass of wine should be okay."

Dinner was surprisingly edible, although the carrots might have been a bit mushy and the potatoes could have benefited from more seasoning. Brian didn't seem to notice; he just tucked into the meal as if it was the best thing he'd had in weeks. Sophie gave him points for that, even if such behavior was probably normal for him.

She offered the wine again, and he shrugged and filled both their glasses.

"I'll probably regret this, but just this once."

"Is it because of your head injury?" she asked. "I'll understand if you can't."

He waved her off. "No, it's because of my insomnia. The doctor warned me that alcohol triggers sleeplessness." He raised his glass to clink against hers. "But I probably won't be sleeping much tonight anyway, so cheers." His green eyes were warm.

What did he mean? She decided not to think too much about the possibilities. "Can't you take sleeping pills for insomnia?"

Brian shook his head. "That's a slippery slope. Most sleep medications are habit-forming, and I don't want to depend on them. Besides, there's a reason for the insom—" he broke off. "Never mind, it's nothing." He took a longer gulp of his wine.

Sophie never pried. It was safer not to know the inner workings of other people's lives. But this time, this time, she *wanted* to know. There was something bothering Brian Maclean, something broken inside. It called to that secret place inside her own heart that held the unspeakable. The secret that had crippled her life and destroyed her future—the one she had never told anyone.

Something told her that if she pressed, if she ventured beyond the barrier and asked, his truth would demand that she share hers. And she didn't think she could do that.

He was staring at her, green eyes hooded. As if he was guarded but still hopeful.

She took a deep breath and closed her eyes against the bleakness she saw there. "Besides what?" There, it was out.

He stood up, and she thought she'd lost him. He was leaving, and it was what she deserved for stepping out of her comfort zone. He shoved his hands into his jeans pockets and walked three feet. Then he turned, retraced his steps, and sat down again. His voice, when it came, was low and rough, and Sophie thought she heard a tremor in it.

"I told you I was a teacher, right?"

She nodded but said nothing.

"I taught math at my local high school. Ninth to twelfth grade. For eight years, right out of college." He looked up, and Sophie thought she could see anger sparking in the green depths, mixing with the pain. She held her breath.

"Just before the end of school this last term, one of my students developed a crush on me. I wasn't sensitive enough to understand how fragile she was, and I reacted . . . badly." He was silent for a long time, but Sophie, who understood silence, who lived with it and embraced it, said nothing. After a moment, he went on.

"She was hurt. She told her parents that I made— that I made an advance." Sophie could read anger and shame in his expression, and his voice had sunk to a whisper. "The school didn't stand behind me, so I quit."

"And that's why you can't sleep?" Her voice felt rusty, as if she hadn't used it in a long time.

"Does there have to be more?" The words dropped into the quiet of the kitchen. His hands curled into fists. "I lost my career. Isn't that enough?"

Sophie sat immobile, paralyzed by the emotions that hung over the table like a cloud. A voice slithered into her mind. *What if he's lying? Why would he quit his dream job if he was innocent?* She tried to push the voice down, but it coiled around her brain and whispered in her ear. *What if that girl was the victim . . . like you?*

Nausea threatened to overwhelm her. Her mind was at war with itself. On the one hand, she knew she was channeling her own experience. She'd only known Brian Maclean for a few short weeks, but she knew this man wasn't like *him*, that he would never do such a thing. But the part of her mind that relived that night over and over in her nightmares—that part was pushing her to get out of here, put miles between her and this-this—

She didn't have to decide. Brian's eyes widened and she could read the horror in them. He stumbled to his feet, knocking the chair over. With a muffled curse, he picked the chair up and placed it carefully in its place. Then, without another word, he strode to the door, opened it, and left. The slam against the doorframe reverberated through her mind—final, unforgiving.

And suddenly she was on her feet, running. She threw the door open and raced after him, heedless of the evening fog that shrouded the street with a blanket of grey.

"Brian!" she called into the darkness. "I'm sorry!"

But he was gone, swallowed up by the mist as if he'd never existed. She realised she was crying, tears of grief and remorse coursing down her cheeks and dripping onto her jumper. She kept walking toward Fiona's house, knowing that it was useless, that she'd lost something precious tonight and it was her own fault.

She almost tripped over him. Brian lay face down on the pavement, eyes closed. She knelt beside him, fumbling desperately for the mobile that she knew was back home on the counter. She turned his head to the side and saw that his eyelids were moving, like they had that night in the hospital.

Had he hit his head again? Sophie felt around for an injury, but there was no lump, no bleeding. She scanned the street in desperation, but the fog made it impossible to see. Down the street, impossibly far away, music spilled out of The Dancing Unicorn. She sent a silent plea in that direction, knowing it didn't matter. She couldn't move him, and she couldn't leave him here.

Please, please! Mary, Caomhainn! Somebody!

A shape emerged from the gloom. Biscuit's yellow eyes glinted in the murky light of the streetlight as she stared at Sophie, and then at Brian.

"Biscuit, go get help!" Sophie heard herself say. *As though a cat could—*

The animal turned and disappeared up the sidewalk toward the pub, and Sophie sighed. Maybe a service dog, but . . .

Moments later she heard footsteps pounding on the pavement, and Caomhainn appeared out of the grey murk.

"I've got this," he said, and scooped Brian up in his arms as if he were a baby. Without asking, he strode back toward Sophie's house, opened the door, and deposited his burden on the couch.

"He'll be fine," he said.

"How do you know? Why's he unconscious, then? Are you a doctor?"

"Trust me," he said simply. He stood up. "Just keep him here. Dinnae fash, he's not hurt, he's . . . away. He'll wake up when he's ready, aye?" And he was gone.

Sophie stood in the silence of her home, listening to Brian's even breathing. His eyelids continued to twitch and his chest rose and fell, but those were the only indications that he was alive.

Trust me.

He's not hurt; he's away.

She had no idea what that meant, but she did trust him. She had to. If Caomhainn said so, Brian would be fine.

CHAPTER 26

ARGYLL, SCOTLAND, 1648

BRIAN

The pounding was relentless. This was the worst headache he'd ever had, even worse than the one he'd woken up with after the boom hit him. And this drubbing didn't come from just one place on his skull. It was everywhere. Deep, reverberating booms, punctuated by the incessant rattling of gunfire, threatened to tear his head apart.

Gunfire?

Brian opened his eyes. He was lying on hard-packed earth, rocks poking into his back. He lay still for a few minutes and assessed the pain. Nothing really hurt except for his head, and that feeling was fading as he became more aware of his surroundings.

He sat up slowly and strained to see through smoke that held an acrid stench reeking of gunpowder. *Weird. Where have I ever smelled gunpowder?*

But the horror that met his eyes drove the thought away. Around him men grappled with each other, stabbing and slashing. Guttural oaths he couldn't understand, ground out in a harsh language that seemed alien yet familiar.

Other sounds filtered into his consciousness. Moans from men lying on the ground, writhing in pain. Screams, cut off with a terrifying finality. No sound at all from those who lay still, blood seeping from ghastly wounds.

Someone directly in front of him fell across his legs. The man rolled over onto his back, and Brian looked into eyes that would never again see the light of day.

"Crìsdean!" A hand gripped his shoulder. "Git ye up, lad! We cannae stay here!"

The voice was familiar, but he had no time to search his memory. The other man had grabbed his forearm and was hauling him to his feet, pulling him away from the dead man. Then they were running, an instinct for survival he hadn't known he possessed driving him back into the trees. The sounds of gunfire and the tang that accompanied it faded.

"I got 'im," the voice gasped, and others crowded in around them.

"Is he hit?"

"There's nae blood 'at I c'n see."

The voice of his rescuer. "I dinnae thynk he was hit. He jist fell."

The man let go of his arm and, deprived of the support, Brian let himself sink onto the ground. He leaned back against a log and gazed around at the worried faces before him.

He knew these men. He'd seen them not long ago, standing in the great hall of an ancient castle. The one who rescued him just now had been dressed then in a white shirt with ruffled cuffs and a tartan sash with a badge.

Clan Maclean. "*Mebbe he is a lass, Mam,*" the man had taunted.

The sash was missing. Stains he didn't want to think about marred the once white shirt that hung now out of torn trews. Mud and grime streaked the man's face.

All of them looked like that—like they'd been in a television bar fight. But he knew that wasn't it. Brian could no longer fool himself into believing this was a reenactment or even a dream. The empty, staring eyes of the dead man who had fallen into his lap would stay in his memory forever.

He was back. The castle was gone, but these were the men who had been training in its yard that first time. The now familiar nausea rose in his gut and he turned and vomited into the grass.

What had he been thinking, wishing to travel back in time again? Safe and sound in Inverness, he'd thought it would be nice to see the castle once more. Not this. Never this.

"Git it all oot, lad." The new voice came from a tall man with black curly hair and clear blue eyes that reminded him of Sophie's.

"Where am—" he stopped. Some instinct of self-preservation told him to be quiet.

The man's eyes searched his face and then widened. He patted Brian on the shoulder. "Are ye awright, lad? We have t' git back t' th' fight—" Giles' words cut off at the excited voice of another man who rushed up to join them.

"They're retreatin'! It's over!" The youth's smile died as he looked around in alarm. "Where's Dànaidh?" he demanded.

"I'm right here, Ealar. Hauld yerself t'gither." A narrow-faced man with light brown hair and bleary hazel eyes clapped him on the back.

"Wha's wrong wi' Crìs?" asked the one called Ealar.

The black-haired man gave Brian a warning look and turned back to the others. "He'll be fine," he said. "Let's gie home, aye? 'Tis a long way back."

"Wha'ever ye say, Giles," said the man called Dànaidh. Brian thought he detected a sneer in the man's voice before he turned his back and began walking away, spine stiff. The others exchanged glances but said nothing, and followed in his wake.

Giles pulled Brian to his feet. "Dinnae say anythin' t' th' others," he said. "We'll talk as we go, eh?" He began walking toward the rest of the men, and then turned back. "Are ye comin', lad?"

Brian took a deep breath and fell into step beside him. The nausea receded along with the last remnants of his headache as they walked, leaving that odd feeling that his brain was being squeezed into a space too small to accommodate it.

Giles slowed their pace and dropped back from

the others until they were out of earshot. "Who are ye?" he said quietly. "Ye're no yerself, are ye?"

"What?"

"Kenna telt me. I didnae want t' believe 'er, th' wee midgie likes t' pull a prank now an' agin', ye ken? An' it's been a long time since, so I thought . . ." He looked for some reaction, but Brian returned a blank stare.

Giles sighed. "But she's a smart 'un, an' I c'n see whit she meant. Ye ken whit I'm talkin' about, d' ye no?"

Brian hesitated, then nodded. "My name's Brian." When there was no reaction from Giles, he added, "This has happencd before. Kenna's the girl who likes to dress like a man, right?"

Giles smiled. "Weel, aye. Bit nobody else kens, 'cept th' three o' us." He gave Brian a steady look. "Me, Kenna . . .'an Cris. You." He paused, as if surprised at what he was saying, and then added, quietly, "I'm Giles."

"What year is this?" Brian asked suddenly.

Giles started, then gave a wry smile. "Sorry. I cannae get my heid 'round this. 'Tis th' year o' our Lord, 1648."

Brian was quiet, his thoughts racing as he tried to put the picture together. 1648. Last time this happened, the girl named Kenna had said it was 1647. So time here moved differently than his reality. The first time, in the yard at Duart, it had been 1646. *Two years have passed in the space of two months.* None of this was possible, but it was happening anyway.

Giles let him be, walking quietly beside him when he had to be teeming with questions. Brian admired the man for it, and he was grateful because his brain was spinning faster than he could keep up.

What had happened in the year 1648? Jeremy Brown had said this period was called The Wars of the Three Kingdoms—a very romantic name for the horror he had witnessed today. War wasn't like TV at all. It was a conflagration of sound and pain and desperation, with death waiting at the end. He swallowed something sour and was grateful for his now empty stomach.

Brian glanced at Giles. It would do no good to ask *him* what today's battle had been called; he was pretty sure these guys wouldn't have bothered with fancy names for the never-ending bloodshed. But he did know where they stood in the conflict, thanks to Jeremy.

The Highland clans took sides based on their own loyalties and needs, as they always had. Jeremy had said that the Macleans were Royalists who stood behind their king, a decision that hadn't proven the best choice historically speaking. Brian let his brain filter the information, and slowly the picture emerged.

Charles I would be executed by his own parliament in 1649—only one year from now--ushering in a decade in which the unthinkable had happened, total abolishment of the monarchy in Britain.

These Macleans would never believe such a thing could happen. Should he tell Giles what he knew? Brian didn't know how this was supposed to work, but wouldn't sharing historical information with those living it mess with the future? It was called a time paradox or something. He'd never really liked time travel movies because they seemed full of romantic drivel, but now he wished he'd paid more attention.

But wait—he hadn't traveled. Or at least, his body hadn't. So, if this wasn't time travel, what was happening to him? There was too much detail. He didn't know these people, this place. He had never experienced battle, and the reality of that stranger's violent death was something he could never have imagined just from watching movies.

His breath hitched. Was this the result of brain damage, like the doctors in both hospitals had told him? Would it get worse? Would the episodes lengthen until his mind was trapped in this time forever?

Worse, what if he'd been shot in that battle? If he'd been the one who fell lifeless on the battlefield, did that mean he would die in his own time? The nausea crept back.

Suddenly, Giles turned and pulled him toward a small stream they'd been following. He pointed to the slow-moving water and pushed Brian's head down so that he was staring into its shimmering depths. "Look."

Brian found himself peering into a face that wasn't his. Reddish brown hair like his, green eyes. Except it wasn't his hair or his eyes. He was looking at a stranger. He turned and retched, but his empty stomach produced nothing but bitter bile.

"Who is that?" he asked, his voice breaking.

"Crìsdean," Giles said quietly. "Ye *are* Crìsdean, dinnae fash. Whitever is happenin' t' ye, ye must ken 'at."

Brian tried to stem the hot tears that rose behind his eyes. The empathy and kindness offered by this young man, a peer in age but vastly older in experience and wisdom, threatened to undo him.

The man was wrong, though. As the two tramped along in the wake of the other Maclean clansmen, the truth wrapped around his brain like a viper and squeezed.

No matter what Giles said, he wasn't Crìsdean Maclean of Duart Castle on the Isle of Mull. This body, trained in swordcraft and muskets, wasn't his. He had to hold on to that, keep the knowledge close, or he really would go insane. And if he wasn't the man who owned this body and these clothes . . . where was the real Crìsdean?

CHAPTER 27

MULL, SCOTLAND, 1648

KENNA

The men had returned last night, exhausted from the battle and the long trek, and gone straight to bed. It wasn't until late morning that Giles had pulled Kenna aside in the hall and whispered in her ear, "Th' library—noo."

She knew what it was before he opened his mouth. It had happened again—Crìsdean was someone else. It had been over a year since the last time, and as days and then months went by with no hint of change, she had dared to hope it was over, that whatever the cause of his mental confusion, it had run its course. Heart in her throat, she faced his older brother's worried eyes.

"I didnae b'lieve ye, lass," Giles said. "E'en wi' th' proof walkin' right b'side me, I didnae thynk it could be. But he spake almost in a diff'rent language. I had t' listen hard t' unnerstand him at all, an' I almost wisht I hadn't."

Giles ran his hand through his hair absently, like Crìsdean did—like all the Maclean brothers did when upset. He looked her in the eye and spoke quickly. "He's awright noo, lass, dinnae fash. He was back t' himself by th' time we reached home, bit—"

"Did he get hit 'n th' heid? Did he fall unconscious? Did he tell ye a diff'rent name?" Kenna interrupted.

"Whoa, lass, slow doon!" Giles was making a veritable nest out of his hair; it stood up in every direction like the spines of a hedgehog. "I didnae see whit happened; we were fightin', ye ken? Ever' man fer himself. 'Twas Pàdraig found him, half-sittin', lookin' brain-cracked an' starin' at a dead man like 'twas th' first time he seen one." He paused for a minute. "Ahh—does Crìsdean ken enybody named Brian?"

Nausea rose in Kenna's throat. "'At's th' name he called himself. Brian Maclean."

Giles paced around the small alcove. "Why would 'e say 'is name was Brian? Why would 'e talk so strange? An' . . ." He stopped again. " He asked me whit year 'tis."

Kenna nodded. "He asked me 'at too." She held both hands out, palms up. "I cannae make it out. Both 'o th' other times, he didnae get hit. Nuthin' happened t' him a' tall. He just passed oot, an' when he came to, he was sumbody else."

She took a deep breath. "He didnae *thynk* he was some'un else. He *was* some'un else. He didnae ken anythin' Crìsdean kens, an' he talked th' way ye said—like he was from some'ere far awa'. I took him round th' castle, an' he seemed surprised t' see ever'day things. I thought he was playin' a prank, but he wasnae. He was skairt, Giles. Really, truly skairt."

"I'll keep a watch on 'im, lass, in case it 'appens agin, bit it seems this Brian is fair canny. He kens much abit Duart, an' that's on account o' ye. I dinnae thynk he'll gie himself awa—least no if he can help 't. Giles grinned at Kenna. "With th' both o' us watchin', our Crìs cannae come t' trooble, aye?"

Kenna felt tears of gratitude fill her eyes and blinked, unable to speak.

"'Scuse me."

They turned to see a stranger standing in the doorway. She smiled. "I didnae ken enybody was up here."

Kenna and Giles stared at the young woman. She was plump and short of stature, dressed in a simple gown of light brown with a pristine white apron. Her straight brown hair was held back in a white kerchief, and her wide mouth curved up in a smile.

"I'm Lili," she offered. "Lili MacPherson. I'm here t' be th' governess t' young Annie Maclean," The smile widened, lending sudden warmth to her plain face. "Although, I cannae thynk why Miss Frances needs a governess fer a four-month-old bairn. I guess I'm more a nanny. Bit she'll grow; then I'll be a governess."

Giles smiled at the newcomer. "Welcome t' Duart. I'm Giles, Annie's uncle. She's a darlin', aye?"

Lili laughed. "Thank ye. An' we'll see if she's a darlin, will we no? I've never minded one so young, bit I like 'n adventure." She looked around the library. "I'm up here lookin' fer somethin' t' read t' wee Annie. It's nivver too soon t' introduce a bairn t' readin', aye?"

Oh Lord, she's just Giles' kind o' person, Kenna's face split in a grin and her irritation at the interruption drained away. *Another 'un thynks books 'r the fountain o' life.* And indeed, Giles' face was alight with a joy that only another book lover would understand. He smiled at the new addition to Duart's family.

"We dinnae have books fer bairns, but mebbe some poetry'd do. It's almost akin t' music, an' wee 'ns like music, aye?" He led Lili toward the shelf that housed the castle's small collection of poetry tomes, and soon the two were in deep conversation, having completely forgotten Kenna.

She stood alone in the alcove and smiled to herself. It was a good thing wee Annie was going to be the recipient of all this bookishness, instead of her. She couldn't think of anything more boring.

Poor bairn. But you never knew, maybe she'd grow up wanting to wield a blade. Kenna thought about that, and a smile spread over her face. Annie could become her squire and learn the art of swordcraft. Oh, Frances would hate that! The image of the wee bairn chasing her mother around the castle with a broomstick was splendid.

She sighed. She knew she was deliberately distracting herself from the problem at hand. It was obvious the discussion of Crìsdean's peculiar attacks was over for the moment, but it hung like a sodden raincloud over her mind. She left the library and made her way down the spiral staircase to the ground floor and out into the courtyard.

It was empty today. The men having just returned from a battle, there was no stomach for sparring. She'd wait until Crìsdean woke up and judge for herself if he was all right.

She had nothing else to do but worry. Lachlan had returned from the battle with his son and nephews, and Mary was too busy making up for lost time to need her ward. At loose ends, Kenna wandered out to the edge of the peninsula and climbed atop one of the rocks at the water's edge.

Across the sound she could see the mountains of the mainland, standing tall and rugged as they had for thousands of years. Behind her, Duart rose in defiance, like a young upstart out to challenge the mountains for supremacy.

The men who had built her four hundred years ago probably thought they could defeat nature. Fools! Duart was *built* from nature, from rocks like the one on which she stood. And men were always wrong. The castle would surely crumble into the ground someday like other man-made creations, leaving the mountains to their rule.

Kenna squeaked as a pair of sturdy arms went around her.

"Whit're ye thinkin', lass?" Crìsdean murmured into her hair. He rested his chin on the top of her head. "Did ye miss me?"

"Aye," she said, and turned to look deep into his eyes. *Crìsdean's eyes.* "I missed ye terr'bly. I hate this damn war; when'll it end?"

Crìsdean shrugged. Kenna sat down on the rock and pulled him down beside her. "Is it no goin' well, then?"

"Weel, we won this time, but I'm that worrit about th' future. Ye ken th' king was captured th' year gone, aye? By Scotsmen, too—th' bastards—an helt by 'is own govermint fer months. He jist escaped in November."

Crìsdean turned worried eyes on Kenna. "I should-nae speak ill o' th' king, an' I'll never tell another soul a'sides ye, but Charles doesnae seem t' be thinkin' straight. He's fightin' wi' his own parliament, wi' th' Campbells, an' wi' th' church. I want t' wed ye next year, but—"

"Wha?" Kenna searched his face, eyes wide. "Wha'd ye say?"

"He's fightin' wi'—"

"Not 'at, ye eejit. Th' other thing!"

Crìsdean grinned. "Ach, aye. I want' t' wed ye. Ye ken 'at, no? Year next, when ye turn seventeen. Does 'at suit ye?"

Kenna lunged at him, wrapping her arms around his middle, and tumbling them both off the rock onto the grass. Her lips found his, and she kissed him until he pushed her away, gasping for air.

"Kenna! I have t' be alive t' wed ye!"

She sat back and gazed at him, taking in the flya-way auburn curls, the laughing green eyes, and the dimple on one side of his mouth. This man was her past, her present, and her future, and she would pro-tect him with everything she had.

Seven, his mother called him. Anna had told everybody who would listen that Crìsdean was spe-cial because he was the seventh son. He might be a healer or have the second sight, she would say, with a glare that discouraged argument. Her listeners knew to nod obediently and reserve their comments for later.

She hadn't done him any favors with the claim; when his mother wasn't around, his brothers teased him until he couldn't take it anymore and almost chopped off Fergus' foot with a sword. All of this had taken place long before Kenna's arrival at the castle, but the story was a part of Maclean lore, much to Crìsdean's chagrin. At least now, only his mother dared to call him Seven.

Her heart felt as if it would leap from her chest and fly into the grey sky. He *was* special, no matter that there had never been a sign of magical ability in him. He was special, and he was hers.

Keep ye away, Brian Maclean. I mean it, keep ye away fra' my man.

CHAPTER 28

INVERNESS, SCOTLAND, PRESENT DAY

The worst part of holding the memories
is not the pain. It's the loneliness of it.
—Lois Lowry

Brian lay still for a moment, wondering what was different. The last he remembered, he was marching through midge-infested bogs and forests that seemed to have no end. The air was heavy with unshed rain, but spirits were high despite the dismal weather.

They had won. He kept his eyes closed and wondered about that. Won what? He had no recollection of playing a game. The only sport he took part in was sailing, but he had seen no water in this place.

Memories surfaced with annoying sluggishness. Shouts, screams, curses. Not the kind you heard at a sporting match—these were frantic, tinged with desperation as if the score was as important as life itself.

An image drifted into focus. Eyes, staring at the sky, glazed and fixed. Dead eyes.

Brian's own eyes snapped open. He was lying on a couch, covered with a wool blanket. The room was dark, but a soft light shone in the distance. It came from a table next to an armchair in which a woman sat, reading. Kenna.

No, Sophie.

The memories crashed in on him with the force of a Nor'eastern gale. Overcooked meat, mushy carrots, Sophie listening as he told her his bitter truth about the incident that had cost him his job and ripped away his self-esteem. The look in her eyes—doubting him, judging him.

He gasped and struggled to untangle himself from the rough wool. Sophie's head jerked up. She threw the book onto the side table and stood. Her eyes met his and she froze as though her feet were glued to the floor.

She was afraid of him.

Shame and anger surged through him. He made it to his feet, still clutching the edges of the blanket. With a furious thrust, he rid himself of the thing and started toward the door, only to realize that his shoes were missing.

"Where are my shoes?" The words were clipped and harsh, but he didn't care. He had to get out of here and away from Sophie MacArthur, before he came apart at the seams and melted into a puddle of ichor right in front of her.

The words seemed to break the bonds that held her to the floor. She approached Brian slowly, hands held out, and stopped inches in front of him.

"I-I'm sorry," she said, her voice on the edge of a sob. "I'm so sorry. I didn't mean—"

"It's all right." His own voice sounded dull and defeated to his ears. "It doesn't matter. I need to go—can you please just give me my shoes?"

"No." The word had the ring of finality. She stood her ground, eyes searching his face.

"Fine," he said. He started for the door again, but a surprisingly strong grip on his arm stopped him. He whipped around and jerked his arm out of her grasp.

"Don't touch me!" he said. "I might hurt you, right?" Sarcasm dripped from his lips, poisoning the air between them.

Sophie's eyes darted away and then back. She took a deep breath, walked to the door, and placed her back against it.

"Please, Brian. You can go, but please listen to me first."

It was the plea in those words that stopped him. He stared at her for a long moment, then turned and sat down again on the couch.

"Fine. Talk." He crossed his arms and leaned back against the soft cushions. "I'm listening." As *if anything she could say would change the memory of that look in her eyes when I bared my damn soul.*

Sophie stayed where she was, hands clasped behind her.

"Something happened to me," she said, and stopped.

He said nothing.

"Three years ago." Her words came slowly, as if every fibre of her being was trying to hold them inside.

Brian felt some of his anger dissipate in the face of her struggle. He leaned forward on the couch.

"Go ahead," he said, more softly.

"I-I was attacked." Her voice was a whisper.

Brian's head jerked up. "What?"

"There was a man," she said, and then the words flooded out in choking gasps. It was as if a dam had broken and all the debris, dirt, and mud was pouring out in a torrent, carrying everything away in its path.

"I met him in the student center at uni. His name was Luke, and he was a musician too—piano. At the Conservatoire everybody is in music, of course. He'd heard me play in a concert the week before, and he said he admired me for my talent. He wanted to meet with me, talk about our music—" her voice cracked but she kept going, as if stopping was impossible now.

"He invited me to rehearsal for a ballet perfor-mance the dance department was putting on, said he was playing in the orchestra, and would introduce me to the rest of the musicians."

She was trembling, her hands kneading the mate-rial of her sweater. Brian picked up the blanket and crossed to where she still stood against the door. He wrapped the wool around her and led her to the couch, pushed her down gently and sat next to her, careful to maintain a distance. She didn't seem to notice; her eyes were focused inward, on something he couldn't see. He wondered if she even knew he was there.

"It wasn't a date, just a meeting. But he was so nice, and he had such lovely dark brown eyes. And it was about music. At least, I thought—" A shudder rippled through her slight body.

Brian wanted to reach out, pull her in, and com-fort her, but a new awareness told him that was the worst thing he could do. So he stayed perfectly still. It took everything he had, but he waited.

"Wh-when I got there, the theatre was dark. There was no one on the stage, no one in the pit. No music; no sound at all. I thought I'd gotten the place or the time wrong, so I turned to go."

For a moment she was silent. When she spoke again, her voice wavered. "He came at me from a seat in the back row. He grabbed me and hugged me. I tried to pull away, but he wouldn't let go. He told me I was b-beautiful, that I was just the girl he'd always w-wanted, that it was love at first sight."

Sophie's haunted eyes were fixed on the wall behind him, and the last of Brian's anger drained away in the face of the misery he saw in them.

"I told him I wasn't interested," she said. "That I thought we were there to talk about music. She shuddered. "And he . . . laughed at me. Then he-he started-s-started-he started k-kissing me. I looked into his eyes, and they weren't brown after all; they were black. Like a demon's eyes." The shuddering intensified.

"I fought him—I did!—but he just held me tighter." Her knuckles were white where her small fists clutched at the blanket, but she went on. "He called me a tease, said I shouldn't be like that. He said I needed to be punished."

For the first time since beginning her story, Sophie looked at Brian, and in her eyes he saw something more than the agony of remembering. He knew that look—he'd seen it in the mirror. It was shame. He felt sick. The coward in him didn't want to hear any more, but he pushed it down ruthlessly.

He reached out slowly, as if she were a small kitten that might dart away at any second, and touched her fingers. They were like ice.

"What . . . happened?" he asked, his voice barely a whisper.

Sophie looked at him again, and the blue eyes filled with tears. She swiped them away with the back of one hand.

"The door was so close! Only a few yards away. But it was no use. He ripped my blouse and tried to push me down on the floor in the aisle. He would have been able to; he was so much stronger than me." Her breath hitched and tears were running down her face, but she swiped them away and continued.

"Someone opened a door somewhere in the theatre. I didn't see anybody, but it distracted him for a second. I jerked myself free and ran out the door, and I never looked behind me until I reached my flat. I dropped out the next day."

Brian hadn't realized he'd been holding his breath; now he let it out in a long sigh of relief. So the bastard hadn't raped her. He wanted to shout for joy. He wanted to hug her to him and tell her he would protect her. He wanted to kill the son-of-a-bitch in the most painful way possible.

"You didn't report it to the police?"

She stared down at the hands fisted in her lap. "No. I was too ashamed. I left Glasgow so fast, tried to leave it all behind me. Anyway I'd just met him; I only knew his first name, and I couldn't even tell them what he looked like. I never really saw his face; it was dark in the theatre, and when I met him, he was wearing a mask." Sophie wrung her hands. "It was during the pandemic and we all had to wear them." She shuddered. "All I remembered was his eyes."

Sophie's voice sank to a whisper. "I've never told anybody about it, not even Deirdre. There was nobody in my family I could tell. I didn't want anybody to know. I was afraid I had caused it somehow, made him think I—"

"Stop it!" Brian's anger surged again. He made a supreme effort and forced himself to speak calmly.

"You did nothing wrong," he said, and now he took both of her cold hands in his and forced her to look him in the eye. "He was a predator. He knew exactly what he was doing; he'd probably done it before. If he hadn't been distracted, he would have done whatever he wanted to you and never had a moment's remorse for it."

And that's why she gave you that look, his inner voice sounded in his ears. *There you were, telling her your sad, pitiful story about how you were violated by a student, wah, wah, poor you—when what she'd faced was so much worse! What a fool you are, Brian Maclean. What a self-pitying, loathsome jerk.*

"I'm sorry, Sophie. I didn't understand where you were coming from. I thought—never mind, I'm an idiot."

She laughed, a small hiccupping sound that had no mirth in it. "No, you're not. You were right to be angry."

He opened his mouth again, and she held up a hand. "Don't talk. Let me get this out. I need to."

He nodded, and she gave him a wan smile that disappeared as soon as it came, like a winter sun sliding behind the clouds.

"I did wonder—when you told me about that student—I wondered if you could be—" She paused and then finished in a rush, "—like him."

Brian flinched, but held his face still and managed a nod. "I get it," he said. "I do. I just didn't know why you would think that of me. It hit me in a place that I didn't know was so sensitive, and—" he stopped.

She said nothing, just watched him with those amazing eyes, and he realized something else about Sophie MacArthur. She was very good at waiting.

"And I wanted you to think better of me." The words tumbled out into the space between them. He felt like a steam train that has run out of fuel. The memories of the battlefield, the dead man, and the endless walk sank to the back of his tired mind, forgotten. He could deal with that later. It had been a *very* long day.

"That's all," he finished. "I'm sorry I ran out like an ass. Forgive me?"

She smiled, a real smile this time, and it took his breath away. "Forgiven." She took a deep breath and sat back against the couch cushions. "Now, can we talk about why I found you passed out on the pavement?"

Luke Cameron's lip curled as he looked down at the girl. Why had he thought her pretty? She was a mewling, whimpering mess. Blonde hair straggled across a face puffy from crying, and her blue eyes gaped at him vacantly as if she wasn't sure what had gone wrong. He put his hands around her throat and finished quickly, suddenly repulsed. He turned away and stepped into the small toilet, washed his hands, and dried them on his jeans. Without a backward look at the girl on the bed, he left.

It was raining, of course. At this hour he had the street to himself; everyone was taking up stools in the pubs and taverns, or home trying to put cranky children to bed. Normal people, living normal lives. Mindless sheep.

The energy drained out of his body, leaving him empty and wanting. The thing that was always there returned, growling and gnawing at his gut. It was happening more often now; his control was slipping.

It was *her* fault—all of it. All these pathetic girls were shoddy imitations of the one he really wanted. He remembered as if it were yesterday instead of three years ago. The moment he saw her in the student center, he'd known she was the one. The woman who would change him, make the squirming thing inside him go away. The one who could calm his hunger, cool the heat that was burning him up and tearing away his control with jagged teeth.

But she'd betrayed him. Denied his need and run away. Left him fighting a surging maelstrom of confusion and desire that had grown until it threatened to consume him. It was all her fault.

He blinked the drops out of his eyes and scowled into the mist. He hated Glasgow. It was always raining, always chaotic. It wasn't home, though he'd spent four years here at the Royal Conservatoire. Home was where *she* was. Having to waste time here fed his frustration and fueled his rage.

He'd spent long enough leaving crumbs for the cops, leading them by the nose. It was time to get back to Inverness.

CHAPTER 29

INVERNESS, SCOTLAND, PRESENT DAY

*There are far too many fish in the sea to waste
time chasing one that doesn't want to be caught.*
—Unknown

Deirdre stared miserably into her wine glass and let her thoughts simmer like a poisonous stew. She wanted to throw something at the cheerful waitress and watch that stupid smile slide off her insipid face. She wanted to scream at these happy, yipping people to shut up. She wanted to drink until her favorite pub went out of business.

It was so fucking hard being Sophie's best friend. Deirdre had resisted calling her for a week. Since that day she'd stopped in and found out that Brian Maclean was coming over for dinner. Innocent Sophie, *beautiful* Sophie, had somehow done it again, and she probably didn't even know.

If she were honest—much as she didn't really want to be—none of this was Sophie's fault. Deirdre hadn't told her friend about her crush; if she had, Sophie would probably have backed off immediately. She was the most loyal person Deirdre knew.

And it wasn't like she'd gotten any encouragement from Brian. She'd totally misread that one. She was the one who'd called—she cringed, thinking how many times. He'd answered the first few calls, but then his phone was eerily silent.

Deirdre glared at her image in the wine glass. She always jumped in with both feet and then wondered why she was alone, treading water. The truth was, it wasn't the first time she'd scared a man off with her enthusiasm. If she were attracted to a lad, she always assumed he'd like her back if she persisted.

Brian *had* seemed to like her though, that night at the Dancing Unicorn. Well, she'd done all the talking—*and why the hell can't I ever shut up?*—but he'd smiled and seemed interested. Truth was, he was probably there to listen to Sophie and her damned human violin. Like every other man in the place.

There's nothing wrong with me, Deirdre told herself. *I'm sociable. I like people, and they like me. Men like me. They say I'm cute.*

So what was the problem? Deirdre fiddled with the vinegar bottle on the table in front of her, making it roll on its edges like a top until it fell over and leaked pungent drops onto the wooden surface. She picked it up and slammed it back into place. The vinegar matched her mood. She picked up the paper serviette and began shredding it, while giving the fork a malevolent glare. *You're next.*

She *was* cute. Yes, and Sophie was gorgeous. Never mind that she was completely unaware of her looks—probably didn't even want them—those huge blue eyes were like beacons to the male species, and women flocked to beauty salons to get that perfect shade of blonde hair that Sophie had naturally. *Damn it.*

Deirdre sighed. She knew she was being unfair. Sophie had never sought the attention. She avoided it as much as possible, really. She hid out in her house, reading and playing the violin, and she'd probably never come out if her best friend didn't intervene. Her social skills were negligible, and Lord knew she hadn't a clue how to flirt.

I'm my own worst enemy, Deirdre thought. *If I didn't insist on dragging Sophie out into society, we'd both be perfectly happy doing our own thing. She could fraternize with that violin and I could frolic in the sea of humans. Human men.*

Except somehow Sophie had wound up playing at the Unicorn. Deirdre stopped punishing the tableware and thought about that. It was so uncharacteristic of her—not only to venture into a pub in the first place, but to take a job. In a band, no less. Playing in front of a crowd of strangers, all staring at her. It was as mysterious as the pub itself.

So it wasn't her fault. She hadn't made Sophie go there, and Brian was her sister-in-law's brother, so of course they would have met eventually. Fate was a bugger.

A giggle began somewhere in the nether regions of her stomach and worked its way upward. All this aggravation was no use; she was incapable of holding a grudge so she might as well give it up. If Brian Maclean could help pull Sophie out of herself, all the better. Maybe it needed more than a best friend to fix such a lost cause.

And anyway, she should stop fooling herself; just because she was attracted to him, it didn't mean he had to reciprocate. There were plenty of nuts in the tree, and Deirdre Clarke wasn't about to whine about one that whacked her on the head and rolled away. Men were all mindless numpties when it came to female looks; she'd just find another one sooner or later.

A soft classical melody reached her ear, and she looked up to see that a young man had taken his place at the piano in the corner. He launched into the beginning of Pachelbel's Canon, embellishing the simple chords with difficult fingering that gave the well-known piece new life.

He was good, very good, and Deirdre felt the last of her frustration seep away. She should get out of there, get some air, maybe stop in at the Unicorn. But she remained at the table, watching the man's supple fingers glide over the keys.

The waitress approached her table, and now her smile seemed more genuine. Maybe it was the music, but Deirdre felt better. She smiled back at the young woman and ordered the potato soup. It was still early, there was plenty of time to get to the Unicorn. A week of sulking was long enough. She found herself looking forward to seeing Sophie, and if Brian was there, so be it; friendship was better than love, every time.

The food came and she tucked into it with enthusiasm. Her foot tapped to the music and her heart felt lighter than it had in a week. There was no sense in indulging a broken heart from a romance that never was; she simply didn't have the wallowing gene.

The music stopped and the man pushed the bench back and stood up. Deirdre pushed the empty soup bowl back and beckoned the waitress over. She pulled her credit card out, but a hand intercepted and placed another card on the tray. She looked up, startled.

The piano player stood next to the table. He handed the tray with his card on it to the waitress and turned back with a smile.

Up close, he was handsome. Very handsome. Tall, with a slim build and muscles rippling under his white shirt. His sandy hair was artfully messy, and his brows lifted over lovely hazel eyes that glinted with appreciation when he looked at Deirdre.

A born flirt, she thought. *Knows he's hot . . .I need to be on my guard with this one.* She smiled back, relishing the challenge.

"Hullo," the man said. He had a faint accent—Western Isles, maybe. His voice sounded just like his playing, low and musical. Deirdre felt her insides go warm and gooey, like the sauce on a sticky toffee pudding.

"I saw you sitting here," he said, "and I wondered why such a beautiful lass was all alone. It's almost a crime." He gestured to the chair opposite Deirdre. "Do you mind if I join you?"

He called me beautiful. Not cute—beautiful. Oh, he's good.

She nodded, unsure whether words would come out if she tried to speak.

He pulled the chair out and folded himself into it, his movements fluid and graceful. Then he smiled again and extended a hand across the table. She took it with care, noticing the beautiful lines of his long fingers, the well-manicured nails.

"I'm Sam. Sam Douglas."

"Deirdre Clarke," she said, feeling suddenly breathless. "You- you play beautifully."

"Thank you." His answer was simple and unaffected, as if his talent was unremarkable, just something he'd picked up along the way. Deirdre could feel her heart take flight, and she let it. *Let's just see where this goes,* she thought. *Don't rush it this time like an eejit.*

He was a good listener. He asked her about her life, about where she went to school, what food she liked, and what music she loved.

"I like all kinds of music," she told him, enjoying the way his warm hazel eyes softened when she talked. "Classical isn't really my favorite, but hearing you play might change my mind."

Oh God, I'm flirting with a total stranger, she thought. It felt good, and he didn't seem to mind a bit. After all, he was the one who'd approached her first.

"Where did you learn to play like that?" she asked.

"I've been playing since I was a kid." He shrugged. "It's second nature. But I got a scholarship to uni for it, so music has been good to me."

"My best friend went to school for music," Deirdre said. "I guess I must be attracted to musicians."

He laughed. "And I'm glad you are. Where did your friend go to school?"

"The Royal Conservatoire. It's in Glasgow."

He whistled. "That's an amazing school. Wish I'd gone there. She must be good."

Deirdre smiled. "She's wonderful. She plays the violin. Hey!"

He tilted his head. "Eh?"

"Why don't you come with me to The Dancing Unicorn? She plays in a Celtic band there." *And she has a boyfriend—at least, I hope so.*

Sam looked at his watch. "Aye, I can do that. Is this pub local? I don't think I've ever heard of it, but I've only been here a few months."

"It's up on Ardconnel, just above the castle," Deirdre said. "I don't think it's been there that long, even though it looks old as hell."

"Let's go, then." Sam stood and came around to help her on with her jacket. "Gets pretty nippy at night, with the wind off the river."

Deirdre put another tick in her mental "pros" column. *A gentleman.* And added another when he took her arm as they left the pub. Deirdre couldn't remember another time when the pavement seemed to be made of clouds.

The music reached them before they got to the top of the Market Brae Steps, and light spilled out into the street from the pub's open door.

Sam looked at Deirdre and smiled. "Is that the band your friend plays in? They're really good."

Pride swept through her. "Aye, they are."

At the bottom of the steps leading into the pub, she stopped and turned to face him. "Everybody is nice here, except for one. Don't try to pet the cat."

Sam shuddered dramatically. "I hate cats. Nasty, slinky things." Then he grinned. "Kidding; I'm just allergic to them, so thanks for the warning; I won't be getting close."

Deirdre smiled. "Then, let's go. You're in for a treat. This place is spooky magical."

She ignored Sam's arched eyebrow and pulled him into the taproom of The Dancing Unicorn. All the tables were full, as usual, but Wee Caomhainn caught her eye and grinned. He waved a dishcloth toward the back corner.

Deirdre followed his gesture and froze. Brian was there, alone. He hadn't seen them; his attention was on the stage, where Sophie was playing another reel. His mouth was open in a wide smile and his hand tapped the table to the beat of the music.

Deirdre sighed. Then she thrust her shoulders back, grabbed Sam's hand, and led him to the table.

"Hi, Brian."

A slightly nervous smile crossed his face, and then he spotted the man holding Deirdre's hand. His face cleared, and he gestured to the three empty seats at the table.

"Hi, Deirdre. Have a seat. I think Sophie's almost finished with her set."

Sam sat down across from Brian and angled his chair slightly to face the stage. Deirdre took a seat between the two men. "Sam, this is Brian Maclean—Sophie's-friend. Brian, this is Sam Douglas—*my* friend."

If the emphasis on those last words was notable to anyone but her, it wasn't apparent. Brian took the hand that Sam offered and shook it heartily. "Hi. Have you been here before?"

Sam looked around the taproom. "No, I haven't, but I'm not originally from around here and I work in a pub, so I tend to avoid them in my free time." He grinned. "Have to admit, though, this place might change my mind."

Deirdre looked covertly at both men, and decided that Sam more than held his own in the looks department. He looked good in the white shirt, with that light brown hair. It set off his beautiful hazel eyes . . . eyes that right now were looking at her. A small smile played over his face, and Deirdre felt a shiver of pleasure arc through her.

"Sam plays piano over at Simon's Bar, on Academy," she said. "He's amazing."

Brian nodded politely, and then his eyes brightened. The music had stopped, and Sophie was making her way toward them. She gave Deirdre a wide smile.

"I wondered where you've been," she said. "Haven't heard from you in a week." She caught sight of Sam and her eyebrows went up.

"This is Sam Douglas," Deirdre said.

Sophie nodded. "Nice to meet you." She sat down in the empty chair next to Brian and shot her best friend a questioning look.

Deirdre grinned and glanced back at Sam. He was looking at her. *Her*, not Sophie. She realized that she'd been holding her breath and let it out slowly.

This one might be a keeper.

CHAPTER 30
MULL, SCOTLAND, PRESENT DAY

*Moments would stutter and hiccup
and falter and repeat. Time seemed
to be breaking down entirely.*
—Neil Gaiman

Sophie stared out at the choppy water of the Sound of Mull and wondered what the hell she was doing, chasing a nightmare with this man she barely knew and wasn't sure she even liked.

Oh, stop it. That ship has sailed further than this one. She stole a sidelong look at the man standing next to her at the rail of the ferry. He was staring out at the waves, lost in thoughts of his own.

What was she to do? She did like him, but he was destined to be disappointed if he wanted something permanent with her. A loner from a cursed family was nobody's idea of the future. He'd figure it out, go home to Canada, and she'd be back where she belonged—in her own home, alone.

A strange new feeling rose up, a mixture of resignation and hope. She turned it over in her mind and examined it, and the answer came. Truth was, it didn't matter what happened next. Brian Maclean had inserted himself into her life, and all the fantasy men in her novels had packed up in a huff and moved out.

"There it is." His tense voice penetrated her thoughts. His body was stiff, hands clenched tightly on the railing. She followed his gaze to the castle that stood against the blue sky like a proud sentinel.

"It's the right castle," Brian said again. "At least, I think—" he broke off.

"Duart," Sophie said. She wanted to put her hand on his to reassure him, but she didn't dare. Their relationship—whatever it was—was too new, too fragile. Every glance, every interaction, was fraught with a strange tension, like Oliver's strings when she wound them too tight.

She was afraid that this could all dissolve into nothing any minute. Anything she might say would be the wrong thing, any touch could send one of them running.

He'd told her about his dreams or visions or whatever they were. She'd listened, at first dubious and then fascinated. He thought they were real, that he'd actually been here—at Duart Castle—in the past. Three times. So now they were on a quest to visit Brian's dream castle, to see if walking its parapets and climbing its stairs would dislodge a memory.

Of what? Sophie stared at the castle as the ferry drew closer to the Isle of Mull. A *memory of a dream?* She'd listened to Brian's story and hadn't believed a word of it. But it was true he kept losing consciousness, the last time for no discernible reason. He swore he hadn't hit his head, and she did believe him about that. She'd been there; there was nothing that could have caused his collapse, no sign of injury, and when he came to, he was fine. It was just that his story was so ridiculous.

Not like hers. Since letting her story out, the nightmares had slowed their frequency, but she knew they were still there, still waiting. Each one was different—sometimes the janitor didn't interrupt, sometimes she was a second too late, or the door to her escape was locked. It always ended with her sitting bolt upright in bed, tears running down her face, her body coated in sweat. Every time, she saw those black eyes, glinting like some feral creature.

Maybe she should have shared the memory of that night with another person long ago. She should at least have told Deirdre, her best friend. But she had walled it up and denied its voice, until Brian Maclean. And he had listened. The only reaction he had was the horror in his eyes at the evil of the man who had almost raped her, who had stolen her innocence.

He had understood, or at least it seemed so. When he asked, *Did you report it?*, there was no judgement in his clear green eyes. He'd been angry—at the man who'd dared to commit such an act, at himself for jumping to conclusions about her reaction. And he'd been proud of her courage in telling him, when she hadn't told another soul.

There was a jolt and Sophie's attention snapped back to the present, surprised to see that the ferry was docking at Craignure on Mull. Brian hadn't moved. His hands were still locked on the railing, his posture ramrod straight.

"Brian?" she said softly. "We should get downstairs. The foot passengers get off first."

"What? Oh, yeah." He looked at her and managed a smile. "I was thinking."

"Aye, that you were," she said, and smiled back before moving ahead of him to the metal staircase that led down to the line of disembarking passengers.

"No taxis today; they're all out on tours," the woman at the information center told them. "You'll have to walk. It's just over three miles to the castle, along the main road here. Won't take ye too long. But be back by half-three, aye? There's only the one ferry back."

They set out along the curving road, and within minutes were breathing heavily. The road rose and dipped, and though they could see the castle in the distance, it never seemed to get any closer. Occasionally a car passed them, but for the most part, they were alone, except for the sheep that glanced up curiously and then returned to their grazing.

"We have to have gone at least three miles already," Brian grumbled. "I don't think we're ever going to get there."

"And we have to walk back, remember?" Sophie said. "The same hills, same sheep. Are you sure you want to do this?"

He grimaced. "Absolutely. There's no way I'm turning back now. We'll make it somehow, if it kills us."

He took her hand. A tingle ran up her arm and Sophie froze for a second, but nothing disastrous happened so she allowed him to tow her along. He was holding her hand, and no one had run away yet. Maybe it would be all right.

And they did eventually reach the castle. There were only a few vehicles in the small car park, and small clusters of tourists wandered about the grounds. From up close, Duart Castle was impressive. Massive sandstone walls reached into the sky as if grasping for the clouds that hovered just out of reach. On the side nearest the road, modern scaffolding crawled up the side of the building, giving the impression that the castle was straddling time, balancing between past and present.

Brian sighed. "Let's get this over with." He grabbed her hand again and pulled her toward a small gatehouse in front of the building's arched stone entrance.

The gatekeeper was a white-haired old man who looked as if he might have been constructed with the castle. He gave them a cheerful smile from a mouth that was missing quite a few teeth.

"The tour is self-guided," he said, handing them a pamphlet. "Map's inside, and there're guides who'll answer your questions. Fancy a photo with a real member o' Clan Maclean?"

Without waiting for an answer, he came out of the tiny booth. Close up, he was resplendent in a white shirt, wool vest, and well-worn Maclean tartan that came to his knobby knees and put his skinny bowed legs on display. He called to another staff member who stood at the entrance to the keep itself, and waddled over to place himself between Brian and Sophie, with a bony arm slung over her shoulder.

Sophie fished out her mobile and handed it to the staff member, who snapped several shots of the three.

He handed it back and whispered loudly, "Ye'd better come with me, or auld Simon here'll keep ye prisoner and ye'll never see the inside of the castle!" He winked at them and then at his colleague, who pretended to be affronted before backing away and returning to his gatehouse.

"I'm Nathan," said the staff member. "I'll leave ye to tour on yer own, but I'm here if you have questions."

Sophie nodded and started through the archway toward a manicured lawn surrounded on three sides by castle walls, with the entrance at their backs. She turned at a sharp intake of breath to see Brian transfixed in the doorway, green eyes wide and face drained of color.

"What is it?" she asked softly.

For a long moment, it seemed as if he hadn't heard her. Then he blinked. "It's the yard," he whispered. "Where I woke up the first time. It's not exactly the same—there was no grass, just dirt. Jeremy showed me pictures, but they weren't clear. But it's the yard, Sophie! There were men with swords all over the place, whacking away at each other."

Brian's voice had risen and he sounded on the edge of panic. He looked around and saw that they were alone in the yard. "Come here," he said, and walked to a spot near the edge of the square, about ten yards from a side door into the castle. He sat on the grass and leaned back to gaze up at the sky.

"I was right here," he said, under his breath. "Just for a few minutes, but I was here, and that girl was holding me. You know, the one who looks like you. Kenna."

Sophie stared at him with concern. He'd told her about her doppelgänger, a young girl he'd seen in his odd dream before he'd even met her, but she hadn't believed him. Because it was impossible. It had to be some sort of déjà vu, a trick of the brain probably caused by his head injury.

But now, looking down at his unguarded, honest face, so anxious—no, so *frightened*—she allowed a sliver of doubt to crawl into her mind. If it was an aberration caused by his concussion, it had probably been a terrible idea to come here. But if it wasn't . . .

"Brian, I believe you," she heard herself saying, and she sank down beside him on the grass and put her arms around his shaking body. "I believe you." And she realized with a shock that she really did believe him. Something had happened to this man—something real. His eyes searched her face and cleared slowly.

"Are ye okay?" Nathan's concerned voice intruded on her racing thoughts. "Is the lad sick?"

Sophie stood up and pulled Brian up with her. "No, he's all right. He just had a bit of seasickness on the ferry, and I guess he's still feeling a little queasy. He'll be fine." She smiled at the man and pulled Brian toward the entrance to the keep itself. *And when did I become such an accomplished liar?* she wondered.

They followed the route outlined in the pamphlet without talking. Brian studied everything but said nothing until they arrived at the bottom of a spiral stone staircase. Then he clutched at her elbow.

"I remember this," he said. "Kenna took me on a tour of the castle, and we went up and down these steps. *These* steps!" he repeated. "She said the stairs were built to turn clockwise, so that the clansmen wouldn't be hampered if they had to defend against an enemy because they could hold their swords in their right hands." He turned to look into Sophie's eyes, as if searching for something. Understanding? Belief?

"Did you see a picture of Duart's stairs online?" she asked, trying to keep her voice calm. "Or did Jeremy show you one from a book?"

Brian's shoulders slumped. "Yes," he said. Then he clutched her arm. "But when Jeremy showed me the image, I recognized them. I'd never seen these stairs before, but when I saw the photo, I knew them."

Sophie realized he was shaking, and she put a hand on his arm to steady him. "Are you all right?" she asked softly.

He looked at her, and his eyes came into focus. "Yes . . .no . . ." His face was drawn. "I need air." She nodded and led the way back outside.

"Should we check out the gift shop?" Sophie asked, pointing to a small building across from the castle entrance.

"No, let's go look at the sound," Brian said suddenly. He grabbed her hand and took off almost on a run, pulling Sophie behind him and putting distance between them and the castle.

I feel as if I'm in Through the Looking Glass, *being pulled along by the White Queen,* she thought. *Alice would understand.* None of this made sense, but for his sake, she wanted to believe.

They walked along the rocky shoreline and watched the spray hit the huge boulders and recede into foaming pools before it rejoined the black waters of the sound.

Brian stopped so suddenly that Sophie nearly ran into his back. His hand tightened on hers with such force that his nails bit into her flesh.

"Look." His voice was raspy and thick, as if he was fighting a cold.

Sophie followed his stare. There, right in front of them, figures had been etched onto the rocks. The outlines were primitive and almost lost to the ravages of time and weather, but there was no doubt what she was seeing. A lighthouse and a sailboat, three stick figures in tee shirts and shorts.

She glanced at Brian to see his face washed of color, his eyes nearly bulging.

"Some tourist, probably a kid," she said, but he was already shaking his head.

"No." The words were soft but sure. "Look at the sailboat." He pointed to a series of letters barely visible along the side of the small carving.

Sophie knelt to study the letters. "M-l.-e-n, another n, I think," she read.

"U-m-D-p-h-n." Brian's voice came from behind her, "*Millenium Dolphin*." As if he were a marionette whose strings had been cut, his legs folded and he collapsed into a sitting position on the grass. "That's the name of our sailboat, back home in Baddeck."

CHAPTER 31

MULL, SCOTLAND, 1649

FRANCES

I hate 't here.

Frances sat with the other women in the solar and tried to keep her inner thoughts from showing on her face. She forced stiff lips into a fixed smile and widened her eyes in pretended fascination, as if their prattle about fashion and tea and children was the most engrossing thing she'd ever heard.

The light conversation was covering a deep fear. Things were not right in the house of Maclean. Sir Lachlan, the laird and chief of the clan, was ill, and the castle's residents went about their days under a cloud of uncertainty and worry. Except for her. She simply didn't care.

Normally the talk would have been all about the war—these eejit women loved to prattle on about it—but apparently that subject was taboo now for this family of Royalists. Their ruler, Charles I, had been executed in January, accused of treason by his own parliament. His son, Charles II, held a precarious grip on the throne for the moment, but he might be toppled at any time. No one knew what that Oliver Cromwell would do next.

Well, Cromwell could come marching out to the tip of the peninsula in person and take over the castle, for all Frances cared. The Macleans were fools to keep backing the king, and if she had cared a whit about what was going on in the world, she would have told them so. But she paid little heed to those things. None of it concerned *her*, so it was meaningless.

She looked around desperately. If something interesting didn't happen soon, she was sure she'd go mad. These damned Macleans were heathens and louts, and their women simpering, domesticated cows. She hated them all. Their children were just smaller, noisier versions of them.

Including her own. Annie was a year old now, a wee charmer who had all the brothers wrapped around her tiny finger. All except her own father— and Frances knew why. A sly grin crossed her face.

Annie's eyes were blue, and her hair, though black like her mother's, sprung up in wild curls all over her small head, and bounced when she toddled across the room. Bright blue eyes, black curly hair. Just like Giles.

She knew what Dànaidh was thinking. He had idolized his small daughter when she was born, carried her around everywhere like a tiny trophy. He had smiled more, laughed more. The baby had smoothed his rough edges.

But then her hair grew and became springy ringlets, when neither of her parents had curly hair. Her eyes stayed a brilliant blue. And Dànaidh had begun sending dark looks between his daughter and his older brother Giles, who had springy black curls and bright blue eyes. His distrust surged up out of that black place inside him, and the old, suspicious Dànaidh returned.

Frances had enjoyed laying kindling on that fire, for a while anyway. She could have told her husband that her mother and two of her sisters had curly hair and blue eyes, but it was too much fun to watch the brothers' animosity deepen, to imagine they were fighting for her honour.

Her smile morphed into a tight frown. *If only t'were true.* But Giles had resisted every attempt she made to get close. It was only in Dànaidh's head, placed there by Frances' clever tongue, that there was anything between them.

Dàinny's a fool. An' Giles d'serves it for rejectin' me.

The frown deepened. Perhaps it was not such a good idea to play with the brothers' emotions, after all. Giles avoided her now as if she carried the Black Death—the coward. He scurried away like a wee rat when she invaded his damn library, making it impossible for her to talk to him alone.

And he had comrades in his little game—that beastly Crìsdean and his beloved brat, Kenna. They watched her and warned Giles when she approached. She was sure of it. She imagined strangling the wee witch in her sleep, but it was small comfort.

Giles would have come to her in time; she was sure of it. Frances had never met a man who could resist her when she wanted him. She would have worn down his resistance eventually.

But then Dànaidh had hired that nanny. *An' 'tis my own fault.*

She was probably the only one in the castle who hadn't succumbed to her daughter's charms. Truth was, she hated the squirming, squalling, smelly thing. She told Dànaidh that Annie was too much work for her and she was afraid she might fall ill. At first she'd liked his choice—a simple, plain young woman from the Western Isles. The woman doted on Annie, and after a few failed attempts at conversation, she had left Frances alone.

Lili MacPherson loved to read, and she thought her young charge should be read to as much as possible. Which meant she spent all her free time in the library.

Frances wasn't concerned at first. Lili was short and stumpy and plain. With drab brown hair and huge brown eyes, she looked like nothing more than a small fat mouse. Invisible, irrelevant. Easily gobbled up if she became a nuisance.

Frances wrinkled her nose. The woman was always a mess too. Her gowns were dull and coarse and usually covered with sticky fingerprints or baby goo of some kind. No man would choose someone like that over her.

No man except Giles, who apparently had blinders on when it came to beauty. He and Lili had struck up an immediate friendship, discussing politics and history and whatever the hell else they found between the covers of those damn books.

Frances had seen them walking, laughing, talking, and gesticulating wildly along the parapet or near the rocks at the shoreline, and thought she might lose her mind over their single-minded enjoyment of each other's company.

Dànaidh had seen their burgeoning friendship too, and he looked happier than he had in months. He stopped drinking so much and was kinder to his small daughter. He sought his wife out frequently and grew more amorous as the weeks went on. As a result, Frances had missed her courses, her breasts were tender, and she had difficulty keeping down her breakfast. She was almost certainly with child again, and she wanted to cry for the unfairness of it all.

Another mouth, mewling and crying and sucking the life out of her. *I'm twenty-seven years, 'tis too auld t' be havin' a bairn.* Her brows knitted and her hands clenched so tightly her knuckles turned white. How did women like Anna do it?

If *she* had seven children, she would have drowned some of them in the loch. Unless they were Giles'. Frances allowed herself to float on that idea for a few minutes and then rejected it. No. She wasn't made to be a mother, not even for him.

If only Dànaidh were gone. The thought hovered, dark and sinuous and exhilarating. She would be a widow and everyone would pity her for her loss. Giles would no longer need to avoid her for honour's sake, and he would be free to stop pretending and come to her.

Every time the men went out to battle, she prayed that her husband would catch a musket ball in the heart, or take a sword between his ribs. But her prayers fell on deaf ears. It seemed God had no interest in helping her.

Why had she ever agreed to come here? She knew the answer of course, but it didn't help; she'd had no choice. The wedding of Frances Cameron to Dànaidh Maclean was just an excuse to get rid of an embarrassing problem.

Her brother's best friend had been handsome, rich, and ardent when in his cups. He was also betrothed, which meant little to Frances, but quite a lot to her family. When the two of them were discovered in the stables, covered with hay, the incident was hushed up, the young man bundled back to his family, and she was sold off to the nearest neighbour, a Maclean of Duart.

Dànaidh had been besotted with his new bride, and for a while, she thought he would do as well as any. He was handsome enough, with his tousled brown hair and pretty hazel eyes, and like all the Maclean brothers, he was magical with a sword in his hand. But still Frances felt something was missing, and she realized what it was when she first saw Giles.

Every man she had seen or conquered in her past paled in comparison to Dànaidh's older brother. His black curls fell carelessly onto his forehead, and his brilliant blue eyes pierced her soul. She knew why she had been sent here—it was not a punishment; it was God's plan for her.

The idea that God might not find it amusing for one of his children to wed one brother and seduce another did occur once or twice to Frances, but she brushed it off. Giles was the one for her, and all she had to do was make him understand. Fate would take care of the rest.

She hadn't counted on Lili MacPherson, though. Just the thought of that small fat mouse in Giles' company was torment beyond belief. Something black and metallic rose in her throat.

I willnae let this go on. The thought put down tiny roots in her mind. She recognised it, embraced it, and set herself to letting it grow until she was ready. *I'm goin' t' take care o' th' problems, one at a time.* She looked across the room to where Anna was laughing with the other wives over some trivial nonsense.

Ye have seven sons, ye auld witch. Ye shouldnae miss one, aye?

But first, the mouse.

There was a knock on the door, and Kenna entered. Her already pale face was white as table linen, and her hair had come loose from its snood.

Nuthin' new there, Frances thought. But then she saw the tears streaking the girl's pale face, the huge blue eyes watery from grief, and she knew before Kenna spoke.

"He's dead," Kenna said, forcing the words out on a sob. "Sir Lachlan died. Hector's th' chief noo."

CHAPTER 32
MULL, SCOTLAND, 1649

CRÌSDEAN

Crìsdean gave his cousin a worried look. "'Tis been a hellish year, aye?"

Hector Maclean said nothing. His deep-set brown eyes were hooded, and new lines seemed to have appeared overnight on his face, making him look far older than his nine-and-twenty years. He sat with his arms balanced on his thighs, hands dangling between his knees, and nodded.

So much responsibility, Crìsdean thought. *Where'll we go from here?*

The world was falling apart. King Charles was dead, and while the Macleans of Duart were still reeling from the ramifications of a ruler's execution by his own parliament, Sir Lachlan had arrived home burning with a fever, the same one that had carried off Crìsdean's own father just last month. He was gone in less than a week.

"All those battles, all 'at glory 'n sacrifice," Hector muttered darkly. "An' for what? T' be brought doon by a fever?" His voice was thick. "I dinnae thynk Ma'll survive this. She waited so long for 'im t' come home, only t' lose him. Damn this war!" The young chief gave a shuddering sigh. "Damn th' king an' 'is treasonous parliament! Damn Cromwell an' his lackeys. Damn 'em all t' hell!"

Crìsdean knew Hector was speaking from grief, but he had to admit that in some ways, it *was* the king's fault all this had happened. If he hadn't been so stubborn, so set in his ways, and unbending, he might not have run afoul of that pompous collection of old men down in London. They were unwilling to listen to their own king, but they hung on every word that fell from the mouth of that dangerous upstart, Oliver Cromwell, swallowing his self-serving lies like starving dogs.

"I dinnae thynk I can do this, Crìs." Hector choked and swiped away the tears that had gathered in his eyes.

"Ye can. Ye must." Crìsdean let the words hang in the air. He held his cousin's gaze, and after a long moment, Hector nodded slowly. He stood and began pacing the small room. Crìsdean watched, wanting to help the cousin he idolized but knowing there was little he could do or say.

Hector was clan chief now; they were no longer on the same level. It didn't matter if he wanted the position; it was his, and Crìsdean had meant it when he said he could do it. Hector had learned leadership at his father's knee, gone into battle beside him. He believed in Sir Lachlan's teachings, as they all did. The Macleans had always been Royalists, loyal to a man. *But loyal to what? To whom?* The bitter thought rose, unbidden and unwanted.

Hector stopped pacing and fixed the younger man with a gimlet eye. "I ken wha' yer thynkin', cousin," he said. "But dinnae fash. Charles II is our king noo. Clan Maclean 'll keep fightin' in his name, aye?"

Crìsdean nodded, but he couldn't speak over the lump in his throat. Fighting. Always fighting. Kings came and went, and the world went on fighting. Even though the Scottish parliament had recognized Charles' oldest son as the new king of the Three Kingdoms, the Covenanters of Scotland refused to acknowledge him unless he caved to their demands to establish Presbyterianism as the only true religion. From the news that filtered into the west shores of Scotland, negotiations weren't going well for the new king.

And then there was Cromwell, waiting for the chance to take down yet another king. One might think he wanted to abolish the monarchy completely, the treasonous snake!

Hector was watching him, his expression contrite. "I'm sorry; I'm puttin' all this on ye, an' forgettin' ye've lost yer own father. Dinnae mind my rantin'; I feel I can talk t' ye afore anyone else." He clapped Crìsdean on the shoulder. "Let's talk o' happier things, aye?" He strode to the sideboard and poured two cups of amber liquid from a cask. "Shall we share an *Uisge Beatha* afore goin' on?"

He handed a cup to Crìsdean and winked. "Ye'll need it fer my next words. Wha's goin' on wi' ye an' yer wee lass? Aren't ye thynkin' o' gettin' marrit?"

Crìsdean blushed and took a gulp of his whisky.

Hector laughed. "Should we hae a weddin', then?" he asked. "It can be my first werk as chief, aye? Walkin' wee Kenna t' ye?" He paused. "My first werk after buryin' my father, 'at is."

Crìsdean took another drink. "Aye, I'd like 'at, but after th' mournin' is done, o' course. Mebbe next fall?"

"Done," the chief grinned at him. "Next fall 'tis, then. She'll be a bonny bride." He winked at his cousin. "Jist try t' have 'er wear a gown, aye?"

Crìsdean choked up a mouthful of whisky, and Hector laughed. "Didnae thynk I kent, did ye?" He pivoted and strode to the door, but turned at the last second. "I'd like t' say 'tis b'cause I'm the chief, lad, bit th' truth is, everbody kens." He laughed and was gone.

Weel, I'm happy ye can laugh, e'en if 'tis at me. Crìsdean stood alone in the room for a few minutes and then straightened his shoulders and went in search of his lass.

He found Kenna in the nursery, listening to Lili MacPherson telling a story to the children. That was no surprise—the nanny often had a gaggle of children gathered around her, and frequently a few adults as well. They loved listening as she told stories in her soft, melodic voice.

Crìsdean knew Kenna loved Lili for her kindness. He suspected she also appreciated the young woman because she was good for Giles. And sure enough, there was the man himself, sitting off to the side and grinning like a besotted sheep as Lili's voice gathered them all in. Crìsdean found himself smiling as well, watching his older brother in a rare moment of happiness.

Everyone in the castle knew there was something between the two. Giles was spending more and more time out of the library these days and was often seen strolling the grounds or deep in conversation with the nanny, whose plain face lit up and became almost beautiful when she was in his presence.

Despite the grief of their recent losses and the fear of the unknown that lurked outside, everyone inside the castle was happy to see the transformation. Crìsdean spied a familiar figure in the shadows, and his brow wrinkled. *All but one.*

Frances stood rigid against the wall, her fists clenched at her sides, and glared at the storyteller. These days her face habitually wore a pinched, angry expression that did nothing to enhance the beauty she was so proud of. Crìsdean didn't understand it. In his opinion, she looked like a witch with that black hair and those greedy black eyes.

"Some'un should tell 'er she doesnae look so pretty wi' that jealoos face," Kenna had told Crìsdean yesterday, after Frances swept by, pretending she didn't see them where they stood in the hall. "She allus looks like she ate somthin' sour. An' she better take care—does she thynk Dànaidh doesnae see 't?"

Crìsdean shoved Frances to the back of his mind and moved to seat himself on the floor next to Kenna, marveling anew at how beautiful she looked in her simple gown, with her long blonde hair caught up in a snood.

"She's tellin' th' one abit th' Ghillie Dhu," she whispered. "'Tis their fav'rit."

"Th' wee bairn's name was Annie," Lili was saying. She winked at the tiny lass on her lap. "Aaa-ie," the child parroted, showing her four teeth in a huge grin.

Lili laughed. "Aye, lassie. Annie kent she was lost, 'an she sat doon 'an began t' cry. 'Why are ye greetin' so?' said a voice, 'an the wean turned t' see a verra tiny man, dressit in moss 'an green leaves."

"'Twas th' Ghillie Dhu!" shouted a small lad in the front. Hector's three-year-old brother was bouncing up and down in excitement. "He'll save 'er!"

"Who's tellin' this story, Sir Allan?" Lili asked the child. "D' ye want t' hear th' rest, or no?"

"She sounds like Mam," Crìsdean whispered to Kenna. "She could nivver git out a whole story wi'out one o' us breakin' in. Nae me, o' course." He put a hand over his heart.

Kenna snorted. "O' course."

Crìsdean grinned and whispered, "Ready?" They made their way out into the hall and up to the top floor of the castle, where they stood on the parapet looking out at the sound.

"How's Hector?" Kenna asked.

"I'm worrit about 'im," Crìsdean admitted. "'E's puttin' on a braw face, but I ken he's greetin' inside."

Kenna's hand found his. "Ye ken what 'at's like, aye? Ye've jist lost yer own da."

Crìsdean looked down at the lass he loved more than the world. "Aye, but I have somethin' t' protect noo, 'an Da is watchin' t' make sure I do it right." He leaned down and placed a soft kiss on her forehead.

"Hector says we c'n get marrit in th' fall."

Kenna wrapped her arms around his waist and laid her head against his broad chest, where she could hear his steady heartbeat through the homespun shirt. A rumbling began deep in Crìsdean's stomach, and she pulled her head back and looked up at him suspiciously.

"Are ye laughing? Be there sommat amusin' about marryin' me?"

He ignored the dangerous tone in her voice and grinned at her.

"Well—um—he also said he'd consider it a favor if ye was t' wear a gown fer yer weddin'."

Kenna glared into his laughing green eyes. "Why would he say sich a thing?" Her eyes grew wide. She put her hands on her hips and glared at him. "I havenae worn trews under my gowns 'n this year gone!" She paused. "Well, only a wee few times." She rounded on him again. "Did ye tell 'im? I'll kill ye!"

Crìsdean put both hands up in a gesture of self-defense. "Nay! I never! I dinnae fancy dyin' in my sleep." He danced back and out of her reach. "He says everbody kens."

He bounded away and around the corner, his laughter trailing behind.

CHAPTER 33
INVERNESS, SCOTLAND, PRESENT DAY

One of the deepest impulses in man
is the impulse to record, to scratch a
drawing on a tusk, or keep a diary . . .
—John Jay Chapman

The noise of another band tuning up filled the vast park area, competing with the shouts and laughter of hundreds of concertgoers who wandered the grounds behind St. Andrew's Cathedral. Mothers chased children sugared up by the strawberry shortcake and cookies provided by the food trucks that lined the area, and the rich odor of fried food emanated from at least two fish and chips wagons.

A line of adults snaked through the roped-off maze in front of a huge tent that offered whisky and beer. Groups of older men, some in well-worn kilts, talked politics while waving cans of beer to emphasize their points and cursing when necessary.

Brian looked around the wooden picnic table they'd been lucky enough to snag when an American family left to meet their tour bus. The Gathering, apparently a big deal in Inverness, had called out a great many foreign visitors intent on experiencing the Highlands music scene. The prime tourist season was over now, but September was still a lovely month and the city known as the capital of the Highlands was a year-round tourist destination.

Brian was having trouble paying attention. How could the Gathering compete with time travel—or whatever the hell was happening to him? He wondered what would happen if he announced suddenly, "I don't know if I'll be here next week. I might be in the seventeenth century." *That* would be a conversation stopper, for sure.

To be honest, it probably didn't much matter if he said anything anyway; Deirdre and Sam were doing a fine job carrying the conversation all by themselves.

"I'm really here for Tidelines and the Red Hot Chili Pipers," Deirdre was saying. "The Pipers are heading off to the States to tour after this, so we shouldn't miss the chance to hear them right here at home. And I really like Beinn Lee; they're coming on big. Oh—they're from Uist, I think—aren't you from the Western Isles, Sam?"

Sam Douglas smiled. "Aye, from Lewis. The Outer Hebrides have a lot of great bands these days; maybe I should have followed their lead and gone into pop music instead of classical." He shook his head and gestured to the stage, where another band was tuning up. "I might be headlining at the Gathering instead of playing piano in a pub."

"Well, I'm glad you're playing in a pub," Deirdre said. "I might not have met you otherwise."

Brian felt a hand clasp his under the table, and looked sideways into Sophie's clear blue eyes. He gave her a weak smile and was rewarded with another squeeze and a nod. Deirdre's words repeated themselves in his head. *I might not have met you* . . . Relief filtered through him—relief that he had met Sophie MacArthur, that she understood what he was feeling, and that she *believed*. He wasn't sure he'd be so trusting were she the one in his situation. She was a miracle.

Who else would believe, without asking questions, when a man told her those pictures on the rock had been made in 1646, and not by a modern-day tourist? He hardly believed it himself, but every time he closed his eyes, he saw the crude carving of a sailboat, and the letters he was sure spelled *Millenium Dolphin*. And yet he hadn't done those carvings. He was sure of it.

Brian had spent hours trying to recall the finer details of his trips to Duart Castle The first time had lasted only minutes, and all he'd seen was the yard. The second time had been longer, almost a day. Kenna had taken him around the castle, shown him the spiral stairs, and he'd met that nasty black-haired woman. *Frances*, Kenna had called her, right before she stomped on his foot and he woke up in Raighmore Hospital. No—he was sure they had gone nowhere near that rock.

The third time he hadn't been at Duart at all. Brian shuddered at the memory of those dead eyes that haunted his sleep. Thank God he'd missed most of the battle; it was nearly over when he found himself on the killing field. The march home had taken the better part of three days, while the clansman called Giles tried to take the edge off his incipient hysteria. If it hadn't been for Giles...

And Kenna. Those two had kept him alive and sane in the seventeenth century. They had known he was a stranger in their midst but still accepted and protected him. Just like Sophie was doing now. He looked at the woman beside him, clear blue eyes focused on him, and an idea emerged. He sat up straight and tightened his hand on Sophie's under the table. "Let's go!"

Without a second's hesitation, she stood up from the picnic table and announced, "We'll be right back—carry on." Ignoring the surprised faces on the other side of the table, she allowed Brian to pull her across the crowded field, through the exit, and out onto the street. When they reached Ness Walk, Brian kept going until he found a bench facing the river. He pulled her down beside him and gazed into her eyes.

"Kenna is your ancestor, Sophie. I'm sure of it. I think that's why I'm being pulled into the past."

She blinked at him. "Okay, but so what? You're being pulled into the past to meet my ancestor. Why?" She shook her head. "I don't get it, Brian. I'm sorry."

He sighed and leaned against the hard wooden back of the bench. "I don't know, but there has to be a connection. Every time I wake up in the 1600s, she's there, and I'm in the body of someone named Christian Maclean. I saw my reflection last time, and it wasn't me. He looked kind of like me, but it wasn't *me*!"

Sophie studied his face. "Then, do you think this Christian could be *your* ancestor?"

Brian closed his eyes and thought. "I don't know. Possibly . . . probably. He has the same hair, only longer and a bit wilder, and his eyes are green, like mine." He grabbed his own hair in both hands and yanked at it, as if doing so could pull the truth out of his memory. "He's younger though, maybe early twenties."

"Brian?" Sophie was staring at the river. "Where do you think he goes . . . the real Christian?" She turned back to him. "When you're in his body, where is he?"

Brian laughed, a rough, bark of sound that had no humour in it. "How the hell do I know?" he asked, but then his eyes sharpened and focused on her. "Wait! He's still there, inside his own body. When I'm there, it feels as if I'm all stuffed up, like I have a head cold. Like my brain is squished in a space too small for it."

"What?" Sophie's brows furrowed. "How is that possible? You said you're in his body, seeing and hearing everything. How can he be there too?"

"I don't know!" Brian's nostrils narrowed on a sharp intake of breath, and his answer was a frustrated growl. "How is it possible? How is it possible that a man can be transported out of his own body to a time almost four hundred years ago? If we believe that, how hard is it to believe that two souls can exist in the same body? Jeez, listen to me!" He looked at the people strolling down Ness Walk. "Anybody but you would think I was nuts!" He furrowed his brows and let out his breath slowly.

"I'm sorry," he said. "This is just so bizarre. I'm having trouble believing any of it myself, and I was there. Three times now.

"Let's take it one thing at a time," he said, in a calmer voice. He put up a hand and raised his index finger in the air. "I'm myself, or at least my head is, when I wake up in the past." He raised his middle finger to join the first. "This Christian guy is still there because he's the one who drew the images on that rock. It had to be him; I was never there by the water during any of my trips." Brian looked to Sophie for confirmation, and she nodded.

"Time moves differently then," he said slowly, putting up his ring finger. "I never really gave it much thought until last time, but I've traveled back three times in a couple of months, and yet *a year* has passed each time I go back. It must mean something, right?"

Sophie said nothing, and after a moment Brian continued. "There has to be a reason. What does Christian think when I'm there? What does Kenna think? She *knew* it wasn't him with her. Does she ask him later when I've gone? Wait!"

Sophie sat still and waited. *She is so very good at waiting,* Brian thought. He couldn't imagine what she was thinking about all this, but she hadn't run away. That had to be good, right?

"Wait," he said again, more softly. "This happens frequently to me, but to Christian and Kenna, months—even years—pass between my visits. Surely they must believe each time is the last. And Giles knows now. Do others? Does that Frances person know?"

"Frances?" Sophie asked. "That nasty woman you met at the castle?"

"Yeah. She seemed to be in a snit about something." A sour smile twisted his lips. "I think she must've had a thing for Giles because Frances came down from the library in a huff and Kenna said, 'Good for you, Giles,' or something. Like she was proud of him. And Frances was really pissed off."

Frances. There was something about her that kept tickling at his brain. Black hair, eyes so dark they were almost black, pale skin. She had delicate features, probably quite attractive when they weren't twisted in anger. Not his type, but he could see where some men would find her beautiful.

There was something familiar about her, though he'd only seen her the one time. Was she part of the reason for his trips to the past?

"I think I need to see Jeremy again," he said. "Will you come with me?"

"Of course."

As if he had willed it, Brian's cell phone trilled. He pulled it out of his pocket to see Jeremy Brown's number displayed on the screen. He held it up for Sophie to see, and then answered.

"Brian, I think I've found something," Brown's voice said. The excitement in his tone reverberated through the phone. Brian put the phone on speaker and placed it on the bench between Sophie and himself. "Go on," he said. "You're on speaker; my friend Sophie is with me."

"Okay. Remember how I said that only the important members of a clan tend to be recorded in its histories? Unless something momentous happens to them, the others are forgotten. Well, I found one of those happenings."

"Yes?" Brian sucked in his breath and waited.

"Anyway," Brown said, "this was one of the more interesting bits in Maclean lore; don't know how I missed it. Well, in my defense, you were looking for names, and there wasn't much to go on there. Wasn't important in the grand scheme of things happening in Scotland, but to Clan Maclean it's the stuff of legend."

Brian sighed. Would the man ever get to the point? He looked over at Sophie, who was grinning. *Academic*, she mouthed.

"So," Jeremy went on, "in 1651, there was a battle—a rather famous one. The monarchy had been abolished in 1649 with the execution of Charles I and Cromwell was firmly in control, but clans like the Macleans, Royalists to the bone, were still fighting. They recognized Charles' son as king and formed an army."

Brian could feel his impatience rising, and he tamped it down with difficulty. Sophie laid a hand on his arm and gave him an encouraging smile.

"Anyway," said Brown, "Cromwell didn't like that idea at all, so he invaded Scotland in 1650. The Scottish army was defeated once or twice, and by July of 1651, they were pushed back from Edinburgh to the edge of the Firth of Forth, where they regrouped near a small village called Inverkeithing. Are ye still with me, lad?"

"Yes," Brian said, between clenched teeth. Sophie giggled at his expression.

"This is all important," Brown said, "because a part of the Royalist force included the Macleans of Duart."

Brian perked up. "Yes?"

A delighted laugh came over the line. "Aye, the very ones. The clan chief was a young man named

Hector, who'd only been chief for a little over two years. He was only thirty-one. He and his clansmen were pursued for six miles before turning to engage the enemy. Almost all seven hundred of Duart's Highlanders were wiped out; only forty managed to make it back to Mull.

"So," Brian said. "Sad, but why is it important?"

"Because . . ." Jeremy Brown let the words draw out for a minute. "Because the bravery of Hector's clansmen was so exemplary that it's become part of clan history. Even had a song written about it."

"What did they do that was so brave?" Sophie cut in. Her eyes were round with excitement.

These Scots and their battles, Brian thought. *Dad is just like this.* For the first time, he felt a stirring of something in his own veins, where the blood of hundreds of Macleans had combined to produce a Canadian math teacher. He sat up straighter and waited, nerves tingling.

"They were outnumbered and had no chance. Hector was felled by a musket ball. Some of his men stood guard over their wounded leader, even knowing it was futile. Each one stepped up in turn and shouted, '*Fear eile airson Eachuinn!*,' which means 'Another for Hector!' in Scottish Gaelic, before being cut down by sword and musket. In the end, Hector also died, but the courage of those clansmen lives to this day. *Fear eile airson Eachuinn!* has been the clan battle cry ever since.

Brian was silent. Something was trying to make itself known, something he had heard in the past. A *name?*

"Did you find any of their names?" he asked.

"Sorry, lad. I told you, none of their names made it into the history books, except for Hector's. His four-year-old brother Alan became chief after him. There was no mention of the other clansmen, either. Only that there were seven, and they were Macleans from Duart."

Something fell into place. A woman, holding him in her arms in the great hall at Duart Castle, a worried voice murmuring a name. *Seven*, she had called him.

CHAPTER 34

INVERNESS, SCOTLAND, PRESENT DAY

*Remember. Just because you don't believe
in something doesn't mean it isn't real.*
—Katherine Howe

Sophie sipped her coffee and looked across the tea table at her best friend. It seemed ages since they'd found time to just hang out, talking about nothing. Deirdre did most of the talking, as usual, and Sophie took care of the listening. They fit together like puzzle pieces, content to be what they were meant to be in the relationship. Perfect.

Except that Deirdre's conversation seemed to be almost exclusively about one thing these days—Sam Douglas. According to Dee, the man was perfect. He was handsome, considerate, talented; he laughed at her jokes so he was obviously discerning, and above all he had eyes only for Deirdre.

Sophie *tried* to listen. She was a good listener, honed by years of having little to say. But Sophie's skill seemed to have gone on holiday lately, because while her friend listed Sam's marvelous qualities, she found her thoughts meandering all over the place . . . thoughts that inevitably came to rest on the image of another man.

Fortunately, Deirdre seldom checked, which left Sophie's mind free to wander. She had nothing to talk about anyway; there wasn't much she could say about Brian without getting into the realm of fantasy, an area totally alien to Dee.

People and things that never existed, she remembered her friend saying scornfully, not too long ago. She wondered what Deirdre would think about Brian's forays into the past, into the body of his ancestor. A small smile spread at the thought; no, better not to mention such things. She forced herself to tune in again to the one-sided conversation.

"Do you know what he said just yesterday?" Deirdre was saying. "He said he's going to compose a piano piece just for me, and only we two will know what it means. Isn't he romantic?"

"Hmmm, aye," Sophie said.

"He said he loves my hair," Deirdre went on. She pulled at a red curl and let it spring back. "*This* hair! I've hated my hair and freckles all my life, but Sam says freckles are adorable."

"Well, I've always loved your curls and your freckles," Sophie said.

Deirdre waved her hand in dismissal. "You don't count," she said. "You love me no matter what I look like." She leaned forward conspiratorially, as if they weren't the only two in the room.

"Did you know I had a tiny crush on Brian for a second or two? Of course, I could see he was perfect for you; after all, he seems a little boring. I mean, a math teacher? What do you even talk about? Square roots and right angles?"

No, we talk about past lives and time travel . . . and other things. Sophie shared a delicious grin with her inner self, but she said nothing. Deirdre didn't notice—it was one of the brilliant things about her best friend—nothing was ever required.

Deirdre's mobile rang. Her face broke into a wide smile as she looked at the display. "It's Sam."

Well, duh, as Fiona would say. Sophie excused herself to go refill their coffee mugs, but Deirdre's voice stopped her before she got to the kitchen.

"Soph? Sam wants us to meet him at the Victorian Market."

Sophie turned. "I dunno, Dee. I'm pretty sure he means you, not both of us. You go ahead, I have some reading to do."

"Well, if you insist . . . but Brian's with him." Deirdre wore a smug look on her face.

"Oh. Well, okay, then. Let me just rinse the mugs." She placed the mugs in the sink and sneaked a look at herself in the hall mirror on her way back to the sitting room. She rummaged in her handbag for a lipstick and returned in what she thought was record time.

Deirdre's smirk was annoying. Sophie parked a pleasant smile on her face, determined not to rise to the bait. "Ready?"

"Sure. He said they'll be waiting outside the Academy Street entrance."

They walked to the Market Brae steps and crossed the High Street to where it met Inglis Street. Being a Saturday morning, tourists thronged the area in front of the train station on Academy, and taxis buzzed in and out like bees on their way to the hotels and guesthouses along the river.

Sam waved as they approached the Victorian Market. Brian looked up from his mobile and the smile that crossed his face had Sophie's knees turning to jelly. An answering smile parted her lips and worked its way up to her eyes, and she let it stay. Never had she known that another human being could curl her toes like this, never had she thought any man could take front and center in her life. *But there ye go,* she thought; *life is funny.*

And never had she been so grateful to have a talkative friend. They sat down at the coffee shop in the back of the market with their lattes and the bakery's signature chocolate chip cookies and let Deirdre carry the conversation. Brian reached over and took her hand in his, and for the first time in her life, chocolate chips took a back seat in her heart.

She wished they were alone. They had so much to talk about, so many things to work out, but extra ears prohibited any conversation on the topic foremost in their minds. So they contented themselves with banal talk about the music festival and sailing and how hard it was to cook carrots just long enough so they weren't mushy.

"Sorry, I have to go," said Sam.

Sophie's head jerked to where he sat across the table. She'd forgotten he was there. She hadn't really paid much attention to Sam Douglas the first time they'd met. Now her mother hen instincts kicked in and she gave him a covert once-over.

He was slender, with long, supple musician's fingers. His light brown hair fell carelessly over his forehead, and his hazel eyes crinkled as he smiled at Deirdre's disappointed face. *He does have nice eyes,* Sophie thought. *And Deirdre's an adult; she doesn't need me to worry about her love life.*

Still, Deirdre was spending all her free time with him. She crossed her fingers under the table. *I hope he's the one. I'll kill him if he hurts Dee.*

Sam stood. "I have to go in early today, remember?" he reminded Deirdre. "It's Saturday. Want to walk me to Simon's?"

Deirdre's frown disappeared like magic. She grabbed her coat and shrugged into it, took the hand Sam was holding out, and blew Sophie a kiss. The two left, Sam leaning in and laughing as Deidre talked.

"They seem pretty close," Sophie muttered under her breath.

"Huh?" Brian looked up. "Oh, yeah. Good."

"You think? I guess so. It's just that I've never seen Dee fall for a lad this hard."

"Is that a bad thing?" Brian shrugged. "Sam seems really into her."

"Aye, he does." Sophie watched as the two disappeared onto Academy Street. "I just worry about her, the way she gets excited about a lad, then she's so depressed when it doesn't work out." Sophie sighed. "And I get to be the shoulder she cries on."

Brian shook his head. "Well, I hope it works out with Sam because you're going to be too busy to lend your shoulder if it doesn't." He stood and pulled her up beside him. "Where d' ye want t' go, lassie?" he said, in his best brogue. "Th' day is sae braw, aye?"

"Stop that," Sophie said, wincing and shaking her head. "You'll never pass for a Scot."

"Weel, Ah'm that insulted," Brian said. "I'll have ye know I'm from *Nova Scotia*. That means 'New Scotland,' in case you dinnae ken yer Latin."

"I ken it fine, and I'll bet nobody talks like that in New Scotland, either."

"Well," he said, going into what Sophie could only assume was teacher mode, "did you know that there are parts of Cape Breton Island where Gaelic is the first language?"

"No, I didn't know that. And do you speak the auld tongue, sir?"

"I do not. But Fiona does, and our Dad. I told you my father was the dean of the Gaelic College, right? Fee used to teach there."

"That I did know," Sophie nodded. "Now she teaches online Gaelic courses for the university. She's become a real Scot."

There was no answer, and when Sophie stole a sideways look, she saw that a cloud had passed over his face.

"What's wrong?" she asked.

He didn't answer for a moment, and then he sighed. "You're right, I'm not a Scot."

Sophie picked up an odd tone in his voice, but she said nothing. It was his battle; there was nothing she could do. She knew him well enough now to understand that this had little to do with time travel; his pride was involved. He was essentially a man without a country—no job, no prospects, and an uncertain future. He couldn't face going back, and he couldn't stay in Scotland forever as a visitor.

A dull ache lodged in the region of her heart. *Couldn't stay in Scotland.* In a few short weeks, he had become more than Fiona's brother; he'd become . . . necessary. When did it happen? And more importantly, what was she going to do about it?

"Walk me home."

"What?" he said, sounding surprised and a little hurt.

She turned on the pavement and looked deep into his eyes. "Trust me. I'll tell you later." She grinned at him. "Dinnae fash, laddie."

Forty-five minutes later, Sophie was sitting at a round table in the corner of The Dancing Unicorn, across from Wee Caomhainn, Mary and Henry Duncan, and Betty MacBain. The pub wouldn't open for another hour, so they had the place to themselves.

"So, lass," Mary said, "out with it."

"Brian needs a job."

Not a single eyebrow lifted, no emotion at all showed on the faces around the table. It was as if they had known all along, as if they had been waiting. She marveled again at these people who had appeared in her life with their strange little pub, as if out of nowhere.

Then Betty said, "Murray's due for some time off."

The others nodded. "That'd work."

Mary smiled at Sophie. "Can your lad be ready next week?"

"Um, I don't know. I haven't talked to him about it." She felt a shiver of fear slide through her. *What the hell am I thinking, getting into someone else's business like this? What if he doesn't want to stay? What if this is all in my head?*

"It isn't, lass." Caomhainn's deep voice boomed across the table.

Sophie blinked. How the hell did he know what she was thinking? And yet, Caomhainn's words were like a brolly on a dreich day, keeping the rain and the wet from touching her. These people were safe; she'd always known it. She wondered when she had begun to take it for granted. After all, it was why she'd come to them. So now all she could do was trust that the Players would come through for her—and for Brian.

A thought struck her. "What's the job?" It seemed like a reasonable question, but the faces at the table registered surprise that she had bothered to ask.

"Secondary maths teacher, of course." Mary shook her head as if Sophie were slightly addled. "At Highlands Academy."

Henry spoke for the first time. "Tell your lad to present himself on Monday next. Murray will sort him out. He'll need a visa, of course, but Caomhainn can take care of that."

Sophie put her hands up to brace her head, in case it should take off on its own. Something soft landed in her lap, and she looked down to see Biscuit curled up like a small cushion. The cat's tail brushed across her face, and then the animal jumped down and padded across the floor toward the bar.

"Your Brian," said Henry, "is necessary."

She heard the echo of her own thoughts. Not pleasant, not a good lad, but *necessary*. Sophie opened her mouth to ask what Henry meant and then closed it again. It didn't need to mean anything. She was the one who had asked for their help, after all. They were odd, to be sure, but there were a lot of strange people in the world. The Highlands probably had more than its share of mysterious folk.

They had saved her life. The words sounded dramatic and silly in her memory's ear, but she had no doubt it was true. Someone had been following her that night. She'd seen The Dancing Unicorn shining like a beacon in the darkness, and since that night she had felt safe.

How much magic was at work in this small pub? Was it all planned somehow? The poor lad who couldn't master his fiddle, the barman who seemed to know things before she said them, the cat who didn't act entirely like a cat.

Was Brian a part of it? Was there a reason Fiona and Ewan had brought him to this pub that night? She sat up straight and her eyes widened. Were Brian's bouts of unconsciousness, his adventures in the past, tied into this?

She stared at the Highland Players. Four sets of eyes gazed impassively back at her. She was pretty sure that, were she to look toward the bar, a fifth pair would be staring from a furry face.

CHAPTER 35

INVERNESS, SCOTLAND, PRESENT DAY

*Only once in your life, I truly believe,
you find someone who can completely
turn your world around.*
—Bob Marley

"They said *what*?" Brian gaped at Sophie. "What did you tell them? How could you do that without discussing it with me?" He ran both hands through his hair until it stood on end. His green eyes shot sparks and his nostrils flared. "I don't *believe* this!"

Sophie sat across from him, eyes on the floor, shoulders hunched, and hands fisted in her lap. Brian felt a moment's contrition, and then he remembered what she'd done. His glare deepened. Outrage, fueled by desperation and fear, surged through him.

She'd taken it upon herself to find him a job, and not just any job—*teaching. Math. High School.* Never mind that he had no idea what was taught in a UK high school, how to grade it, or even what the graduation requirements were. Never mind that not long ago, it would have been a dream come true.

He knew he was making excuses for his anger. He had confidence in his teaching abilities; he could pick up any curriculum and make it his own. The problem had nothing to do with math—or maths, as they called it here.

I don't know if I can do it, he had told his sister. *Walk into a high school classroom and stand in front of teenagers. Teenage girls.*

Why had she done it—overstepped like this? He hardly knew Sophie MacArthur, really. Sure, they'd gotten close, very close, really, in the last few weeks. He'd trusted her, shared his innermost fears with her, told her things he'd never dared do with another human being, not even Fiona. And she'd taken that information and run with it to a bunch of strangers at that damn pub of hers. How *dare* she? He felt violated, his mind laid open to anyone who wanted to see his shame and fear. His cowardice.

Brian's thoughts caromed off each other and rebounded from the inside of his skull. She'd done the unthinkable, invaded his privacy and trampled over the place where his deepest heartache lay. It was a betrayal of the worst kind—couldn't she see that?

Realizing that there was no sound in the room, he looked at Sophie again, and his heart lurched at the hurt on her face. A single tear was making its way down her cheek, and her lips were sealed tight but still trembling.

The tear did it. His face flamed and shame washed through him, carrying the anger away with it. What the hell was wrong with him? She cared about him; she thought she was helping. This was the second time he'd reacted violently to something she'd done. She was probably waiting for him to run out of the house again, like a petulant child.

He wasn't this kind of man! It wasn't his personality to jump to conclusions, to react with anger to a situation. He was calm, even-tempered; everyone told him that. Laid back to the point of disinterest. *Oblivious,* his sister's voice echoed. He didn't like this new version of himself at all. What the hell was he doing?

You're caring about something for once, his inner voice said with derision. *You care about this woman. So go fix it, jackass, before you lose everything.*

The truth hit him like a slap in the face. He cared about her. No, it was more than that. Unless he was very much mistaken, he loved her. He was in love with Sophie MacArthur. Everything was new and raw and untested, and his emotions were racing around like marbles in an arcade game. He was a certified idiot.

He crossed to her chair and dropped to his knees in front of her.

"I'm sorry, Sophie." He took her hands in his. "I'm a fool. I know you meant well." He looked into her blue eyes, brimming with unshed tears, and suddenly everything burst free from its constraints, and he was babbling like a child.

"I don't know what's wrong with me, why I'm acting like this. I think some of it is the time jumps, but that's not an excuse. I can't control my emotions anymore, especially with you. *Only* with you. Because everything about you is the most important thing in the world to me. I don't know if I'm coming or going anymore because it's all so raw." He held her gaze, and the words tumbled out on a sob. "I think I love you. No, I know I do. I love you, Sophie MacArthur, and I'm so, so sorry."

He put his head down on her lap, unable to witness the result of his confession. His breathing was ragged and his breath came in small gasps, as if he'd run a marathon. His thoughts swirled, fueled by regret and remorse and bitter apology. He hadn't given in to tears once before this—not when he was unfairly accused by Meghan Reynolds, not when his principal looked at him as if he were a criminal, not when he'd summarily quit his job. But now he let go for the first time, let the tears come, careless of the fact that he was soaking her jeans. He couldn't have stopped if he tried. The catharsis of unfettered grief carried him away, and he let himself go.

He felt a hand on his hair and realized she was patting him on his head. Then she put her head down against his, and the relief threatened to send him off again. He took a long, shuddering breath and held still.

"It's okay, Brian. It's okay," she murmured into his hair. "I was just so scared, and it made me realize that I . . . I feel the same way. So I think I have to accept your apology, aye?"

Brian lifted his head and dared to look again at her face. Her eyes were wet with tears, but she was smiling. He let his breath out slowly and pulled her down to him again, covering her mouth with his in a kiss that was tentative at first, and then filled with a rising need that eclipsed anything he'd ever felt before. Her lips were soft against his, finding their place and claiming him with a ferocity that was as surprising as it was thrilling.

He could hear his own heartbeat, feel the blood pounding in his temples, taste the tears on her face, and it all felt so good. He wanted this to go on forever.

But it couldn't, of course. There were still things to be said, and this was the most frightening knowledge of all. Now that he had accepted the feelings he'd been denying, he couldn't afford to make any mistakes.

"I'm sorry too," she said. "I never do that."

Disappointment coursed through him. She was sorry? He didn't want her to be sorry, dammit.

His voice was thick. "Sorry?"

"I shouldn't have overstepped like that. I should have talked to you first. It's not like me at all, but . . ."

Brian was floundering in confusion. She should have talked to him? About what? Kissing wasn't something you discussed beforehand!

"It was just that I didn't want you to leave," she was saying. "I knew you couldn't stay in Scotland forever as a visitor, and . . . I didn't want to say good-bye to you. I guess I panicked."

The relief that enveloped him was overwhelming. She wasn't talking about the kiss! He struggled to get his mind back on the rails. It seemed hours ago that she'd told him about the Players and he'd gone off like a lit rocket. It was all so meaningless now, in the scheme of things; he couldn't fathom why he'd been so angry.

Reluctantly, he pulled himself to his feet, crossed back to the couch, and sat down. He patted the seat beside him. "Okay, tell me again what those lunatics at the pub did."

"They got you a job at Highlands Academy."

"Hmm. And is it public or private?"

"I don't know. I never heard of it before." Sophie's brows furrowed. "That's strange too. I've lived here all my life. There's Inverness High, behind the cathedral. There are a couple of schools for special needs students, and the Royal Academy, over on Culdathel. I went to the Academy; all the MacArthurs did. My father was on the board. But I don't remember a Highlands school, except for the university. Odd."

"Everything about your Highland Players is odd, Sophie," Brian said. "I'm supposed to just show up on Monday? Did they say where it is?"

"Nope. They said you can google it. You're replacing a teacher named—umm—Murray."

"Why?"

"What?"

"I mean, why am I replacing him? Where's he going?"

"I don't know. Henry said he's one of them, whatever that means. They don't say more than they have to, and everything always seems loaded with a deeper meaning. They just said the lesson plans for the first week would be there for you." Sophie gazed earnestly into his eyes. "So, you're okay with this?" Her voice sank to a whisper. "You're staying?"

Brian looked away, over her shoulder, and then back at her. "I guess . . . hell, yeah. I'm staying. But don't I have to get a visa?

"Oh, Henry said something about that too. He said Caomhainn would take care of it."

Brian gave her a puzzled stare. "What would a bartender know about visas?" Then he put up a hand. "Sorry, forgot. More weird stuff."

Sophie giggled. "I wouldn't have been surprised if they said Biscuit would take care of it." Then she sobered. "I never told you what happened that night you—er—"

He smiled in self-derision. "The night I ran out of the house like a mad bull?" He shook his head. "No, I was too busy hanging out on a battlefield with the Maclean brothers right then." A shudder ripped through his body, and he looked at Sophie seriously. "And do *not* ask me anything about that. I can barely face the memory myself."

She nodded. "I won't. But that's not what I was talking about. When you . . . left the house, I ran after you, but I thought you were gone. That's why I almost tripped over you. It was foggy and pretty dark, and you were just lying there on the pavement, not moving." Her eyes darkened.

"You told me that," Brian reminded her. "I'd be just as happy if we both forgot, to be honest."

"What I didn't tell you," she said, and it seemed to Brian that her attention was directed inward, as if she were searching for something. He decided to take a page from her book and practice waiting.

"I didn't know what was wrong with you, she said finally. "I checked you for injuries to your head." She brightened for a moment and a sly smile flitted over her lips. "You know, because that, um, seems to be where you like to get hurt." A small snort of laughter escaped her and she put a hand over her mouth. "I'm sorry, I couldn't help it."

"Let's move on, shall we?" Brian tried to keep his tone crisp, but he was enjoying how much fun Sophie seemed to be having. To see her face light up like that, even at his expense, was worth any amount of mortification.

"Oh, aye. Well, the fog was getting worse, and there was nobody on the street. I called for help in my head, and in the next minute, Biscuit appeared. I've never seen her leave the pub, but there she was—staring at me with those yellow eyes that look as if they're piercing right into your soul. I was so desperate, I told her to go for help."

"And?" Brian had become caught up in the story.

"And she did." Sophie sat back and gave him the full force of those amazing blue eyes.

"Come on now!"

She leaned forward, capturing his gaze and holding it. "She ran up the pavement . . . and Brian, Biscuit does *not* run. She saunters, at most." She paused and took a breath. "And a minute later, Caomhainn was there. I didn't think about it before, but how did he know?"

Brian thought for a moment. "Okay, that *is* weird. But honestly, the whole damn bunch of them is weird." He reached forward to gather Sophie into his arms and leaned back against the couch. "Didn't Scotland have a problem with witches back in the day?" He grinned into her hair. "Maybe that whole lot is part of a coven of witches. They travel around in a flying pub, and Biscuit is their familiar."

He could feel Sophie quivering with laughter. It felt good. "Go ahead, laugh. You won't be so amused when it turns out that your mysterious Highlands Academy is a training ground for witches. They'll force me to work for them and teach me spells. You'll see!"

Sophie put her head up and gave him a look of profound interest. "Really? Will you teach me how to ride your broom?"

CHAPTER 36

MULL, SCOTLAND, NOVEMBER, 1650

KENNA

She should have been getting ready for the wedding. *Her* wedding, hers and Crìsdean's. *I'm gettin' marrit t' Crìsdean Maclean,* she told herself over and over. *I'm t' be Kenna Maclean, wyfe t' th' best o' th' Maclean brothers.* She wrapped her arms around herself and tried to hold the joy inside.

Kenna was eighteen now, nearly an old maid. It seemed as if she and Crìsdean had been waiting forever for this day, but autumn had finally come, and with it the wedding Hector had promised. Royalists like Clan Maclean were waiting to see what would happen with the new king, but the young chief of Clan Maclean had refused to rejoin the war until his favourite cousins were wed.

The war took no notice of his opinion; the killing went on outside the castle walls as always. English battling Scots for power and political supremacy, Ireland struggling with England and Scotland over religion, the old men in Parliament fighting each other over the monarchy itself. But here, on this small outcropping in the Sound of Mull, the Macleans of Duart carried on with their lives as they always had.

They knew this time of peace would be short; as Royalists, they were at the behest of their king, another Charles. This one was fairing no better than his father, but at least he was still alive.

And, thought Kenna, *he can damn well wait.* She was marrying the love of her life, and nothing was going to stand in her way. A giggle escaped as she caught a sudden vision of Charles II, arrayed in all his royal glory, being chased out the front door of Duart Castle by a small lad brandishing a broomstick. And she would do it too.

"Whit're ye sniggerin' about, ye wee fool?" Giles strode into the room, close on the heels of Lili MacPherson. "Dinnae ye have work t' do t' git ready fer th' weddin'?"

"Leave 'er be, ye great ruffian!" Lili told him. She turned her attention to Kenna. "I've come t' help ye wi' th' plannin', an' I dinnae ken why this un is fol-lowin' me."

Kenna gave the girl a sardonic smile. "Ye dinnae ken? Hmm."

Lili blushed to the roots of her brown hair. She turned to Giles and pushed him toward the door, putting a frown on her face that fooled no one.

Laughing, he put his hands up in defeat and allowed himself to be ejected, his steps fading away down the hallway.

"If this keeps up, ye'll be gettin' marrit afore me," Kenna said, shaking her head. "D' ye come from a family o' witches? I've ne'er seen Giles so happy. What kind o' magick did ye work on 'im?"

Lili blushed again and laughed. "He is a pure delight, aye? But I'm no here t' talk about Giles—it's yer hansum Crìsdean 'at's th' king o' Duart these days. He's been struttin' about like a prize cock; I thynk he's grown e'en taller in th' last few days." She took both of Kenna's hands in her own. "Are ye that blissful, lass?"

"Aye," Kenna said, the words catching in her throat. "I am that blissful."

"Weel, then, afore I have t' see t' young Annie and wee Master Coll, let's check on yer gown an' make sure nuthin's missin'. Although I dinnae s'pose Crìsdean cares much what yer wearin'. He just wants ye th' way ye are." She wiped a hand across her brow and took a deep breath. "Jist let me sit doon fer a minute, an' I'll get busy."

Kenna pulled her head out of the clouds long enough to notice that there were new circles under Lili's eyes, and her normally ruddy complexion was pale. *That Frances,* she thought, *why cannae she ivver look t' her own bairns? Lili's fair exhausted.*

The girl's workload had more than doubled with the addition of Frances' second child. While wee Annie had always been a sweet, obedient lass, her young brother was another story. He was due to turn one year old in a few days, and he'd been walking . . . or running . . . since nine months. He was a true Maclean, having been caught just yesterday waving one of his grandmother's knitting needles around as if it were a sword and nearly stabbing his sister in her behind.

The changes wrought by the wee lad were astonishing. Dànaidh had been transformed by the arrival of his son—a son who looked just like him. Dàni seemed to have buried his ill will for his brother Giles, and the two could often be seen heading together toward the nursery, albeit with different goals in mind.

It's all down t' Lili, Kenna thought, as she watched the girl shake off her fatigue and begin laying out the parts of the wedding gown. *She's changed th' verra air in th' castle. Ever'un loves her.*

As if to give lie to that sentiment, a strong scent of perfume wafted in through the door, followed by Frances. Lili looked up from her task and gave her mistress a weary smile, which was ignored.

"I hate t' be th' bringer o' bad tidin's, Kenna, bit yer goin' t' have t' do yer own plannin'. I heard Coll wailin' 'n his cryb, an' he kens he cannae get up wi'out the nanny." She gave Lili a sour look. "Unless I be mistaken, 'at's what yer here fer, aye?" She turned and flounced out the door, turning up the hall in the opposite direction from the nursery.

"I may be courtin' ill tidin's sayin' this," Kenna muttered, "but I cannae bear that odyous woman. She doesnae lift a finger for her own bairns, an' leaves it all t' ye and Dorcas. I sometimes wonder if Annie an' Coll ken who their real mother be. Or care."

Lili gave her a wan smile. "She's right, though; 'tis why I'm here." She straightened to go, and turned at the door. "Frances isnae so bad, really. Ye ken she's wi' child agin, an' 'tis keepin' 'er out o' sorts. But she's been quite kind t' me o' late; has a nice cup o' tea waitin' when I've put th' bairns t' bed."

Seeing Kenna's skeptical expression, she smiled. "Gie on wi' ye, ye'll be th' most beautiful bryde whether I help or no, 'an I'm that happy for ye."

Kenna went back to work on the gown, but her mind was not on her task. Lili really didn't look good. Her skin was pallid and her hair limp. The circles under her wide brown eyes were becoming bags.

Was it really just her duties with the two children? Coll wasn't *that* bad, and Annie was more help than hindrance. No, there was something more going on here. After the wedding, she was going to talk to Giles about it—there wasn't much that one missed when it came to Lili MacPherson.

She saw little of him, or Lili either, in the next few days. Why was there so much to do just to get married? At least time flew when you were busy, because before she knew it, she was standing before the minister in the chapel of Duart Castle, with Crìsdean at her side.

She looked down at her wedding gown, a work of art painstakingly stitched by Mary Maclean's loving hands, and brushed a hand over the soft pale satin. Woven in stripes of sage and cream, the simple garment flowed from her waist to just above the embroidered satin slippers. It was heavy, but somehow it seemed as if she were floating on a cloud.

She felt a hand slip into hers and turned to gaze into a pair of brilliant green eyes. Had Mary matched her gown to Crìsdean's eyes on purpose? Kenna wouldn't put it past her; the woman was a godsend.

Crìsdean smiled, and she clutched his hand to keep from floating up into the rafters.

The minister cleared his throat and began the time-honored introduction from *The Book of Common Prayer*. "Dearely beloved frendes, we are gathered here in the sight of God . . ." Kenna tried to listen, but her mind wouldn't stay in one place.

This isnae happenin'. It cannae be, no one should be allowed t' be this happy.

The minister cleared his throat again, and she came back to earth to find him staring at her, a resigned smile on his face. Apparently the man was used to dealing with brides. She smiled back at him and he nodded and turned to Crìsdean.

"Wilt thou have thys woman to thy wedded wyfe, to lyve together after God's ordynaunce in the holy estate of matrimony? Wylt thou love her, comforte her, honour, and keepe her, in sickness, and in heal-the? And forsakyng all other, keepe onely to her, so long as you both shall live?"

Crìsdean's voice rang through the hall, loud and true. "I will." Cheers from the back of the hall, where his brothers stood, were quickly hushed by Anna. Their mother had taken a firm stand in front of Pàdraig and Fergus, knowing whence any untoward behavior would come and prepared to squelch it.

Kenna's turn came and, determined not to be outdone by her bridegroom, she announced in a clear voice that only shook a little, "I will." And within moments, the ceremony was over. She was a married woman.

In a daze, she allowed herself to be herded into the great hall and seated at the long table. Around her were the people she held dearest to her heart, all gazing at her in awe as if she had somehow turned from a reckless maid with tangled blonde locks into a princess, every hair tucked neatly into place by the clever hands of Lili MacPherson.

Kenna turned to look for Lili, and found her seated at a small table at the side of the room with her two charges. Her eyes were dull, but she caught Kenna's eye and smiled. In contrast, wee Annie's eyes were huge blue orbs in her tiny face. She sat like a small queen, back straight, hands folded neatly in her lap. This was the most exciting thing that had ever happened in her three years of living.

Coll was not so impressed. His nanny had him firmly imprisoned on her lap, and no amount of squirming was working to set him free. Every time he opened his mouth to complain, Lili shoved a piece of bread into it. Kenna grinned and turned back to the table.

Suddenly, Coll tumbled to the floor and let out a screech. Lili was bent double, clutching her stomach. Loud retching noises came from her mouth, and as everyone turned in shock, she slid from her chair onto the stone floor and curled into a ball of keening misery.

Giles was the first out of his seat. He raced across the room and lifted Lili into his arms. "Wha's th' matter, love?" He pushed back her hair and peered into brown eyes clouded with pain. "Where does 't hurt?"

Lili shook her head. "I dinnae . . . I din—" Her gasp was cut off as her body seized and convulsed. Annie burst into tears and Coll, quiet for the first time in his life, sat on the floor next to his beloved nanny, eyes huge with fear.

The others looked on in speechless horror as Lili thrashed wildly. Her body arched at the height of a convulsion and stiffened, and then her eyes closed and she went limp in Giles' arms. Silence fell on the room that moments ago had resounded with joy and celebration.

"She isnae breathin'!" Giles cried out in terror. "She isnae breathin!" He clutched her body close and rocked her in helpless agony, refusing to acknowledge the unbearable truth. Kenna pulled her eyes away and looked around at her shocked wedding guests.

Mary was sobbing, great tears rolling down her face. Dorcas had pulled herself together and rounded up Annie and Coll. She held them firmly against her chest so that they could no longer see the excruciating tableau on the floor. The Maclean brothers were silent, eyes shifting to each other in confusion and dawning grief.

Another figure caught Kenna's attention. Frances sat still, hands folded in her lap, her face expressionless. As Kenna watched, one corner of her mouth quirked upward. Just for a second.

Someone else was not watching the sad scene. Dànaidh sat rigid, eyes locked on his wife, brows furrowed, and lips turned down in a frown. Slowly, he turned his gaze from Frances to Giles and Lili, and back to his wife again. The frown deepened.

Something Lili had said, just days ago, ran through Kenna's mind. *She's been quite kind o' late; allus has a nice cup o' tea waitin' when I've pit th' bairns t' bed.*

A sliver of dread worked its way through and joined the grief.

No, impossible.

CHAPTER 37

MULL, SCOTLAND, JANUARY, 1651

CRÌSDEAN

Crìsdean stood at the shoreline with his arms around his wife and gazed out at the choppy waters of the Sound of Mull, but his eyes saw none of the majesty before him. They were turned inward, where he kept seeing Lili's awful last moments over and over again, like a scene out of time.

A scene out of time . . .

His eyes went to the rock upon which he had made carvings four years ago. A sailboat, a lighthouse, crude figures wearing short trews. A scene out of time. He hadn't experienced that suffocating feeling in nearly two years, but he'd never forget it. That last time was the worst, standing on the battlefield and suddenly knowing that although it was his hand that held his sword, his mind wasn't in tune with his actions.

As if he were at war with himself. The sensation had lasted longer than the others, the presence Kenna called Brian leaving suddenly after two days of marching, as if it had never been there. He hoped it was over, that he would never have to feel that pull on his mind again. He didn't want to feel the man's fear and anxiety, his helplessness to understand what was going on.

He'd thought nothing could be as bad as that, but he'd been wrong. This was worse. A pall hung over the castle, as if the keep had trapped everyone inside in a never-ending cycling of images. It had been so sudden, so shocking. Everyone still expected Lili to bounce into the room, her small charges in tow, and her laughter filling the space.

Dorcas had taken over the bairns' management and Dànaidh seemed relieved to let her do so. Nobody had thought to consult their mother. The wee ones were moving on with the resilience of the very young, although Annie cried more frequently over nothing, and Coll kept asking where his *NaNa* was. As for Frances . . .

"I thynk ye're right, lass," Crìsdean said into Kenna's hair. "There be somethin' wrong wi' Frances."

Kenna said, without turning, "Aye. I used t' thynk she was jist selfish an' mean, bit there's more."

"She's evil." Crìsdean's voice was flat.

"Wha'?"

"Ye thynk she had somethin' t' do wi' our Lili's death," Crìsdean said. It was not a question. Kenna burst into tears, and her husband pulled her around and sheltered her face in his shirt, feeling the dampness soak through the fabric.

Kenna's muffled words drifted to his ear. "I kent there was sommut wrong weeks ago. She was sick an' gettin' sicker an' I was too busy. I was goin' t' talk wi' Giles efter the weddin'. It's all my fault, and now Giles willnae talk t' enyone. He's back 'n the library, an' willnae come out." She looked up suddenly. "How did ye guess?"

Crìsdean held her shoulders and forced her to look into his eyes. "Ye telt me Frances was bein' kind t' Lili." He rolled his eyes. "Frances? Kind? Impossible."

Kenna nodded. "She hated Lili, but she was bringin' her tea every night, after th' bairns were abed. Why would she do 'at?"

"Ye wunner was somethin' in th' tea." Crìsdean's tone was flat. "Poyson."

"'Tis no possible, aye?" Kenna said. "'Tis th' stuff o' wild tales."

"Where d' ye thynk those wild tales hie from?" Crìsdean asked her. "People 'ave been poysonin' their rich rel'tives fer hunnerds o' years. 'Tis th' nature o' humankind."

"It has a name . . . th' poyson."

The two turned, startled, to find Giles standing behind them. The change in the man in just two weeks was shocking; he had lost weight and his skin was pallid and dull. His hair was greasy and his blue eyes were sunken holes in his head.

"I heared whit ye were sayin. 'Tisnae yer fault, Kenna; 'tis mine. Lili telt me abit Frances servin' her tea, an' I didnae thynk on it. B'cause t' do that is t' admit somethin' monstrous."

Crìsdean gave his brother a look of gratitude. "Thank ye, Giles. Kenna's been that worrit on it."

Giles nodded. "Bit when I did let myself thynk on 't, I started t' do some readin'. An' yer right, Crìs, there be a poyson like ye said. Tis arsenick. Sometimes 'tis called 'Inher'tance Powder.'"

"Arsenick? Kenna asked. "Isn't 'at what Cook uses 'n th' kitchen t' kill th' rats?"

"Aye. Easy t' get, an' doesnae have a taste, so t'wouldn't be noticed if someun was t' put it in food, or in . . ."

"Tea." Crisdean and Kenna spoke in unison. Silence fell on the small group gathered at the shoreline.

Kenna furrowed her brow. "Bit Giles, Frances doesnae read. How would she ken about arsenick?" She spread her hands wide. "I cannae b'lieve I'm e'en speakin' this!"

Giles' visage was grim. "She doesnae have t' read. Frances is clever, we allus kent 'at. She'd ken if 't kills th' rats, it might kill a person, no?" His face was set. His words, when they came, were ground out through gritted teeth. "Maybe she only meant t' make Lili sick, bit arsenick 'as been used t' kill for centuries. What did she have t' lose by tryin'?"

Suddenly his legs gave out and he folded to the ground, where he sat with his head in his hands. "Why didnae I see whit was happenin' t' Lili?" he moaned. "She was so brave, she didnae wish t' bother me wi' her problems. I'm such a fule!"

Crìsdean gave Kenna a helpless look. She shook her head, and they waited. After a while, Giles looked up with damp eyes that shone with new purpose.

"I'm goin' t' find th' truth o' this. If Frances did 't, if she poysont my Lili, she willnae get awa' wi' "t." He scrambled to his feet and strode off toward the castle, shoulders hunched and hands fisted at his sides.

Something was niggling at Crìsdean's brain. He pushed it around and shuffled it until it came into focus.

"Th' question be," he said softly, "why would Frances hurt Lili?"

"B'cause she hated 'er," Kenna said. "B'cause Giles liked Lili, not her."

"Bit . . ." Crìsdean shook his head. "At makes no sense. T' take sich a riske, t' kill somebody . . . whit would she gain by 't?"

Kenna opened her mouth, and shut it again. "I dinnae ken."

"I mean," Crìsdean went on, "she wanted Giles. We kent 'at, she made a right fule o' herself o'er it an' she must've been mad as a chylled hen when he fell fer Lili, bit she could ne'er have what she yearned fer, could she?" He spread his hands out. "She's *marrit*."

They stared at each other for a long moment. Kenna's eyes widened.

"Marrit, aye. T' Dànaidh."

"Ach, God, Kenna," Crìsdean breathed. "Whit if Lili was jist th' first? Whit if somethin' were t' happen t' Dànaidh?"

"Dinnae fash, love," Kenna said, her tone dismissive. "Giles would nivver be wi' Frances. He cannae bear 'er. Frances would be mad t' think sich a thyng possible."

Crìsdean arched one eyebrow. "Mad enough t' kill?" he said.

Kenna's face drained of color. She clutched her husband's forearms, fingernails digging in like talons. "We need t' warn Dànaidh! She could gie him enythin', an' he'd nivver ask on 't!" She began to tug him toward the castle.

Crìsdean pulled her back and wrapped her in his arms, holding her against his warm body. "Thynk, love. We cannae do 'at," he said. "What d' ye thynk would happen if we was t' dander up t' him an' say, 'Ho there, Dànaidh, yer wyfe 'at ye love so much, she be thynkin' o' sendin' ye off?'"

A long sigh escaped Kenna. She pushed herself away, wrapped her arms around herself, and walked in a tight circle, her brow furrowed.

"Ye're right. O' course ye're right. He loves 'er, willnae see fault in 'er. So . . . whit do we do?"

"We watch," Crìsdean said. "Giles 'll help, an' Ealar fer sure. He has no love fer Frances, an' ye ken he thynks Dàni c'n do no wrong. No th' rest; Fergus an' Pàdraig cannae be trustit t' keep quiet, and Bearnard has his heid t'gither wi' Hector these days, talkin' o' war."

He paused and managed a weary smile. "We'll likely be goin' t' th' war soon, love." He shook his head. "Nivver thought Dànaidh would be safer in battle than here t' home."

Kenna stopped pacing and came over to stand in front of Crìsdean.

"Ye ken I dinnae want ye in battle, but 'tis th' way o' th' world now. An' ye'll be fine, b'cause ye're no jist pretty, ye're smart. But let us no talk o' war th' noo, aye?" She raised on tiptoes and kissed the tip of his nose.

"An' I want t' do my parte, so I'm goin' t' be nice t' Frances." She shivered. "E'en though ever bit o' my soul is fightin' it. If I git close t' her, I can keep an eye on 'er."

Crìsdean's face paled and he grabbed his wife by her shoulders. "Whit're ye thynkin'? I dinnae want ye enywhere near Frances!"

Kenna patted his arm. "I only mean t' be nicer, no t' drink tea wi' 'er. None o' th' other wyves like 'er, so she's allus alone. I can do "t—didnae I keep ye safe when Brian was here wi' ye?"

Crìsdean's eyes flicked to the carvings on the rock. "Aye," he said, slowly. "Ye did. Bit . . ."

"I'll be careful, I will." She put her hand over her heart. "I promise ye."

Crìsdean was still staring at the rock. "Kenna," he said after a moment, "why d' ye thynk Brian was 'ere, inside o' me?"

She blinked at him. "I dinnae ken. An' mebbe we'll nivver ken. 'Less he comes back."

Dorcas appeared suddenly in the castle's doorway. Her face was drawn and pale, and there were tear streaks on her face.

"'Tis wee Annie. She's fevered an' ravin', callin' fer Lili." She gulped and wrung her hands. "An' I thynk Coll's sick too."

Crìsdean and Kenna looked at her in helpless horror. The fever that had carried off Lachlan and Arthur Maclean was back. It seemed more and more that God was punishing the Macleans of Duart.

CHAPTER 38

INVERNESS, SCOTLAND, PRESENT DAY

*"He can occasionally see to an enemy,"
she conceded. "If he manages to get his
sword pointed in the right direction and
the enemy does him the favor of falling
upon it in precisely the right way."*
—Lynn Kurland

"The only thing ye have to remember is that th' pointy end goes int'a th' other guy. If ye get that down, th' rest is a bonus," Harry MacBain said, and waved his sword in the air for emphasis.

Brian rolled his eyes. Did everybody involved with the Highland Players have to look and talk as if they'd just walked out of the past? Here he was, standing with a group of about ten men on a church lawn in the center of Inverness, and his instructor was dressed like an escapee from *Outlander* in a great kilt, sporran, knit bonnet—the whole lot. The others wore similar costumes, making Brian feel like the odd man out in his jeans and sweatshirt

Well, your accent isn't quite right, lad, he thought, but decided not to voice it. The man didn't have the advantage of time travel, after all; perhaps he could be forgiven for mispronouncing the odd word or two. Besides, even though their weapons weren't real, these reenactors seemed to know the business end of a sword, and that was what he was here for, right? To learn?

He studied the sword in his own hands. It was light and easy to lift, not surprising because it had been ordered online from a training site and was made of wood covered by foam. It looked legit, though. The thought of facing a real one in battle had the sweat running down his neck in spite of the chill in the air.

What the hell am I doing? he thought. *I'm not likely to wind up in the middle of another battle, am I? And I'm only there for a few minutes.*

But it hadn't been only a few minutes, the last time. The aftermath of that battle, the two-day march back to Duart, the blank staring eyes of the dead man, were as real as this sword in his hands was fake. The time spent in another man's body was increasing with each visit, and so were the chances of facing the enemy in battle, if Giles wasn't exaggerating.

Giles. The man was as real as the instructor facing him now. He'd learned a lot about Giles Maclean in the two days they'd spent tromping over the Highlands on their way back to Duart. The man would much rather have been spending time in his library than swinging a sword or shouldering a musket. He wanted to be a writer, add to the story of his family and see his own books on the shelves. It was admirable . . . and sad.

If what Jeremy had told him was true, Giles would be killed on a battlefield in 1651, defending his chief. As would all his brothers. Every one of them would die, including the man whose body he'd been borrowing.

Christian Maclean—spelled *Crìsdean* in the old tongue, Giles had said—was the youngest of seven brothers, born to Anna and Arthur Maclean of Duart in 1629, which meant he'd been only nineteen years old the last time Brian occupied his body.

Nineteen, and yet already battle-hardened. A warrior like his brothers. Like all those men he'd seen on that battlefield, fighting each other with a desperation impossible to understand by watching movies. They fought to stay alive, to protect their way of life and their fellow clansmen. They didn't go into battle to win honour or go down in history, and they knew every time they pulled a sword from its sheath or loaded a musket, it could be the last.

The empty eyes of the unknown dead man rose in his mind again, and Brian shivered. There was nothing glamourous about a real battle; no standing up and washing off the makeup and fake blood. It was real and visceral, and somehow he'd been transported right into the middle of it.

The chill spread. Was that why he kept travelling to the past? Was that his mission—to stop the brothers from being killed in that last battle? Inversomething, Jeremy had called it. Inver-keithing. A minor battle in the scope of world history, but one that would change the future of Clan Maclean. A singular act of bravery would erase the seven men he'd come to know—his kinsmen—from the pages of time, and almost no one would remember.

But how was he supposed to help? In his sojourns back to the past to reside in Crìsdean's body, he'd realised two things: Crìsdean Maclean was in much better shape than he was, and he knew how to wield a sword. Brian would have to make the decisions, though, and no matter how adept Crìsdean's body was, Brian's lack of knowledge would hamper him. A split second of indecision in a real battle, and both of them would die.

He'd shared his fears with Sophie, and unsurprisingly found himself at the Unicorn. He'd long since stopped wondering why; the pub seemed to be the center of all things weird and bewildering.

Of course, the Players hadn't batted an eye. "So 'tis sword fighting ye need help with?" Mary had said, as if such an idea was the natural progression of things. "We've done a wee bit o' re-enacting in our time," she added, sharing a look with her husband. "We ken just the people who can get ye ready for battle."

Brian gaped at her. *Of course you do.*

Mary was a force not to be denied, so now here he was, clutching a wooden sword and facing a very real-looking Highland warrior who looked eager to cut him in two.

"An', yer deid," the man said calmly. "Ye cannae let yer attention wander when yer holdin' a blade, lad."

Brian looked down to see the blunted point of

the man's wooden sword lodged against his ribs. He sighed.

"Let's try it agin," his adversary said calmly. "An' this time, pay attention, aye?"

Brian grasped the sword the way he'd been shown, his right index finger over the outside of the hilt and around the heel—he ignored the flash of pride at remembering that one—and his thumb on the other side. Then he carefully placed his feet shoulder-width apart, so that his right foot faced forward and his left turned ninety degrees away. He straightened his back and lowered his body slightly, as he'd been taught.

When he looked up, he saw that his trainer was leaning on the pommel of his own sword, grinning.

"The battle 'll be over, lad, before ye get yerself sorted out. An' ye'll still be deid."

Sophie arrived an hour later to find Brian nursing a dozen bruises and rubbing a stinging wrist.

"Yer lassie's here; same time next week?" Harry MacBain grinned at him.

Brian groaned and nodded, and the man laughed. "Yer no so bad, lad; ye have good reflexes an' yer footwork is comin' along fast."

Brian smiled weakly and limped over to the car. He eased himself down into the passenger seat, leaned back into the headrest, and closed his eyes.

"That bad?" Sophie asked, as they pulled out of the car park. "I saw the last few minutes; you looked as if you were holding your own. Very dashing, I thought."

"You're just being nice," Brian said, his eyes still closed. "Let me tell you, if anyone ever says foam is soft, they're lying. Ouch!" he gasped as they hit a pothole. "Go easy on a dying man."

"Sorry," Sophie laughed. "When we get home, I'll put an ice pack on it and give you some paracetamol. And then we're due at the Unicorn."

"How many ice packs do you have?" Brian groaned. Then he sat up straight. "Ow. Why are we due at the Unicorn?"

"Because I have to work tonight, and they want to know all about your training. We can grab fish and chips there, unless you just want to stay home and rest."

"With fish and chips on offer? Are you serious?" Brian looked considerably happier. "I'll even put up with the Players syphoning out my brain cells for that."

Sophie shook her head and patted his hand. "Thought that might do it."

"So who are these reenactor friends of yours?," Brian asked Mary, as he decimated a plate of chips. "And why are they so bloodthirsty? They had no pity for me at all!" He fed a chip to Biscuit, who had appeared next to his feet. "You understand, don't you?" he asked the animal hopefully. The cat accepted his offering and stared at him with unblinking, yellow eyes.

"Shoo, cat," Mary said affectionately. Biscuit cocked her head as if considering the order, and ignored it in favor of another chip.

"If ye're going to defend yerself properly," Mary resumed, her tone crisp, "ye need t' learn from th' best."

"An' to answer yer first question," Betty spoke up, "Harry MacBain's my cousin, an' the others 're related 'n other ways." She waved a chubby hand in the air. "Highlanders 're all kin somehow or other, ye ken."

"So," Mary took back the reins. "How d' ye feel?"

"Like every muscle in my body is threatening to go on strike," Brian said. "But Sophie took care of me, and I guess I'll live."

"Looks like th' muscles o' yer right arm work jist fine," Henry noted, pointing to the nearly empty plate of fish and chips.

"I can see I'll get no sympathy here," Brian said. He turned back to Mary. "To answer your question truthfully, I feel fine. Everything aches, but it's a good ache. I think I could hold my own in a battle with a three-year-old now, and maybe a five-year-old in a few weeks."

Mary snorted. "Ye'll do fine, long as ye dinnae get too full o' yourself, lad. Ye havenae seen our Highland three-year-olds."

The ensuing laughter was interrupted by a blast of cold air as the door opened to admit Deirdre and Sam Douglas. Biscuit arched her back and fled to the bar, where she sat with narrowed eyes, her tail swishing.

"That cat hates me," Sam said, and shrugged his shoulders. "Guess it can tell I like dogs."

Mary stood up. "Time to get busy," she said. Her tone sounded terse, and Henry and Betty joined her as if it had been an order. The Players disappeared into the kitchen, leaving the two couples at the table.

"Something I said?" Sam said. "Isn't it okay to like dogs better than cats?"

"Not here," Deirdre laughed. "And Biscuit isn't a cat. She's family. You'll learn."

Sophie's band mates began to appear from the rear

entrance. She kissed Brian on the cheek and stood to go. "I have to work," she said. "See you later?"

Brian grinned. "I might be asleep later. Wake me up, okay?" She gave him an answering smile and crossed to the stage.

Deirdre fixed Brian with a sharp look. "Are you two living together?"

Brian flushed. "Well, kind of. I've been—I guess—well, yes." His glance flicked to Sam, who was watching him with amusement. "A little help, maybe?" he asked hopefully.

Sam put his palms up, hazel eyes glinting in the light from the candle on the table. "Sorry. I can't stop her when she has her detective hat on."

Deirdre laughed. "It's fine, I was just asking. You two have gotten awfully close, that's all." She gave him a rare serious look and said softly, "Be good to her, aye? She's my best friend, and I don't want to see her get hurt."

"I have no intention of hurting her," Brian said, his voice stiff. "She's very important to me too." He stood and shrugged into his jacket. Then he paused and gave Deirdre his full attention.

"I appreciate your concern," he said sincerely. "But you have no worries from me. Like you said, we've gotten very close."

Later, as Brian soaked in Sophie's tub, his memory kept returning to that last few words at the pub. Something was prickling at his tired brain, trying to wiggle in. Something about Deirdre?

She was understandably protective, he reasoned. She'd been teasing, but there was real concern in her brown eyes. She'd be a force to reckon with if something threatened her friend, and for that he was grateful.

He could feel his mind drifting as the warmth soaked into his sore muscles. *Eyes. Deirdre's brown eyes . . .*

He shook his head and decided he'd better get out of the tub before he fell asleep. He threw on some sweats and lay down on the couch. His thoughts swirled and reformed and ebbed again.

Eyes danced through his head. Mary's little bird eyes. Sophie's beautiful blue, Deirdre's brown, Sam's hazel. The eyes paraded by as if trying to tell him something, faded into the mist, and he slept.

CHAPTER 39
INVERNESS, SCOTLAND, PRESENT DAY

When we least expect it, life sets us
a challenge to test our courage and
willingness to change. The challenge
will not wait. Life does not look back.
—Paulo Coelho

ophie studied Brian's face over her morning coffee. It seemed lit from within, his eyes glowing. When she'd met him at the Unicorn, on the night that would live in infamy forever, she would never have guessed Fiona's grumpy brother could possess such a gorgeous smile, but now it danced across his face as he told her about Highlands Academy.

"They're no different, Soph! Eager, scattered, brilliant, morose—just like the kids back home. They're amazing!" He waved his hands as he talked about his new job, his classroom, the curriculum.

He was born for this. No wonder he'd been so depressed. Teaching to Brian Maclean was like breathing; having it ripped away must have been worse than death. She sent a prayer of thanks to the Highland Players for knowing exactly what he needed, and for thinking him worthy of their trust. Then she gave herself a little pat on the back for taking a risk for the first time in her adult life.

She wondered how the administration of his former school could make such a colossal mistake. To lose such a treasure—did they even realise what they'd thrown away? She even mustered a moment's pity for the girl who'd filed that false report. A child, really—a young, barely formed human made of confusion and angst and teenage ideas of love.

Thank you, Meghan. If you hadn't done that, he'd still be in Nova Scotia, teaching and sailing. I never would have met him. Her heart faltered at the idea. The thought of the old Sophie MacArthur, holed up in her lonely house with only Oliver and her books and an unmanageable AGA for company, was inconceivable now.

She took a sip of coffee, considering her next words. "So, you're okay with those teenage girls? They have raging hormones over here too, you know, and part of that interest you're chuffed about is down to their maths teacher being so handsome."

A shadow passed over Brian's face, and then he grinned and the sun came out again. "So, you think I'm handsome?"

Sophie cocked her head and pretended to study him. "Weel, lad, ye'll do." She shot him a look. "Pay attention and answer the question. Are you okay?" *It's all right, laddie. You have me now, and woe be it to any little brat who thinks different.*

He nodded. "Believe me, I won't let that happen again. Part of what happened was my fault. Fiona always told me I was oblivious, and I hate to admit it, but she's right. I should have paid more attention; I mean, I wasn't a newbie teacher." He gave her a solemn look. "I promise, I won't be meeting any little Scottish lasses alone after school. I'll send them to my teaching partner; she'll deal with them."

"She?" Sophie's eyes narrowed. "Your partner is a woman? Why didn't you mention that before?"

Brian gave her a serious look. "Yes. She's quite lovely. Great sense of humour, smart, and so kind. Brings me homemade cookies-er-biscuits . . ." He caught a murderous glint from the blue eyes across from him, and chuckled. "Her grandchildren love her baking, she says."

"Ach, you!" Sophie reached across the table and swatted his arm. "I think I liked you better when you were oblivious."

Brian stood and came around the table. He cupped Sophie's face in his hands and kissed her full on the lips. "Nicest thing anybody's ever said to me," he said.

Sophie grinned and pushed him away. "Get on, now. You'll be late for those wonderful bairns and your sexy partner."

"I didn't say she was sexy; I said she was lovely. And she is. She's been at Highlands Academy since Robert the Bruce ran Scotland, but you'd hardly know it to look at her. Very elegant woman, is Morag MacGregor." He ducked Sophie's punch and made for the door, turning at the last moment to blow her a kiss. "See you later. I love you."

Sophie puttered around cleaning up the breakfast dishes, did some laundry, and dusted the already clean bookshelves. Mindless chores, little tasks that had once seemed so important.

I really was pathetic, she thought as she polished the tea table, an heirloom from some MacArthur ancestor. *I was barely living, and I didn't even know it. All because I let that thing—that monster—control me. I needed someone to show me that life can be fun, exciting . . .normal.*

She collected Oliver and sat with him in her lap, thinking back to the morning conversation. "He's so easy to talk to," she told the violin. She ran a scale absently, tuned a string, and put the bow down across her lap. "I used to hate meaningless conversation, remember? I couldn't see the point in it; talking to other people takes so much *work.* But did you hear us? We were teasing each other! I feel different with him—I feel *needed.*"

Oliver said nothing. Like his owner, he didn't need to talk to make himself understood, which was why she loved him. He'd been with Sophie since she was a small child, just learning the scales. He'd talked a lot in those days, she remembered—loud shrieks of agony as the bow was pulled across his strings like a carpenter's saw.

Sophie grinned at the memory, picked up the bow again, and began to run through the pieces she would play tonight. Her precious sidekick responded with the precision they had learned together over the years, as the joyous melody of a reel swirled through the huge room. A Cape Breton reel. For Brian.

Lost in the music, she almost missed the knocking. Startled, she looked at her watch. Half eleven—who would be calling this time of day? Everybody she knew was at work. She stood and placed Oliver carefully on the floor next to the chair. Maybe one of the Highland Players? But why would they be here now? She was due at the Unicorn tonight; they'd all see her then. An emergency—had something happened to Brian?

The knock was repeated, and Sophie realized she was still standing rooted to the floor. Heart in her throat, she ran to the front door and flung it open. Sam Douglas stood on the step, arm raised to knock again.

"What's wrong?" Sophie demanded. "Is Deirdre hurt?"

"Hurt?" Sam blinked. "No, she's fine. In fact, I'm here about her—I need your help. Um, may I come in?"

Other than Brian and Caomhainn that one time, no man had crossed Sophie's threshold for years. Ewan didn't count; he was family. Every hair on her neck was standing at attention, and for a split second, she wanted to slam the door in Sam's face and run back into the safety of her home.

Instead, she gathered her courage and stood aside to allow him entrance. She pointed to the couch and took a seat in her armchair, which was twenty feet away from him and the closest piece of furniture to the door. Courage only went so far. Sam sat down and placed his rucksack on the floor next to his feet.

"What can I help you with?" Sophie asked.

Sam's smile was shy. "I-um-I want to propose to Dee," he mumbled.

Sophie's fear drained away and she clapped her hands. "Really, Sam? That's wonderful!" She laughed. "But I don't know how you think I can help; I probably know less than you do about proposing."

"No, no," he waved a hand. "I can handle that part myself. What I need help with is the ring, and you're her best friend. And a girl." He smiled. "Do you have time? Are you sure I'm not bothering you?"

Sophie gave him an answering smile. "I don't know much about diamond rings, either," she said, "and Deirdre's and my taste are wildly different, but I'll give it my best."

Sam breathed a sigh of relief. "Thanks. I brought some ideas . . ." He pulled a stack of pamphlets out of his rucksack. "I've been to three jewelers, and there are so many options I'm getting a headache. I don't know what she likes, so I thought of you. I'm desperate!"

Sophie felt a surge of joy for her friend. "Happy to help. Would you like a cup of tea?"

"Sure." Sam spread the pamphlets out on the tea table, and Sophie hurried into the kitchen and filled the electric kettle. She pulled teabags out of the tin on the counter and threw them into a pot, and then went rummaging for biscuits.

Sophie's kitchen had changed since Brian's arrival. The cupboards and the fridge were now full of things men liked to eat. The tea towels, featuring a field of thistle and a Highland cow, were Brian's contribution. Found in a souvenir shop on the High Street, they matched the new salt and pepper shakers.

"Scottish people don't buy Scottish souvenirs," Sophie had told him, but here they were, claiming pride of place in a Scottish kitchen. She grinned and put the teapot, biscuits, and serviettes on a tray and took them out to her guest.

Forty-five minutes later Sam left, his choices circled on the pamphlets. Sophie wandered back to the kitchen to clean up, wondering why entertaining strangers was so draining. She rinsed the teacups and put everything away and then stood in the empty house, imagining Deirdre's reaction when Sam proposed.

She decided to go to the Unicorn early, get some lunch. *I wish I could tell them about Deirdre and Sam.* But he'd sworn her to secrecy, although it wouldn't be at all surprising if the Players already knew—they seemed to know everything. She dressed for work, pulled her coat out of the closet, and grabbed her handbag from its spot near the couch.

She rummaged in the bag for her house key, but it wasn't in the pocket where she usually kept it. She dumped the contents out onto the floor—no key. *Dammit.* Had Brian taken it this morning, thinking it was his? No, he kept his key on a pewter ring that featured the Maclean crest. Hers had a silver-toned treble clef. There was no way he'd make that error. She texted him to be sure, and almost immediately, a message came back—*Nope. Do you have a spare? I can come back on my lunch if you need mine.*

Sophie texted him back. *It's okay. I do have a spare. Thanks, come to the Unicorn after school?* A heart emoji appeared instantly. She fetched the spare, locked the door, and walked the few hundred feet to the pub. Maybe the key had fallen out of her handbag somewhere. If someone found it, they wouldn't know what lock it belonged to, but still . . . if it didn't turn up, she'd have to change the locks. That was a nuisance, but years of running scared had honed her instincts. You couldn't be too careful.

Sam Douglas let himself into his flat and threw his rucksack onto a wooden chair. He fetched a beer from the fridge—a little early, but this was a celebration—and took it with him into the bathroom. He stared at his reflection in the mirror and then washed his hands and carefully removed the contact lenses he always wore when he left the flat. He put them into their case and stowed it in the medicine cabinet and then looked at his reflection again.

Dark brown eyes, irises nearly black, gazed back at him under the sandy mop of hair he'd worked so hard to achieve. It had taken three boxes of hair color to alter his black hair to light brown, but it had done the trick. She'd never recognized him.

His mouth twisted. How *could* she recognize him—she barely looked at him. The bitch's eyes were all for that Canadian bawbag. It had been hell watching the two of them acting all lovey-dovey right in front of him. His hands clenched; he imagined strangling the prick right in front of her, watching the light go out of his eyes while she screamed and begged. He took a long breath and forced himself to relax. Soon.

He picked up his beer and returned to the tiny room that served as kitchen, sitting room, and bedroom. He picked up the rucksack, reached into a side zippered pocket, and extracted a key on a silver treble clef ring. He held up the ring and dangled Sophie's house key.

It had been easier than he thought. Why did women insist on keeping their handbags in plain sight? Didn't they know it made them easy prey for a criminal? He laughed at his joke, removed the key from its ring, and threw the treble clef on top of the pamphlets. He'd dispose of the lot in a public rubbish bin on the High Street, so no one could ever connect them to him.

Luke Cameron could feel the need uncoil in his gut. It wanted out, and soon he'd let it loose. He could have had her today, but he wanted her to see *him*. He couldn't do much about his hair, but when he was ready, he'd leave the lenses out and she'd see him for who he was. He wanted to watch the look of terror transform her face the moment she recognized him and knew she was lost.

It had been such a long time waiting. He *deserved* this.

CHAPTER 40

INVERNESS, SCOTLAND, PRESENT DAY

*Seven. That's the magic number. There has to be
seven of us. That's the way it's supposed to be.*
—Stephen King

It was raining—again. Clouds covered the tops of the distant mountains with a blanket of grey, and a cold wind tore the last autumn leaves off the trees, sweeping them down Ardconnel Street.

Brian pulled the hood of his parka up and hunched his shoulders against the weather. *Dreich*, the Scots called it. Dull, gloomy, chilly, damp. In short, Scottish weather at its most wretched. The word itself was harsh, guttural, unpleasant to the ear, and difficult for a foreigner to pronounce. Brian loved it.

He loved the feel of the word, the rasp in his throat as it worked its way up and grated off his tongue. *Dreichhh. Drrreeicchh.* It was perfect. The weather was perfect. Scotland was perfect.

A noise that sounded like a very unmanly giggle gurgled through his stomach and out into the street.

He'd bet he was the only one out today who felt this way. The Scots had so many words for weather, and almost all of them described the misery of it. Oorlich, plowetery, smirr, stoating—the kids in his classes loved to challenge him on words they knew he couldn't say and laugh at his pitiful attempts to guess what they meant.

He didn't mind. The kids were perfect too. Everything about his life right now was perfect. He hadn't lost consciousness for a month, he loved his job, and he was living with the love of his life in a mansion that overlooked a castle. He pushed up the sleeve of his parka and gave himself a pinch. Nope. Not a dream.

Grinning, he sloshed up the steps and into the Unicorn. The band was in the middle of a spirited reel. Sophie spotted him from across the room and smiled, and his heart did a somersault at the look in her blue eyes.

Caomhainn beckoned him over to the bar and put a glass of whisky in front of him. Brian frowned and pushed it away, but Caomhainn slid it back in front of him again.

"Ye're going to need it, lad," he said, and something in his tone set the hairs on the back of Brian's neck tingling. He had a feeling his perfect day was about to go south.

Biscuit left her place at the end of the bar and meandered over to give him a soft pat on the nose. He looked at the cat warily, and she stared back at him with unblinking, yellow eyes. "Thanks," he said, and then—*What kind of world is this, where I'm relying on a cat for support?*

"Get going," Caomhainn said, and jerked his head toward the corner table. Brian followed the gesture and saw Mary, Henry, and Betty ranged around the table, all staring at him. The usual smiles were absent, and anxiety slid back into his stomach and took root.

Brian looked for Sophie, but she was immersed in her music, eyes closed. He sighed, stood, and picked up his whisky. He made his way slowly to the table, feeling as if his world was slipping out from under him.

"Sit, lad," Henry said, and Brian sank into one of the two empty chairs.

He looked at the Players. "What?" he croaked. Dread had settled in his stomach like a brick.

Mary pointed to the untouched whisky Brian had put down in front of him. "Drink."

The chills intensified. This was all wrong. The Players knew about his condition. They'd been spectators at the most embarrassing moment of his life, and they knew what the doctor had said. If they were urging him to drink . . .

He picked up the glass and downed the whisky without allowing himself to think further on it. "What?" he said again, his voice tight.

Mary cleared her throat. "When you go back in time . . ." Brian gaped at her, and she rolled her eyes.

"Back in time?" he said. "How-how did you know?" He was losing control of this situation fast. He grabbed for his empty whisky glass. Caomhainn appeared at his side and poured a generous draft, and Brian downed it in two gulps.

The Players were all looking at him with the same expression—as if they had no time for this, as if he was a fool to think they wouldn't have known.

"There are no coincidences," Mary said. "The world goes round, and people repeat. Good is good, and evil is always evil. It's all related, lad."

"You mean—" Brian tried to hold onto the edges of the conversation, but the edges were getting fuzzy. "Are you talking about . . . reincarnation?"

Betty laughed, a warm chuckle that broke the tension for a moment. "Now don't be silly. We're talking about ancestry. Nothing magical about that, is there?" She snorted. "Reincarnation. *Really.*"

Right, and there's nothing magical about time travel or possession or whatever it is. And nothing at all magical about you people. Brian studied them through narrowed eyes. He realized suddenly that their heavy accents were gone, and somehow that was more frightening than anything else.

Mary cleared her throat and took back the reins of conversation. "Don't make fun of the lad, Betty. This is all very strange to him, and we don't have time."

Brian reached for his glass, but it was empty. "Time for what?" he asked dully. He turned around and looked toward the stage in desperation. Sophie gave him a wide smile and launched into another reel.

"Pay attention," Mary said, in her best school teacher voice. "When you go back, you must remember this. There are no coincidences."

Brian gaped at her, and then at the others. They were nodding sagely, like those bobble-head dolls people put on their truck dashboards. He opened his mouth, then closed it again. He was suddenly very sober.

Mary nodded in approval. "Good lad. Now listen. There is a reason for everything. There's a reason you have gone back, something you must do."

Brian stopped wondering how the Players knew what they knew. "And you know what it is, right? So tell me."

"We can't do that, lad," Henry said. "There are rules."

"Rules?"

"Aye. There are things we can't tell, things you can't do with time. For example, you can't change history that's been recorded."

"What does that mean?" Brian said. "You mean the time paradox?"

"In a way." Henry waved a hand. "You can't change major events in history. For instance, you couldn't go back in time and kill Hitler. Too bad about that." He shook his head. "You can't alter the outcome of a major battle, or change who won a war."

"So what can I change—and why should I?" Brian heard his voice and wondered what the hell he was doing. These people sounded like lunatics, and he was going along with them! He fisted his hand under the table, and looked at the stage again. *Sophie, save me!*

"I'm sorry," Henry said. "You'll have to figure it out for yourself." He shrugged.

"Another one of the rules?" Brian asked.

The Players ignored the sarcasm in his voice. They all nodded in unison, as if it were obvious.

The music stopped, and a moment later, Sophie appeared next to the table and slid into the empty chair. Brian grabbed for her hand and clutched it, and she gave him a look of surprise.

"Now there are seven of us," Mary said in satisfaction. "It has to be seven."

"Seven?" Brian said. "I count only three. Oh," he amended, as Caomhainn appeared next to the table. "Four, with Caomhainn."

"There's you and your lass."

"That's six," Brian argued. He didn't know why it was important, but math was his thing. It was not to be trifled with.

Mary rolled her eyes. "And Biscuit, of course." At the sound of her name, the cat sauntered over from the bar and jumped onto the table. "Seven."

It was Brian's turn to roll his eyes, but again he was ignored.

"All right," Mary said, "let's talk about Sam Douglas. I believe you know him, Sophie."

Sophie looked at Mary in surprise. "Know him? Of course I know him. He's Deirdre's boyfriend. In fact, he's going to propose to her."

Mary shook her head. "No." Her voice was flat. "He is not." She cocked her head.

Sophie stared at Mary Duncan. She looked around the table for some clue, but the Highland Players' faces were expressionless, all eyes trained on her.

"Is-is there something wrong with Sam Douglas?" she said in a low voice. *Oh no! Deirdre!* She felt her stomach tumble. "What do you know?"

Mary's bright black bird's eyes pierced Sophie's. "Have you never felt something odd about him?"

Sophie thought about last week, about Sam

standing at her door. His warm hazel eyes, shy expression—at odds with the chill that had crawled up her spine. "I—had a feeling," she said. "Only for a second, and then it was gone. I know I've never seen him before, but for that second, it seemed as if I knew him from somewhere. As if he knew *me*."

Her mobile rang. Sophie looked at the display and exhaled in relief. She spoke into the phone, "Hold on, Dee, it's too noisy here." She stood. "It's Deirdre. I'll take it outside."

"Don't—" the noise of the pub drowned Mary's words, as Sophie wove her way through the tables to the front door and pushed it open. Outside, she put the device back to her ear. "Dee. Where are you? Didn't you say you were coming to the Unicorn?"

Deirdre's voice on the other end sounded thick, as if she were fighting a cold. "I'm at your house. C-can you come home? I-I have a surprise for you."

Sophie pulled the mobile away from her ear and looked at it in confusion. Then she put it back and spoke in a puzzled voice. "Dee, I'm working; you know that. What's going on? Is Sam with you?"

"N-no."

Deirdre was her best friend, and Sophie knew when she was lying. Her memory served up Mary's words just minutes ago. *Have you never felt something odd about him?* "Hang on, Dee, I'll be right there!"

Deirdre's voice broke into sobs. "No! Sophie, don't! Don't come! H-he's—" A choking gasp came through the line, and then the mobile went silent.

Sophie ran toward her house, heedless of the fact that she'd left her coat at the table. Rain soaked through her performance costume, but she didn't notice. Her heart pounded and she could feel the blood hammering in her ears. What had happened? Had that bastard hurt Deirdre?

A hand grasped her arm and pulled her around. Brian was coatless, his brows furrowed over worried green eyes, russet hair shedding water droplets that trickled down his face.

"Sophie!" He held both of her arms in his. "What's wrong?"

"It's Deirdre. I think she's in trouble!" She was panting, her breath fogging the night air in little puffs. "I need you to go back and tell the band I can't play anymore tonight. Please!"

"Are you serious?" Brian gaped at her. "They can figure it out for themselves. You're not going any-where without me!" He grabbed her hand, and they ran the rest of the way to Sophie's house.

"She's not here," Sophie said, as they stood on the doorstep. "She said she was at my house, but she doesn't have a key—damn! Neither do I . . .it's in my handbag, at the table."

She pushed Brian back toward the pavement. "Can you get it? Please? Hurry!"

Brian took a deep breath and turned to sprint up the pavement. "Stay right here! I'll get it and be right back. I mean it. Don't move!" He disappeared back toward the pub.

Sophie stepped closer to the door. Had she left it unlocked? Had Deirdre found it open and gone inside to wait? She pounded the door knocker. "Dee? Are you in there?"

Silence.

"Dee?" Her throat closed on a sob. "Please, open the door if you're in there!"

Footsteps sounded on the wooden floor, and the door eased open. Sam Douglas stood in the doorway.

"Where's Dee? Why are you here?" Sophie demanded. She pushed him aside and ran into the sitting room and froze in shock at the sight that met her eyes. Deirdre lay face down on the carpet, unmoving. Blood pooled around the handle of a kitchen knife, buried to the hilt in her back. Through the drumming in her ears, Sophie heard the front door slam shut.

"She didn't do as she was told," Sam's voice said from the doorway. Sophie turned to face him, shock making her movements slow. His handsome face wore a look of supreme boredom. "Bitch tried to ruin everything." His mouth stretched in a wide smile. "But you came anyway, so it's all right—and three's a crowd, right?" He walked around Sophie to pull the knife from Deirdre's back. "She won't be needing this, I guess." Then he turned to face Sophie again.

"Don't you remember me?" Sam's brow wrinkled. "That's disappointing. I certainly never forgot *you.*"

Sophie stared into his eyes. His black, fathomless eyes, and her throat closed. They were the eyes she saw in her nightmares.

"L-luke?" she managed, just above a whisper.

"Aye, that's my lass!" Luke Cameron grinned at her. "I knew you couldn't forget me."

A key turned, and Brian stood in the doorway, holding Sophie's handbag in one hand and the house key in the other. "Sophie? Sam? What—?" Then he saw Deirdre on the floor, and his eyes widened.

"Watch out!" Sophie screamed at him. "It's Luke!"

Luke pushed past Sophie and strode to meet Brian where he stood in shock in the doorway. "And we certainly won't be needing *you*," he snarled, and whipped his hand forward.

There was a thud and a ping as the handbag and key hit the floor. Brian's hands moved up slowly to wrap around the handle of the knife buried in his abdomen, and came away slick with blood. For a moment that seemed an eternity, Sophie's world stood still as the man she loved stared into the face of her worst nightmare. His eyes sought hers for the briefest flicker of time, and then she watched the consciousness drain from them. His knees buckled and he collapsed to the floor and lay still.

Luke put a hand out and grabbed Sophie as she ran toward Brian, sobbing. He clamped his arm around her waist and put his mouth close to her ear.

"Shhh, lass," he whispered. "He doesn't matter anymore." He reached behind to push the door shut and turned the bolt. "I'm here."

CHAPTER 41

MULL, SCOTLAND, APRIL, 1651

BRIAN

"Crisdean?" A soft voice sounded in Brian's ear, and a small hand patted his cheek. He rolled over to stare into Sophie's sleepy blue eyes. As he watched, the eyes cleared, then filled with alarm..

"Shite!" She scrambled to sit up and push herself as far away from him as possible, pulling the blanket up to her chin. She stared at him and her face paled. "Ach, no!" she moaned. "*Brian?*"

The shadows swirling through his brain lifted for a moment. Not Sophie—*Kenna.* Brian pulled his eyes away from her and looked around. Wan light filtered from a small open window set deep in grey stone walls. Tapestries hung on three walls, and the fourth featured the familiar Maclean crest carved into a stone fireplace. He was back at Duart Castle.

Memories flickered like an old silent film, teasing for a second and disappearing. An image crawled into his mind—his own hands, covered with blood, clutched around the handle of a knife.

He'd been stabbed. He tried to wrap his mind around it, and another picture emerged out of the fog. *Sam Douglas.* Brian's eyes flew open and he stared at the wooden beams above his head, trying to understand what had happened. With agonizing sluggishness, the memories came crawling back. Deirdre's boyfriend Sam Douglas, black eyes lit with a demonic glee as he plunged a knife into Brian's stomach. Deirdre, lying motionless on the floor. Sophie, her eyes huge with terror.

Panic gripped him. He struggled out of the blankets and found his footing on the stone floor. He looked down at himself, at the long cotton nightshirt that tickled his knees. His feet were bare. *Crìsdean's* feet were bare.

Kenna jumped out of her side of the bed and came around to stand in front of him. She took his large hands in her own small ones and squeezed them. "'Tis me—Kenna." She shook her head. "Ach, this be a nichtmare!"

Brian took several deep breaths and considered her words. A nightmare. It made sense. He looked down at himself. There was no blood on his hands, none on the nightshirt. It was all just a traumatic dream. A piece clicked into place.

Trauma. His trips to the past had all been caused by physical or emotional trauma. But a nightmare—was that enough to send him back?

A crash in the hallway jerked both their heads in that direction. A man's voice, raised in anger, echoed down the stone corridor.

"I've telt ye, an' I'll no tell ye agin!"

"Hush, now, ye'll wake everbody." A woman's voice, silky, cajoling,

Kenna's face darkened. She threw on a robe of some heavy material and marched to the door. Brian, left alone, followed in her wake.

Giles stood amid the wreckage of pottery, cutlery, and some sort of tea-soaked pastry now strewn over a pile of books scattered on the floor. Frances faced Giles, her hand outstretched toward his arm. She saw Crìsdean and Kenna in their doorway and pulled the hand back, a pout spreading over her face.

Other doors opened, and the Maclean clans-men spilled out into the hallway in various states of undress. Giles flushed and turned to go up the stairs, but before he could get to the first step, a fist caught him in the jaw and he went sprawling. Dànaidh stood over him, arm raised to strike again.

"Leave 'er be, ye bastart!" he snarled.

Frances slid up against Dànaidh's side and put her hands around his arm. "Thank ye, Dànaidh," she purred. "I dinnae ken whit happened. He jist willnae leave me be."

"That's a lie." Kenna stepped out of the shadows in her doorway and faced the taller woman, hands on her hips. "Ye've been stalkin' efter Giles since ye came t' Duart. 'Tis plain t' see for enyone wi' eyes 'n 'is heid." She turned her focus on Dànaidh. "Are ye such a besotted numpty that ye cannae see what yer wife be up tae?"

With whiplike speed, Frances brought her palm around sharply. Before it could connect with Kenna's cheek, her wrist was grabbed and held in a firm grip.

Brian's eyes widened. He saw his own hand holding Frances' wrist and found himself staring into the angry black eyes of Dànaidh's wife. There was something off about this woman—*something familiar*. He dropped her wrist as if her touch burned him, and backed up next to Kenna. His thoughts whirled. *Something familiar . . .*

Giles had regained his feet and was facing Dànaidh, fury etched on his face. His blue eyes shot sparks. "I'm that tired o' this, Dànaidh," he ground out through gritted teeth. "Are ye so daft that ye still thynk I'm wantin' yer woman? Truly? I wouldnae touch 'er if she was th' only woman in Scotland!" His face wrinkled in disgust, and tears welled in his blue eyes. The next words came out on a strangled gasp. "She kilt my Lili!"

Silence fell in the hallway. Some faces registered shock at Giles' accusation; others wore no expression at all. Ealar's brown eyes were fixed on Frances, whose pretty face had assumed a look of hurt innocence. She leaned into Dànaidh and buried her face in his arm.

Kenna caught Giles' eye, shook her head, and looked sideways at Brian. Giles' blue eyes widened.

"I'm sorry, Dàn," he said in a low voice. "I spoke wi'out thynkin'." He gave Kenna a tiny nod, bent, and picked the books out of the mess on the floor, and started up the stairs. "I'll be in th' library."

Dànaidh stared at his brother's back for a long moment. Then he peeled his wife's hands off his arm and turned to stare at her as if he'd never seen her before. "Is 't true? Ye kilt Lili?" He looked at her and his face drained of colour. "'Tis. I wunnerd, bit I didnae thynk . . ." His eyes widened. "An' whit about wee Annie an' Coll? They had th' fever, bit they were gettin' better. Surely ye didnae . . .ye couldnae . . . yer own bairns . . ."

Frances was silent.

Dànaidh's voice sank to a whisper, and he backed away from his wife, eyes huge with horror. "Ye didnae grieve. Ye didnae grieve . . . no. I cannae believe it, I willnae believe." Dànaidh whirled away from Frances and stomped unsteadily down the circular stairs toward the ground floor, weaving like a drunken man and hanging onto the rope rail with both hands. Frances stared after him, an unbecoming flush rising on her face.

Kenna pulled Brian back into the room and closed the heavy door. "There be a lot ye dinnae ken," she whispered. "Wee Annie an' Coll died o' th' fever last winter, an' noo Frances is five months gone wi' child agin. She's no kind o' mother, but fer Dànaidh t' say wha' he did—" She shook her head.

Brain planted his feet. "I'm sorry, Kenna. That's sad, but I don't have time for all this drama. What if it wasn't a nightmare that brought me here? What if Sophie's in real trouble? I have to get back!" He looked around in desperation, and then his shoulders slumped. "But that's not how it works, is it?" he said, his voice dull. "I can't just go back when I want to."

Kenna looked at him in frustration tinged with sympathy. "Brian, I dinnae ken how ye come an' go."

She gave him a somber gaze. "'Tis years between." She sighed. "Ye seem a nice lad, bit I wisht ye nivver came back. I wisht' on it an' prayed on it so much! I-I'm sorry." Her blue eyes shone with unshed tears.

Brian went over to the bed and sat down. He put his head in his hands and tried to make sense of all this, but the pressure on his mind was too much.

"I need t' thynk," Kenna said. "Bide here." The door closed softly behind the woman who was probably Sophie's ancestor. Brian wondered how many incarnations of Sophie MacArthur had graced the earth over the years and through the generations . . . how many men had been lucky enough to gaze into those amazing blue eyes and find love.

Eyes. Something about eyes. Blue eyes. Hazel eyes. Black eyes, filled with unholy lust, with the need to hurt. He forced himself to sit very still and think, taking a lesson from Sophie in patience, letting his memory deliver the answers he needed. And when they came, they nearly undid him.

He knew why Frances seemed familiar—it was her eyes. He had seen them just today . . . they were Sam's—no, *Luke's* eyes.

His thoughts stretched further. If Kenna was Sophie's ancestor, Frances must be Luke's! His brain was racing now, putting pieces together like a malevolent jigsaw puzzle. *The world goes round, and people repeat. Good is good, and evil is always evil. It's all related.* Mary Duncan's words slid into his memory. *Evil is always evil.* Panic slithered back like a viper and wrapped itself around his lungs, squeezing the breath from him.

Frances wasn't just nasty, she was evil. Something Giles had said. *She kilt my Lili.* He didn't remember anyone named Lili, but if Giles was right, Frances had nothing to lose. She must hate Kenna for outing her in front of everyone like that. And Kenna was out there somewhere in this damned huge castle. He jumped up, ran out into the hallway, and stopped. Where could she be?

Frances knew every inch of this castle; of course, she would know where Kenna might go. He pictured the woman stalking her prey like a black wolf, and the panic squeezed tighter. He walked a circle in the hallway, trying to think, but the thickness, the weight of something pressing on his mind, made everything sluggish and dense.

Something pressing. A thought filtered out of the mess that was his brain . . . the brain he was sharing with the person who cared more about Kenna than anyone else. He closed his eyes, put his fingers to his temples, and pressed, ignoring the pain.

Crisdean! Help me! Help me save the woman you love! He pushed the words into the darkness inside himself, praying that the man who owned this body would hear them, that he would know what to do. The fog swirled, deepened, resisted. And then the answer drifted up like a whisper and planted itself in his mind.

He tore up the spiral stairs to the next floor and the next, heedless of the fact that he was still barefoot and wearing nightclothes. At the top of the staircase was a door leading out onto the parapet, and he took it without thinking. Kenna had showed him the first time, told him it was her favorite place to be alone and think.

He opened the door and looked out, but no one was in sight. His heart lurched, and he took the stone walkway to the corner on leaden feet, sure he was wasting precious time.

A voice came from around the corner, and he froze.

"Ye wee bitch—it be yer fault Giles wouldnae come t' me." Frances rasped, anger choking the words out. "I rid him o' that ugly creature he liked so much, but he still didnae come t' me! 'Twas yer fault!"

"Ye cannae have everthin' ye want in this world," came Kenna's voice—calm, reasonable. "Ye had a good man. He loved ye, but ye still wanted more. An' noo ye have nuthin'. Ye'll be goin' t' prison, ye wickit witch. Giles kens ye kilt Lili and so does Ealar an' if it be true ye kilt yer own bairns—"

"Shut yer mouth!"

Brian put his head around the corner and saw Kenna, her back pressed against the stone rail. She looked impossibly small in the shadow of her deranged adversary, but her chin jutted in defiance.

"I hate bairns!" Frances shouted. "I didnae kill 'em, bit I'm glad they're gone. Snivelin', mewlin' wee rats. Bit Dàinaidh wouldnae leave me be, an' noo there's anither rat brewin'." She looked at her stomach with disgust. "Giles hates me an' now Dànaidh willnae have me an' it's all yer fault! Why should ye have th' man ye want? 'Tis no fair!" she advanced on Kenna. "I'll shut yer nasty mouth fer guid!"

"D' ye thynk ye can git awa wi' murder—agin?"

Kenna said, her tone calm composed and unwavering.

"Ye ruint my life!" Frances yelled over the wind. "A' least I can make sure yer precious Crìsdean doesnae have his wee brat. Fair be fair, aye?" She lunged forward, wrapped her arms around Kenna's waist, and hoisted her up toward the edge of the stone rail.

Brian felt his muscles—Crìsdean's muscles—tighten, and then he was running the length of the walk toward the women. Kenna struggled, but Frances had the strength of the insane and Crìsdean's movements were hampered by the other man inside his head.

I'm in the way here! Brian pushed his own thoughts ruthlessly aside and let Kenna's husband take over.

Crìsdean caromed into Frances with a force born of desperation, slamming her into the wall with an ugly thud. Kenna hit the ground and rolled. She curled up like a small hedgehog as Frances grappled with her husband, snarling and scratching like a wildcat. The woman's teeth sank into his arm and he cursed and shoved her away. She stumbled into the wall, hit the edge of the parapet rail, and went over with a scream, her arms cartwheeling uselessly in the air. She disappeared into the mist and landed with a thud.

Kenna scrambled to her feet. She looked over the parapet at the body that lay below, arms spread eagle and black eyes staring at an unforgiving sky. Then she turned and threw herself into Crìsdean's arms, sobbing.

"Uhh, Kenna?" Brian said. "It's me. I'm still here."

CHAPTER 42

JULY 20, 1651

KENNA

Moonlight glinted off the waves in the Firth of Forth. Water lapped lazily against the sides of the flat-bottomed boats carrying Cromwell's invaders across the water, propelled by long poles that made no sound in the darkness. Throughout the night and early morning, fifty boats made their way across the firth on their way to a small town called Inverkeithing.

To the great firth, the spectacle of men setting about the business of killing each other was nothing remarkable in the grand scope of existence. After all, battle was nothing new here. Men subjected their own kind to an endless display of greed, betrayal, and lust for power, ignored by the sparkling water that rolled on toward the sea, as it always had.

To the north, the Royalist forces, some four thousand strong, advanced through the hills and waited for the English as the sun rose. Among these were five hundred Highlanders under the command of Hector, chief of Clan Maclean of Duart . . . and one very small lad in oversized trews and floppy bonnet.

Kenna was exhausted beyond reckoning. None of her practice with the tiny sword Crìsdean had fashioned had prepared her for thirty days of marching across Scotland, with no one to talk to and nothing to keep the midges from burrowing under her shirt and biting the tender skin under her breast wrap until she wanted to tear everything off and run naked.

Crìsdean had never told her that being part of an army consisted of marching until the blisters on your feet became the only way you knew you still *had* feet. He hadn't told her about the mud and the prickly gorse and the heat. But she could forgive him, for one reason.

He didn't know she was here.

If he had known, he would have locked her in Duart's dungeon to keep her from following the clan. He would have clamped her in leg irons before he'd allow her to put herself at such risk.

But he couldn't know because he wasn't himself. Brian Maclean, a man with no experience of this time, was still firmly embedded in her husband's head. Over the past weeks he had sunk into depression and become a thin semblance of the man he'd been when she'd first met him. The strain of living a life not his own was taking its toll.

Since Frances' death, Brian had waited to leave, to return to his own time and the woman he called

Sophie. But nearly three months had passed, and he was still trapped in another man's body. She tried to imagine how he must feel, but her patience was as fragile as his.

Why *was* he still here? "I was sent to protect you," he'd said. "You're Sophie's ancestor, and if something happened to you, she wouldn't be born. She wouldn't exist." His sincerity, the certainty that flashed from those green eyes that were Crìsdean's but not, squeezed her heart and made her wish he was right.

He *had* saved her. Frances was dead. His work was finished, and he should have gone back long ago. He was a man out of time, occupying a body that wasn't his. Keeping up the facade was destroying them both.

Kenna missed her husband. Tears sprang to her eyes and blurred the path ahead. She missed Crìsdean's ready smile, the dimple that flashed on one side of his lips when he was teasing her. She missed his conversation, his appreciation—the way he looked at her as if she were the only woman in the world. She missed his body.

And it mattered not that he was still there, lost somewhere inside that body. He was still Crìsdean Maclean, the man she'd fallen in love with when she was fifteen years old. She felt sorry for Brian, but she wasn't going to allow him to get her husband killed. She couldn't let him give in to despair, and she was afraid he was doing exactly that.

When the order came down that the Macleans of Duart were to travel across the country to support the Scottish army in their fight against England, Brian had reacted calmly—too calmly. He'd gathered his clothing and his weapons without a word, his movements wooden. As if his soul was gone.

Kenna had pulled him aside the night before they were to leave and forced him to look her in the eye. "Ye cannae gie up, Brian! If ye try t' fight like ye are, ye'll be kilt." She grabbed his arms and shook him, and he gave her a bleak, unfocused look. "Ye'll get Crìsdean kilt!" Tears swam in her eyes and she swiped them away angrily.

His answer was flat, emotionless. "I'm sorry, Kenna. But it's over for me. I—I don't think what happened was a nightmare, not anymore. I think I died there, in my time; that's why I'm stuck here. Everyone I ever knew is gone. Sophie is gone!" His words oozed out like poison.

"Bit Crìsdean—"

"Crìsdean is going to die!" he snapped. Kenna stiffened, her fingers locked on his arm. Brian winced and went on. "I'm sorry, nobody's more sorry than I am, but they *told* me. The Players did. You can't change history that's been recorded. This is 1651, and they're—we're—all going to be killed at a place called Inverkeithing. All seven of us—and your chief." He closed his eyes against the horror he must have seen on her face.

"No!" Kenna stomped a small foot. "Yer lyin'! Why're ye lyin'?" Tears streamed down her face. "I hate ye fer this, Brian Maclean. I hate ye!"

He had turned away without another word and made his way slowly down the spiral stairs toward the yard, head low. A stubborn resolve bubbled up in Kenna's chest. He was wrong. Damn history! She needed to get ready; she had her own battle to fight.

BRIAN

Heat crept beneath Brian's collar. Sweat beaded on his forehead and dripped onto the already soaked shirt. He blinked away the swarms of midges intent on eating him alive.

Alive, but not for long. This running was futile, a retreat from sure defeat. It was a complete rout, just like Jeremy had told him.

Kenna's face rose and hovered in his mind; her anger and fear clouded his memory. It had been cruel, what he'd said to her, even if it was true. He knew the end of this story, and he wanted nothing more than to stop and just get it over with.

Still, for her sake he would try. He was a Maclean, after all. They could not last much longer in this heat, but stopping was no longer a choice. Close behind, Brian heard the pandemonium of men crashing through the brush, fed by the anticipation of victory. A ravenous army intent on delivering the final blow to an enemy outnumbered ten to one.

He wondered what it would be like—his last moments on earth. Certainly he'd never imagined dying four centuries away from home, in a battle that wasn't even his. Hell couldn't be worse than this.

He wiped the sweat from his eyes and tried to focus on the way ahead. The sounds of pursuit had diminished; the men ran without the constraint of gorse and bramble thickets that had impeded their escape until now.

There was something odd about the wilderness here. Ash, birch, and elm stood alongside a pathway that meandered through a carefully tended woods. Sophie had taken him on a tour of Cawdor Castle, just outside Inverness, and its manicured gardens had looked something like this. Ahead, an opening in the trees beckoned.

The exhausted men burst from the trees and stood, panting. Across a vast lawn stood a castle. Symmetrical, with gabled roof and dormer windows on the upper floors, its two wings reached out to the sides as if to enfold them in its embrace. The small windows on the ground floor and lack of an obvious entrance suggested that this place had been built as a fortress and might provide safety from their pursuers.

Hector strode to the base of the castle and called for help in the name of their king, his voice ringing with the strength borne of his heritage and responsibility. They waited in a silence heavy with anticipation.

Brian allowed himself a sliver of hope; maybe they would find sanctuary here, among fellow Scots. Maybe the history books were wrong, and it was *other* Macleans who had been killed on this day. Maybe . . .

A face appeared in a window. In the next second, a stone fell from the parapet above, striking a clansman on the shoulder and sending him to the ground. The face disappeared and a shutter closed over the window.

Trapped and helpless, Hector Maclean's men turned to face their adversary. Government soldiers poured from the woods and paused at sight of their quarry, right out in the open and waiting like lambs in the slaughter pen. Brian watched in despair as the enemy moved forward almost leisurely, weapons held loose in their hands.

With a muffled curse, Hector drew his sword and held it high. "*Bàs no Beatha!*" he roared. Brian knew that one. "Death or victory!" The war cry of Clan Maclean.

More men emerged from the woods and the lawn became a frenzied mass of screaming, cursing bodies as the two sides engaged. In moments, the grass was slick with Highlander blood.

Brian dodged the thrust of a pike and winced as a sword nicked his left arm. Muskets thumped. "The chief!" came a cry, and they all turned to see Hector go down, clutching at his stomach. As if galvanized by the wounding of their enemy's leader, soldiers converged on the fallen man.

Bearnard Maclean stepped forward to stand in front of his chief. "*Airson Eachuinn!*" he roared. Brian remembered Jeremy telling him it meant something like "For Hector!" The oldest of the seven brothers stood, legs braced apart, and stared fearlessly into the face of his enemy.

There was a pause, and then three swords met the challenge. Like a slow-motion movie, Bearnard sank to the ground beside his chief and was still.

Giles stepped forward, sword drawn. "*Fear eile airson Eachuinn!*" he shouted.

No! Brian's mind screamed. *Not Giles!* But the man who had walked with him through this alien world, who had sheltered and protected him, stood his ground in defiance, until a musket ball tore into his chest, and he sprawled across the body of his brother.

Four times more the cry was heard, as one by one the Maclean brothers took their turn to stand guard over their wounded leader. As Brian watched in horror, the men he'd come to know and respect were dispatched, one by one, by the sheer power of the opposing force. Dànaidh, Ealar, Fergus, and Pádraig—all of them gone, into the pages of Jeremy's history books.

His own voice sounded in his head. *I don't want to die!* For the briefest of moments, he wavered. Then Brian Maclean, high school math teacher from Nova Scotia, stepped forward to take his place, sword held before him.

"Another for Hector!" he called. He parried a thrust from one, dodged another. He thrust, heard a grunt of pain, and watched one of his adversaries go down. *Th' pointy end goes int' a th' other guy . . .*

A soldier loomed in front of him and swung his sword almost lazily, in a great slicing arc. A pain worse than anything he could have imagined burned through his stomach. The sensation dissipated as quickly as it had come, and he was floating above the scene. Curiously detached, he looked down to see Crìsdean's body sink to the ground. The soldier held his weapon in both hands and lifted it once more.

A shrill scream rose above the grunts of men and clang of weapons. A small figure raced through the crowd of warriors to stand over Crìsdean Maclean. She raised a small sword and brandished it in front of her, face set in determination. Kenna's bonnet had come off, and her glorious golden hair flew around her face as if it had a life of its own.

The enemy stood still, stunned at seeing a woman on the battlefield, humbled by the courage of this tiny lass. They looked around at each other in confusion and disbelief, and then one by one, they sheathed their weapons and turned away. In moments, the clearing was silent.

The scene receded. Brian found himself fading into a familiar darkness, but this time he embraced it for what it was.

I'm going home.

CHAPTER 43

INVERNESS, SCOTLAND, PRESENT DAY

It takes one person to rewrite the history book.
—J.R. Rim

Brian struggled against the shadows swirling around him. As quickly as images formed, they dissolved into the mist, just out of reach. Trees, thistle, men playing at swords like those reenactors the Players had hooked him up with. One thing he'd learned: swords were nothing to mess with. You could get seriously hurt if you weren't careful.

Sounds emerged, a cacophony of screams and clangs and thunder. It sounded as if the kids had finally mutinied; exams were coming and they were all on edge. He'd have to give them another pep talk tomorrow, to settle their anxiety.

Something tickled his nose, and he brushed it away. The light was too bright; he squeezed his eyelids tighter against it, and groaned.

"Wake up, sleepyhead," a feminine voice murmured next to his ear. It sounded sexy; he should check it out. Brian forced one eye open to see a woman smiling at him. Oh, yeah, definitely sexy. This was a great dream. He closed his eyes again.

Something soft bounced off his head. His eyes flew open again to see Sophie, holding a pillow high in the air. He put both arms over his head to deflect the blow. Then his mind cleared, and he gaped at her.

"Sophie! You're all right. Thank God!" Brian felt a rush of emotion that brought tears to his eyes. He swept her up and crushed her to his chest until she squealed and pushed him away. She leaned back and frowned.

"Brian! Are you crying? What's wrong?"

"H-how did you get away from him?" he asked.

She looked at him in confusion. "What?"

The memory of that day surged back. The look of terror on Sophie's face, the excruciating pain of the knife as it sliced into his stomach. The pain . . .

There was no pain. Had he been gone long enough to heal? Brian lay back down, put his hand under the quilt, and pushed on his stomach. Nothing hurt. He threw the covers off and stared at his abdomen. Nothing. No blood, no scarring . . . nothing.

"How long was I unconscious this time?" he demanded.

She laughed. "If by unconscious you mean dead asleep . . ." she thought for a moment. "Well, you passed out on the couch halfway through *Eastenders*, although I don't know how anyone can sleep through all that drama. You woke up long enough to crawl into bed, and now it's half eight. So, about nine hours?"

Nine hours? He'd been asleep for nine hours, while three months had gone by in 1651. It didn't match his other travels at all. But that didn't matter. It had been late evening when he'd walked into Sophie's house to find Deirdre on the floor with a knife in her back and Sophie in the clutches of that monster, Sam—no, *Luke*.

"How did you get away from Luke?" He pushed himself to a sitting position in the bed and grabbed her arms.

Sophie's expression was blank. "Luke? Who's Luke?"

Brian gaped at her. Of all possible responses, he hadn't expected *that*. She wasn't messing with him; she wouldn't do that. Even if she were a practical joker, which she most definitely wasn't, she'd never kid around about that.

Everything about this was wrong. She didn't know who Luke was. She didn't remember the man who had attacked her in college, caused unspeakable trauma, crippled her life.

A line from Sherlock Holmes slid into his mind. *When you have eliminated the impossible, whatever remains, however improbable, must be the truth.*

No shit, Sherlock. Help me out here; I'm not as smart as you.

He swung his legs off the edge of the large four poster and slid his feet into his slippers—Highland cows with tartan bow ties and yarn hair over their button eyes. Sophie had a matching pair, only hers had pink hairbows instead of the ties. "Couples' coos," he'd told her when he presented them. "Everyone should have them." The slippers grounded him, fixed him in the here and now. At the moment, they were all that was tethering him to reality.

"Brian?" He turned to see Sophie still crouched on the bed. Her eyes were wide, her brows creased. He stood and pulled her up with him.

"I have some questions," he said, "and I want you to answer honestly, okay?"

"O-okay."

"Was Sam Douglas ever at your house? I mean, besides the time he came to ask you about engagement rings?"

Sophie eyed him warily. "What are you talking about? Who's Sam Douglas? What engagement rings?" Then her eyes went round. "Engagement rings? Are you proposing to me?"

Brian's eyes widened in astonishment. "No! I mean, yes . . . of course, eventually, but that's not what this is about!" He grabbed at his hair with both hands and pulled it. It hurt, but it didn't help. Had Sophie fallen and hurt her head while he was gone? Did she have amnesia? No, that stuff only happened in movies. But then, why was she acting like this?

He tried another tack. "Sophie, it lasted three months this time. I thought I was stuck there; I thought I'd never get back to you." Remembering, Brian crushed her to him again, and then pushed her back far enough to look into bewildered blue eyes.

"Stuck?" She studied him cautiously. "Stuck where?"

Brian stared at her. A frisson of unease rippled through him. Why would she joke about the time travel? She knew how wrenching it was for him to find himself in his ancestor's body, four hundred years in the past.

"It was awful," he said. "They're all dead. Giles, Dànaidh, the twins—all of them." He choked the words out past the lump in his throat. "They all died, right in front of me."

Sophie reached for his hand and held it tightly. "Brian, I think we'd better have the doctor look at you. Maybe this is still from that sailing accident you had back in the summer. These weird dreams—they're not normal."

Brian's brows furrowed. "But they weren't dreams, you *know* that! I was *sent* back . . ." He paused, uncertain of his footing, and then plunged ahead. "And now I know why. It was to save you."

"Save me from what? Brian, you're scaring me!"

"Stop it! This isn't funny, Soph!" He glared at her in frustration. "Not exactly *you*; I had to save your ancestor, so you'd be born!"

Even as he said the words, Brian realized how crazy they sounded. People would think he'd lost his mind if they heard him. But Sophie—Sophie should know. She'd said she believed him.

"Remember the etchings on the rocks by the sound?" he asked suddenly. At her blank expression, he sighed. "Never mind. Will you go to the castle with me? I mean, can you take time off from the band?"

"The band?" Sophie's blank look deepened. "You mean the orchestra? You know we're on break right now. The new season doesn't start till May." Her face had paled. "You *know* all this." The look of fear deepened on her face.

I need to be careful, Brian thought. *We're not on the same page here, and if I keep asking questions, she'll have me up at that psych institute on the hill!*

"Sorry," he said, and gave her a wan smile. "I must still be half asleep."

"Well, you'd better wake up. You'll be late for school if you lag about any longer." She wrinkled her nose. "And you need a shower. Whatever that dream was, you woke up covered in sweat. Hurry up. I'll drive you there."

When had she learned to drive?

Thank God she did, Brian thought later, as he made his way up to the front door of the school. *I never would have found it. Sophie's right. I'm in serious trouble.* He stopped and stared up at the coat of arms that adorned the front of the school. It featured the Scottish saltire on a shield, with a crown at the top and the heads of a camel and an elephant on the sides. The cat at the bottom reminded him of Biscuit.

Very impressive. Very nice. The only problem was that it wasn't his school. The large three-dimensional letters to the right of the coat of arms read "Welcome to Inverness Royal Academy" in English and Gaelic. *What had happened to Highlands Academy?*

Heart in his throat, he entered the modern school building and stood in the large, open lobby. Teachers and students rushed by on their way to class.

"Mornin', Brian!"

"How about that match, aye?"

"Good morning, Mr. Maclean!"

Brian teetered on the edge of panic. What was happening here? Everybody knew him, but he'd never seen this place or these people in his life. A new fear surfaced—where was he supposed to go?

"Mr. Maclean, I forgot my notebook," a young boy said. "Can I walk with you to your room to get it?"

Brian took a deep breath. "Sure." He let the student take the lead, and eventually found himself in a room that looked like any other math classroom. The feeling of familiarity helped dispel the fear building inside him, but not by much.

None of the students he met that day seemed to notice that he didn't call them by name. They all seemed to expect him to be here. He followed the manual and managed to deliver a credible lesson, but the effort of trying to adjust left him exhausted by the end of the day. When Sophie picked him up, he collapsed into the passenger seat of her Volvo and closed his eyes. He kept them closed until they reached home.

The house was like an island of normalcy in an insane world. Oliver leaned against his wall, right where he should be. The carrots were still mushy, the potatoes lumpy. After supper, when they retired to the sitting room, he sat down and took both of Sophie's hands in his.

He had to face this, no matter what happened next. There were too many unanswered questions, too many pitfalls. If there really was something seriously wrong with him, he should find out and get it treated.

"Sweetheart," he said carefully, "I know I haven't been myself today. But I want you to listen and try to give me the benefit of the doubt—even if it doesn't make sense. Just pretend it does, okay? Then I promise I'll go to the doctor like you said."

She nodded and grasped his hands. "Okay." She gave him the full wattage of those brilliant blue eyes. "I love you, Brian. I'll always be here for you, no matter what. You know that, right?"

He nodded, unable to speak for a long moment. Then he took a deep breath and began. "Remember the night you shared your experience back in college?" He cleared his throat. He'd promised himself he'd never bring that night up again, but everything about this was just so . . . wrong. "You know, when you dropped out, after Luke?"

She was shaking her head. "Brian, I told you, I don't know anyone named Luke. I never dropped out of uni—why on earth would I? How would I have been able to get into the Royal Orchestra if I didn't graduate?"

She looked at his face and took a deep breath. "Go on."

Brian sat still for a minute and then said, carefully, "Is Deirdre all right?"

"Of course she is! I met her yesterday for lunch. She was going on about some new lad she met—Colin something."

"What happened to Highlands Academy?"

Sophie blinked at the abrupt change in subject. "Never heard of it. Where is it?"

Brian's head was pounding from the effort of holding in his emotions. Somehow, while he had been off fighting the Battle of Inverkeithing, everything had changed. A thought occurred to him, and he grasped it like a lifeline.

The Highland Players would know.

"Sophie, let's go to the pub."

"Now? On a school night?"

"Yes, now. I think the Players 'll have the answers."

"Who? Never mind—okay," she said. "Which pub?"

"The Unicorn, of course." He jumped up and started for the front hallway where they hung their coats.

"Is it close?" Sophie threw on her jacket and followed him out the door. "Can we walk?"

Brian stared at her as if she'd grown an extra head. "The Unicorn. Just up the street."

"Never heard of it. There's a pub on our street? Brilliant!"

A feeling of dread slid up Brian's spine. "What— never mind, let's go." He all but dragged her up the pavement toward the Unicorn. Then he thought of something. "Wait." He turned to face her. "Shouldn't you be playing there tonight?"

"Playing? At a *pub*?"

Brian opened his mouth to answer, and then closed it again and stared in disbelief at 26 Ardconnel Street. Where The Dancing Unicorn should be was a vacant lot. Weeds and long grass grew in scattered clumps, and odd bits of what looked like burned wood lay at angles in the brush. An old rusted fence sagged away from the pavement.

In the center of the lot sat a black cat.

"Biscuit!" Brian called. The cat looked at him with unblinking, yellow eyes.

Eyes. Golden eyes, blue eyes . . . black eyes. In a torrent, images rushed at him. Frances' black eyes, so like Luke's. He stared at the empty lot, and the answer came. He'd had it four hundred years ago; he just hadn't realized it.

He'd thought he was sent back in time to save Kenna so that Sophie would be born in the twenty-first century, but that wasn't it. The key wasn't Kenna; it was *Frances.*

Black eyes.

Frances was Luke's ancestor. And because he had gotten Crìsdean up to that parapet, Frances had died, right in front of him. Which meant that the child she was carrying would never be born. Her line had ended on that stone walkway at Duart Castle— because of him.

The truth crashed in like the waves on the Sound of Mull. Frances had died, which meant Luke would never be born. Sophie wouldn't meet him, wouldn't be attacked by him, *because he had never existed.* Deirdre hadn't been killed; he hadn't been stabbed.

Mary Duncan's words came to him on the wind that blew through a vacant lot that should have been a pub. *There are no coincidences.*

Brian could sense his old memories softening, becoming misty around the edges and fading away as those of his new reality replaced them. He looked once more at the black cat sitting in the middle of a vacant lot. The animal stared back at him, and then one yellow eye closed in what looked very much like a wink. The cat turned, sauntered to the back of the lot, and disappeared down the stone steps that led to Castle Street.

Brian turned to Sophie and took her into his arms. It seemed as if he'd been holding her like this forever . . . and maybe he had. He smiled and kissed the top of her head.

"Let's go home."

JULY, 1651

he battles went on; muskets thundered and swords clanged. Bodies stepped and dodged and whirled in the never-ending dance of death. Man killed his own and was killed in turn, for an idea, a lie, an obsession.

But in the clearing where one hundred Highlanders slept, the silence was profound. For the Macleans of Duart, the war was over. They lay where they had fallen, no longer caring who won or lost in the end. Even the birds had abandoned this cursed place; the leaves on the trees were still.

The day bled into nightfall. In the weak light of a gibbous moon, something stirred in the clearing. Kenna sat up and gazed with bleary eyes at the bodies of the men who had once been her family. The stench of death was unimaginable, as if the whole world was rotting away. She stifled a whimper—there was no time for such things—and turned to the man who lay next to her.

Her small hands probed the ragged area where the sword had sliced into his flesh.. She held a finger under his nose and sighed in relief. He still breathed. Crìsdean Maclean's face was pasty grey and the movement of his chest nearly imperceptible, but he was alive.

She placed a hand on his forehead and then her own. He was fevered, burning from within. Kenna struggled to her feet and made her way to a stream that ran past the edge of the estate. She tore off a bit of her filthy shirt and soaked the cloth in the cold water, then returned to Crìsdean and wiped his face. If he didn't wake soon, the fever would carry him off and she would be truly alone.

Kenna closed her eyes against such negative thoughts. Fear would not help either of them. She turned her face to the cloudless sky and sent a prayer to whatever gods might be listening. Probably none of them; surely no god would allow such atrocities as these. A tear escaped and rolled down her face, and she let it go unimpeded.

Something pulled at the tattered edge of her shirt, and she looked down to see a hand clutching the hem weakly. Crìsdean's eyes were open; hollow green pools in his pale face. As she watched, they cleared in recognition, and he blinked. His hands scrabbled in the grass and he struggled to sit up.

"Crìsdean!" Kenna held him down with the little strength she had left. "Dinnae try t' move. Ye're bad hurt, love. I've stopt th' bleedin', an' pit a cold cloth fer th' fever, bit ye cannae move or 't will all be fer nought, an'—"

His hand moved to cover her mouth, and a weak smile creased his face. "Kenna. My Kenna. Will ye stop talkin' fer jist a minit an' let me look at ye?"

Kenna's tears were running unchecked now, fear and joy mingled together in a torrent of emotion. She bent over and placed the softest of kisses on his warm brow.

Crìsdean moved his head to the side and froze. Giles lay not two feet away, blue eyes open and staring at the night sky as if it held all the wonders of the books he held so dear. Beyond him was the body of Fergus, his hand outstretched toward his brother Pádraig. Crìsdean wrenched his head away and retched, dry heaves shaking his body.

"Dinnae look!" Kenna held him still. "Ye cannae do enythin'. They're gone."

Crìsdean's eyes fixed on hers. "All?" he whispered. "An' Hector?"

She nodded, unable to lie to this man no matter the pain it caused.

"I'm . . . th' last." The words were so low she had to bend close to his lips to hear them.

"Aye."

She held his hand while he cried, bitter tears of grief and regret shaking his body. Finally the harsh sobs subsided, and he used the hand that was not clutching hers to swipe the moisture from his eyes.

Kenna watched, and when he looked at her again, she forced her voice to sound as matter of fact as she could manage. "Weel then, yer mam'll be expectin' us home. So ye may want t' quit lyin' abed an' get goin'. We have a long way t' go."

Crìsdean's stared at her and then his face creased and he was laughing. It was a fragile thing, a thin, gossamer wheeze of breath. But it was real and true, and suddenly, the night air was filled with sound, as if nature was witness to a miracle and wanted to be a part of it.

By morning his fever had broken. The long gash in his stomach was not as deep as had seemed at first, and youth and conditioning took care of the rest. A week went by before he could walk more than a few steps, another week before he had the strength to bury his brothers and his chief, but the day came when they set out across Scotland once again.

They stopped at villages sometimes to work for food, often staying a week or more. Crìsdean helped in the rigs, and Kenna mended bairns' torn trews, but many times they were given bread and fruit out of kindness. They slept in cots, in stables, but most often made their bed under the stars.

On a cool morning in October, Crìsdean and Kenna Maclean boarded a skiff in the small fishing village of Oban, and as the shadows came down over the Western Isles, they disembarked and stood at the rocky edge of the sound, gazing at Duart Castle.

"Home," murmured Crìsdean. Pain coloured his voice. "How do we tell Mam?"

Kenna took his hand and squeezed it. "It'll be terr'ble hard, aye. Bit . . ."

She pulled him around to face her and looked into his clear green eyes. "Afore we go, I have somethin' t' tell ye," she said, her voice uncharacteristically shy. She took his hand and placed it on her abdomen.

"Ye're no th' last."

Crìsdean's eyes grew round. He dropped his pack and took her into his arms, tears pouring down his face. When he finally released her, she gave him a determined look.

"If it's a lad, we're namin' him Brian," she said. "If he'd not bin there, I wouldnae followed ye. So 'twas him saved ye, when all be said."

Crìsdean smiled. "Awright." His brow wrinkled. "Long 's he stays out o' ma heid."

ACKNOWLEDGMENTS

arl Dannenberger - My amazing husband. His tireless work to publicize, market, and promote the books allows me to live my dream. Because of him, I can just write.

àiri MacKinnon – Kinswoman and friend. My expert on Invernese – always there even for the ridiculous questions (and an expert on the sweary words)

enny Tomasso – Minister of Mayhem. Helps me to understand exactly where to stab someone in the most dramatic way, how to blow things up spectacularly, and where to hide the bodies. No matter the method, he's the expert.

athy Kiel – Unflinching beta reader, that greatest of friends who will be honest without worrying about the consequences.

Steve and Mary Maclennan – Highlanders for Hire and the inspiration for my Highland Players. Check them out here if you want to set up an ambush or watch a reenactment of Scottish history: https://www.facebook.com/highlanders4hireltd/

Victor Cameron – The first friend I met in Scotland, who introduced a stranger to Rait Castle. He is always ready and willing to take me on another journey into the heart of the Highlands, and infuses his love for his country's history into everything he does. Author of Walk History and Time Facebook page: https://www.facebook.com/profile.php?id=100091411576014

Caomhìn MacFhionghuin (Kevin MacKinnon) – another kinsman I was lucky to meet in Inverness, he is a walking Highlands history book, always willing to share his huge knowledge base and love of his country's past. The inspiration for Wee Caomhainn.

Reid Blyn – Our landlord in Baddeck, Cape Breton Island, he was a crucial resource on the art of sailing and the Bras d'Or Regatta. Without his expertise, Brian could never have made it into the head of his ancestor.

Andrew Saul, Duart Castle Guide – Without his analysis and advice, my understanding of Clan Maclean would be sorely lacking.

Even though the MacKinnons and Macleans were not the best of friends at certain points in Scotland's history, he was willing to let bygones be bygones and share his vast knowledge of the castle and its occupants, as well as the clan badges and mottoes.

The Staff at Inverness Royal Academy – for sharing valuable information about their school and its workings, so that Brian could feel at home in his new facility.

Giovanni Dannenberger—one of my youngest beta readers. He is responsible for the addition of Biscuit, the Highland Players' mystical cat, who sauntered her way into the hearts of readers and earned her creator this accolade.

DUART CASTLE

Duart Castle sits on a high crag of land which juts into the Sound of Mull. Built by Chief Lachlan Lubanach Maclean sometime in the 14th century, it is the seat of Clan Maclean of Duart. It can be accessed by ferry from Mull and then by taxi (if you're lucky) or a lovely three mile walk.

More here: https://duartcastle.com/

9 781965 253168